JOHN BROWN'S WOMEN
A NOVEL

SUSAN HIGGINBOTHAM

ONSLOW PRESS

ISBN: 978-1-7374749-0-6 (paperback)
ISBN: 978-1-7374749-1-3 (e-book)

"People who never did a heroic thing themselves are very particular as to how heroes behave."

—Annie Brown Adams interviewed by Katherine Mayo, October 2-3, 1908.

A Note on Place Names

In writing about the raid on Harpers Ferry, I have used the form that was current in John Brown's day—"Harper's Ferry," with the apostrophe. Likewise, I refer to "Charlestown," now known as "Charles Town." Both Harpers Ferry and Charles Town, of course, are now part of West Virginia, which was carved out of Virginia during the Civil War. Charlestown should not be confused with the West Virginia capital of Charleston, hundreds of miles away.

Part I

Mary

1

January 1833 to July 11, 1833

Mary Day was not supposed to be the wife of John Brown. That was her sister's place. Betsy was in every way superior to Mary—older, livelier, better schooled, and, above all, prettier. It didn't matter that the recently widowed Mr. Brown hadn't actually asked her to marry him; everyone assumed he would, once a few more months had passed. Why would a man keep paying a housekeeper as competent and congenial as Betsy to care for his five children when he could take her as a wife instead?

Nor did anyone expect Betsy to refuse a proposal, even with those five children—four of them boys. Mr. Brown was a godly man, well respected in their Pennsylvania community near the Crawford County seat of Meadville, and his tannery employed fifteen men. It would be foolish to say no to that, at least for a girl from a large family where money was always tight.

So, when Mary came to Mr. Brown's house, it was just to help spin wool and flax, and maybe to stay on to help Betsy with her ready-made household after she married. Mary would sit quietly behind her spinning wheel just like she did at home, saying little and being spoken to even less. Mr. Brown would get so accustomed to her, he'd likely forget she was there, except when the wheel ceased to hum. She would be useful and earn her keep, and she would never have to worry about being left alone in the world, even if she didn't marry.

As it turned out, she was wrong about at least some of those things.

~ ~ ~

Mr. Brown wasn't a stranger to Mary. He was good friends with Thomas Delamater, whose wife, Martha, was yet another older sister of Mary's, so naturally, Mary had encountered him at various gatherings—church and the like. She doubted he had remembered seeing her; they weren't the sort of meetings that one did recall, and Mary tended to blend into the background anyway. She wasn't exactly homely, but she certainly wasn't pretty. The one thing people noticed about her, if they noticed her at all, was her height; she was taller than most women, and since she was still a few months shy of her seventeenth birthday, it was entirely conceivable that she might grow some more. Some women might have fretted about this, but Mary couldn't see the point in bothering. She was what she was.

For her own part, she recollected Mr. Brown quite well. He was in his early thirties, tidily but very plainly dressed, with dark hair he simply brushed back off his forehead. Wiry and of medium height, he had but one striking feature, but it was all that was needed: his eyes, blue and piercing. They made her sneak several glances at him on those occasions where she found herself in his presence, and even led her to wonder what she might feel if those eyes were turned straight on her—as they were now.

Mr. Brown stepped forward to welcome her to his house. "You're here," he said, not so much brusquely as simply stating a fact.

Mary withstood his gaze. "Yes, sir."

"Well, Betsy will show you everything and tell you what to do." He hesitated and added, "Welcome."

"Thank you, sir," Mary said. She was relieved that Mr. Brown hadn't made more fuss over her.

Inside the house, Betsy, smiling almost possessively, led forth two small children, while three older boys stood at attention. Mr. Brown's face softened somewhat as he looked upon them.

"My oldest, John Jr." He indicated a sturdy boy of eleven or so, who made a courtly bow. "Jason." The middle boy, with lighter blond hair than his older brother, shyly nodded. "Owen." The third lad gazed at her from underneath a thatch of red hair. Fewer than four years separated the oldest of the trio from the younger, Mary guessed, and would later learn that to be true; from the way they stood close together surveying her, she also guessed that this was a tight-knit crew.

Mr. Brown turned his attention to the two on either side of Betsy. "Ruth." A girl of about four, the family's other redhead, gazed warily at her. "And Frederick." The youngest, no more than two, hummed, stopping when his father gave him a look. Despite his motherless state, he looked healthy, as did all the children. Lively too—Mary hoped that she was not expected to discipline this brood, as she was acutely conscious that only about five years stood between her and the oldest boy. She probably didn't need to worry, as this was surely a task that Betsy would reserve for herself.

They sat for supper soon after Mary arrived. Mary helped her sister serve, of course, but she was surprised to see the older boys spring up to help as well. There would be no idle hands here, even if it meant that a male did women's work.

Mr. Brown said grace, and there followed a meal, with Mr. Brown leading the conversation and none of the children talking out of turn. The table being cleared, again with general assistance, Mr. Brown turned toward a shelf on which a number of well-worn Bibles were kept and distributed them to all. Mary was not surprised at this proceeding, having been advised by Betsy, who had said with a certain air of resignation, "There will be a Bible reading before breakfast and one before supper every single day. Every single day, without fail. Now, I am no heathen, but still . . . But there are a lot of worse things a man can do at his home."

Despite this warning, it had not occurred to Mary that Mr. Brown would expect her to join in on her first evening at his house. But he did, and there was nothing Mary, who read her Bible every day but had not read anything aloud in years, could do but comply. Mercifully, the verse assigned her was a simple enough psalm—no long words, none of the ridiculously complicated Biblical names that Mary couldn't have pronounced even if the Lord himself had asked her to do it—but even so, she stumbled over her verse, acutely conscious that no one else came close to reading so badly. Mr. Brown read his verse with a great deal of feeling, and John Jr. with a good deal of flare. Owen and Jason managed theirs smoothly, if somewhat mechanically, and little Ruth, who was not yet reading, carefully repeated her verse after her father.

No one said anything after her dismal performance, but Mary could only imagine what the young Browns were thinking. "I made a fool of myself," she whispered to Betsy as they settled to bed that evening in the room they shared with Ruth and Frederick.

Betsy yawned. "Well, I doubt Mr. Brown cares, as long as you tried."

"Well, I do."

So, the next morning, Mary crawled out of her bed, went downstairs, and laid a fire in the kitchen, then took out her Bible and began reading it aloud.

"Miss Day?"

She started to find Mr. Brown looking at her.

"You like your Bible, I see."

Mr. Brown looked at her so approvingly, Mary felt that simply saying "yes" would be dishonest. "I was just practicing for the next reading, so I wouldn't stumble so."

"Ah, I see. Well, read to me, and see if you can do so without stumbling."

Mary obeyed. It took a while, but after some hints from Mr. Brown, she at last had it perfect.

When she thanked him, he asked, "Have you much schooling?"

"No. Just a couple of years in New York before Father had to—before we moved."

Mr. Brown looked at Mary sympathetically. He probably knew, through the Delamaters, that Mary's father, having once been fairly prosperous, had lost everything by signing notes for some friends who had betrayed his trust.. Finally, he had moved from New York to Pennsylvania in hopes of improving his situation. Mary's studies, such as they were, had ended with that move. "Well, I will be happy to help you whenever you like."

Mary thanked him just as Betsy came down to start breakfast with her help. Evidently, Mary would be doing much more here than the spinning—not that she minded, for she didn't like to sit idle.

Soon the children were ranged around the table, a position that emphasized the gap in age between nine-year-old Owen and four-year-old Ruth; the boy who had come between them had died. A newborn boy had died the previous August, followed soon by his mother, Dianthe. Poor Frederick, gingerly lifting a cup of milk, must have barely been weaned when he lost his mother.

Betsy had told Mary that Mr. Brown had taken his wife's death hard, even though gossip had it that Dianthe had not always been in her right mind. One time the Browns had attended church with the Delamaters, whom Mary had happened to be visiting, and there she had seen Dianthe, a small, plain woman. Mary couldn't say that she was cracked, but there had been something about her. She had a lovely singing voice, but she had sang with a fervor that was somehow disturbing. Afterward, she had come out, wearing a pretty woolen cloak that she must have made herself and taken pains over. It had fallen off her shoulders, and Mr. Brown had tenderly settled it back upon her. She had thanked him, and then, not five minutes later, it had fallen again. Mary was sure that she'd swept it off herself. She had walked placidly on, while little Ruth cradled the cloak in her arms.

After Dianthe died, taken by the childbed fever, Mr. Brown had taken his motherless children and gone to stay with one of his tannery employees. But the employee was a newlywed, and Mr. Brown hadn't wanted to overstay his welcome. So he had brought the children back home and, through the Delamaters, had found Betsy to care for them and the house—a rehearsal, one could say, for their marriage. So far the rehearsal appeared to be going well. The children munched their bread contentedly and kicked each other under the table cheerfully, and everything in the modest house shone with cleaning.

Except, Mary found, for the spinning wheels—a great one for wool and a smaller one for flax. Dusty and forlorn, they sat in a corner, not touched since poor Dianthe had felt the first pangs of labor.

Mary felt a little strange about taking this dead woman's place at her wheel, so she waited until the three older boys had started off for school, then scooted the wool wheel over to another part of the room, where it at least didn't radiate so much Dianthe. With that out of the way, she set to work. Some women found spinning tedious and tried to do it only in the company of others to better while the time away, but Mary could spin for hours in utter silence and only know that time had passed by the setting of the sun.

She was still at work, pacing back and forth alongside the great wheel, when Mr. Brown came home. "Ah, I've missed that music."

"Music?"

"The music of the wheel. Hard work has its own special music, I think. And it looks like you've been quite productive."

Mary nodded shyly.

"Well," said Mr. Brown after a long pause. "Carry on, Miss Day."

~ ~ ~

Mary had been at this for a couple of weeks when Mr. Brown announced that he had to go to Ohio to visit his father. The night before he was supposed to leave, he came home, frowning, and called his oldest son to him. "There's a shipment coming in, probably tomorrow night. Can I trust you with it?"

"Yes, Father."

Mary had expected Mr. Brown to go on more about the importance of the shipment, but he simply nodded, and John Jr. went back to his book. She wondered what the shipment was. For the tannery? But surely one of the employees there could handle it? Young John did help out at the tannery when he was not in school, but when school was in session, he tended to that and to his chores at home. Frankly, from what Mary had seen, he wasn't the most dependable worker, preferring to sneak off and read.

It wasn't for her to tell Mr. Brown how to run his life, though. The question didn't occupy her thoughts for long, in any case, as she and Betsy were busy getting Mr. Brown's clothing together for his trip. He dressed very plainly, in suits of black or brown, but he was particular about his clothing, especially his shirts, which he liked crisp and neat.

The sisters sent Mr. Brown on his way well-supplied with shirts. His absence created a bit of a holiday feeling, at least among the older three boys. Although Betsy made a half-hearted attempt to do a Bible reading in Mr. Brown's place, the boys ran through their verses so quickly and so badly that she gave it up and contented herself with telling a fairy story to Ruth and Frederick, who clearly hadn't heard of such before and, to the best of Mary's belief, never heard of such again. Mr. Brown wasn't keen on fairy stories.

Deep in the night, something awoke Mary—a light playing on the walls of the room where she slept. She looked out the window and saw a lantern-carrying figure—nay, two figures— heading in the direction of the barn. Presently, the two of them disappeared into the barn, and after a longish interval, a single figure headed back from whence it had come. Mary heard the door open and a quiet step make its way to the room where the three older boys slept. Silence fell upon the house.

Mary lay back down and frowned up at the ceiling. She was certain the figure that had stayed inside the barn was a woman, and if she were not mistaken, the other figure had been John Jr. But why on earth would he sneak off with a woman? If he had been a few years older, the answer would have been shamefully obvious, but he was not even twelve yet and did not strike Mary as being a particularly worldly youth anyway. Mary was tempted to wake Betsy, who would not have hesitated to barge into the boys' room and find out what was going on, but she did not want to get young John in trouble with his father. Betsy had informed her that Mr. Brown was a strict disciplinarian, though Mary had yet to see him whip one of the children.

Nothing was amiss when Mary woke the next morning. John Jr. was as bright-eyed as ever as Betsy served him breakfast. Still, Mary noticed that he did not eat his bread and butter; when he left the table, he wrapped it up in a napkin and left the house.

Mary was quiet, but she was as curious as any other sixteen-year-old girl. After a decent interval, she left the house. Sure enough, John Jr. was walking to the barn.

Mary followed at a discreet distance. She and Betsy were opposites in almost every way, but they had one thing in common: the Brown children hadn't really warmed to them. Oh, they were polite, and they did what Betsy bid, but it was clear their hearts weren't in it. Mary could understand; their mother had been dead for less than six months. She and Betsy were poor substitutes, and hired substitutes at that. Even the younger two children treated them warily, although Frederick, who had a fey quality about him, would occasionally forget himself and snuggle in Betsy's lap. The chances of John confiding in Mary were not high.

When John Jr. went inside the barn, Mary remained outside—there was such a thing as being too obvious. Finally, he reappeared, and she tried to look as if it was pure chance that she happened to be outside the barn.

To her surprise, John hastened up to her. "Miss Day, how fast can you make a dress?"

"If I had the materials, in a single day, I suppose. Why?"

"I need one—for someone. Can you make it today?"

"I don't have the materials. Most of the wool I spun is at the weaver's. Until that comes back, or unless I can buy some cloth in town, I can't make anything."

"Drat," John said. He shuffled from one foot to another. "Can you keep a secret?" he finally asked.

"For a good reason, I can."

"All right, then, but you mustn't tell or—or there will be dire consequences."

Mary nodded.

"Father helps smuggle escaped slaves to safety. There's one hiding in our barn. A girl about your age."

Dumbstruck, Mary stared at him. Slavery was something she knew little about; indeed, she'd never seen a slave. If Mary had been asked for an opinion, she would have probably concluded that being free was better than being a slave, but needless to say, no one had asked. She knew vaguely that the topic was talked about, but she seldom read a newspaper. The idea that someone might actually do something to help the slaves was entirely new to her.

But Mr. Brown had impressed her as a kind man, and if he was helping the slaves, surely that was a good thing.

"She's wearing this thin dress," John said. "I guess it did well enough when she left, but she's cold now, and she'll only get colder when she goes farther north. So, I was hoping—"

"If she's smaller than me, John—as most ladies are—I can give her one of my dresses. I can fit it to her."

"Really? Thank you, Miss Day." He smiled at her for the first time.

"I'll go get it."

Mary wasn't a saint. Returning to the house, she chose her least favorite dress, a brown wool that had seen its best days, and brought it back to the barn, along with a quantity of pins. "So, where is she?"

"In the haymow."

Mary looked up and saw nothing but—unsurprisingly, really—hay. "Can I see her?"

"I suppose, but you'll have to climb."

Mary snorted at the obviousness of this remark—where did he think she had been raised, Philadelphia?—and quickly climbed the ladder, worrying a little bit about what a slave might look like. Would she be wearing shackles? A brand? It was reassuring to hear that she was at least wearing a dress.

Once they were both in the haymow, John Jr. neatly pushed some bales aside, revealing a door large enough to accommodate a man who had sense enough to duck his head. "Cromwell," he called.

Mary heard someone unbolt a door, then a face appeared, lit by a skylight in the room. It belonged to a girl who was probably about Mary's age and, to her immense surprise, not all that far off from her color. There were no shackles, and the girl's calico dress, though too thin for a Pennsylvania winter, was perfectly ordinary, even pretty. "This is Miss Day," Johnny said to her. "And this is Josie."

"Pleased to meet you, ma'am."

"Johnny said you needed a warmer dress." Mary displayed the one under her arm. "If you let me try this on you, I can cut it down and have it ready by the morning."

"That's kind of you, missus. But ain't no need for you to do the work. I've been sewing since I was a little bit of a thing. Sewed for my mistress, and she was right particular. If you bring me a needle and thread and shears, I'll whip this out in no time. It'll pass the time here too."

"All right." Mary looked around the room. It was small but adequately ventilated and supplied with a feather bed and heaps of warm blankets. Clearly, this space had been the result of careful planning. "How long have you been . . . escaping?"

"Lord, miss, I've lost all track of time. Been a good two months, I guess. Started out in Maryland."

"What made you decide to run?"

Josie looked in John Jr.'s direction and shook her head.

"John, could you get my sewing things so I don't have to go up and down this ladder again? You know where I keep them all."

John Jr. obeyed. When she and Mary heard the sound of his feet descending the ladder, Josie said, "Master was looking at me the way he looked at all of us girls when we started getting a shape to us, miss. I knew he'd be doing more than looking soon. So I lit out to a place I'd heard about, and here I am."

"It must have been hard leaving your family."

"Ma died years ago."

"Your father?"

"You might say Master is my father, miss."

There were so many layers of awfulness here, Mary could hardly unpack them. Josie shrugged. "That's the way it is, miss. At least in my place. Some masters leave us girls alone, but others don't. If a girl complains, if she's fool enough, she gets beaten or sold to someone even worse. Or both."

Mary tried to imagine what "even worse" might be and decided to stop trying.

Over the next day or so, Mary visited Josie as often as she could without being too conspicuous about it. Josie redid her dress so wonderfully it almost looked pretty—indeed, she put Mary's sewing to shame—and it was a good thing she was quick about it, for Mr. Brown came home shortly afterward. The next evening, he left on another trip, with Josie—as John Jr. told Mary later—concealed beneath some hay, bound for Ohio. Mary had sent her off with her warmest shawl, knowing she could soon knit herself a new one.

A few days later, Mr. Brown returned from his journey. The morning after his arrival, he caught Mary alone at her spinning wheel. "Miss Day, John told me that you helped with the delivery the other day, and you gave away your shawl and dress."

"Yes. I felt so terrible for the poor creature." Too late, Mary thought she should have kept talking in code, but Mr. Brown just nodded, and there wasn't anyone around but two of them anyway. "She told me that her master would have— I can't say it, sir."

"Used her as his concubine?"

Knowing the meaning of the word from the Bible, Mary nodded. "She said it happens often."

"It does. Go to a plantation and you will see slave children nearly as white as yourself, fathered by their masters and with masters among their grandfathers as well. Every aspect of slavery is vile, but that to me is one of the vilest of all. A man satisfies his lusts, and at the same time, breeds up more slaves for himself."

"That's cruel, and so very wrong. Someone should put a stop to it."

"That practice, or slavery altogether?"

"Well, both, I suppose."

"When?"

Was he teasing her? Testing her? "Now is as good as any time, I guess."

"Should the slave owners be compensated for their loss?"

"I hadn't thought about it, sir. But it seems that it would almost be a reward for their sin, so I would say no."

"I agree with you. It appears that you are an abolitionist, Miss Day. A rather hard-shell one too."

Mary couldn't spell the word, much less explain its meaning at the time, but she nodded. "I suppose I am."

Mr. Brown gave a quick smile and walked away, and Mary resumed her work.

~ ~ ~

A few days later, Mary finished her spinning. There wouldn't be any more for her to do for a while, but Mr. Brown told her to stay around and help with sewing and whatever else was needed, so she did. It was about all Mr. Brown said to her, because ever since their conversation about Josie, he had been spending a lot more time at the tannery, and when he was home, he was quiet and thoughtful. It was his habit to take the younger children upon his knee before their bedtime and sing a hymn to them—which was usually quite an occasion, accomplished with great enthusiasm—but once or twice lately, he had let the song trail off in midair. While Mary wouldn't say there was anything lacking in his Bible readings, he did seem to be choosing shorter verses. Betsy was a little snappish with everyone, especially Mary, but Mr. Brown didn't seem to notice.

After about a week of this, Mr. Brown thrust something into Mary's hand as she was heading off to bed. "Please read this at your earliest convenience," he said almost gruffly and walked away.

Mary's heart thumped as she stared at the letter he had handed her. Was he sacking her? But he hardly needed a letter for that; all he had to do was tell her that she was not needed anymore. Reprimanding her? Mary could think of nothing she had done wrong; to the contrary, he'd seemed quite pleased, and he was quite particular about housework. Had it to do with the children? But they were Betsy's charges.

There was only one possible explanation that came to Mary's mind, but it seemed so unlikely, it didn't even bear thinking about.

Except that she couldn't stop thinking about it.

Betsy was brushing her hair when Mary came to bed. With her sister so occupied, Mary slipped the letter under her pillow and slept, though not very well. She couldn't get past the strange notion she had of what the letter might be.

The next morning, Mary put the letter in her pocket and walked to the well under the guise of going for some water. Having checked to make sure she was unobserved, she took out the letter.

It was what she had both suspected and doubted: a proposal of marriage. Mr. Brown wrote that Mary had gained his respect and esteem, not the least because of her compassion for the poor slaves. He was aware that he was twice her age, but the disparity would be less noticeable as she grew older, and besides, his being older meant that he had already made most of his youthful mistakes. He recognized that the responsibility of five children would be a large one, but they were good children, for the most part, and he would make sure they obeyed her. He was not a rich man, nor likely to ever become one, but he believed there were more important things, as he believed Mary did as well. Finally, so Mary might be better able to give early instruction to Ruth and Frederick and any children Mary might bear him, he offered to send her to school for a short time to repair any lack of which she might be conscious.

How many girls got slavery mentioned in their proposals? How many girls got proposed to *in writing?* And the part about bearing children—how strange to picture Mr. Brown begetting them upon her, when she had expected to die an old maid!

Mary put the letter in her pocket and stared down into the well. Should she refuse for Betsy's sake? But it wasn't as if Mr. Brown had courted Betsy in any fashion, as far as Mary could tell; he treated her kindly, but not much differently from the men in his tannery who sometimes joined them for meals. And what would refusing accomplish? Betsy certainly wouldn't want him to pick her just because Mary had turned him down—even if Mr. Brown were inclined to take one sister instead of another.

And the plain fact was that Mary didn't want to refuse.

She didn't love Mr. Brown, but that was fine—she didn't expect to. As she would often tell her granddaughters, people, at least their kind of people, were more practical in those days. They looked for certain qualities in a person, and when they found someone who possessed them, they snapped up that person and let love find its way in later. What mattered to Mary was that Mr. Brown was a kind man, and one who was well thought of by his neighbors. He was sober—something that meant a lot in a time when it was common to see men staggering about the streets, even in a small city like Meadville. Mary had never wanted to be the woman who had to greet a creature like that every evening. As a bonus, she liked Mr. Brown's looks: those rare smiles that transformed his face, his blue eyes that blazed with anger when he spoke of slavery, his lean figure, his tidy—"tasty" they called it in their part of the country—way of dressing.

She did wonder, though, what he saw in her.

Mary heard a step behind her and turned to see Mr. Brown. "You read the letter?"

"Yes. Why didn't you propose in person?"

"I am very bashful around women. It is a peculiarity of mine. The finer the lady, the more tongue-tied I am."

"Well, I am no fine lady."

"In the respects that are important to me, you are."

"Did you propose to your first wife by letter?"

First wife, practically an admission that there was to be a second. He shook his head. "There was no need; my father managed most of the business. I was quite young—only twenty—and he more or less chose her for me. Not that I was opposed in any way; she was a fine woman and an excellent influence over me. She made me a better man. In any case, he spoke to me, and then to her mother. Then at last I spoke to her, and it was all arranged. But you are entirely my own choice. So, will you marry me?"

"Yes."

"Good." He hesitated, then he kissed her—a careful kiss, but one that seemed capable of turning into something more if he didn't keep himself in check. He drew back as Mary blushed. "I think you had best go back to live with your family until we are married."

~ ~ ~

"Why is Mr. Brown going to Meadville in such a confounded hurry?" Betsy stopped in her tracks as she entered their room. "And why are you packing?"

She couldn't put this off any longer. "Mr. Brown asked me to marry him."

"You?"

Mary nodded. "He asked me this morning—well, last night, really, when he handed me a letter—and I have accepted. He is going to ask Father's permission and take me home to live until our wedding." She hoped she did not sound triumphant.

"He asked you before he asked permission of our father?" Betsy's lip quirked upward.

"I guess he supposed Father would agree."

"Yes, he undoubtedly will. Still a bit presuming, if you ask me."

"You're not . . . angry?"

"With you? No. It's not that you have any womanly wiles or art about you. Maybe that's what Mr. Brown liked. Who could have guessed?" Betsy sat on the bed, the better to think. "Of course, his first wife wasn't a beauty by any means ei— I mean—"

"I know what you mean," Mary snapped.

"Well, I'm sure you'll make him a good wife," Betsy said more kindly. "Mind you, I don't envy you those five children. They might take well enough to hired help, but a brand-new mother is a different thing altogether."

Mary suspected Betsy could have gone on like this for hours had Mr. Brown not called for her to go. Betsy said in parting, "Mr. Clark at the general store has been very friendly to me lately. And he's quite handsome and well-to-do, I hear."

~ ~ ~

A few days after her departure from Mr. Brown's house, Mary began going to school—not with Mr. Brown's children, which would have been too awkward for words, but in Meadville, where she boarded with the teacher. It was a tactful arrangement, which Mary appreciated, and she did her best to show Mr. Brown that his efforts were not wasted. She learned to read better, to compose a respectable letter, to write a nicer hand, and to keep to a household budget. But she often caught herself daydreaming about Mr. Brown when she should have been reading, and she spent far more time sewing pretty undergarments and a new dress—made with materials bought in Meadville with the money she'd earned working for Mr. Brown—than was really necessary.

Maybe she'd been fonder of Mr. Brown than she'd realized. Or maybe she was just growing fonder of him as time went on.

Once a week, Mr. Brown's duties as postmaster of his village brought him to Meadville to pick up the incoming mail from Pittsburgh. He got into the habit of stopping by to visit Mary. Not a man to sit in a parlor, he would take Mary out walking and inquire about her progress, giving no outward sign that he was her future husband, although anyone who saw them together must have guessed that something was out of the ordinary. As a result, they were getting to know each other better. Mary didn't talk much about herself beyond her studies—really, what was there to say?—and she could not have flirted with him to save her life, but through what could best be called judicious listening, she eased him into talking about himself.

He had been born in Connecticut, but at age five, had journeyed with his parents to Hudson, Ohio, where his father still lived. For years, he had worked in his father's tannery and farm, but his dream as a youth had been to enter the ministry, a goal which had seemed within reach when he enrolled in school in New England with the plan of preparing himself for college. But a series of misfortunes—an inflammation of his eyes, an economic downturn, perhaps his innate restlessness—had intervened, and he had returned home. Finally, he had decided to move to Pennsylvania and start his own tannery. So far, the venture had been successful.

"Have you had any shipments lately, sir?" Mary asked as they walked through Meadville. Really, it was more of a lope, with Mr. Brown slightly ahead of her in his favored position with his hands held behind his back. Mary quickened her pace as Mr. Brown looked back at her, his puzzled expression changing to a smile as he understood her meaning. "One, a young man. By the way, the one you helped with arrived safely, I have learned."

"When did you become interested in these poor people?"

"My father has always been a strong anti-slavery man, and he taught me and the rest of his children to think likewise. But I suppose the first strong feelings I had was when I was a young lad, during the last war with the English. I had the task of driving cattle to an army camp for my father. At one point I stayed at an inn with a man who owned a slave, a boy of my own age who quickly became my friend. His master was all kindness to me, praising me for doing so well traveling on my own with my herd, giving me sound advice on how not to be cheated of anything. To his slave he was all cruelty, kicking the lad for the slightest misstep. That awoke me to the full horrors of slavery."

"I am glad that you are doing what you are doing. I will help when we are married."

"It's good to be of use, but I cannot deceive myself; those few I have helped smuggle to safety are nothing compared to the millions still trapped in slavery. It's not enough." He slowed his pace to look into her eyes. "I believe, Mary, that my life will have been a waste if I do not strike a great blow against slavery. One day, I hope I will have an opportunity to do it."

That sounded almost presuming, as Betsy put it. But Mary could not quarrel with the sentiment.

~ ~ ~

"Miss Ames thinks you have made good progress," Mr. Brown informed Mary in early July. "She does not feel that there is any need for you to remain at school and"—he looked away—"I am quite ready to start our married life. So, unless you wish to stay—"

Mary shook her head. "I am ready too." Daringly, she took Mr. Brown's hand, the first such gesture she had made, and was relieved when he did not pull away. Thus emboldened, she asked, "Have you told the children?"

"Not yet." As if reading Mary's thoughts, he added, "But I will tell them before the wedding. I do not think it right to simply turn up with a new wife on my arm."

"They must miss their mother very much."

"Yes. As I missed mine. I must tell you that I didn't warm to my stepmother, although she was an excellent woman. I fear they may be slow to accept you, but you must take it in stride."

"My mother did the same, you know." Betsy, Martha, and three others were the products of her father's first marriage. If they had given her mother difficulties, Mary didn't know about them. In any case, although the prospect of taking over the care of the five youngsters was a daunting one, it was far better than returning to what she had come to think of her half-life at home. Yes, it was high time she ceased being Miss Day and became Mrs. Brown. "I can manage the children. When shall we marry?"

~ ~ ~

They married on July 11, 1833. Mr. Brown simply picked her up at school, where Mary sat waiting in the teacher's little parlor, her modest trousseau neatly packed in a small trunk. She wore her Sunday dress, a light blue calico print with Crawford County's subdued version of gigot sleeves. Guided by *Godey's Lady's Magazine*—the last thing she and her teacher had studied together—she had dressed her dark hair high and added a couple of ringlets with her teacher's help. Mary was not certain Mr. Brown would approve of all this fuss, but it was, after all, her wedding day,

"You look very pretty, my dear."

"And you look fine too, sir."

Mr. Brown had donned his best Sunday coat for the occasion. Mary wondered, a little guiltily, if Betsy had brushed it for him.

The Delamaters had offered their house near Meadville for the wedding, it being conveniently located for the small number of guests who attended. As was common, a justice of the peace performed the ceremony. It was a swift and simple one; before Mary had a chance to get nervous, Mr. Brown slid a thin gold band on her finger, and they were pronounced man and wife.

Betsy, her days as the Browns' housekeeper officially over, was at the wedding, chatting with her brothers and sisters. To Mary's relief, she did not act the least bit like a rejected bride. Martha had made a fine wedding cake, a few pieces of which Mary saved for her new stepchildren, who were being looked after by a neighbor. She had been rather relieved to find that they would not be at the wedding; she was content to leave the task of mothering them for the next day.

The last of the guests having waved goodbye, it was time to go to bed in the guest room that had been allotted for the newlyweds. Martha, who thought of everything, had set up a folding screen, the purpose of which Mary did not divine until John indicated the screen and said, "Why don't you get ready for bed, my dear?"

Thus concealed, Mary removed her dress, stays, and petticoats and brushed out her hair, debating whether she should braid it for the night or leave it long and flowing. Having chosen the latter, which seemed more appropriate for the occasion, she emerged in her thin linen shift to find John awaiting her in a dressing robe. He looked her over and nodded his approval. "You're a sturdy girl."

"Yes." Tall, wide of hip, and ample of bosom since her thirteenth year, Mary never had been the wispy type.

He stepped up to her and touched her cheek. "But I know you're young still. Don't be frightened. I'll be very gentle with you."

"I'm not frightened. People do this every day."

"True." John smiled and took her hand. "Then come to bed, wife."

2

December 1833 to May 1834

Mary settled into marriage as easy as an old shoe, to use a favorite phrase of John's. Oh, John had his peculiarities, but Mary supposed she had some of her own. He liked things done at a certain time and in a certain way—his way, naturally. Mary had been in his household long enough before their marriage to know that, so it didn't come as a surprise to her. It was also true that he had strong opinions about things that most people didn't have opinions about at all. For instance, he disapproved of bright colors, especially red, something Mary had to keep in mind whenever she bought or dyed her cloth. (Even when she was a gray-haired woman, she felt somewhat guilty when one of her granddaughters flitted by her in red.) He didn't care for butter. *What on earth is wrong with butter?* Mary often wondered. But at least he didn't make the rest of them use lard, as he did.

Other things had been a surprise to her—in a good way. Maybe it was the knowledge of his bashfulness around women that made Mary bolder, but from nearly the beginning, she had found pleasure in the marital act, and this in turn had pleased John. Even in this area, though, John tended to stick to a schedule, as he was a man of routine.

But there was one place where the shoe didn't fit so easily: the children. The older boys weren't much of a problem. They were polite to Mary, and she was wise enough not to expect more for the time being—after all, there were only eight years separating her in age from Owen, the youngest of the three. As for the younger two, Frederick was the easiest of her new charges. He was a sprite of a child, given to moods of silence and moods of affection. When he was in the second mood, he would often let Mary cuddle him, although he generally preferred Ruth or his father. Occasionally, he had truly wild moods when Mary couldn't do a thing with him—but then, John too had trouble at those times. He seemed to realize even then that there was something amiss with Frederick, as there had been with Dianthe, and he never disciplined him as severely as he would the older boys.

But Ruth plagued Mary so much, she canceled out all the good from the other four children. Nothing Mary did could please the little girl. Mary didn't cook like Mama. She didn't fix her hair like Mama. She didn't make her clothes like Mama. She couldn't even cook, fix hair, or make clothes like Betsy. Mama had a pretty singing voice; Mary croaked. (There, Ruth was correct—at least about Mary.) Mary was ugly and fat.

In short, Mary was completely worthless.

When John was around, of course, Ruth was all politeness to Mary, because he certainly would have punished her otherwise. His father had not spared the rod on him, and he did not spare it either. Once or twice, Mary had witnessed the boys being whipped, especially for lying—the worst offense they could commit in John's eyes—and she had no desire to see little Ruth punished likewise. So, she said nothing to John about Ruth's hatefulness and tried to tell herself that it would pass. After all, Ruth had been Dianthe's only daughter, and Dianthe had not even been a year in the grave before Mary took her place.

One day shortly before Christmas, following another go-round with Ruth—Mary had braided her hair too tight—she decided to do some sewing, which always gave her a feeling of peace. She began searching through Dianthe's rag bag. For some reason, although Mary had stuck a few things in there from time to time, she had never given it a thorough looking over. There were the usual things—shirts that had made their way down through the boys and were now unfit for anything but handkerchiefs, and a coat of John's that the moth had gotten. But there was something else, folded carefully—a simple but quite pretty linen dress that could have belonged to no one but Dianthe.

There was a trunk in which some of Dianthe's possessions—her famous shawl and her Bible, among other things—were stored. Why this dress wasn't with them, Mary didn't know, and the truth was, she didn't care. She was so tired of Ruth finding her at fault for not being Dianthe; even John had let it be known once or twice that Dianthe had her ways of doing things that Mary would do well to emulate. So, without further thought, Mary spread the dress upon the table and got out her scissors.

"You can't do that! It's Mama's!" Ruth ran up and snatched the dress, almost cutting herself on the scissors. "You—you monster! You stupid monster! I'm telling Father!"

She ran off in the direction of the tannery and returned, panting, with John in tow. "What is this all about? A dress?"

"Mama's dress! She"—Ruth's voice quivered—"she was going to cut it to pieces!"

"It was in the ragbag," Mary said.

John looked at her half kindly, half reprovingly. He held out the dress, letting it unfold gracefully. "Surely, my dear, you must have realized that this didn't belong in the ragbag?"

Mary felt small and, yes, stupid, as if she were being disciplined like one of the children. "I wasn't thinking."

"No, I don't think you could have been. But no harm done." John refolded the dress and nodded at Ruth. "Put it with your mother's other things. And now I must get back to the tannery. I hope this sort of interruption won't become routine."

Ruth trotted off with her precious dress in her hand and her little nose in the air, and Mary put away the ragbag and found something else to keep her busy. But she was hurt because she had not wanted the dress for her own use, but for the child she was carrying.

Coming from a large family, Mary wasn't ignorant of such things. She knew what to look for, and even though she had noticed only one real symptom—her lack of monthlies—that seemed quite enough. She didn't feel sick or tired, but she did feel somehow different. Just the other day, she'd had to loosen her stays despite all the hard work she was doing around the house that should have kept her trim. Still, she hadn't yet told John. She hoped he would be pleased, but she couldn't forget that childbirth had killed Dianthe—just as it could kill Mary. She decided not to think of John waiting a decent interval, then handing another woman a letter and following her to the well.

But she had missed four courses, so it was probably time she told John. So that night, as she and John lay in each other's arms—it was Friday, one of their usual nights—she said, "I wanted that dress for a reason."

"My dear, there is no need to keep discussing this."

"I wanted to make baby clothes out of it. Our baby's clothes."

"You are with child?"

Mary was pleased that he hadn't asked whether she was certain, as if she were such a ninny as not to know. "Yes. I think I am about four months along."

"I suspected as much."

"How?"

"I am a father many times over, my dear. And I have noticed that you have not been troubled by your monthly courses for some time."

"Oh," Mary muttered. It was annoying, being found out so easily.

John kissed her tenderly. "But I am very glad to hear my suspicions were right. We must pray for a safe delivery. As for the child's clothing, I suppose that the things handed down from my children are getting a little worn"—here, Mary nodded vigorously, not that John could see her in the dark—"so if you cannot weave enough linen to supply your needs, we will get what you need in Meadville."

So, they made up from what Mary considered their first quarrel.

~ ~ ~

As Mary's time approached, Ruth began to warm up to her a bit, drawn at first by the growing pile of baby things in Mary's work basket. Poor Dianthe, Mary had learned by then, had been ill during most of her fatal pregnancy and hadn't made many preparations for Ruth to admire. Perhaps she'd had her suspicions that they wouldn't be necessary.

"I can sew a little. Can I help?"

"Of course, but I want you to practice on some hand-kerchiefs first."

Ruth obeyed and was soon quite capable of hemming baby gowns. They began sewing side by side, much to the pleasure of John, who must have noticed more of the tension between them than Mary had realized.

"Are you having a boy or a girl?" Ruth asked during one of their sessions.

"I won't know until I have the baby."

"Oh." Ruth contemplated this for a while before adding, "Well, I hope you have a girl. There are plenty of boys."

Privately, Mary agreed with her—not, of course, that she would object to a child of either sex, but there were already four sons to carry on the Brown name. "Well, we will see."

The next day, when Mary braided Ruth's hair, she pronounced her work almost as good as Mama's. It was a sweet moment.

~ ~ ~

On May 11, ten months to the day after Mary's wedding, Mary was awakened by a horrible pain that ceased for a while only to be followed by another. After a few minutes of this, she shook John awake. "It's my time."

He shot up. "I'll get the midwife."

"And my mother." Mary winced. "And Martha. And Bet—"

"I'll get as many as I can, my dear."

The midwife—simply a neighbor who had fallen into the way of delivering babies because there were so few others around to do it at that time—soon arrived, followed later by

Mary's mother and older sisters. By the time the family turned up, though, Mary was far along in labor. At least, the midwife pointed out cheerily, she was not taking forever, as so many women did with their first babes. Mary was not particularly grateful, though.

To Mary's mind, she raised an uncommon commotion in childbirth, groaning and demanding to know when the business would be over. Yet when all was over, the midwife pronounced her the quietest patient she'd ever had, although she seemed to think this more of a peculiarity than cause for praise. Not that Mary cared, for she was hugging the beautiful little girl the midwife had put into her arms. With only slight help from the midwife, the baby soon found her way to Mary's breast and settled contentedly to her meal.

John had retreated to the tannery after Mary was safely in the hands of the midwife and remained there until Martha fetched him. By then, Mary was cleaned up and sitting upon fresh linen. "What a lovely girl you have given me," he said, stooping to kiss them both. "You are feeling well, my dear?"

"Yes."

"Good. Your mother and sisters have told me that they can stay as long as you need them. I don't want you up too soon."

He took the baby, whom they had already decided to name Sarah, and rocked her gently in his arms before handing her back. "God has been good to us."

Just then, the children trooped into the room. The older boys, well used to this ritual, gave their new sister a nodding glance before running off, but Frederick stared in fascination at the newcomer, and Ruth said, "Good. A sister, just like I wanted."

Mary's ordeal had made her a little bold. "Does that mean I can stay?"

Ruth thought it over for a moment. "I suppose."

3

September 1842 to December 1843

Sitting with her seventh child, Austin, at her breast, Mary gazed at the list of belongings that the bankruptcy court was allowing the family to keep—pretty much everything inside the house, she discovered as Austin, who had arrived in the world on a fine September morning just days before the court had taken its inventory, gave a contented snort. She had been worried about the spinning wheels, which she had finally started to think of as hers about a year into her marriage. But they were safely on the list, as were almost all the other meager furnishings in the house.

Six bedsteads, old ... one writing desk ... six feather beds, old & poor ... Only a couple of sturdy pieces of furniture had been deemed worth seizing by the court.

John had hoped for something different, of course, when he moved them from Pennsylvania to Ohio, where his father lived and where other family members were scattered about. He had planned to operate another tannery, grander than the one in Pennsylvania and with the backing of a partner. But the partner had taken his son into the business instead—not much to be done about that. John had then put his hopes into investing in land, counting on the construction of a canal to make its value soar.

For a time, things had gone their way. At one time they had owned not one, but four farms. Mary had caught herself thinking of the larger house they would build, with a real parlor like the one in which she had been married. There would have to be a parlor set to furnish it, of course—maybe even a piano. Ruth longed for one, Mary knew, and Sarah would surely enjoy it as well. There had been no rush, of course; she could wait a few years until they could safely afford these things.

But slowly at first, then relentlessly, all had changed. The planners of the canal decided on another course. The national economy had taken not one but two dives, once in 1837 and again in 1839. John had relied on credit to finance his ventures, and now all had come due with no means to repay it. Mary had lost track of all the lawsuits filed against her husband.

Not that John had simply admitted defeat; that wasn't in his nature. At various times, he had bred cattle, racehorses, sheep—anything on four legs, it had seemed. He had gone East, venturing into New York City, following up one prospect and then another. Finally, he'd been given a handsome sum by a firm in Connecticut to invest in sheep for them. He'd not had bad intentions in doing what he had done next: desperate to pay a looming debt, instead of using the money as intended, he had appropriated it for his own use, planning to repay it from a bank loan that was coming any day.

But the loan had never come through, and John—ashamed and as cast down as he must have been when

Dianthe died—had had no choice but to assign his goods to his creditors. The best of their goods and livestock had been auctioned off.

Yet all hadn't been lost: a sympathetic creditor, Heman Oviatt, had arranged for John to keep his sheep and to tan hides for him in Richfield, Ohio, not far from Akron. This had eased the burden upon the Browns until a fresh round of lawsuits left John with no choice but to declare bankruptcy, pursuant to which a man had come to the house in Richfield and inventoried their possessions. Forced to do his work amid a swarm of children, with Mary and her brand-new babe lying in one of the beds he dutifully counted, he had clearly not relished his task.

If she had bought that parlor set, no doubt it would have been gone and sold by now.

Frederick ran in, tailed by Mary's boys. "Ma! They're taking away the oxen!"

"Yes, your father said they probably would."

"But they're mine!" Frederick's eyes widened. "I helped train them! And they won ribbons last year. They can't take them away! I won't let it happen!"

Before Mary could stop him—not that she could have, lying in bed with only one hand free—Frederick rushed to the door, only to be stopped by John as he came in from outside. "Now, what's this?"

"Pa, you promised me they wouldn't take the oxen."

"I told you we'd try to keep them if we could. We can't. They're too valuable."

Frederick stared straight ahead. Sometimes, when disappointed, he would simply shrug and go about his business; at others, he would go into a screaming, howling fit. No one in the family—not even his father, not even his older brothers—was adept at predicting which course he would take.

Sarah—the only girl Mary had borne—sat beside Mary's bed, industriously hemming a blanket for the newcomer. (The bankruptcy man hadn't bothered with the baby things.) She rose and pulled at Frederick's hand. "We'll have others someday. Even better ones."

"Indeed, we will," John said. "This is just a transitory state of affairs." He smiled in his almost imperceptible fashion. "After all, we do have an ox cart left to us. Something will have to draw it."

"And we have each other," Mary said. Perhaps it was a trite thing to say, but whatever the upheavals of the past few years, she could still find comfort in looking around her. John Jr. was gone from home, teaching school in hopes of raising funds to further his education, Ruth was off on some errand, and Jason and Owen were out in the fields, but Frederick and the children she had borne John were all before her: Sarah, Watson, Salmon, Charles, Oliver, Peter, and now Austin. Some took after her in looks, some took after John, and one or two didn't look much like either of them. There was every shade of hair from light blond (Sarah) to red (Salmon) to dark brown (Watson), and every shade of personality from her sweet Sarah to her grumpy Salmon. Oh, they kept her busy, and they weren't always well-behaved (even though John was still strict with his offspring, he couldn't be everywhere at once, and Mary tended to be soft-hearted), but they were her greatest blessing, something that no court could take away. The Bible warned against pride, and Mary generally heeded it, but she could not help but feel a bit of it when her brood ranged themselves around the table with John and her stepchildren. They were so squeezed together that it was hard for them to not elbow each other in the ribs, although admittedly some, like Salmon, didn't try that hard to avoid it.

She patted Frederick on the arm and nodded at Watson and Salmon. "You boys go do your chores now. There are plenty creatures left to take care of here."

~ ~ ~

"Please pass the biscuits, John," Jason said to his brother as the family breakfasted. When this produced no result, he added, "Please pass the biscuits within my lifetime, John."

"Oh. Sorry." John Jr. reached for a plate of biscuits, still hot and delicious smelling, but was preempted by Salmon, who grabbed one for himself before passing the plate to its destination.

"Are you well, John?" Mary asked her stepson. "You've been acting like you're somewhere else these past few days."

A year had passed since the bankruptcy, and the family was getting on well enough that John had been able to give a little money to John Jr., who would be leaving after breakfast to return to Grand River Institute in Austinburg. "Quite well," John Jr. said.

"Well, you certainly don't act like it."

"Something's ailing him, Ma, but it's not what you think," Owen said as he buttered his biscuit. "He's in love."

"Owen!"

"Well, it's true."

"You didn't tell me," Ruth protested.

"Or me," their father said. "Is Owen right, son?"

"I merely wrote to a young lady I had met at school last term to ask if she would be returning, and I got a reply that she would be. That's all."

"You took it less calmly yesterday," Owen said. "*Oh, my beautiful Adelia will be coming back* was what I heard."

"Is she beautiful, then?" Ruth asked.

"She's pretty," John Jr. said.

"*Sparkling blue eyes, curly blond hair, and the face of an angel* is how you described her yesterday."

Normally, John would have elevated the conversation at such a point, perhaps turning it to one of the issues of the day, but instead, he said, "I do hope her character is as fine as her looks, son."

"It is." John Jr. put down his knife with a sigh. "She's perfect."

"Are you going to marry her, then?" Sarah asked. "I think you should."

"She sounds nice," Charles said.

"I've got a ways to go before I can do that," John Jr. said. "First, we have to get to know each other bet—"

"And to kiss," Frederick said.

"Yes, well, I suppose a kiss wouldn't be out of line at some point."

"No, indeed," Jason agreed.

"A kiss, then, but more important, we have to fall in love—"

"Before or after the kiss?"

"Before," Mary said firmly.

"Yes, before. And then I would have to get her father's permission to marry her, and I would have to prove that I could support her. And, of course, I have to get her to say yes."

"That's a lot to do," Sarah said.

"Yes, it is a rather daunting task. I would like to undertake it. But since I have to be back at school to do anything about it, I'd best be on my way."

John Jr. gathered up his belongings, and the family gathered around to say their goodbyes. Finally, John Jr. said,

"Well, I'll see all of you at the end of the term." He smiled at Mary, who was six months gone with child. "And one besides that, I trust."

"God willing," John and Mary said, almost in unison.

~ ~ ~

Mary wasn't unduly worried when Charles complained of a pain in his stomach a few days later. With eight children under age thirteen in the house, seven of them boys—some of them going to the village school to trade illnesses back and forth, some eating too much or eating the wrong thing—there was always a bellyache somewhere. Still, the Brown children were a hardy crew who usually shook off illnesses and injuries quickly, so Mary got out her usual remedies without feeling more than her usual concern.

They didn't work. Nor did her prayers. Nor did John's.

Charles grew no better; instead, he developed the bloody flux. Although John had always preferred his own doctoring to others, he allowed a medical man to be fetched, but the doctor could do nothing that was not already being done. A week later, on September 11, Charles was dead. He would have been six in November. Always a brave boy, he had suffered in silence until delirium mercifully took hold of him.

Mary, tears streaming down her cheeks, dressed him in the pants he'd recently started wearing, just like his older brothers Watson and Salmon. He had been so proud to leave off his babyish frock. John, no less sorrowing than Mary, built him a coffin and managed to bury him nearby, but there was no time to mourn further, not even time for a simple funeral. Hours after Charles died, Ruth, Oliver, Frederick, Sarah, Peter, and Austin had fallen ill, and when John returned from his dismal task, he could barely stand and had to take to his bed as well.

Neighbors—at least those who dared to walk into a house where sickness raged—came to help Mary as she moved from sufferer to sufferer in a fog of grief and exhaustion, sleeping only an hour or two at a time. John and Ruth, less sick than the others, staggered up whenever they could to give someone a drink of water or to wet his or her forehead. But all of them combined could not save Austin, who died on September 21, Peter, who died on September 22, or Sarah, who died on September 23. Austin, who had spent his first birthday crying in agony. Peter, who though not yet three, had promised to be the best looking of the Browns. Sarah, Mary's firstborn.

Never before had she had the experience, so common to so many, of losing a child. She'd not even miscarried one. Now she had suffered the loss fourfold.

John had recovered sufficiently to help Jason and Owen build three more small coffins while Mary laid out the children for burial, ignoring the neighbors' pleas for her to rest. Carefully, she dressed them: Gowns for Austin and Peter, who would never live to wear their first pants. Sarah's favorite dress and the dainty pantalettes of which she had been rather proud. Alone of the four children, she had known that she was dying, and though she had died a most exemplary death from a religious point of view, she had also found the strength to insist that she be buried in her best dress, a green calico, and with her favorite doll. Mary carefully tucked it under Sarah's arm.

There was at least a funeral, conducted by the minister of Richfield's Congregational Church. The diminished family listened to a short service, curtailed because so many were still weak from the illness that had cost them so much. It was a fine day, warm yet with a hint of fall in the air, but Mary could take no comfort from her surroundings.

Beside her, Oliver—at four, the youngest surviving child—stood staring as the last coffin was lowered into the ground. The illness had nearly carried him off as well. Since recovering, he had walked around like a baffled puppy, trying to comprehend the fact that his closest playmates, Charles and Peter, were gone, along with the baby he had considered a curiosity and the sister who had toted him around like a doll in his infancy. "They're not coming back, then?" he asked as they walked back to their house.

"No, Oliver," Mary said.

"Never?"

"Never." She looked to John on the other side of her for some comforting words, but he was silent. Had he stooped before, or had he just begun to?

It was left to Ruth to take her little brother by the hand. "They have gone to see God, and they are very happy in a very beautiful place."

"I wish they were in Richfield."

~ ~ ~

They came home to a clean house and a good meal, thanks to their neighbors. Mary tried not to notice the odd gaps at the table. No one wanted to move over to fill the accustomed spaces of those who had gone.

After a mostly silent meal and the usual evening prayers, John sat down at the desk to write to John Jr., who had not been informed that anyone in the family was ailing. John had insisted that he not be told, reasoning that if he knew, he would surely come home, putting yet one more person in danger. He wasn't writing home much anyway; the one letter they had received from him in the midst of all their troubles said that he was busy attending to his studies and perhaps

41

also to his romance, happily unaware of what had befallen his family. After John's pen had scratched for a while, he asked, "Mary, would you like to see the letter?"

She nodded, and John handed it to her.

God has seen fit to visit us with the pestilence since you left us, and Four of our number sleep in the dust, and Four of us that are still living have been more or less unwell but appear to be nearly recovered. . . . This has been to us all a bitter cup indeed, and we have drunk deeply, but still the Lord reigneth and bless be his great and holy name forever. In our sore affliction there is still some comfort. Sarah (like your own Mother) during her sickness discovered great composure of mind, and patience, together with strong assurance at times of meeting God in Paradise. . . . We fondly hope that she is not disappointed. They were all children towards whom we might have been a little partial but now they all lie in a little row together. . . .

Mary wondered how much comfort her stepson would gain from Sarah's good end. Since he had turned nineteen or twenty, he had regularly clashed with his father about religion, much to John's despair. She could hear him ask, *What just and merciful God would snatch four young children from their parents?*

Indeed, she had been silently asking the same question.

"Jason said he wanted to add a line or two. Would you like to?"

"No. I don't have anything to say."

"Very well." John handed the letter to Jason, then turned back to Mary. "You look very worn out. Go to bed. You must keep up your strength."

She nodded and let him lead her to the bed they shared on the first floor of their little house, one that up until now had felt crowded. He helped her out of her dress, then, after she braided her hair for the night and donned her night cap, helped her settle into the freshly laundered sheets—the neighbors had taken care of everything. It was a chilly night, and he tucked the covers around her. "Are you warm enough?"

"Yes."

"Good." He kissed her on the cheek. "A brighter day will dawn, Mary."

~ ~ ~

There was something to be said for living on a farm in times of sorrow: no matter what one's misery, cows had to be milked, chickens fed, and eggs collected. There was winter clothing to be made, baby clothing to be sewn. And there was the Browns' special business to see to as well. Whatever had befallen the family over the years, wherever they had dwelt, their home had remained a stop on what was now called the Underground Railroad, and every few months, runaway slaves arrived to be sheltered and fed, then helped to freedom.

If the Lord had meant to punish them for having too much pride in their children—the only rationale Mary would think of for His taking four of them—He might have at least set off their good works in helping the slaves. But she was trying not to question the ways of the Almighty, partly because she had been brought up not to do so, and partly because it seemed such a hopeless task.

There were her surviving children to attend to as well, of course. Here she had some cause for gratitude. Wild and strange as Frederick could be at times, he had proven to be the best of brothers to Watson, Salmon, and particularly

Oliver, letting the latter pester him as much as he wanted. Ruth, feeling the lack of a little sister to pet, openly hoped that Mary would bear another girl, but in the meantime, she took much of the heavy work upon herself so that Mary could rest. Jason and Owen spent most of their time working on the farm, but they too were humoring their brothers by allowing them to share their sleeping quarters in the loft in the adjacent barn, a mark of manhood which the older of Mary's boys had always envied. John Jr. had written a beautifully consoling letter from school, though not as religiously orthodox as his father would have preferred. Gradually, everyone had shifted their positions around the table, so a stranger entering the room would never have guessed that four more people had sat around it just weeks before.

So, she managed to get through her days, though there were times she would find one of the children's possessions—a garment on a hook or in a drawer, a toy—and wonder at such pain a mere inanimate object could cause.

It was Sarah's things that had the power to hurt her most. With so many boys so close in age, Mary had got into the habit of making their clothing in duplicate, and everything had been handed down so much that there was nothing in Charles or Peter's clothing to tear at her heart. Most of their toys had been owned in common with their surviving brothers. Likewise, most of the baby clothing that Austin left behind had nothing unique to him about it. What was not destined for the ragbag would go to the next infant. But Sarah was a different matter. No one else had worn those dresses of hers, which Mary had spent more time than necessary trimming. No one else had used that little calico bonnet that Sarah had made herself, with only notional help from Mary. And there were those rag dolls that kept popping up around the house. Sarah had not picked up after herself as well as Mary had thought.

Her grief was of a quiet sort. On some days, she would sit in her rocking chair, cradling her swollen belly. At other times, maybe once or twice a week, she would find herself wandering to the spot where her children lay buried. Sometimes she would simply sit there, other times she would weep.

She doubted that she was the only one who made these pilgrimages. John Jr. had once told her that not long after Dianthe died, he had seen his father lying prostrate at her grave, his shoulders heaving. John Jr. had then slipped away, not wishing to disturb the solemn majesty of such sorrow.

But if John was making such visits now, Mary never saw him. Like her, he bore his burden silently. In one respect, though, he had changed: he had become far more lenient with the children. Even Salmon had not been able to provoke a whipping lately, and goodness knew sorrow had not kept him out of trouble.

It was a sign of this altered state of affairs that two days before Christmas, Mary and Ruth were busily preparing for the feast to come. Like many of Puritan stock, John looked askance at that holiday, but a number of their neighbors in Richfield, including the boys' playmates, had begun to make a great fuss over the occasion, even hanging up stockings for Santa. In his softened state, John—in the face of Oliver's pleadings—had weakened his stance enough to permit a Christmas dinner with oranges and nuts for the children to enjoy, although the chimney would remain barred to Santa.

But the meal would not be of Mary's making. Just as Mary was beginning to set out the ingredients for a pumpkin pie, she felt the familiar pangs of labor.

One of the boys fetched a midwife and a neighbor—one of the women who had helped tend the dying children, although Mary preferred not to dwell on this—then disappeared with his brothers and John into the barn or into the fields. Ruth, who had finally been granted the privilege of assisting, scurried about, obeying the commands of Mary's attendants. But her help was not required for long. In a couple of hours, after a comparatively easy labor, Mary was delivered of a daughter.

The women who generally saw fit to pronounce upon such things had warned Mary that the baby might be a puny little thing, stunted by all the sorrow she had passed through. But the girl the midwife put in her arms, though admittedly a little smaller than her previous children, was sturdy and squalling. After an extended show of indifference, she took to Mary's nipple eagerly, even greedily.

John, summoned by Ruth, came to admire his latest contribution to the world. "Are you feeling well, my dear?"

"Yes."

"Good. I had been worried about your health after—" A shadow passed over his face, and instead he took the baby. "A lovely girl," he said as the infant glared up at him with an expression that was anything but endearing. Mary could not help but smile. "God has been merciful to us by giving us another daughter to cherish."

It was the first inkling Mary had that John realized how particularly she had grieved for Sarah. She held the infant—Anne, they decided—tightly after John passed her back. "He has indeed."

For the first time in months, she believed those words.

4

October 1846 to February 1847

Although Mary was more comfortable going to the servants' entrance of the Perkins mansion to pick up the Brown family's mail, which for reasons best known to the postmaster had to be delivered in care of the Perkins family, Mrs. Perkins had made so much fuss the last time she had used it that Mary went to the front door, even though the Irish servant girl who opened the door was arguably better dressed than Mary. Instead of just handing her the mail as she usually did, however, the girl said, "Mrs. Perkins wants a word with you, ma'am," and turned to fetch her, assuming that Mary would not refuse. So, she waited as the sheep baaed in the distance.

Not long after the birth of Anne, John had entered into a business partnership with Simon Perkins of Akron. The "of Akron" wasn't necessary; anyone in their part of Ohio knew about Mr. Perkins. His father had founded Akron, and between the two of them, it was now a thriving city. A rich man in his own right, Mr. Perkins had married the daughter of David Tod, a prominent and wealthy politician in the state.

He and his bride had built a handsome stone mansion on a hill just outside of Akron. Deciding to add sheep-raising to his numerous enterprises but knowing little about matters of breeding, he had cast about for an appropriate partner and had hit upon John, who, even in the midst of all of his business troubles, had gained a reputation as a man who knew mutton.

In the spring of 1844, the Browns had moved from Richfield to Akron, into the simple frame house in which Mr. and Mrs. Perkins had stayed while they were building their mansion. Now the expanse between the houses was filled with the flock of Perkins and Brown, admired throughout the state and even outside it for the quality of the wool it produced. Residents of Akron had christened the incline Mutton Hill.

Though Mr. Perkins had taken most of the financial risk upon himself, he largely deferred to John's judgment, and so it had come about that the partners, at John's urging, had opened a wool commission house at Springfield, Massachusetts to sort, grade, and sell wool from Ohio and other western states. John had been in Springfield since the summer, having come home to Akron only briefly, when the Browns' latest daughter was born in September.

With him in Massachusetts was a highly reluctant John Jr., whose heart was in Ohio with Miss Wealthy Hotchkiss, a young girl he had met at school the previous year through Ruth, her roommate there. Miss Hotchkiss's widowed mother insisted that she not marry until she was eighteen, or at least within comfortable sight of her eighteenth birthday. That struck Mary as a bit foolish, as she had married young with no ill effects, and she suspected that Mrs. Hotchkiss was simply reluctant to let her daughter go.

That Mary could understand.

After those dreadful days of loss in 1843, followed by Anne's birth, she had borne John two more girls: fourteen-month-old Amelia and six-week-old Sarah, the latter named after her dead sister. Anne, however, had become "Annie" while Amelia had been transformed somehow into "Kitty"—all the doing of John, who had previously not been one for nicknames or diminutives. He'd also eased up quite a bit in disciplining Watson, Salmon, and Oliver. In fact, some might say he had eased up too much on the three boys, at least in Salmon's case. Certainly Mrs. Perkins would; indeed, Mary had spent most of 1845 and 1846 apologizing to her for Salmon's pranks. She hoped her son hadn't pulled yet another one.

Mrs. Perkins glided to the door and nodded at Annie, whom Mary had brought with her. "Good afternoon, dear."

Annie fixed Mrs. Perkins with her usual penetrating glare, her default expression for most people outside of the family. Only Watson, whom Annie adored, and Annie's father had never received the glare. "Good afternoon," she said crisply.

Mrs. Perkins wisely turned her attention to Mary. "How is the new little one?"

"Very well," said Mary. "She'll be wanting to nurse in a bit."

"Well, I won't keep you. I did have a concern . . ."

"Salmon really has been trying to do bet—"

"Salmon? No, he's been on his best behavior since the incident that shall not be named." This would be the time Salmon, embittered after some of the Perkins servant girls reported that he had been seen stealing cherries from the Perkins orchard, put itching powder on the seats of the outhouse they used. "My daughter Anna told me that she saw some *black* people around your house a few days before."

"Black people," Mary said evenly. John had not hidden his abolitionist sentiments from Mr. Perkins, who did not share them, but nor had he let it be known that the Underground Railroad now had a stop at the house on Mutton Hill. With John and John Jr. in Springfield, Jason traveling to and fro on his father's business, Frederick tending the flock that remained at Richfield, and Mary tied to her new baby, most of the conductor's work had fallen upon Owen, who apparently had not been as careful as he should have been, although the people the nosy Miss Perkins had seen were safely on their way to their next destination. With a mix of guilt over lying and pride over finding a lie, she said, "I believe my sons were putting on a minstrel show the other day."

"For just themselves?"

"I don't think they got very far with it."

"Still, I would take care that the house is well secured at night. Akron has acquired a number of desperate characters over the years."

"I will."

"Well, you had best get back to that baby of yours."

Clutching her mail with one hand and little Annie's hand with the other, Mary bade Mrs. Perkins goodbye and walked back to her house. Despite Mrs. Perkins' prying and what Mary suspected had not been a convincing lie, it was a pleasure to be out, as it was a crisp autumn day and she had been confined longer with her new Sarah than with her last few pregnancies. Only in the past few days had she felt herself again.

At home, Ruth emerged from the kitchen. "The baby's been sound asleep, but Kitty is about to drive me mad. She's everywhere and into everything. Why, she almost spilled ink on herself."

Kitty, whose curiosity had tripled with her newly perfected ability to walk, smiled angelically at Mary.

"Come, Kitty. Get out of Ruth's way."

Ruth scowled. "I wish I'd gone back to school."

"Your father said you could go back next year."

"That's next year."

"Well, I am thankful that you agreed to help out here instead. And it would have lonely for you there, with both your brother and Miss Hotchkiss gone." Miss Hotchkiss was teaching district school as part of her campaign to prove herself mature enough for marriage.

Ruth snapped, "I had other friends at school, you know."

"Of course," Mary said mildly. "Would you like me to fix supper?"

"No, Mother. You rest. You shouldn't have got out of bed in the first place."

Obediently, Mary sank into a chair and closed her eyes. How long did she doze? Ten minutes? A half hour? All she knew was that the sound that awoke her was one that she had never heard before and one that she would spend the rest of her days praying to never hear again. A crash, then a piercing scream, then another, followed by a moan.

All was a blur after that. Mary running into the kitchen to find Ruth crouching on the floor amid quantities of red-hot soup, clutching Kitty in her arms and weeping. Owen rushing in from outside, yelling for Watson to get help from the Perkins house. The baby awakening and crying piteously, joined by Annie. A physician shaking his head and saying that there was nothing to be done except to make the poor little mite comfortable with laudanum. Mary holding Kitty through the night, long after Kitty had gasped out her last breath, until Mr. and Mrs. Perkins gently pried her from Mary's grasp and forced Mary to take a draught of the same laudanum and lie down.

The soup had burned Kitty so badly, Mr. and Mrs. Perkins could hardly bear to look at her. But Mary could scarcely bear to look away.

~ ~ ~

Groggily, Mary awoke to an eerily quiet house. Mr. and Mrs. Perkins had taken the children to their mansion and had even located a wet nurse for Sarah until she could be reunited with Mary's breast. Meanwhile, the Perkins' hired girls had cleaned the kitchen and prepared breakfast, though none of the remaining Browns—Mary, Owen, and Ruth—could do anything but rearrange their food. Mr. Perkins had arranged for a funeral and a suitable burial place, and his workmen were building a small coffin. Two neighbors sat watching over the still figure covered with a snowy linen sheet. There was nothing for Mary to do but remember the horrors of the day before and blame herself for her short nap.

With the pretense of breakfast over, Owen said, "I'm going to write to Father."

Ruth wrung her hands. "Don't tell Father what I did."

"I'm just going to write the facts," Owen said, getting out pen and paper. In the detached manner she had viewed everything since awakening and finding that the events of the last day had not been a nightmare, Mary thought it was a shame that Jason or John Jr. weren't there to write the news; their handwriting was much better than Owen's. John might have to read the letter twice over to know what had happened.

"Please, Owen!"

"Would you rather he hear it from Mr. Perkins first? You know he'll write. I'll be fair."

Ruth said nothing but put her handkerchief up to her face.

Mary didn't blame Ruth. No one did. Ruth, busy with her cooking, had turned her back for an instant, and Kitty, no doubt attracted by the smell of the soup, had scurried up to investigate and toppled the pot upon herself. "It could happen to anybody," Mary said hollowly, and not for the first time. "Why, if I had been in the kitchen helping you instead of asleep . . ."

"You were asleep because I made you rest." Ruth started crying again.

Mary couldn't offer her any comfort. It was left to Owen to soothe his sister.

Presently, the workmen arrived with the coffin, followed by Mrs. Perkins, who would have laid out the body, but Mary insisted on performing this task for herself. Her preparations for the short, simple funeral finished, Mary gazed at Kitty, wearing a pretty little sunbonnet with her face tilted at an angle to obscure her injuries. A phrase tugged at her memory—not from John's Bible readings, but from somewhere else she could not remember. Something her teacher had read during her brief time in school, perhaps, or something that John Jr. had read aloud. "May flights of angels sing thee to thy rest," she said softly.

Startled, Mrs. Perkins looked at her. "Did I say something wrong?" Mary asked tiredly.

"No." Mrs. Perkins wiped her eye. "Not at all."

53

~ ~ ~

Soon the letters from Springfield arrived. One was from John directed exclusively to Ruth, who took it outside to read and returned looking more at peace than she had in days. Mary received her own letter from John, along with letters from John Jr. and Jason. They gave her some comfort, but not what she wanted most: John himself, to draw solace from and to solace in return. Although he wrote of divine providence, he also admitted to being struck dumb by the news, and in his next letter, written a few weeks after the first, he confessed to yearning for home. Yet he stayed in Springfield.

Without John, she watched 1846 fade into 1847, and their lives resumed their accustomed pace. Sarah, cheerfully unconscious of the tragedy that had briefly deprived her of her mother's milk, was a healthy, happy baby, easy to please. Watson, Salmon, and Oliver, sobered somewhat by Kitty's death, were making an effort to apply themselves at school and at home. Annie interested herself in a litter of puppies. Ruth began to hum again as she went about her chores.

And Mary? She carried on, still with that same sense of detachment. Mrs. Perkins and the other neighbors could not have been kinder, but Mary suspected that they thought she was lacking somehow—that she should be showing more emotion, dabbing at her eyes as she fed the chickens. But what good would that do? She'd shown plenty of emotion, in private at least, after the children in Richfield died, and it hadn't spared her from another loss.

Finally, in February, John wrote that he was coming home. He arrived a few days later with nuts and oranges for the children, fish, tea, and bolts of cloth for Mary, and a nickname for Sarah, who'd been a red-faced newborn when he last saw her. "Little Chick," he said, patting her fluffy blond head and taking her into his arms.

Annie, jealous, scrambled into her father's lap and began her favorite activity: methodically emptying his pockets. Ruth, who had been the recipient of a tender greeting from John, sat on a footstool near his feet. Mary's three boys munched their oranges and dutifully answered John's questions about their conduct. Frederick, Owen, and Jason reported to John about the sheep operations and joked about the absent John Jr., who was in Ashtabula County visiting his ladylove.

"It's good to be back," John said finally. He gently moved Annie off his lap. "Mary, show me where little Kitty rests."

Mary nodded. Together they walked to Kitty's grave, which bore a wooden marker half covered in snow. John said a short prayer, then brushed at his eyes and cleared his throat. "I admire the fortitude with which you have borne this."

Mary shook her head. "There's no credit in it. With the children in Richfield, I wept, I sorrowed. Now I just feel—I can't describe it."

"Numb."

"Why, yes. That is the word."

"I felt the same way after Dianthe's death. I couldn't understand it. I had loved her; I had been a good husband to her, I thought—not perfect, by any means, as you know yourself, but good enough. I missed her. But I simply felt this deathly calm, which also kept me from attending to my work properly. It lasted for weeks. Finally, I found myself weeping at her grave—young John caught me at it, as a matter of fact. After that, I began to feel more as I should, and I was able to exercise my responsibilities as well. It was not so long after that I hired your sister as my housekeeper, and you know how that turned out. I don't know what brought about the change; I can only attribute it to God's mercy. It is there, Mary."

"I hope so."

"Still, it is better to bear sorrow together. I've missed you."

"And I you."

They stood in silence, staring at the humble grave. "I think she should be with the others at Richfield," Mary said. "She's all alone here, and she was such a friendly little crea—"

She could say no more for the tears that were finally falling. Quietly, John said, "She is with her heavenly father, I trust, but if it comforts you, I will see about having her moved."

"Thank you, John." She brushed at her eyes as he put his arms around her. His steadying embrace was the comfort she had missed most, she realized.

"Are you ready to go back?" he asked after some time had passed.

She nodded. Hand in hand, they walked back to the house on Mutton Hill.

5

July 1847 to February 1848

Mary had never heard such a din as when the Albany-bound train pulled out of the station at Buffalo, throwing off so many sparks that Mary worried that the whole contraption might blow up. John was placidly reading his newspaper, though, so she settled back into her rather uncomfortable seat, holding Sarah with one arm and Annie with the other. Because Ohio had been slow to get railroads built—much to Mr. Perkins's disgust—it was the Browns' first time on the cars, except for John and John Jr., who were already old hands at riding the iron horse thanks to their business travels.

Her boys, jostling for position beside the window, did not seem to share her concerns. "I like the train better than the steamer," Oliver said.

"Well, I liked the steamer better than the train," Salmon countered. Mary knew he was just being contrary.

"You haven't been on the train long enough to know for sure," Watson said. He was the reasonable one.

"Which do you like better, Wealthy?" Frederick asked.

"Goodness, I don't know yet," said the newest member of the family. She looked ruefully at her pretty dress, which was already a little sooty. "I do know I should have worn a dark dress like Mother Brown."

"I always wear dark dresses," Mary said and instantly wished she hadn't. It would have been better to accept the implied compliment.

John Jr. had introduced them to his bride just the day before, he and Wealthy having reached Buffalo a day or so after the Browns arrived. Everyone had seemed to like the girl, a doe-eyed, dark-haired creature. John had welcomed her with a "Well, well"—his habitual greeting for close family members. (John's second son, Jason, had married about the same time as his brother; his bride, Miss Ellen Sherbondy, had rated merely a polite "Good morning," from John.) Mary's boys had regaled Wealthy with their adventures on the steamship, an experience Mary herself preferred to forget, having spent an entire evening huddled in a corner of the ladies' deck, trying to simultaneously nurse Sarah and hold in the contents of her stomach.

Annie had almost smiled at Wealthy, and Sarah had grabbed Wealthy's pretty dress and pulled herself upright just to get a better look at her. Mary tried her best not to think of little Kitty, who had had the same triumphant glint in her eyes when she first stood upon her feet. As for Frederick, he'd already asked Wealthy if she had a younger sister. She did, it turned out, but she was too young for Frederick, or for anyone.

And Mary? Oh, she liked the girl, she supposed, or at least she didn't dislike her. But there had been awkward moments, such as at the hotel in Buffalo when Mary lifted her saucer to her lips and began to drink her tea from it. For just a moment, Wealthy, cup in hand, had stared at her before looking hastily away.

Well. Mary had noticed that Mrs. Perkins didn't drink from her saucer, but she had always assumed that this was because she was rich or close to it. But when she looked around the hotel dining room, most of the other guests weren't drinking from theirs either. At some point, John and John Jr. seemed to have lost the habit themselves, at least in public.

It wasn't just the saucer, though. Wealthy reminded Mary of something else—her rudimentary education. Normally, it wasn't something Mary gave much thought to. She could read and write and do sums, more than enough to get her through. She read the newspapers when she had the time. She listened attentively when John and the boys discussed the news of the day. Her letters might have some misspellings, but no one had ever complained of difficulty understanding her, and her handwriting was clear and neat. She wasn't ignorant, but she knew she was lacking.

At their hotel the night before, without trying to, she had caught a glimpse of a letter Wealthy was writing. Intermixed with her elegant script was a series of characters she didn't recognize. "Phonography," Wealthy had explained, seeing her puzzlement. "My friend from school and I are trying to learn it. Once you learn it, it's much faster than writing."

"What is the use of it?"

"Oh, plenty! Newspaper reporters use it to record speeches, and court reporters use it to record trials, but of course we're just learning because it's interesting."

Because it was interesting.

Looking at her daughter-in-law, busy with whatever she had called it, Mary—though but thirty-one—felt very old. Having not one, but two daughters-in-law—for what else could she call them, having long called John Jr. and Jason her sons?—made her feel even older.

The train chugged heroically on. John bounced a daughter on each knee as Mary took her turn with the newspaper and found her eyelids growing heavy. How sleepy the ride was making her!

She wasn't the only one, it turned out. Wealthy had fallen fast asleep, her head resting on John Jr.'s shoulder. "She had a dreadful trip on the steamer; she barely slept," her new husband explained.

"Poor thing," Mary said politely.

"She looks like a princess sleeping there," Frederick said wistfully.

"I think of her as my princess," John Jr. said.

Mary gazed out the window.

~ ~ ~

It would have been more sensible and economical for the Browns to live together in one big house, but John and his princess (as Mary could not help but think of her) wanted to live on their own, or as close to it as was realistic. So, they moved into a boarding house, and the rest of the family rented a house not far from the depot, as the sound of trains coming and going constantly reminded them until they got used to it.

In many ways, Springfield was an agreeable place. To begin with, this was the largest house in which they'd lived, with a proper, though rather bare, parlor and separate bedrooms—actual bedrooms and not a sleeping loft—for John and Mary, the boys, and the girls. Furthermore, unlike their previous homes, their residence was on a city street, so Mary could talk to her neighbors as they hung out their laundry or walked to the market. Most of them were working people, so she didn't feel the shyness she had always experienced with Mrs. Perkins. Only once was there an awkward moment: a neighbor stopped in to borrow some eggs and found a black employee of John's with the redundant name of Thomas Thomas sitting at the table talking with John and John Jr., perfectly at ease. "Who was that?" the neighbor asked Mary later.

"An employee of my husband's. And a friend of ours as well."

The neighbor looked startled but said nothing more on the subject. People in Springfield were generally anti-slavery—Mr. Thomas, in fact, was a former slave—and those who weren't generally minded their own business, at least.

She wasn't short-handed in Springfield either, as she had feared with Ruth away at school. Because John and Wealthy boarded, Wealthy had little housework to occupy her time, so after studying her phonography and reading her newspapers in the morning, she would come over to Mary's house and help with whatever was needed—cleaning, cooking, or looking after the younger children. She was good with the children and would probably make a fine mother. With this in mind, Mary watched her for signs of pregnancy, but as far as she could tell, there were none.

But there was one shortcoming to Springfield: it was by far the unhealthiest place in which the Browns had lived. Someone was always ailing, including Mary herself, although soon it proved that some of her symptoms were due to her expecting another child in the spring. No one got dangerously ill, but no one ever felt particularly well either. Even the newlyweds seemed to lose a little of their sparkle.

The sickest of all that autumn of 1847 was John Jr., who came down with the typhus fever and was dosed by a physician with calomel—a cure that proved far worse than his illness. To prevent insanity, the doctor had prescribed opium as well, and for two solid days, John Jr. hallucinated while John, ever ready to attend his children in their sickness, sat beside him calmly. Mary took her turn at his sickbed too, but she mostly found herself comforting a frantic Wealthy.

"What if he dies? Mother Brown, I love him so much!"

"He won't die," Mary said. The confidence with which she spoke was genuine; those terrible days in Richfield had taught her what death looked like, and she saw it nowhere around her stepson. She was so certain, in fact, that an astringency crept into her voice which did not go undetected by her sensitive young daughter-in-law. "Now, just sit down quietly and apply these compresses without all this carrying on. He will know you are beside him, and if you are calm, that will help him a great deal."

Wealthy obeyed, and to Mary's satisfaction, her ministrations did help the ailing man. Soon she was nursing him quite efficiently. Rather to Mary's amusement, she took umbrage when Mary, who had been tending her stepsons for years, unceremoniously began to strip John of his nightshirt just as Wealthy awoke from a catnap. "I'll do that, Mother Brown. Goodness."

The calomel treatments finally ran their course, leaving John Jr. weak and pale but blessedly coherent. "Next time, if there has to be one, I'm trying the water cure," he said on the first day he was allowed to sit upright. He smiled feebly at Wealthy, who was plumping his already plump pillow. "I should have done it this time, but there isn't a practitioner in Springfield, and I was afraid I'd die if I didn't get some sort of treatment."

"The water cure?" Mary asked.

Given a chance to expound, John Jr. looked almost well again. He sat up straighter. "It purges the body of impurities. Practitioners use all sorts of methods. Wrapping one with cold sheets, plunges into cold water, treatment with warm water. Father takes a rather dim view of it, as he does phrenology, but after this hell, I'm more than willing to give it a try."

"Well, I certainly would," Mary said, and the not-so-newlyweds looked at her in surprise.

She might not be educated, but she wasn't stuck in her ways.

~ ~ ~

Years before, in the Browns' earliest days in Ohio, before John's bankruptcy, a celebrated preacher from Cleveland had come to give a series of sermons at the church the Browns attended. In those days, the Browns had been able to rent their own pew, and from that comfortable perch, they had witnessed a group of black people, a couple of whom had worked for the Browns, being steered unceremoniously to the rough seats around the stove in the back while the white guests were ushered to the remaining pews. John's expression had grown sterner as more blacks joined the huddle around the stove, but he had held his peace. But the next meeting, at his special request, the black visitors had returned, and this time, as the congregation and minister looked on, John had settled them in the Browns' pew while he and the rest of the family took their places by the stove. The next day, a couple of deacons had come over to remonstrate with John—it just looked odd, they said, for black people to be sitting in the pews surrounded by whites. But John had sent the men away completely confounded, and for three weeks, the Browns had sat by the stove while the new congregants were ensconced in the family pew.

After that, though, the Browns hadn't had much contact with black people, except for fugitives—until they moved to Springfield, which had a thriving community of freedmen, their numbers rapidly increasing due to the railroad. Along with Mr. Thomas, John had hired several of them to work at P&B, and soon they became regular visitors to the Browns' home. So, Mary was not surprised when John suggested that the family worship at the Zion Methodist Church, the black church. Even John Jr., who had seldom set foot in a church since coming of age, announced his intention to go along.

The Free Church, as it was called because of the decidedly abolitionist cast of its congregation, was located in a dull-looking building on Sanford Street. The congregants, however, were in their most festive array, which made the Browns, dressed in their usual plain, dark clothing, even more conspicuous. Only Wealthy, who had not put aside her fashionable tastes when she married, fit in with her surroundings with her elaborately patterned dress and bright bonnet. Mary wondered how many petticoats the girl must wear to make her skirts stick out so. She'd even coaxed her husband into donning a bright necktie.

Mr. Thomas spotted the Browns—not that this was hard to do—and showed them to a pew, which they had to press into tightly to fit as the occupants of the surrounding pews showered nods of greeting upon them. Most seemed to know John, and Mary was surprised to see how many knew her as well.

Despite the friendliness of the congregation and knowing so many there, she felt rather awkward in the midst of so many dark faces. Yet her unease was as nothing compared to what a black person must feel every day, she reminded herself.

Then the choir began to sing—no ordinary song, but John's favorite, "Blow Ye the Trumpets, Blow." Every one of John's children, from John Jr. to little Sarah, had been sung to sleep with it, and John had even sung it to Mary a couple of times when she was ill. Mary listened to the words, deeply familiar but rendered in a style so distinct that it was almost as if she were hearing them for the first time.

> Blow ye the trumpet, blow
> The gladly solemn sound:
> Let all the nations know,
> To earth's remotest bound,
> The year of jubilee is come;
> Return, ye ransom'd sinners, home.

As John Jr. and Wealthy swayed gently to the music, Wealthy's petticoats rustling, Mary let it envelope her.

She felt, in fact, completely at home.

~ ~ ~

Early in January, while John and Mary were lying in bed, he said, "There is something I have been turning over in my mind. You remember Gerrit Smith."

"The man with the land in Virginia." A wealthy man from New York who had inherited considerable real property from his father, Gerrit Smith had given some of his acreage in the Ohio Valley of Virginia to Oberlin College a few years back. Through his father, a trustee of the college, John had been given the opportunity to survey the property in the days before his bankruptcy. The college had agreed to grant John part of the land as compensation for his services, and for a while the family had intended to move to Virginia. But the college, undergoing its own rough spell, had been unable to fulfill its promise, and the plan had been abandoned. Mary had not minded much; years of living with John had made her doubt that she would enjoy being in a slave state, even though the institution was not as embedded in that part of Virginia as others.

"He has land in New York too—Essex County. Mr. Smith has a plan to give land to free blacks there to cultivate and form their own community. But most of these people are unsuited for it, either because they are used to the mild winters of the South or because they have been working in hotels or such in the North. Given my long experience in farming, I thought I—we—might move there and give them some friendly guidance."

"You mean, leave this place? But what about Perkins and Brown?"

"It wouldn't be right away; time enough for us to come to an arrangement. I'm sure we can work out something, especially if Jason and Owen continue to manage the flock in Akron. And, of course, I will have to talk to Mr. Smith to see if he would be willing to sell me the land."

"You are going to write to him?"

"No, such men get so many letters. I will probably just see him. I'm sure he won't object."

Evidently the millionaire Mr. Smith was to have no choice in the matter of seeing John. Mary snorted with laughter, and John took her hand. "You know me, my dear. And I know you. You are very adaptable. Essex County will be quite a change, though."

"It will be a healthy place for the children, at least." Although she had never been to Essex County in the Adirondacks—at least not that she remembered—her brother Orson lived not far off in Whitehall, her birthplace.

"Yes, and the mountain scenery is said to be glorious. I like mountains, anyway. They are not only beautiful, but strategic."

"Strategic?"

"Something that I have been mulling in my head for some time, and probably will for some time to come. But I've kept you up enough, and I need sleep as well. It will wait."

He kissed her on the cheek and rolled over.

~ ~ ~

A couple of years before, a man named Frederick Douglass had published an autobiography about his years as a slave. Needless to say, the eloquent memoir had caught John's eye, and when Mr. Douglass began publishing a newspaper, *The North Star*, a few months after the Browns' arrival in Springfield, John had been an early subscriber. (It was not the only paper to which he subscribed. Sometimes Mary felt awash in newsprint.) Then, in February, Mr. Douglass came to Springfield to lecture, and John, who had met him briefly the year before, invited him to his home to stay the night.

Years later, Mary would learn that Mr. Douglass, having seen the substantial building that P&B occupied, had expected a house in a fashionable neighborhood with comfortable furnishings, as he had encountered when he had visited other abolitionists in America and on his recent lecture tour abroad. But he kept his surprise well hidden, for Mary, serving him the simple meal that the family always ate, noticed nothing amiss.

Mr. Douglass was a handsome man, immaculately clad in a frock coat that, even to Mary's inexpert eye, appeared a cut above anything else in Springfield. She wondered if he had had it made in England. "Were you homesick when you were in Europe?" she asked shyly as she helped little Sarah with her plate.

"Very much so. I missed my wife and children, and, as imperfect as it is, I missed my country."

"I heard you were able to buy your freedom before you returned," Mary said. "It must have been a fine thing, to leave a slave and return a free man."

Mr. Douglass gave her an appreciative smile. "It was, Mrs. Brown."

Ruth was at the table as well, having come to Springfield for her February holiday. Her return to school had done her good; she looked rosy and pretty again, more so tonight with the famous Mr. Douglass at the table. She could not help but feel a little smug, she had confessed to Mary, that she was getting to see the orator while John Jr. and Wealthy, who had picked this inopportune time to travel to Boston, were missing him.

After the simple but hearty meal was over, the boys cleared the table and did the dishes, to the evident surprise of Mr. Douglass. "I see you do not differentiate so strictly between men's work and women's in your house," he said. "That is quite admirable."

"It is more a necessity in our case than a virtue," John said, "but it is true that the boys can fend for themselves in the kitchen."

"But none of them can spin or knit," Ruth said.

"True," John said. He smiled. "Well, perhaps we men are just too clumsy for such things. The first thing I noticed about my wife was how skillful and graceful she was at her spinning."

Mary blushed.

As John had made it clear that he wished to have some private conversation with his guest, Mary, Ruth, and the children left them in possession of the table, where they remained when Mary went to bed.

She woke in the middle of the night to find John's side of the bed empty; sure enough, the conversation was still going on. With no train blasting its horn for the moment and no one passing outside, it was easy enough for Mary to make out the men's words. John must have been discussing the Gerrit Smith lands with his guest, for he was talking about his venture in Virginia.

"When I was surveying those lands," John said, "I began studying maps of Virginia, and it occurred to me that the Alleghany Mountains would be the perfect place from which to strike a crippling blow to slavery. I have since been in that area to buy sheep, and my opinion was only confirmed. Someone could lead a group of hardy men into those mountains, with all their natural hiding places, and begin to entice slaves from those rich farmlands nearby. Those slaves who are not equipped to survive in the mountains could be smuggled up north in the usual way, and those who are of hardier stock could in turn entice more of their brethren to run. Such a plan would have two effects: it would make the ownership of slaves such an insecure proposition that planters would be forced to consider other means of working their land, and it would keep the anti-slavery agitation alive and would lead to laws that would weaken and finally abolish the institution."

"Who would lead this plan?"

"Why, me, of course," John said. "It would take the right men and a good deal of money. I could probably raise some of the first quite easily, but the second—that may take years. But someday—"

A train whistle sounded, silencing the men for a moment. When they resumed talking, it was in lower voices, and Mary felt ashamed of eavesdropping anyway. She rolled over, trying to find a comfortable position for her burgeoning belly. But she could not fall asleep.

This plan might take years to come to fruition. It surely must have been what John had alluded to some days before when he had spoken of the mountains being strategic. Till this evening, she had half forgotten about it, knowing John's tendency to think aloud. It might come to naught, as had some other of his well-intentioned schemes, such as his idea years before to raise a black child among his own children. Still—

The men had forgotten themselves again. As clear as day, Mr. Douglass's fine voice sounded. "But what if your plan fails?"

"Well," John said, "then I suppose I would hang."

6

May 1849 to October 1849

"Look at the grandeur all around us," John said, gesturing at the Adirondack mountains surrounding them as Ruth and the youngest children, Oliver, Annie, and Sarah, obeyed. "Isn't it splendid?"

A chorus of voices agreed, but Mary stayed silent. She turned to make sure that the little coffin, wrapped in carpets and packed in a crate, was secure in its place on the wagon. It contained the body of her youngest daughter, Ellen, known as Nelly, who had not been quite a year old.

Nelly's death, at the end of April, had not been unexpected. The previous autumn, while John was traveling to Essex County and Mary was visiting her brother Orson at Whitehall, the six-month-old baby had fallen sick, and soon after the family's return to Springfield, it had become apparent that she was consumptive. Mary had hoped—they had all hoped—that the move to Essex County, with its fresh mountain air, might improve her health. But Nelly had not been able to hold out that long and had died as the Springfield things were being packed. As no one wanted to leave

71

her behind, they had brought her body to be buried near their new home in New York.

Nelly's birth had been an unusually hard one, and Mary had barely recovered when the little girl became ill, requiring all of Mary's attention. She had had help from Ruth, who'd finished up at school, and from Wealthy, but a weariness had set in that she had yet to shake. It was more than just weariness; some days, she could barely drag herself out of bed.

At age thirty-three, was she reaching the end of her time? Surely the Lord couldn't mean to take her so early. If so, why had He not taken her when Nelly was born? No, it must be the exhaustion of caring for Nelly all these months that was wearing her down, that and sorrow. Nelly had been such a bright little thing for her age . . .

Perhaps this place might do Mary some good, even though they had moved too late to help poor Nelly.

She turned toward Ruth and John, who were walking beside the cart to spare the handsome team of horses they had purchased at Westport. Not yet trusting himself to find his way around these mountains unaided, John had hired a Mr. Thomas Jefferson, a black man who was also moving to North Elba, to drive the team. "Ruth, get in for a while. I would like to walk."

John frowned. "Are you sure, my dear?"

"Yes."

Mr. Jefferson clucked at the horses, and John helped Mary switch places with Ruth, who was looking rather uncertain about her new surroundings; she'd confided to Mary that she was worried she'd be the only young woman around. Just the effort of getting down had told on Mary, but she lifted her chin and plodded along, taking great gulps of the mountain air.

It *had* to help her.

~ ~ ~

Though John had bought some land in nearby North Elba already, he had not had time to build upon it, so he rented a farm from a Mr. Flanders until he could finish up his business in Springfield and construct a home. The Flanders farm consisted of a small cabin—just a couple of rooms plus a sleeping loft—and a large barn. Both were soon full; John had taken care to purchase some milk cows before their arrival, and Owen, with help from Watson and Salmon, had driven some fine Devon cattle over the mountains. A young black man by the name of Cyrus Thomas, a former slave who knew John from Springfield, had turned up at the cabin looking for work, and John had immediately engaged him to help Owen run the farm while John went back and forth to Springfield. Somewhat to Mary's chagrin, he had also found a black woman by the name of Mrs. Reed to serve as their housekeeper. Was she really that poorly? Never in her life had she used hired help for herself. But she couldn't argue with John's consideration for herself and Ruth, whom neither she nor John wanted to see burdened with all the care of the household.

Mary doubted that Ruth would be at home much longer anyway. Although even John had described poor Dianthe as plain, Ruth had not taken after her, but had developed into an attractive young woman, buxom and with a pleasing countenance. Mary was not the only one who was of this opinion; despite Ruth's worries that she would be bereft of companionship, several young men had quickly learned of her presence in the area and were soon making rather foolish excuses to come by the Brown cabin. "Just to check that you're settling in," they would say, when it was quite apparent that the Browns had settled in fine. Still, it kept Ruth diverted, provided her brothers with endless fodder for jokes, and fascinated Annie. Even Mary, still not entirely sure about these young people's need for romance when she and John had managed things so matter-of-factly, found herself keeping an eye on the suitors' progress. At first a Mr. Keese appeared to be in the lead, but lately a Mr. Thompson had been gaining ground. Ruth had remained silent on the matter, but Mary had noticed that she had been dressing rather more nicely than feeding the chickens really required, and she took so much time primping before Sunday meetings that her brothers had to push her away from the mirror.

One unusually hot day in late June, Mary woke from a nap to find Annie and Sarah standing in front of her bed. "There are *men* upstairs," Annie said disapprovingly.

"Men? What sort of men?"

"Hungry ones," Ruth said, coming into the room. "Those men from Boston who breakfasted with us the other way. Villeroy Aikens undertook to guide them around the mountains and got them thoroughly lost. They should have used William Nye instead."

"Or Henry Thompson," Owen called. "Didn't you say he could guide you anywhere?"

Ruth ignored him. "Anyway, they managed to stumble back to our place. They were famished when they reached here, and so eager to eat that I thought they'd make themselves sick, so I gave them plenty of milk and sent them upstairs to the loft to rest. Mr. Jefferson has gone to their inn so a wagon and mules can be sent for them."

"They drank all the milk we put out," Annie said. "Every single drop."

"Well, there's more where that came from," Mary said.

Annie's expression was dubious.

The men were a Mr. Richard Dana and a Mr. Metcalf, who were lawyers from Boston, and their guide, Mr. Aikens, a Vermont judge's son who had declined to follow his father into the law, preferring the life of an adventurer and outdoorsman. Since settling into their farm, the Browns had given meals and lodgings to several such parties of city folk come to enjoy the beauties of the Adirondacks. Though the Browns and their neighbors did not charge their guests, it was universally understood that the guests would present their host with a gift of cash upon parting, so it was a pleasant arrangement for all concerned.

In an hour or so, the gentlemen came downstairs from the loft. They were dressed as they had been when Mary saw them at breakfast the other day, in red flannel shirts, wool trousers, and thin tweed overcoats, the garb of a city gentleman in the country, but their garments were now torn and tattered, and their faces were decidedly sunburned. Evidently their feet were too swollen to fit into their boots, which they held in their hands. They smiled at Mary as Ruth clucked sympathetically. "As you see, madam, we have returned rather the worse for wear."

"I'm glad you were able to find your way here," Mary said. She glanced at the rather sheepish-looking Mr. Aikens. "Even people who have lived here for years get turned about, I'm told."

As the men sat down to await their mules and eat the cornbread Ruth and Mrs. Reed had prepared, they picked up their conversation where they had left off the other day. Owen in particular was interested to hear more of Mr. Dana's travels in California. Even Annie was impressed to hear of oranges ripe for the plucking, and Mary herself ventured a few questions. "Do you think you'll go back to look for gold like so many are doing now?"

Mr. Dana shook his head. "I will leave that to the single men; I have a wife and four little ones at home. But someday I would like to return. It is a place everyone should see."

Presently, a mule wagon, driven by a man Mary knew only as Tommy, came to fetch the footsore travelers back to their lodgings. After some dickering with Ruth, who would have given the men change for the dollar they handed her for her trouble, they departed, only to return two days later at breakfast time to thank the family once again. They seemed momentarily disconcerted to see Mrs. Reed, having prepared the meal, sit down with the rest of the family—as did Cyrus Thomas—but they quickly recovered themselves. Mr. Dana thanked Ruth and Mrs. Reed, then turned to Mary. "I hope we did not put you out too much, Mrs. Brown."

"No, not at all."

Was Mr. Dana simply speaking courteously, or did Mary really appear all that feeble?

~ ~ ~

"Are you going to see the queen?"

"No, Annie," John said. "I told you, Americans have no queen—or king, as the case may be. Your forebears fought to rid us of such."

"But you could see her anyway."

"Well, I doubt that, but in any case, I won't have the chance. But I will bring back something for you girls." When Oliver scowled, he added, "For everybody."

Though P&B's Springfield venture had started out rather promisingly, it had run into trouble. Outmatched by the more powerful wool manufacturers, the partners were finding it hard to bring their wool to market in the United States, so John, with the obliging Mr. Perkins's consent, had decided to sell his wool abroad. He would sail to England in just a few days, on August 15, on the steamer *Cambria*.

Ruth bustled about, getting John well supplied with clothing for his journey, and Mary helped as best she could. As they sewed and mended, Mary remembered the first time she had prepared John's wardrobe for a trip, back in the days when she was merely a hired girl and her sister was John's expected bride. Since then, sending John off had become a ritual of sorts, made easier or harder physically depending on who was there to help her with the preparations. But the act of saying goodbye had become no easier over the passing years; indeed, perhaps because of the children they'd lost, it had become harder. She could not shake off the fear that each goodbye might be the last for one of them.

It was a foolish idea, of course, which was why she hadn't troubled John with it. Still, when the day arrived for him to set off, she insisted on accompanying him as far as Westport.

"It's a tedious drive, my dear," he said.

"I know. But I would like to go just the same."

"Very well."

With Watson accompanying them to bring the team— and, of course, Mary—back, they made the drive to Westport. John, never one to leave anything to chance, took advantage of Mary's presence by reiterating the instructions he had given her and the boys as to the care of the farm. It was just as well that all Mary had to do was listen and respond at appropriate times, because the trip to Westport, the longest she'd taken since they had arrived in Essex County, was beginning to tell upon her. Her back ached horribly, and she felt dizzy and faint.

Getting out of the cart and taking some refreshment at Westport made her feel somewhat better. As John awaited the ferry that would take him to Vermont, from which he would travel to Boston, he took the opportunity to make some purchases for the farm, while Mary bought some material to make clothing for the children and tried in vain to find some fringe for Ruth's green dress, a rather smart garment for Essex County that often made its appearances when Mr. Thompson called.

It being time to board the ferry, John bid Watson a fatherly goodbye, then turned to Mary. As was his habit in public, he confined himself to clasping her hand. "God be with you, my dear. I will write to you often, and I hope you will write regularly to John so he can send me news of you."

"John—" To her mortification, she began to weep.

John pulled out his handkerchief, cutting into the supply Mary had prepared for him. "Mary, this isn't like you at all. Calm yourself, dear. A sea crossing is quite safe these days."

She wiped her eyes. "I know. It is just—"

"What, my dear?"

"Nothing. I'm tired, is all."

John startled her by giving her a kiss on the cheek. "Don't fret, my dear. My business will soon be accomplished, I hope, and in such a manner that I will be able to spend less time away. In the meantime, let Ruth and Mrs. Reed handle the heavy work, as they have been doing. I know Ruth won't take advantage of my absence."

"No, of course not." Having achieved command of herself, Mary took John's hand. "Have a safe journey, John. I will pray for your safe passage."

Having watched John's ferry pull away without further tears on Mary's part, she and Watson stood in silence, Mary regretting her foolish display. Finally, Watson said, "Don't worry, Ma. Father will be fine."

"I know."

"Then what's wrong? You can tell me, Ma."

If asked, Mary would have said that she had no favorites among her children, and the answer would have been truthful up to a point. But Watson, her first son and since the deaths at Richfield, her oldest child, had a certain place in her heart, perhaps not the least because of the quietness they shared. But she could not tell even him that her fears were not so much that John might not return, but that she might not live to see him. "I'm just worried," she said. "After all, he will be an ocean away."

The next day, before retiring to bed, Mary rummaged around in the little bookcase in the parlor and quickly found what she wanted: a copy of *The Water Cure Journal*, a periodical which John Jr. had sent to Owen a few weeks before. In it was a letter written by John Jr. to the publishers, with whom he had become friendly. It was rather florid, as her stepson's letters tended to be at times, but once the writer got to the point, it was clear enough: having suffered yet another bout with typhus in Springfield, he had determined not to dose himself with the doctor's remedies, but to go to a water-cure establishment. Not only had he fully recovered, but the cure had purged the calomel left from his last encounter with the disease.

Mary flipped through the journal. There seemed to be no end of ways that water could be used to effect a cure, nor any ailment to which it might not be applied, but nothing told her whether it might work for her. She wasn't even sure what exactly ailed her; it had been so long since she had felt entirely herself. All she knew was that the life of an invalid did not suit her; she was far too young to sit and watch others work. And she was certainly too young to leave a brood of motherless children behind.

Could she even afford the cure? Dr. David Ruggles' establishment at Northampton, Massachusetts, to which John Jr. had gone, wasn't the most expensive water cure, but it wasn't cheap either. Still, John had left her with a reasonably good supply of money, and if her case seemed hopeless or Dr. Ruggles a quack, it would be easy enough to simply leave and go to Springfield, then back to North Elba.

And what would happen if she simply did nothing?

~ ~ ~

John Jr. and Wealthy boarded with one of John's workers, Mr. Middleton, and his wife. They were an English couple. Mary liked them both, especially Mrs. Middleton, who waved her inside and said in her charming accent, "John and Wealthy aren't here, I'm afraid; they went to Boston to see off your husband. They may well be back this evening, though. Were they expecting you?"

"No," Mary said. "I have something to take care of."

Mrs. Middleton was too English to pry. "Well, come have some tea. There's certainly room for you to stay here if they are delayed a day or two." As Mary followed her into the parlor, Mrs. Middleton said, "I was so sorry to hear of your little girl's death. She was such a sweet little thing."

"We miss her," Mary said simply.

For an hour or so, she chatted with Mrs. Middleton, realizing as she did that she had been missing something else as well—the company of Mrs. Middleton and her other woman friends in Springfield. Though there were neighbors in Essex County, seeing them took more effort, and John's inflexible habit of keeping the Sabbath limited visiting as well. And winter, which she knew was harsh in that part of New York, had not even set in.

A key turned in the lock, and John Jr. and Wealthy, laden with carpetbags and a hatbox that looked suspiciously new, came into the parlor. "Good evening, Mrs. Middle—Mother? What are you doing here?"

Mrs. Middleton having tactfully left the room, Mary came to the point. "I have been feeling poorly lately, and I am getting no better. I want to go to the water cure. The same one you went to."

John Jr. frowned. "Father—we saw his steamer off, by the way—said nothing about this."

"He didn't know."

"And you came all the way here from Essex County? Alone?"

Mary nodded. "It wasn't hard. People were very helpful."

"And Father knows nothing of this?"

"No. And I don't want him to know—for a while, at least."

The young people looked at each other. Mary could guess what they were thinking. It wasn't like her to stir up things. "He would only worry about me, and I know he has enough to worry about with his business."

"You can say that again," John Jr. said gloomily, lowering his voice. "I'm not optimistic about this trip. But do you know how rigorous this treatment is? It's not just soaking in water. It's being plunged into cold water, having sheets wrapped around you for hours—very uncomfortable. It purges your bowels—"

"Yes, I read that in your article."

"Well, I tried to put it delicately there, but it was rather disagreeable. You're willing to put up with all that?"

"I have to get better, or I will die. I am certain of it. Nothing else is working. I don't think even your father realizes how sickly I have felt; he thinks I am just rundown. But I need your help. Dr. Ruggles' circular says that he requires that people write to him with their symptoms, but you know how slow the mail is in Essex—I have a letter from Ruth to you, by the way—and I feared that if I waited, I would get only worse. Since you have been there, can you write a letter for me to give him when I arrive, so that perhaps he will be willing to take me on as a patient immediately?"

It was perhaps the most Mary had ever spoken in a single breath. John Jr. blinked, but then he said, "Of course I will, Mother, if you are determined to go. I hope it will do you good. I would only ask that you rest until tomorrow to give us time to get some things together for you."

"Perhaps Thomas Thomas can speak up for you," Wealthy said. "He happens to be taking the cure himself and would surely be willing to put in a word."

"Excellent idea from my darling wife." John kissed her hand. While Mary couldn't dispute that it was a good idea, she couldn't help but wonder whether this honeymoon would ever end. With no offspring to wear them down, the pair reminded Mary of a couple of children playing house. Her impression was strengthened that evening when, lying in the room adjacent the couple's lodgings, Mary heard a series of unseemly sounds emanating from the room, followed by a girlish giggle and a sheepish chuckle. Evidently bedtime was the most important part of the younger Browns' romps.

All was quiet afterward, however, and the lovers were bright-eyed and helpful the next morning. Wealthy assembled the extra sheets and towels the establishment required, and John escorted her to the depot.

Mary had gathered that Dr. Ruggles was a remarkable man. Born a free man in Connecticut, he had taken to the sea and finally settled in New York City. He had assisted Frederick Bailey, later known as Frederick Douglass, when the young man, newly escaped from slavery, had arrived in the metropolis, and had helped hundreds of others to freedom. When his eyesight had failed, he had come to live at the Northampton Association of Education and Industry, a utopian, abolitionist community that had supported itself by running a silk mill. Though the community—which regarded all persons as equals regardless of race, sex, or religion—had foundered, Dr. Ruggles and many others had remained in the area. As his health grew worse, Dr. Ruggles had attempted the water cure upon himself, and although it had not been sufficient to restore his eyesight, he had at least found some relief. It had inspired him to open his own water cure, which had struggled for a while but now seemed to be flourishing.

As promised in the advertisement Mary had seen, a carriage was waiting at the Northampton depot to convey prospective patients to Dr. Ruggles' establishment about two and a half miles from town. Soon they were at its gates. Mary assumed that the shuttered three-story building housed the patients, while the low-slung outer building must surely be where the various baths were located.

Introducing herself as Miss Gedney, a young black lady showed her in. Shortly after, a boy led in Dr. Ruggles, a handsome, though somewhat frail-looking man in his late thirties who wore the dark glasses of a blind person. He held out his hand, which Mary grasped. "Mrs. Brown, I understand?"

"Yes. I do hope you can do me some good. I realize I should have written ahead, but I felt that I could wait no longer."

"Well, we have space for you, but I won't accept you if I don't feel I can do you any good. How is Mr. John Brown, Jr. doing?"

"He appeared quite well."

"Good, good! Let us go into my office, and I will examine you. Miss Elizabeth Gedney will be present. Should you take the cure, she and her sister Sophia will be giving you your treatments."

Mary nodded, remembering too late that Dr. Ruggles could not see her do so, and followed him and the boy into another room, which was fitted up with books. Miss Gedney stood there chatting with an older woman with a turban upon her head. "Ma's here, Dr. Ruggles. Do you want her to leave?"

"She can stay if Mrs. Brown doesn't mind."

"I don't mind," Mary said. In truth, she was rather relieved to have the older woman present. She reminded her of the many midwives who had attended her over the years.

Miss Gedney waved her behind a screen, where Mary stripped to her shift. When she presented herself in front of Dr. Ruggles, he said, "I imagine you've read that I diagnose by touch. If the lungs, stomach, and wrist are in an electro-positive state, the water cure will benefit a person. If they are not, I can do nothing and will not waste your time or money by pretending otherwise."

"I understand."

Frowning in concentration, Dr. Ruggles conducted his examination. "I do believe we can help you, Mrs. Brown. You have neuralgia, it appears, and the cure is good for it."

"So, I am in an—electro-positive state?"

"Indeed, you are. So, will you be staying? If you do, we can get your treatment started today, although some patients like to settle in a little."

"Might as well get it started now," said the older lady. She had a rich, deep voice as redolent as Dr. Ruggles'. "Faster you start, the faster you'll be out of here. Dr. Ruggles gave me the cure too. I hated every moment of it, but it did me good."

"My friend Mrs. Sojourner Truth speaks the truth," Dr. Ruggles said. "The treatment, provided that you follow it rigorously, will progress to a crisis—"

"Oh, the crisis," said Mrs. Truth—for what else could Mary call her? "You'll want to be put out of your misery then."

"Now, now," Dr. Ruggles said. "Don't scare Mrs. Brown away."

"Scare? She don't look like one who scares easily. Well, I'm off; I just stopped by to see the girls. You take good care of Mrs. Brown, now."

"A remarkable woman," Dr. Ruggles said as Mrs. Truth took her departure. "Born a slave in New York, escaped, and later went to the law to get her son back after he was sold South. Finally found her way to our community in Northampton and stayed in the area when it broke up."

"She should tell her story," Mary said.

"She is," Miss Gedney said. "A lady is writing it for her. Ma can't read or write—neither can I—but she can talk just fine. You don't seem to talk much yourself, Mrs. Brown."

"No," said Mary. "But I listen just fine."

To her surprise, Dr. Ruggles and Miss Gedney both chuckled.

Having dressed herself, Mary followed Miss Gedney to the third floor, where the least expensive rooms were located. To save money, she had come prepared to share a room, but no one else was in the small chamber to which she was led. "You probably won't care for the mattress; it's straw. Ladies always complain, but Dr. Ruggles thinks it healthier."

Mary tested it and found it rather hard, just as promised. Miss Gedney continued on cheerfully, "Supper will be at six. It will be very simple but very wholesome. No butter, and not too much milk."

Thinking of the cows at home and their bounty, Mary suppressed a sigh.

She had unpacked her few belongings and admired the view—the third floor, though a bit uncomfortable, did have its advantages—when she was summoned for her first bath of the day, the sitz bath. It was taken in company with the other lady patients, each of whom sat in her own tub of tepid water, sipping from a tumbler of the same substance. There were a couple of quite young ladies, several of Mary's age, and a rather spry maiden lady of a certain age. Although she knew it was frivolous, Mary had secretly worried that she would stand out too much among the other ladies as a rustic, but here, with everyone wrapped in a sheet and her hair tucked under a cap, it was impossible to distinguish who spent her days laboring on a farm and who passed her time sipping tea in a parlor.

Each woman had her favorite bath, she learned. The youngest of the ladies was fond of the plunge bath, as was, rather to Mary's surprise, the oldest lady. One sang the praises of the wet pack, which Mary had learned she would experience the next morning, and the daintiest of the ladies preferred the foot bath, which the youngest lady thought was really no bath at all.

Just as her companions enjoyed a variety of baths, they suffered from a variety of ailments. The youngest lady had suffered from a bad back since falling off a horse; a middle-aged schoolmarm suffered from rheumatism; and the oldest lady simply thought the cure would agree with her, a point Dr. Ruggles had declined to contest. "What brings you here?" the youngest lady asked.

"I wish I knew," Mary said. "All I know is that I haven't felt myself in months, and I thought I would die if I didn't get a change."

Her companions nodded understandingly, and Mary settled back more comfortably into the tub.

When they had last finished their sitz baths and changed into their clothes in preparation for a walk, Mary was much surprised to receive compliments from the other ladies on her dress, which, though in general keeping with the time, was very plain and somewhat shorter and less full than was stylish. "So sensible! It is so foolish to wear all of those heavy petticoats."

"And no tight lacing either."

Mary considered pointing out that since she lived on a farm, she could hardly function with billowing skirts scraping the ground or laces that squeezed the life out of her. Instead, she simply smiled and said, "Yes, I find it very practical."

Within just a couple of days, she had become accustomed to the routine of the water cure: the wet pack, being wrapped in wet sheets like the Egyptian mummies John Jr. had once told her about, first thing in the morning; a half bath before dinner; a sitz bath in the afternoon; and a foot bath before bed. Sometimes she might get a spray bath instead, and she had even faced the plunge bath, although she had been certain she would drown in it. At all times, a pitcher of water was within her reach, and the baths were interspersed with wholesome, if not particularly appetizing meals, at which wheat and rye bread, vegetables, and fruit abounded. She found herself actually feeling better than she had in months.

Then, in early September, she fell dreadfully ill, not with the crisis that Mrs. Truth had so jovially predicted, but with raging dysentery. A third of the patients were affected.

With the well patients needing their usual attention and the sick ones clamoring for succor, Miss Gedney and the other servants had their hands full, so Mr. Thomas, at Mary's request, wrote to John Jr. to send Wealthy to assist her. For hours, Mary tossed and turned between fits of sickness, fretting that Wealthy might not come. Perhaps she was visiting her people in Ohio, or gallivanting up to Boston or suchlike, or . . .

"Why, Mother Brown! At the water cure, and your glass is empty! I'll go fill it."

"You came," Mary mumbled.

"Well, of course I did," Wealthy said. "I got on the train as soon as John told me of your letter."

She bustled around, whacking Mary's pillow into shape, emptying the chamber pot without even wrinkling her pretty nose, and giving Mary a sponge bath, all the time commenting on the view from her room and chatting about Mrs. Truth, whom she had apparently met while fetching Mary her water. Soon she had decided that Mary would be better off with the room rearranged—"John says I like to change things about, and he is right!"—and had effected the transformation in moments. As Mary lay in her bed, now placed by the window, clad in a fresh chemise, she was utterly exhausted from her daughter-in-law's exertions, but she could not deny she was more comfortable.

The next morning, Wealthy had a good breakfast waiting for her when she awoke. "Dr. Ruggles will be up to see you shortly," she informed Mary. "I told him all about your condition. You look a little better this morning."

"I feel better." Mary nibbled at some toast and drank some water—evidently, this part of her regime was not to change. "I suppose it is far too early to have heard from my husband."

"Yes, though I would expect something soon. John just sent a letter to London and will be writing to him each week, in plenty of time to catch the weekly mail packets. He did not tell him that you are here, although when we heard you were ill, we thought perhaps he should have in case—"

She wisely did not finish her thought.

Dr. Ruggles arrived a little while later with encouraging words. To recompense Wealthy for her trouble, he offered to let her use the facilities when she was not attending Mary, and soon Miss Gedney was wrapping Wealthy in wet sheets while Mary drifted in and out of sleep.

In a couple of days, Mary, though weak, was feeling so much better that she could dispense with Wealthy's services. "I'll be sorry to go," Wealthy said as she gathered her things together. Although she had always been a healthy-looking young lady with a bloom on her cheeks, taking brisk walks and cold baths had given her the appearance of a living advertisement for the water cure. "This place is so healthful; I just wish John could come back. He's never been entirely well in Springfield, and I don't think New York City is going to improve his health. But he has longed to study phrenology there for so long, I wouldn't dream of standing in his way."

"Are you still planning on going to Essex County?"

"Yes, Ruth advised us to go before the cold sets in. Or I should say that Henry Thompson advised Ruth, and that is what she advised us." Wealthy smirked. "Ruth wants us to move there, but I don't know if I want to live quite that far out, even though I do think I would enjoy being back on a farm. There's not much for me to do in the city. I wouldn't mind so much, perhaps, if I could go back to teaching just to fill the time, but of course no one will employ a married woman. Sometimes I think perhaps we should go ahead and have a child instead of waiting as we have been."

Mary opened her mouth and closed it. All this time, she had assumed that Wealthy's childlessness was an unfortunate state of affairs, one that she would not give her daughter-in-law pain by discussing. "You mean—"

Wealthy nodded. "John and I would like to have two or three children at most."

"How?" Mary blurted out.

"There's the tried-and-true method, of course, but it's rather unappealing. Fortunately, there's the douche and the sponge, and there is keeping careful track of one's cycles. Dr. Frederick Hollick has lectured about the subject. John and I went to one of his lectures and learned so much." Wealthy consulted the little watch that hung at her waist, a gift from John Jr. for her last birthday. "I suppose I had better be off if I want to catch the next train. We can discuss this more when I next see you if you like. Of course, some of the ladies here are knowledgeable too, no doubt."

"No doubt," Mary said faintly.

Wealthy kissed Mary lightly on the cheek and took her departure, calling out goodbyes as she made her progress down the hall.

Two or three children at most? It was true, Mary supposed, that her years of nearly constant childbearing had affected her health; Dr. Ruggles had tactfully told her as much. But even so, those terrible two weeks in 1843 had taught Mary that so many could be snatched away so quickly. Why tempt fate?

~ ~ ~

Soon news arrived from two directions: from John Jr., who reported that John had arrived safely in England and was attending to his business there, and from Ruth, who reported that all were well in Essex County, including little Annie and Sarah, who missed her but were bearing up and being good girls, save for Annie's incorrigible tree climbing, which left her dresses in perpetual need of mending. The tidings made Mary, who was rapidly improving, feel even better.

September passed into October. The cold baths became rather less agreeable, but Mary kept on with her routine. At 142 pounds, she was thinner than she had been in years—not a bad thing—and she no longer had to stop to rest when she strolled around the grounds, now brilliant with color.

And then, at the end of October, she returned from a walk to find John waiting for her.

Surveying him as she did so, she clasped his hand. He looked tired, no doubt from the long voyage and the rail journey afterward, but in good health. "It is so good to see you home safe. Was your trip a success?"

"Sadly, no. The wool didn't sell for what we had hoped, and most did not sell at all. There is a great deal of pigheadedness against American wool. We will have to redouble our efforts at Springfield."

"At least you tried."

"I was much surprised to learn from John that you were here. You had not said a word to me about such a plan."

"I did not make the plan before you left. It came to me after you left that if I did not do something, I might not see you again. I knew the children would be in good hands with Ruth—I have never blamed her for poor Kitty—and that Owen could manage the farm. And everything has worked fine. I feel much better."

"You do look better. So, you will be coming with me to Essex?"

"No. Dr. Ruggles advised that I stay a couple of more weeks."

As Mary spoke, she realized that she had not asked John's permission to stay. She did not amend her answer, however. In reply, John said merely, "Very well. I have little money on me to give you, so if you need any, you can write to John, and he or Wealthy can get it to you."

"Thank you, John. Will you be able to stay overnight? I know Dr. Ruggles won't mind, especially as you are both friends of Mr. Thomas."

"No. I should get back to the office and see what has transpired in my absence. From what John has told me, it won't be pleasant."

He sighed, and Mary patted his hand.

As they waited for the carriage to take John back to the train station, Mary showed John about the grounds and introduced him to some of the other patients and Dr. Ruggles, who was ill and could speak with him but briefly. When the carriage pulled into view, Mary said, "We are to hear a young woman, Miss Lucy Stone, speak in a few days. She has done much good for the anti-slavery movement. It will be interesting to hear a woman speak in public. I have never done so before."

"You do plan to come back, don't you?"

"Why, of course."

"Good. I know you have never cared for Essex County, and with our business reverses . . . Well, some of the women at these cures have rather unusual notions about marriage, I have been told."

"Not me, John. I will be back in a few weeks, I promise."

"I will look forward to it. I have missed you."

He kissed her on the cheek and climbed into the carriage. Mary watched as it drove away. Smiling to herself, she briskly walked back to her quarters.

Part II

Wealthy

7

1845 to 1854

It was in the summer of 1854 that John Brown, Jr., had caught the Kansas fever. He'd come home from a lecture, his face aglow and his coat pockets bulging with pamphlets. "It's the place for us, Wealthy. Rich land, there for the taking. And we can strike a blow for freedom too. Where better to settle?"

Had Wealthy been married to a different man, she would have pointed out that they were already settled—at Vernon in Trumbull County, Ohio. To be more precise, in Wealthy's childhood home, purchased from her parents' estate just a couple of years before.

But she knew better, for if there was one trait the Brown men had, it was restlessness. Since she and John had married in 1847, they had lived in Springfield, New York City, and various places in Ohio. Lately, however—as recently as the day before—John had been talking of moving to North Elba in Essex County, New York.

Wealthy had first visited Essex County in October 1849, while Mother Brown was at the water cure, and she could still remember the blizzard that had forced her and John to trudge the distance to the ferry at Westport while snow blew into their faces and seeped into their clothing. She had required an entire day before a roaring fire to thaw out. Even the prospect of living near Ruth, who had since married Henry Thompson, had not increased Wealthy's enthusiasm for the frosty climes of the Adirondacks—although when the temperature in Ohio hovered in the high nineties and the crops shriveled that droughty summer, she had been on the verge of reconciling herself to the idea.

But all that year of 1854, Kansas, a place she had managed to get through life without thinking about at all, filled the newspapers, especially the abolitionist ones to which the Browns had faithfully subscribed since their marriage. A senator from Illinois, Stephen Douglas, wanting to see the area known as Nebraska opened for settlement as a territory, had proposed that the area known as Kansas also be made into a territory. To win support from his Southern colleagues, Senator Douglas had made the unholy bargain that the people of each territory would be allowed to decide whether it would allow slavery within its borders. This "popular sovereignty," as the smooth-tongued senator called it, in effect upended the Missouri Compromise of 1820, which had prohibited slavery north of the 36° 30' parallel. The Kansas-Nebraska Act, as it was known, had delighted Southerners and infuriated abolitionists, including the Browns. Since then, settlers had streamed into Kansas, some intending to make it into a slave state, others intending to make it into a free state, and still others simply looking for a new start or an adventure. Added to that were a group of people who did not intend to settle at all—the so-called Border Ruffians, Missourians who crossed over into the territory only to make trouble.

John was not a domestic tyrant. "Of course, we'll go only if you want to go. I know it's nowhere like we've been before. We'll be in a tent for a while, no doubt."

"I suppose I could live with that. But aside from the Border Ruffians, there will be Indians."

"We can live as friends together."

"I would miss my sisters very much."

"Who knows? Eunecia might join us once we get settled. Hannah, I rather doubt, but the railroads are bound to be extended there eventually, and then it won't be a hard journey at all."

"Eventually."

But she wasn't putting up much of an argument. She too had read the newspaper articles about the fertile soil of Kansas, the praise for its climate. She too had watched helplessly as the merciless sun wiped out months of work on their small farm. She too wanted to see a blow struck against slavery; John's abolitionist sentiments were one of the first things that had drawn her to him. And as much as she loved her family, it was shrinking; both her parents and her older sister Mary were dead, leaving Hannah, who was married with a passel of children, and Eunecia, who would no doubt marry soon as well. Even if Wealthy stayed in place, who could guarantee that her loved ones would? And had not her Connecticut forebears settled Ohio when it too was wild and dangerous? Surely her generation could show similar gumption. "Nonetheless, I am willing."

John hugged her, his pamphlets rustling. "I knew you would agree. I knew when I examined your head that you had pluck."

"Well, at least it's not North Elba."

~ ~ ~

Wealthy hadn't been so foolish as to fall in love at first sight, but she had liked John's looks the first time she had seen him in the Grand River Institute's Ladies Department. Normally the Ladies' Hall was barred to those of the male species, but on that August day in 1845, the halls had thundered with masculinity as fathers, brothers, uncles, and the occasional hired man lugged young ladies' trunks to their lodgings while the preceptress, Miss Betsy Cowles, soothed parental fears. Men could only call in the parlor, she assured parent after parent, and only at designated times and under the strictest supervision. An efficient woman, Miss Cowles issued reassurances while at the same time welcoming back old pupils and greeting new ones, not to mention assigning them to their rooms. "Yes, Mrs. Green, any young man caught with spirits in his room will be expelled immediately. Why, Miss Abernathy, so lovely to see you back! Miss Hotchkiss, you'll be in room five. You'll be with Miss Brown, who just arrived a short time ago."

A pretty, red-headed girl of about sixteen, Miss Brown was accompanied by her brother and her father. The brother, in his early twenties, was stockily built, with gentle blue eyes under a shock of blond hair. He could not have looked more different from his father, a whippet-thin man in his forties with blue-gray eyes that blazed, even as he said in a perfectly mild voice, "Miss Wealthy Hotchkiss. A fine Puritan name."

"Yes, sir," said Wealthy, reduced by those intense eyes to a state of simpering demureness.

The younger man—like his father, he bore the utterly ordinary name of John Brown—said, "We were just telling Ruth how privileged you ladies are to have a table in your rooms. We men have no such convenience but must eat standing or balance our plates on our laps."

"Do you attend school here, then?"

"Yes, I've been here for a couple of years." As if sensing what Wealthy was thinking—that he was rather older than most students—he added, "I got a late start, but it's better late than never."

"Oh, I agree," Wealthy said.

"John helped me with my affairs until he was of age, as was proper," said the older man. "Very capably too. His delay is not from want of application or desire on his part."

John Jr. gave Wealthy a sheepish smile, undetected by his father, which she returned.

But she hadn't fallen in love with him right then. Maybe it was a little later, at chapel. They had chapel every afternoon, and for many students, it was the most important part of the day—the time when the entire student body came together, officially to give thanks to the Lord and unofficially for the Men's Department and the Ladies' Department to study the other and be studied in turn. While this struck Wealthy as rather frivolous—she had not come here to make eyes at young men, but to improve herself—she nonetheless found herself attending carefully to the arrangement of her dark hair as she prepared to follow the other girls to the hall. And when Ruth's eyes naturally turned to look for her brother at chapel, how could Wealthy's not do the same?

It had pleased her to see that Mr. Brown was not the only student of his age, though it distressed her to see that his clothing, while neat and clean, was somewhat shabby compared to that of his classmates. When it came time to sing a hymn, she found that she could distinguish his voice from the others quite clearly; he was a perfectly good tenor and would have been better with proper training.

Someone with a fine soprano voice was trilling along, singing the wrong verse in the hymnal—that someone being Wealthy herself. Blushing, Wealthy turned her thoughts to the music and found her lost place. She would not let herself wonder if Mr. Brown might have been listening for her voice as avidly as she had his.

But no, although she had certainly been distracted, she couldn't say for certain she had been in love. Was it that evening, when she and Ruth had talked through the night and Ruth told her that the Brown family helped slaves to freedom, that she had fallen in love? A few days later, when John turned up to keep her company as she was peeling potatoes, part of the chores that all the students had to do? Or had it been during the weeks when it seemed that she and John would be no more than friends, as were Ruth and Wealthy?

Ruth had told her that a couple of years before, John had fallen in love with another classmate with the pretentious name of Adelia, and she had broken his heart. For one thing, she had told him his head was in the clouds, and she didn't think he would ever earn enough to keep her in the comfort she expected. For another—and here Ruth had turned grave—there was poor Frederick, their younger brother. "He has these crazy spells every few months when he gorges himself with food, has blinding headaches, can't sleep—just goes wild. The rest of the time, he's quiet and pleasant and hardworking. John told Adelia about this as well. He wanted her to know these things, but I think he hoped that she would overlook them for the sake of love. She couldn't."

"The wretch," Wealthy said. Maybe it was then, thinking of John's honesty being rewarded so unfairly, that she fell in love.

Most probably, she had been in love by late December. By this time, she, Ruth, and John had fallen into the habit of walking from chapel together, sometimes accompanied by others, but always at minimum a trio. As the three of them were trudging through an early snow—John had taken her arm, but since he had Ruth on the other arm, Wealthy couldn't draw any hope from the gesture—John cleared his throat. "I've an odd request to make of you, Wealthy. Remember last week, we spoke of phrenology?"

"Yes, it was very interesting."

"It's something I'd like to study one day; not on my own as I have been doing, but with a qualified practitioner. But since I have been studying on my own, I'd like to practice doing some readings. I've done some of the men in my hall but no ladies. Except for Ruth, and that was when I was first beginning. Would you be willing? The books advise practicing on someone known to us, and I know you are receptive to new ideas, so you would be ideal."

At least he thought she was ideal, if not precisely in the way she wanted. And going off to study phrenology was most likely not something of which the wretch Adelia would approve. "I'm very willing."

"Wonderful! Saturday night, then, in the parlor of the Ladies' Hall? Ruth may come, of course, as an observer. I would advise wearing your hair down, or at least plaited."

Although Wealthy had not had the opportunity to receive a gentleman caller in the parlor, those classmates who had done so complained that it was less than satisfactory, at least when the caller was of the interesting sort. At any given time, there might be three girls receiving visitors, and Miss Cowles or a teacher made a point of breezing in and out to make certain that the young ladies' virtue was not being compromised and that conversations were seemly. So even if Ruth had not joined her as she walked downstairs to the parlor, Wealthy was not expecting a great deal of privacy; indeed, the two sofas were already occupied by awkward-looking couples.

Freshly arrived, John stood beside the fire, rubbing warmth into his hands. Nodding his approval of Wealthy's unconfined hair, which she had decided to plait instead of exposing in its full glory, he gestured toward a chair. "First, I will take some measurements. Then we will proceed to the actual reading."

As it was not every day that a young lady's head was measured in the parlor, the couples ceased their courting and turned their attention to John, who had taken a tape measure from his pocket and twined it around Wealthy's cranium. Meanwhile, Miss Cowles peeked in. "A phrenological examination, Mr. Brown? Do let me sit in."

John nodded. His measuring complete, he scribbled on the form he had brought with him. "Now, hold as still as you can—as if you are having your daguerreotype made—and look straight ahead."

Obeying, Wealthy trained her eyes upon the flickering fire as John ran his left hand, then both hands over her head, pausing now and then to take notes. By now, virtually the entire Ladies' Hall had squeezed into the parlor. Their presence did not distract John, who diligently went about his task. At last, he pronounced, "Finished. Now, if Miss Hotchkiss consents, I will be happy to share some of my findings."

"I consent," said Wealthy, knowing that the girls would give her no peace if she had not.

"But what is this good for, Mr. Brown?" Louisa Barbour, a particular friend of Wealthy, asked.

"Well, first, it's always good to have insight into one's character. But beyond that, it can be used to help one settle into a profession, or to help one improve in one's profession. It can even be used to determine whether one will be compatible with one's sweetheart. Or a prospective sweetheart." Amid a giggle or two from his audience, John added, "Now, if I were a professional, I would take some time to analyze my findings before presenting—"

"Oh, but please don't make us wait," one of the younger girls said.

"Well, I can give some general impressions. First, let me say that although this science can reveal the depth of certain faculties, they are not immutable. Once you have the knowledge of these faculties, you can develop the better ones and work to suppress the worse. To just touch on the most interesting findings, Miss Hotchkiss's faculty of benevolence is quite marked, as is her faculty of adhesiveness. Unfortunately, her quality of acquisitiveness is marked as well—"

"I knew it," whispered Miss Bartholomew, who was immediately silenced by a look from Miss Cowles.

"Her faculty of tune is very high—"

"We certainly know that from our hymn-singing," said Miss Barbour sweetly.

"Her faculty of self-esteem is high, which could be either an ill or a good thing; she must cultivate the good aspect of it."

Miss Bartholomew maintained a judicious silence.

"The rest I shall allow Miss Hotchkiss to read for herself."

Amid the entreaties of other girls to have their heads examined, to which John gave in, Wealthy studied the chart John had handed her. There was nothing terribly shocking in it, or sadly, nothing that she knew to be untrue (how she loved it when she got a new bonnet!), but there was an omission: the line for "Amativeness" had been left blank. Probably John had thought it unseemly to evaluate this faculty, given Wealthy's maiden state. Or had he evaluated it and simply not decided to reveal his findings? It was disconcerting to think that he might have knowledge that he was withholding. She scanned to the bottom of the page. Next to the date, John had written, "A fine brain."

How could she not be in love after that?

In February 1846, the school recessed for the winter. Wealthy had come home to Trumbull County to find her father looking frail and drawn. Her older sisters, both married to physicians, had brought their husbands by to sneak a look at him, but their confirmation was hardly necessary. Even little Eunecia, the youngest of the Hotchkiss sisters, could guess that he was dying of consumption. The only debate between the two physicians had been whether he had weeks or months to live, and in the end, both had been proven wrong. He was dead within days.

Wealthy was sitting dejectedly in her parlor when their hired girl stepped in and said, "A caller for you, miss. A Mr. John Brown, Jr. He was most particular about the 'Junior.'"

John, calling? The weather outside was frigid and the ground blanketed in snow.

Bundled up in winter clothing, John came into the parlor. Handing his coat and other things to Bessie with a nod in acknowledgement of her services, he said, "I heard from my sister Ruth that Mr. Hotchkiss had died. I wanted to express my sympathies to Miss Hotchkiss—and to the rest of the family."

Wealthy's mother smiled wanly. "That is very kind of you, sir. Do sit down, you look frozen. Did you come from a great distance?"

"Akron. I got rides here and there, but I footed it much of the way."

"You walked?" Wealthy asked.

He nodded. "I'm an inveterate walker. It's invigorating."

"Well, you must stay for supper after all that walking," Mother said. "And stay overnight, unless you have made other arrangements."

John shook his head. "No, I was going to find a tavern rather than impose."

"Goodness, no," Mother said. "There's certainly no need for that."

Wealthy listened as her mother launched into her favorite topic—temperance. It was the most animated she had seen Mother in days, and she was pleased to see John making such a good impression, even while hardly getting in a word edgewise.

Early the next day, after a hearty breakfast and a disquisition from Mother about healthful eating, John rose and prepared to go. "Ruth said that you would be returning to school. Am I right, Miss Hotchkiss?"

"Yes, Father wanted me to finish what I had started."

"Good. Then I'll see you back there in just a few days."

Knapsack in hand, John bade them farewell. The weather outside could hardly look any less inviting. They hadn't even been able to bury Wealthy's father, the ground had been so hard; they had had to place his body in the cemetery's holding vault until conditions improved. "Wait," Wealthy said. "I'll walk with you for a bit."

"Dear! You'll catch your death of cold!" Mother protested.

Even John asked, "Are you sure?"

"I won't be out but for a minute." Before her mother could say more, Wealthy gathered her cloak around her and enveloped her head in its warm hood.

It was even colder than she had supposed, but she grimly faced down the wind as John said, "I was glad to see you're not in deep mourning."

"Mother said I was too young to assume it, though I believe I'm quite old enough."

"Well, I think it unnecessary no matter a woman's age. Unnecessary and unfair, really, as no one expects a man to drench himself in black to prove his grief."

"I hadn't thought of it that way."

"My mother died when I was twelve, as I guess Ruth has told you. None of us put on mourning—not even an armband for Father—but it didn't mean we didn't grieve. Once or twice, I found Father sobbing at her grave. I wept there as well." He took Wealthy's gloved hand. "You'll miss your father a great deal in the days to come, but don't fear; after a while, the grief does settle down. It becomes something that you always carry with you but doesn't obtrude upon you."

"Thank you." She shivered.

"Do go home, Wealthy. Your mother's right; you'll catch cold."

"I will after I ask something. You came all the way here in the freezing cold just to give me your sympathies. Why?"

"I guess I was afraid that Ruth was wrong about you going back to school and worried that I'd never see you again." He hesitated. "It's the wrong time to say this, I know, but I love you."

She stared up at him. "I love you too," she breathed.

"Well, good." After another hesitation, he put his lips to hers, oblivious, as was she, of the wind howling around them.

How that next year and a half had poked along! Once in a while, they'd stolen some kisses in the parlor at school, but when the term ended in July 1846, it had meant their separation, as John had to work for his father in Springfield and Wealthy had to return to her mother's house in Vernon. When he returned for one last term, the winter of 1847, Wealthy hadn't been there; with her father dead, money had been tighter, so she had gotten a job teaching district school instead. It was a subject on which John had been able to offer a good deal of helpful advice in his letters. By then, they had agreed that they would marry when Wealthy turned eighteen at the latest, although she had hopes of persuading her mother to give her consent so that they could wed a little earlier.

In the meantime, Wealthy read up on the subject of marriage, thanks to her older sisters, who were kind enough to lend her books from their husbands' medical libraries. She and John further improved their knowledge in May, when he walked down from school to visit, although their private time together had entailed nothing more than some kissing and petting in the barn while the horse and cow looked on reproachfully. But the visit had been successful in another way: Wealthy's mother had agreed that they could marry in July, two months before Wealthy's eighteenth birthday, after which they would move to Springfield and remain there until John's father no longer needed his assistance.

Eons passed, and finally, on a July day in 1847, Wealthy's uncle Riverius Bidwell led her into her mother's parlor while John, looking fine in a new frock coat, gazed at her proudly. "You're beautiful," he whispered as they took their places in front of the Reverend E. B. Chamberlain. John had suggested a justice of the peace, but Wealthy, knowing the injury this would do to her mother's feelings, had insisted on the minister.

It was a short, simple service, sealed with a thin gold band that John carefully slid onto Wealthy's finger. And then, at last, she was Mrs. John Brown, Jr.

There was a reception with punch and lemonade, excellent food, and delicious wedding cake, but for Wealthy, it was something to be gotten through until night fell and she was finally alone in the guest bedroom with John. "Would you like me to turn my back while you undress?" he asked.

"No. I want you to do it."

He obeyed, valiantly working through Wealthy's layers of clothing. Her pink-and-gray gown, which would serve as a Sunday dress for the rest of the summer, and her uppermost petticoat he managed easily enough, but when he discovered two more petticoats, necessary to give Wealthy's dress its pretty shape, he asked plaintively, "More?" Wealthy's corset, which he arrived at next, elicited a grumbled, "Oh, this thing."

Taking pity on him as he fumbled with the hooks in front, Wealthy quickly divested herself of it on her own account. Then he slipped off her chemise and unbuttoned her drawers, and after that, very little was said between them.

In the hardest days to come in their lives, she would take comfort in her sweet memories of that night: John's caressing hands finally arriving in the place where she most longed to be touched, her clutching him as she abandoned herself to sheer pleasure, his hands guiding hers (not that she really needed that much guiding, it turned out), the moment when they finally became as one, John's own cry of joy, and the delicious rest in each other's arms afterward. Finally, John said, "Was this all your studies promised it to be, my love?"

"No. Better."

"I'm glad to hear that because you were my first. And, I trust, my only."

"The first? Really?"

He nodded. "I went to a brothel once, because I was at the age where I thought I should, just as I'd tried smoking because I thought it was something a man should do. Once I got inside, I found it all rather depressing, but I'd paid up already, of course, so I decided to pass the time in conversation. We had a very nice talk; if I recall, we touched on mesmerism, the effect the railroads were likely to have upon the country, slavery, the rights of women—all sorts of stimulating topics. She was rather well informed for a woman of her kind. I think she found me a rather odd duck, but then again, it's probably the easiest money she ever made. Unless, of course, she found me a bore."

"I didn't think it was possible to love you more, John, but I do."

He positioned her more comfortably in the crook of his arm. "Seeing your entire family here today did give me pause. You're obviously very close to them, and they are very fond of you. Will you get homesick if I take you away to Massachusetts—and who knows where else—in the future?"

"We have plenty of time to decide about the who knows where, and I think I can bear a little change in the meantime." She kissed his cheek. "I want to see some of the world outside of Ohio, and most importantly, I want to follow your fortunes, whatever they may be. Don't underestimate me, love."

Remembering that night seven years later, Wealthy smiled to herself.

But there was someone who hadn't been present on their wedding night, someone whose arrival had been long postponed but then eagerly awaited: their year-and-a-half-old son, Johnny, who half crawled and half walked into the room. He had been slow to walk and talk, to their immense worry, but now he was beginning to manage both. He caught at John. "Pa!"

"Johnny!" John clasped his son. "Did you hear? We're going to Kansas!"

8

April 1855 to May 1855

"Fruit trees and books," Ellen muttered. "If there were any two more impractical men in the state of Ohio than my husband and yours, I don't know where they could be found."

Ellen, who had married John's younger brother Jason just about the same time that Wealthy had married John, was nothing if not practical, which Wealthy was finding rather wearying. "People will want to buy Jason's fruit once they get settled, and John must have his books wherever he goes. Why, when we lived in New York, he stored them at my sister's house, and he was bereft. Anyway, soon they'll be the most impractical men in Kansas."

"Two or three books, maybe, he could have put into a trunk. That would be quite sensible. But three hundred?"

Wealthy shrugged. "There will be many cold nights on the prairie with nothing to do but read." It would have been convenient if the boys, her Johnny and Ellen's Austin and Charlie, provided a distraction at this point, but the three of them, ranging in age from three-and-a-half-year-old Austin to one-and-a-half-year-old Charlie, were playing quite nicely in a corner of the ladies' cabin of their steamboat, bound for St. Louis. There, the Browns—and Jason's fruit trees, sitting in the hold—would board another steamer, which would take them up the Missouri River to Kansas City. John's books had already been shipped there.

John had not been the only Brown to catch the Kansas fever. The first to succumb was John's aunt Florella, a younger half-sister of Father Brown. Florella's husband, the Reverend Samuel Adair, tired of preaching to empty pews in Ohio, had gone to Kansas as a missionary in the fall of 1854. Next, infected by John, had been Owen and Frederick, John's younger, bachelor brothers. Owen seemed determined not to marry, but Frederick had managed to get himself engaged despite the crazy spells that plagued him now and then. He had the idea that Kansas might cure him. The two of them had set off in 1854 with some cattle and horses, wintering them in Illinois before proceeding to Kansas. Soon, Salmon Brown, who was always up for some adventure, had joined them. Even the patriarch of the family, Father Brown, who had ended up back in Akron after his unprofitable trip to England, had considered moving west. Having finally wound up his partnership with Mr. Perkins, however, he had instead decided to stick to his original plan and return to Essex County, where Ruth's husband had erected a house for him. But it was the general opinion of the rest of the family that he might yet succumb.

Jason had caught the fever as well, but like John and Wealthy, he had his affairs in Ohio to settle and his farm to sell, and he couldn't just light off for Kansas the way the bachelors could. Besides, there was the matter of Ellen, who alone of the Browns had remained immune to the allure of

Kansas. She had raised every conceivable objection to settling there, and some inconceivable ones as well. At first, Charlie was too young to risk the journey, which everyone had conceded was a fair point. Then once Charlie shot up and showed every sign of being a robust lad, she worried that traveling with him might be too tiring. The climate was too unlike Ohio's, so they would either freeze to death or roast to death; the Indians were rampant, so they might as well say goodbye to their scalps; there wouldn't be enough women around for civilization, and the women who would be around would be of the wrong sort. On and on the objections went. Some days, she almost managed to talk Wealthy out of Kansas.

But Jason, despite his reputation for being guided by his wife, had held his ground on this particular point, so in April, their affairs as settled as they ever were going to be, they set out on their journey.

Thus far, it had been most pleasant, and even Ellen's grumbling became somewhat half-hearted as they proceeded down the Ohio River. The weather was fine, in contrast to the first steamboat journey they had taken together, as John reminded Wealthy as they stood watching the sunset, Johnny between them. "Remember our trip to Springfield after we married? How sick we were on our way to Buffalo?"

"Yes, casting up our accounts side by side," Wealthy said. "But I prefer to remember how everyone in the boat knew we were newlyweds without having to be told. Remember the captain offering us champagne?"

"I suppose we were a bit obvious. We did stand a bit too close to each other."

"And kiss every chance we had."

"And that little berth in the cabin we shared! It was worth the extra expense, getting a cabin, just to be alone there with you. Quite a contrast to this trip, though not a bad one at all."

They both smiled down at Johnny, who was too taken with the activity about him to attend to his parents' conversation.

This journey, the captain proffered no champagne, but the food was good and abundant, their fellow passengers pleasant. Only when they docked in Louisville and saw slaves hurrying to and from the boat, staggering under loads of cargo and fuel, were they disquieted—for all the fugitive slaves and former slaves they had encountered over the years, they had never actually seen the system in action.

They disembarked in St. Louis, the smokiest place that Wealthy had been in her life, New York City included, and booked passage on the *New Lucy*, one of the packets that traveled the Missouri River. As they had a day to spare, they busied themselves buying the supplies that they had deemed too burdensome to purchase earlier—a plow, some farming tools, and two tents, one for each family. Just the sight of the tents made Ellen's face grow grim. "Surely we'll build our cabins soon once we get our claims," Wealthy said by way of comfort.

"I might remind you that we both had perfectly good houses in Ohio without canvas walls."

Wealthy sighed. "Maybe we can find a stove next."

John coughed. "My dear, we should save what money we have. The stove can wait a little, I'm sure."

"You mean you expect us to cook over open fires? Like savages?"

"Once we get into a cabin, we can buy them at Kansas City."

"But they'll probably be more expensive there. They're expensive enough here. We should have bought one of those nice ones we saw in Pittsburgh."

"I agree; I wish we had bought one back there, although we would had the additional cost of shipping it. But we must economize, dear."

Wealthy scowled, and Ellen shot her a commiserating look. "Those Brown men," she whispered.

Having completed their purchases, they went to the firm of Mr. Slater, a freight agent, to arrange for their transportation to Kansas City. As John signed a paper, Mr. Slater squinted at the signature and said, "Ah, so you're the gentleman from Ohio with the books. They're safely on their way, I can assure you."

"And now we are too," John said.

"Are you taking the stage or steamer?"

"Steamer."

"Passage paid?" They nodded, and Mr. Slater frowned. "Personally, I'd have chosen the stage. The water's still a bit low, I'm told, and sandbars will be a problem. Which steamer?"

"The *New Lucy*," Wealthy said. Another frown. "Is it not a good choice?"

"Well, let me put it this way: she's a beautiful steamer, and fast in season—you won't find a prettier lady on the Missouri River. But the captain caters to more of a Southern clientele. I won't inquire into your politics, but you may want to be discreet if you hold Free-State views."

"We are abolitionists," John said, and the others, even little Austin, nodded. "We make no secret of it."

"Then do yourselves one favor. Say 'cow' for me."

"Cow," the Browns said in unison.

"You say *Ke-ow*. Missourians like a drawled out *Coooow*. They'll find some excuse to make you say the word, believe me. At least say it to suit them, and perhaps you'll be left alone."

"*Coooow*," the Browns repeated.

"That's better," Mr. Slater said, a bit uncertainly. "Well, I wish you a safe journey. Your things will be in Kansas City waiting for you."

They bid him goodbye. When they had cleared the premises, Wealthy said, "That doesn't sound promising, does it? Perhaps we should take the stage? Or another steamer? Or bovine elocution classes?"

"Or go back to Ohio," Ellen muttered.

"I'm not going to be run off a steamer by the slavers before I've even gotten on it," John said.

"But if the water isn't high enough . . ."

"Slaver or no slaver, the captain wouldn't set off if he didn't think he could get us there," Jason said. "Besides, we'll be seeing these people in Kansas. We might as well get used to them."

His argument, delivered in his usual quiet manner, won the day, and the next morning, they boarded the *New Lucy*. Built only three years before, she was a large side-wheeler, glistening white.

They might as well have stepped into a different world. In addition to being piled with freight of all sorts, including livestock, the *New Lucy* was packed with people, few of whom were inclined to give way to anyone, and most of the white passengers were of two classes: Southern aristocrats trailed by slaves, and poor Southerners trailed by tobacco juice. The fine ladies stared coolly at Wealthy and Ellen, who had donned simple gowns and bonnets for the journey, and the poor women, seeing the Brown wives recoil when they took snuff, made a point of spitting it in their direction for the rest of the trip. The men, even of the ostensibly better sort, had bowie knives on one hip and revolvers on the other, and since all partook freely of the vessel's fine whiskey, Wealthy lived in dread of a mortal combat breaking out.

But the Missourians were in good spirits, for just weeks before, there had been an election for the Kansas territorial legislature. Border Ruffians had poured into the territory and cast their votes—if stuffing the ballot boxes, threatening with death any election judges who were brave enough to challenge them, and assaulting anyone who appeared to be casting a Free-State vote could be dignified with the name of "voting." More than once, the Browns heard their fellow passengers boast of their exploits.

The worst of the Missourians was a tall man in a green coat, a cigar perennially clasped between his lips and the usual pair of weapons at his side. Neither the Browns nor anyone else on the steamer, as far they could tell, ever learned his name. He simply called himself "Doctor," although Dr. Sylvester Prentiss, one of the minority of Free-State settlers on board the *New Lucy*, told the Browns later that when Dr. Prentiss asked him a question of a professional nature, the Missourian was unable to muster an answer. Although he had no slaves himself, he did his best to make up for it by lording it over the slaves on board, both those belonging to the passengers and those employed on the steamer as waiters and deckhands, who kept as far from him as they could while performing their duties. It pained Wealthy to see the fear he inspired in those who had no choice but to deal with him, such as those who served him at meals.

The slaves were not the only ones who raised his ire. When the Browns were served at meals—there was no fault to be found with the *New Lucy's* cook—they made a point of thanking the black waiters who set their plates in front of them. "You needn't do that," the Doctor snapped at Wealthy, who through some ill fate he had ended up sitting beside. At least he wasn't smoking his cigar.

"I shall address the waiters as I please."

"You'll just stir them up. You Northerners—"

Before the Doctor could finish his thought, such as it was, there was a thud, and the dishes skittered wildly around the table as the steamer, which had been gliding gracefully down the river, came to an inelegant halt. Their waiter hardly seemed discomposed. "Sandbar," he explained. "Run aground."

"Does this happen often?" Wealthy asked as more waiters hurried in.

"All the time, ma'am, in low water. But they'll put it to right soon."

And so they did, but with so much groaning and puffing on the part of the engine, the Browns and the other novices to Missouri River travel were convinced it would blow up.

It was only the first of many run-ins with the sandbars, extinguishing the Browns' hope for a speedy journey. Worse, the weather grew steadily sultrier, forcing all to drink more freely of the river water.

On a hot day that had been mercifully free of sandbars, the Browns were taking an after-dinner stroll on the upper deck, where they passed the Doctor tilted back smoking in his accustomed chair. Only once, and with a maximum of ill grace, had he been seen to relinquish his favorite perch, that being when the oldest lady on board, deprived of a seat, had fixed her glare upon him. He could not have settled himself in a more inconvenient place, being in a particularly narrow passage. Even Wealthy and Ellen, though eschewing the ridiculously full skirts that the aristocrats favored, had to compress their garments as they squeezed by him.

As the Browns, having cleared the path successfully, leaned on the railing, enjoying the breeze, they saw Ben, a slave of about twelve or thirteen who was employed as a messenger between the captain and the crew, hurry through the passage, so intent on his mission that he failed to avoid the Doctor's protruding foot. With a thump, the chair snapped forward, landing the Doctor in an upright position and nearly sending his cigar flying out of his mouth.

Wealthy could hardly suppress a smile, and one of the ladies seated closest to the Doctor, one who had been much troubled by his cigar, snickered outright. The Doctor grabbed Ben by the collar and threw him to the floor. "Saucy little brat! I'll have you horsewhipped."

"It was an accident!" Wealthy said as John and Jason hastened toward the boy. "The child meant no harm."

The Doctor said nothing in reply but stomped away toward the bar.

Ignoring the cold looks of the passengers around them, the brothers helped Ben to his feet and led him to the captain, who, as John later told Wealthy, appeared to accept their assurances that the lad had been careless at the very worst. So, the matter ended, they thought, until that evening, past sunset, they were headed toward the cabin area, where they heard a dreadful moaning. Barely visible in the sheltered passage was Ben, strung up by his thumbs. "Help me, sir."

Another passenger, a Missourian, was hard upon their heels. Shaking his head, John hurried off as Wealthy wept into her handkerchief.

She had put Johnny to bed in their stateroom and was ready to retire as well when John, who was in the habit of checking their freight on the lower deck, returned. "I found my chance and cut the cords that were binding that poor boy."

"Oh, John!" Wealthy hugged him.

"Being strung up wasn't all that was ailing him. He has cholera; I'm near certain of it."

Knowing that when there was one case of cholera, others would follow, they fell silent. That very night, their fears were proven true when little Austin in the adjacent stateroom awoke in agony.

For two and a half days, his illness raged while the four of them took turns at nursing him and caring for Johnny and Charlie, neither of whom, miraculously, fell sick. Outside the stateroom was no better, as Wealthy discovered the first time she ventured to the deck for fresh air and saw a rude coffin being borne out to the sandbar on which they were presently stranded. The next body she saw was that of Ben. For him, the captain hadn't bothered with a coffin.

The Doctor proved useless in this crisis, even to his fellow Missourians, but Dr. Prentiss tended all the patients, saving many lives and easing the deaths of others. He could not have been more attentive to Austin or kinder to Jason and Ellen, but on April 30, Austin died in his parents' arms. He had been delirious most of the time but had been sensible long enough to kiss his parents goodbye and give them a faint smile.

"You told me this would be a good move for us," Ellen said, staring at the hollow-eyed remains of her firstborn. Her eyes were dry, her voice flat. "You told me that it would be healthier, that we would thrive. Now look at us."

No one could answer her.

They had but one consolation: the last sandbar had proved too much for the rudder of the *New Lucy*, requiring them to lie over at Waverly, Missouri, while the vessel was being repaired. They could at least bury Austin properly in the town cemetery instead of in a sandbar or on the muddy riverbank, as had been the fate of several of their fellow passengers. Although they gave consideration to having the women and children remain on the ship while the men went about their sad task, Ellen could not bear the thought of not seeing her boy laid to rest, and Wealthy was eager to leave the sickness on the boat behind for a short time, even if it meant sleeping underneath the stars for an evening. "What time will you cast off tomorrow?" John asked the captain.

The captain, who had been barking an order to one of the hands, turned his head a fraction. "Afternoon. Get back by noon."

He expressed no sympathy for their bereavement, but the Browns, remembering poor Ben's cruel punishment after the unsuccessful attempt to intervene on his behalf, expected none and would have been at a loss to respond had he offered any. Reassured by the fact that some of their fellow passengers were also taking the opportunity to go ashore, they disembarked. Jason tenderly carried the hastily made little coffin while the rest were laden with luggage, for the riverboats carried a goodly number of thieves who might well be tempted to pilfer in their absence.

As John set off in search of a suitable burial spot, the rest remained under a tree, watching wearily as Johnny played listlessly and Charlie, puzzled at the sudden absence of his older brother, toddled about. It was not John who appeared presently, however, but a young black man with a wheelbarrow. "You folks with the man looking for the cemetery?

From the *New Lucy*? Then follow me. Master thinks a storm is coming up, and he's got a place you can spend the night. Food too."

"There's cholera aboard the ship," Jason said. "My boy died of it."

"Master knows 'bout the cholera, else he'd offer you a room in the house for the night. But this will suit. Unless you're city folk not used to roughing it a bit."

Wealthy smiled. "We've all been farmers."

George, as they found the man's name to be, loaded the belongings onto the wheelbarrow and led them to a mansion on a hill, surrounded on three sides by what Wealthy guessed were slave quarters and a few outbuildings. It was to one of the latter, used as a storeroom, to which George ushered them. It was far from luxurious, but there were plenty of sacks on which to lay their heads. Having got them settled, George returned with bread and coffee.

After buying a plot and a shovel at an inflated price, a weary John returned, and he and Jason set off to dig the grave. They had just disappeared from view when a clap of thunder sounded and rain began to fall in sheets. When the men at last reappeared, they were soaked, and the rain was still falling. Finally, just before dawn, the rain stopped, and the six of them walked to the grave.

Ellen began sobbing afresh as Jason and John carefully lowered the coffin into its resting place. "I can't bear to leave him with these horrid people in this godforsaken state! Can't we carry him with us?"

Jason wearily shook his head. "The captain would never let us back on board with his body. No one would take us anywhere, not with the cholera about. We'll come back for him someday. I promise you. I don't like leaving him either."

John, who had advised Jason against marrying Ellen and had never conquered his disapproval of the match, put his arm around his sister-in-law. "We'll mark it well, so we'll have no trouble finding it."

Having written Austin's name on the rude coffin and marked the grave with a pile of stones, they said a final prayer and departed in silence. As they made their way to their temporary shelter, they found George approaching with a basket full of bacon and biscuits and a pot of coffee. "Master thought you'd be hungry."

The kindness made their already teary eyes fill the more.

"George, is this really your master's doing and not yours?" Wealthy asked.

"It is, ma'am. He knows you're from Ohio, and he reckons you're Free-Staters, but he's a kind man. He's lost children of his own."

John brushed at his eye. "In the past few days, I think I have forgotten that there are good hearts to be found everywhere. Please thank him for us—and please accept a little something for your own trouble."

"I will. By the way, do you know a gentleman with a green coat? Tall and thin, long hair, with a mess of weapons on him?"

John frowned. "Why, that's the Doctor, I think. A man—a cruel one—who was aboard the same steamer. I saw him get off and stagger into an abandoned log cabin."

"That's the one. Well, he's not being cruel no more. They found him dead there this morning. Cholera, they reckon. Master sent some of the hands to bury him on the bank."

"I wish I could find some compassion for him, dying alone and in a strange place," Wealthy said. "I can't."

George bade them farewell, leaving them to eat their meal in private. Then, having written a note of thanks and propped it up where it would not be missed, they gathered their belongings and headed toward the wharf. It was only ten in the morning, plenty of time to board the *New Lucy*.

But when they arrived, they saw the steamer in the process of casting off. "Wait!" John called. "We're coming aboard."

"Too late," Captain Conley said.

"But you told us noon! It's nowhere near noon. And we're paid to Kansas City."

The captain shrugged. "Cast off!"

"You scamp!" Wealthy shook her fist. "How dare you take advantage of a boy's death to serve us so!"

"Stage runs to Kansas City, but it also runs back to St. Louis and to where you damned Free-Staters came from."

There was no point in continuing the conversation. As the steamer resumed its journey, Johnny looked up, puzzled. "Bad man, Mama?"

"A very bad man." She scowled after him. "I hope he—" Catching herself just in time from completing her sentence, she asked, "Well, what now? We could wait for another steamer, but when is the next one?"

"I've had it with steamers," John said. "We may as well take the stage. At least there will be no disease—I hope."

Ellen, who had scarcely said a word since their arrival the evening before, at last spoke. "How many signs do you need? First, we were told not to get on. Then our darling boy died. And now we've been deserted in this miserable town. The captain is right. Why don't we turn around and go back to Ohio, where we have family and friends?"

John shook his head. "Ellen, we've come this far. There's nothing to go back to in Ohio. No farms, no furniture—nothing. Just humiliation at having failed without even trying."

"Then you and Wealthy and Johnny go, if you're so set on it, and the three of us will swallow our pride and go home. The *three* of us." Ellen began sobbing. "There should have been four. Oh, God, there should have been four."

Jason took Ellen in his arms and rocked her gently. "Poor girl," he whispered. "Poor girl . . . I don't know what to do, John. Part of me wants to go on, and part of me wants to go back."

"Whatever you choose," Wealthy said quietly, "it won't bring Austin to life."

Jason sighed. For a good half hour, they sat, awaiting his decision. Finally, Jason said, "Ellen, I think we should go. Nothing can bring Austin back, as Wealthy said. Akron, Kansas, wherever—it'll be miserable without him. But we've come this far, and we might as well press on. At least we can give it a fair try. But I promise you, if you get out there and hate it, I'll take you back to Akron. All right?"

"Do I have a choice?" Ellen wiped her eyes. The last few days seemed to have aged her by as many years. "Do women ever have a choice?"

"You do. I won't make you go, and I won't go alone."

Ellen stared out at the river. "If you want to go, we'll go. I don't care enough to keep arguing."

To their good fortune, the stagecoach to Independence, Missouri, was passing through that very afternoon, and as they told the driver only that the ladies had found the steamboat disagreeable, which was certainly true, they had no difficulty in getting aboard. Once in Independence, however, their luck changed, because there was space on the stage to

127

Westport, Missouri, for only the women and children, and even then Wealthy and Ellen would have to hold their sons on their laps. The men would have to walk to Westport, a distance of about twenty-five miles. From there, assuming all were reunited safely, they would take the mail wagon to Osawatomie, Kansas, where John and Jason's uncle and aunt, the Adairs, had settled.

Ellen received the news of this latest setback with the same indifference she had shown to everything since agreeing to proceed to Kansas, but Wealthy asked, "Can't you wait for the next stage?"

"It's just more delay and expense," John said. In the coach, he had been counting their cash with a look of worry. "Besides, Jason and I are fast walkers. Aren't we, brother?"

Jason nodded with as little spirit as his wife.

"I just worry about you, wandering by yourselves in Missouri with so many unfriendly people."

"We have a revolver and our trusty squirrel rifle. Don't worry, sweetheart. We'll be fine, and the sooner we get started, the sooner we'll be reunited."

Reluctantly, Wealthy let the men depart, John draping a comforting arm around Jason's shoulder. She could only hope that the walk with his brother did the bereaved father some good.

With their boys, she and Ellen squeezed into their seats, each of the women crammed between two people who appeared to have been built specifically to cause their fellow passengers the most discomfort. It did not help matters that Johnny, who lately appeared to be trying to make up for the months he had delayed talking, chattered incessantly. Although it was sometimes difficult for strangers to understand him, the word "Ohio" was perfectly intelligible. Wealthy could only thank Providence that he did not know the word "abolitionist."

At last, stiff and sore, they limped off the stagecoach at Westport, to which it appeared the denizens of the *New Lucy* had been transplanted and multiplied a hundredfold. Wealthy hardly dared to inquire for the mail wagon, but she gathered her pride and finally asked the most respectable-looking and least heavily armed person in sight for directions. To her surprise—perhaps it was the slight drawl she affected, perhaps the two tired little boys, or perhaps Ellen's look of sheer misery—she not only received a cordial answer, but was led directly to Mr. Higgins, the driver of the mail wagon.

It was the Reverend Adair who had recommended the mail wagon as transportation to Osawatomie, so they had no difficulty with Mr. Higgins, who gave them a warm smile after agreeing to drive them the next day. "Free-Staters? Good, we could use more in Kansas. I live there myself, you know."

Following his recommendation, they checked into a hotel known to be hospitable to Free-Staters. There, they settled down for a nap to await John and Jason. In the room were the first proper beds they had been in for weeks, and even Ellen half-smiled when she curled up upon hers. They were deep in slumber when they heard a knock at the door. Wealthy squealed as she opened it a crack. "You're here!"

John embraced her, then Johnny, while Jason followed suit with Ellen and Charlie. "Yes. Tired, hungry—we stopped at house after house to buy provisions, but the minute we opened our mouths and they realized we were from the North, we were told nothing was cooked. We finally sweet-talked a woman into giving us some cornbread for a quarter of a dollar. I don't know what she might have charged for some milk to wash it down."

"That's disgraceful," Wealthy said.

"It's the slavery system that makes them hate us so," Jason said. "It poisons everything. It's a lesson if nothing else."

John nodded. "We'll make Kansas different."

The next morning, they clambered aboard the mail wagon, piled with letters from the east. Wistfully, Wealthy wondered if some of the correspondence might be addressed to them.

Westport was a border town, and knowing that they were at last on the verge of passing into Kansas, all six of them, even little Charlie, sat up straight as the mail wagon left more and more of Missouri behind. "Well, here we are," Mr. Higgins finally said after what seemed an eternity. "Kansas."

"At last," John said. "I thought we'd never get here, and one of us didn't make it. Do you mind stopping a moment?"

"I do it all the time for the newcomers." Mr. Higgins clucked at the horses, who had already shown an inclination to stop on their own.

John handed Wealthy out of the wagon, then lifted Johnny over the side. After a moment of hesitation, Jason did the same for Ellen and Charlie. All around them stretched softly rolling prairie lit by a golden sun. A gentle breeze stirred Wealthy's hair as John put his arm around her. "What do you think?"

"I like it."

"And you, Johnny?"

"I like it too."

"Good, because I like it as well. We'll make it a free state, and we'll prosper." He kissed Wealthy as Mr. Higgins looked on benevolently and Jason put an arm around Ellen, who appeared to be on the verge of tears. "Let's get back on our way, so we can start our new lives all the sooner."

9

May 1855 to October 1855

John and Wealthy's tent at Brown's Station, the name the Browns had bestowed upon their five adjacent claims, had one luxury: the marital bed, constructed of poles and covered with brush, on top of which Wealthy had laid the handsome linen sheets that she had brought to her marriage. Shortly after dawn, just a couple of weeks after their arrival in the territory of Kansas, she rolled out of her bed, careful not to step on Frederick, curled up under a blanket nearby. Just a few days before, she would have shooed out her brother-in-law before getting dressed, but close quarters had made them all less finicky. Instead, after performing her morning ablutions with a crate serving as her washstand, she fastened her corset over her chemise and drawers, donned her petticoat and dress, and stepped outside to cook breakfast, using the kettle that hung over an open fire.

To the Browns' relief and not inconsiderable surprise, their tents and other belongings had made it to Kansas City. Those two tents served as their homes for now, and probably would for the foreseeable future, as the Browns had resolved to devote their attention to planting crops. Of the three bachelor Browns, Frederick shared a tent with John and Wealthy, Owen did the same with Jason and Ellen, and Salmon alternated between the two camps. Wealthy, who had grown up in a family of girls, was certainly getting more acquainted with the male species.

Breakfast would be johnnycake, a meal which little Johnny found hilarious and the rest of the family tedious, but there were wild grapes to liven things up a bit, and Ellen, whose tent was a short walk away, had made biscuits. "Delicious," Owen pronounced as he bit into a warm one.

"Very tasty," Salmon said.

"The best biscuits I've ever had," Frederick said. He was overdoing it as he often did, but at least Ellen smiled. She and Jason were still morose and mostly silent, but there was plenty to keep them occupied.

On this day, the women were planning to do the laundry by Middle Creek. It was a task that was disagreeable enough in a regular home with an actual kitchen, but it promised to be even more disagreeable here, and John and Jason would have to help them take everything to the creek. After the bachelors had gone out to the field to work, the rest of them were gathering up the dirty clothes and the implements of cleanliness when they heard a commotion. "What on earth?" Wealthy asked.

"Indians," Ellen said. "God preserve us."

Indeed, there was an entire line of them, whooping and yelling, wearing full war paint, fully armed, and riding toward the humble Brown tents at full speed. As they advanced, Wealthy had just time enough to consider which would be worse: being scalped or being taken prisoner to live the rest of her life among the savages. What outlandish name might they give her? Determined to go down fighting, she grabbed her washboard, the only weapon she had.

"Put it down," John said. "Come, spread your palms out like this."

"Look pleasant," Jason added.

Grimly, Wealthy obeyed, as did Ellen, who had been reaching for the washtub. As Johnny and Charlie, who had been playing in the tent, poked their heads out in astonishment, the Indians galloped on. Then the chief, with a significant nod, reined in his horse and threw his gun, bow, and arrows to the ground. With a series of clangs, the rest followed suit. Soon the six of them were surrounded by Indians, all nodding friendly greetings or shaking hands.

Wealthy smiled and shook hands all around, although the Indians wore rather less clothing than she would have preferred, which made looking about her rather awkward. When all was over, the Indians had ended up with a bag of flour, and John and Jason with handsome blankets. "These will be fine for the winter," Jason said, draping his on himself. He looked more cheerful than he had in weeks.

"I'm almost sorry it ended so pleasantly," John said. "I wanted to see the ladies wield their weapons."

Wealthy picked up her washboard. "You could still find out," she warned.

A few days later, they were eating dinner, which on fine days they took seated outside at a rough table incongruously topped with a tablecloth from Wealthy's house in Ohio, when they saw a group of men riding up. They were even better armed than the Indians had been, except that instead of bows and arrows, they carried a profusion of guns and knives. They also looked, as they approached, far less friendly. "We're looking for some stray cattle," the most respectable-looking one said more gruffly than necessary. "Seen 'em?"

"No," Frederick said. "And I'm sure we'd notice one that wasn't ours."

Wealthy suppressed a smile. If there was one thing the Brown men were snobbish about, it was their cattle, which admittedly were superior to the rest they had seen in the area.

"Well . . . " The men cast their eyes about. Wealthy wondered if they were going to demand to look inside the tents. "How are you on the goose?"

Wealthy had not the foggiest idea of what they meant, but Jason replied, "We are Free-State."

"More than that," John said. "We are abolitionist."

"Is that a fact?" said the leader. Without another word, he turned his horse around, and the others followed suit.

"What a stupid, vulgar bunch of men," Wealthy said. "Did they think we couldn't see through that story about looking for cattle? They probably look for the same cattle— or *cooows*— every time someone new picks a claim."

"Probably," John said. He rubbed his chin and stared after them thoughtfully. "Sadly, there's plenty more of them."

A few days later, Frederick returned from Osawatomie, ten miles off, where he had gone to the post office and stayed overnight with the Adairs. "Letters for the ladies," he said, handing a couple each to Wealthy and Ellen. "And I received a letter from my own lady," he added with a faint blush.

"Frederick, I wish you had married her and brought her on here," Wealthy said.

"Well, it would have been a bit crowded in the tent. But I wanted to have everything nice for her before bringing her on. A cabin with a stove, at least. And I wanted to see how I did too."

Wealthy patted Frederick on the shoulder.

"Anything from Father and them?" Salmon asked.

"Not yet."

"I wonder if he's still considering coming here instead of North Elba," Owen said.

"You know it takes a long time for Father to make up his mind," Jason said.

"I wish he would," Wealthy said. "And persuade Henry and Ruth to come along with him. And Mother Brown and the children too," she added hastily. She and Mother Brown did not have a great deal in common, it was true, but it would be lovely to have some more Free-State women here, even Mother Brown.

"That brings me to something I wanted to talk to all of you about," John said. "There's something I want to ask of Father."

"Money?" said Frederick.

"No. Weapons. I have been thinking about it, and if the slave states keep sending men into Kansas with no purpose but to intimidate Free-Staters and to force slavery upon this beautiful territory, what are we going to do? We have but a handful of weapons between five men, and the other Free-Staters I've met are no better supplied. Some are far worse. The men doing the bidding of the slaveholders, on the other hand, are armed to the teeth. If there is to be a fight between us and the Border Ruffians—and the longer I live here the more I think there will be one—I want to have not only the right but the might on our side."

"You know I'm ready for a fight," Salmon said. "I have been ever since we went through Missouri."

"And that is where Father comes in. I know he hasn't got the money to send us weapons, but Gerrit Smith does. If Father could ask him or some of the other abolitionists back East for the money and supply us with the weapons, we would be in better straits than we are now. And if the bogus election the Border Ruffians forced upon us is invalidated, as I hope it will, we'll be ready for the next one."

"Then let's write to him," Owen said, and Frederick nodded.

"You, Jason?" John asked.

"I don't care. Ellen and I may be gone by fall anyway."

"Aren't you going to ask the ladies?" Wealthy said.

"Naturally, I was." John looked at Ellen, who gave a mere shrug. "I'll take that as a yes. That leaves you, Wealthy."

"Of course, I agree. I just wanted to be asked."

"Then I'll write to him," John said. "I've no doubt he'll assist us. In fact"—he grinned—"I think he might well decide to come himself."

~ ~ ~

John sent his letter, but as no one quite knew whether Father Brown was in Akron, North Elba, or somewhere in between, no one expected a speedy reply.

Despite the seating of what the Free-Staters called the Bogus Legislature, it was a lovely summer. Although it was hot, the breeze cooled things nicely, and the crops thrived. Tired of having embers from the open fire burning holes in her skirt, Wealthy fashioned herself a pair of bloomers, which John loved, and through working outdoors grew as tan as an Indian maiden, which John also loved. On some warm nights, after a hard day's work, the Browns would go for a swim, and on one memorable occasion, Wealthy and John were able to steal off by themselves and bathe in nothing but what nature had given them.

In June, John walked to Lawrence to attend a Free-State convention there—Lawrence being in essence the Free-State capitol, having been named after Amos Lawrence, an abolitionist who was a prominent backer of the New England Emigrant Aid Company. He returned all afire for the cause and glowing with pride, for he had been made an officer. Meanwhile, Wealthy killed a rattlesnake all by herself.

Jason and Ellen, though still grieving, talked less and less often of returning to Ohio. Little Charlie thrived, as did Johnny, who received a dog as a present from a neighbor. Frederick hadn't had a single crazy spell. Owen was so excited about his claim, he talked in his sleep about it, and Salmon would disappear for days on his claim, planting crops.

To cap things off, Father Brown wrote to tell them that he was indeed coming, with Ruth's husband Henry and perhaps Oliver as well. As John had advised, they would be traveling overland instead of by water. Wealthy couldn't believe that Mother Brown, Ruth, and the children weren't coming too. Had they no sense of adventure? It was true that Father Brown still planned to make his home in North Elba, but perhaps a few months in Kansas might convert him, especially now that the Free-Staters were becoming more assertive.

Then the sickness came.

Beginning in September, one by one, or more accurately two by two or three by three, the Browns fell ill with ague, causing them to shake and shiver, except when they roasted with fever at intervals. They weren't alone; the Adairs in Osawatomie were suffering as well, as were many of the neighbors.

Salmon and Frederick were the first to succumb. Then John, who had set out for another Free-State meeting, returned after barely a mile on the road, sick and listless, and took to the bed. Johnny and Owen were next. Soon, only Wealthy, Ellen, and Charlie were up. The weather turned chilly, windy, and dreary. Lying in bed on a windy night beside a shivering John, Wealthy wondered if their tent was going to collapse around them.

To add to their misery, the laws passed by the Bogus Legislature took effect, including a law that made it a felony to speak out against slavery. On September 15, the day the new code took hold, John, still trembling by turns, managed to dress himself and went for a walk. "Well, I did it," he announced when he returned a few hours later.

"Did what?"

"Found a slave owner—it took some looking—and told him that he had no right to own a slave, that I had broken the law by telling him so, and that I would break the law again. I also told him that if any man attempted to arrest me, I would kill him."

"Surely he didn't try to arrest you!"

"No. He just rode off."

"Perhaps he thought you were touched in the head— and I think you are, darling. You're feverish."

John shrugged and let her wrap a blanket around him. "I just wanted to let him know." His teeth chattered.

Each time one of the men seemed to be recovering and managed to make his way out to the fields to work, another would worsen and take his place by the fire. The only bright spot was that although Johnny and Charlie each fell ill, neither was in danger of meeting poor Austin's fate. Indeed, none of the affected Browns were alarmingly sick; they simply had no energy, no stamina, and no spirit. All they could manage to do was to debate what was making them so ill. Some thought they were too close to the ravine; others thought that it was the same seasoning process that had killed so many of their Puritan ancestors when they arrived in America. "Whatever it is, it doesn't affect you," Salmon grumbled as he looked at Wealthy one evening as they all shivered around the fire and tried to eat the johnnycake Wealthy had made.

It was true. By this point, Ellen had taken ill, but Wealthy remained perfectly healthy—healthier, in fact, than she had ever been.

"She's a witch," Owen offered.

"Well, I'm going to get on my broomstick and clean up," Wealthy said. "Can someone help?"

Feebly, John rose to his feet.

Helping Wealthy with the chores was about all the men were good for these days, save for putting the hay in cocks, watching the boys, and trying to find some stray cattle. The crops were unsecured, they were no closer to having permanent homes than they were when they had first arrived, and the nights were getting colder and the winds sharper. It was enough to make one cry, and more than once Wealthy had done just that when she thought of their cottage in Ohio, plain but not lacking any of the essential comforts of life, and her sisters. She had not seen another woman in weeks save for Ellen and occasionally Mrs. Adair, and Ellen had been so irritable on the subject of their tents lately that she was hardly worth the company.

She scrubbed in silence, too tired for conversation, and in any case, what could she say? Then she heard a rumble and looked up to see a horse and wagon coming over the horizon. "It can't be . . ."

But the conveyance headed straight toward their encampment. Wealthy ran toward it, John wobbling behind. "Oliver! Henry! Where's Father Brown?"

"Resting in our tent a little ways off," Henry Thompson said. "Even he gets tired now and then. He'll be along in the morning."

The men were looking around them. Henry, though a favorite of the Browns, had never lost his family-newcomer manners even after years of marriage to Ruth, and thus maintained a judicious silence, but sixteen-year-old Oliver said, "Is this all there is to this place? No cabins yet? No sheds? You've had all summer."

"We've been concentrating on the crops," Wealthy said.

"Until recently, anyway," John said. "Trust me, it will look worse in the morning."

Oliver simply shook his head.

The next morning, Father Brown himself arrived. As his sharp eyes took in everything—the shivering men, the sagging tents, the fine cattle wandering around aimlessly, the unsecured crops—Wealthy quailed, wondering what he would say to them about having let things get into such a state. "Well," he said after a moment or two, "it appears as if you could use some help. We'll start by unloading the wagon."

It was full of weapons, they soon discovered. The brothers crowded around the wagon, admiring the haul, and even Wealthy and Ellen were impressed. The newcomers had also brought a stove for Jason and Ellen—which brought a smile to Ellen's face—some blankets and other supplies, and even a *Godey's Lady's Magazine* that someone had slipped in for the women. Wealthy didn't even want to think how little she resembled the gorgeously attired creatures in its fashion plates.

Then Father Brown nodded at an object covered with yet more blankets. "Jason, Ellen. I know you were grieved about having to leave little Austin in Missouri."

"Very much so," Jason said, and Ellen nodded bleakly.

"I took the liberty, then, of stopping at Waverly and exhuming him so you could rebury him here."

He carefully slid off the blanket, and they gazed at John's faded handwriting on the lid of the makeshift casket: *Austin Brown*. Ellen, not usually a demonstrative woman, threw her arms around Father Brown and wept while Jason covered his face with his hands. Even Salmon dabbed at his eyes.

"Well, well," Father John said kindly. "Let us find a suitable place to bury the poor lad. And then we shall talk about getting you better situated."

10

February 1856 to May 1856

Wealthy spun around and around, admiring the new cabin from every angle. It wasn't a lengthy process. Consisting of one room and a loft, the cabin was as small as any in Kansas. But after ten months of sleeping in the tent and in a half-face camp, it was quite large enough for her.

John's books, ignominiously boxed up for so long, occupied their own shelves, constructed of shingles and pegs by John. A crate served Johnny as a temporary bed. There was no window, but there were sufficient chinks in the logs to provide adequate light. A bright new quilt, Wealthy's handiwork borne of a long, cold winter, covered the bed John and Wealthy would share. Rag rugs—more products of the winter—dotted the puncheon floor. In the loft, Father Brown and John's brothers could bed down when it suited them. They didn't have the money as of yet, but Wealthy hoped that if John got some surveying work to do or did some lecturing on phrenology, they would be able to buy a couple of upholstered chairs and perhaps even a little melodeon. In the meantime, though, even with their rough-hewn or makeshift furniture, they at last had four walls around them and a solid roof over their heads. Wealthy was not inclined to complain.

Father Brown's arrival the previous October had not improved their situation immediately. Oliver and Henry had fallen ill soon after their arrival—proving, at least, that the illness was connected to the area and not some personal failing of the first wave of Brown settlers. Then there had been the various political stirs. In October there had been an election; it was a minor affair, but the Brown men, taking no chances, had turned up in force with their newly acquired weapons to be almost disappointed when the Border Ruffians stayed at home.

But in December, the Ruffians had threatened to sack Lawrence, and again the Brown men, hearing the news, had rushed to its defense, as had hundreds of other Free-State men. Even Wealthy and Ellen had done their part by baking provisions to keep the men from having to fight on empty bellies, but the preparations had proven unnecessary; Charles Robinson, who had become the unofficial leader of the Free-Staters, had worked out a peace with Territorial Governor Shannon, a process which had mainly involved feeding the governor copious amounts of whiskey.

Then winter, the best of peacekeepers, had set in. Although Wealthy was used to the harsh Ohio winters, she had experienced nothing like that first winter in Kansas. No one, not those settlers who had arrived in 1854 and not even their Indian friends, could recall anything like it in the territory. At that point, John and Wealthy, along with Johnny and an assortment of John's brothers, were living in a half-faced shed and their trusty tent, with a fire roaring between the two structures and blowing smoke into their faces night and day.

A foot and a half of snow blanketed the ground at times, and on one memorable day, the temperature stood at twenty-five below zero. Wealthy and Johnny hadn't even ventured out of bed but had huddled beneath the blankets with Johnny's dog. Poor Oliver had frozen a toe, and John the tip of his nose.

Still, the men had come out in January to cast votes for the Free-State Legislature, not to be confused with the Bogus Legislature. John had been nominated as a legislator, and in February, the Browns received the thrilling news that he had been elected. The election tidings had been received with less joy in Washington, where President Franklin Pierce denounced the Free-State movement. There was a distinct possibility that John and the other Free-State representatives, who were to gather in Topeka in March, might be arrested for treason. John and some of the other Free-Staters in the vicinity were so concerned that they had formed a military company, the Pottawatomie Rifles, of which John had been made captain.

But the troubles in Kansas were the last thing Wealthy had on her mind when John put his arms around her. "Are you pleased, my love? I know it's rough, but we can keep improving it and build a better home for us someday."

"I'm very pleased." Wealthy leaned into his arms. "Especially since you built it."

"With help from my brothers. But I'm willing to take a disproportionate share of the credit." John smiled at Johnny, who was showing his dog the new house. "Do you and Jack like it?"

Johnny considered the matter. "We do," he finally announced.

"Good. Now, here's your uncle Owen at the door. Maybe he wouldn't mind taking you to visit your cousin Charlie for a little bit."

Owen snorted. "Come along, young man."

"That was easy," Wealthy said after Owen, Johnny, and Jack had gone a safe distance.

"Brothers understand," John said as he kissed her, then scooped her up and carried her to the bed. With so many of the Browns shivering together in such close quarters, Wealthy and John had not had intimate relations for months, and it seemed like years. They carried on as they hadn't since Wealthy had become pregnant with Johnny.

"Home, sweet home," John murmured as he pressed inside her.

~ ~ ~

"I just want to remind you how proud I am of you," Wealthy said as John, carrying a carpetbag that contained his best suit and several shirts, set off for Topeka, where the Free-State Legislature was to hold its first session, complete with the new Free-State Governor, Charles Robinson. "Even if you do get arrested."

"I don't think Pierce will carry it that far; I think that's been put about just to frighten us into not coming. But if I do, I'll have plenty of company."

He kissed her and walked away, leaving her to fret.

But John's optimism proved correct, and about three weeks later, he returned unscathed, bearing candy for Johnny that he had purchased when he broke his pedestrian journey in Lawrence. "I've never seen such a fine, brave group of men. Some of them walked twice the distance that I did or more, and in considerably rougher conditions. One lost his nerve and declined to take his oath of office, but he was the only one. We'll meet again in full session in July, but in the meantime, I'll have to go back next month. I've been chosen for the committee that is to codify a system of laws."

"They must think well of you, but I will certainly miss you. So, you had no trouble with the Border Ruffians or the federal government?"

"None. But I would be lying to you if I didn't say there was a sense of unease, particularly in Lawrence. My uncle in Osawatomie is nervous as well. Everyone thinks there will be trouble now that the weather is improving. And even when the weather was foul, there were those murders."

Wealthy nodded. Back in December, a Free-Stater and a fellow Ohioan, Thomas Barber, had been shot in Lawrence by a gang of Missourians the evening before the Brown men and others had arrived in town to defend that city. The January Free-State election, peaceful in the vicinity of Brown's Station, had turned violent in Leavenworth, where a Free-State settler had been murdered—hacked to death and his body dumped on his threshold for his wife to see, the story went. The killers had gone unpunished.

"Do you think we have the resources if the Border Ruffians do cause more trouble?"

"That I don't know. I'd like to think we do, but the sad truth is that for every man who is well armed, there are others who are indifferently armed—and many who are simply indifferent, as long as they are personally not disturbed. All we can do is keep organizing and drilling. And, as Father's favorite saying goes, trust in God and keep our powder dry."

~ ~ ~

In April, word got about that a federal judge with the splendid name of Sterling Cato was to hold a territorial court nearby—not at a courthouse, for no such edifice existed, but at a tavern kept by a pro-slavery settler known as Dutch Henry Sherman, the "Dutch" a nod to his German ancestry. Rumor had it that Judge Cato would enforce the territorial laws, at least against the Free-Staters, a group of whom called a settlers' meeting in Osawatomie—a *male* settlers' meeting, Wealthy noted crossly when the men told her about it. "Why can't we attend? Perhaps the Topeka Constitution should have given us ladies the right to vote."

"Well, if I had had the drafting of it, it would have," John said. "But that might be a bit too radical, even for the radicals."

Wealthy snorted. "It always is."

John and his father went to the meeting, spending the night at the Reverend Adair's, and returned home the next day. "It went well, except for a hard-shell Baptist preacher, Martin White, who stood up and said his piece. Claimed that he was a good Free-State man, but a free *white* state man, and he intended to obey the laws, and the rest of us should as well. So, Father spoke up and said that he was an abolitionist of the old stock, that the blacks were his brothers and his equals, and that he would rather see the union dissolved and the country drenched with blood than pay taxes to support the government foisted upon us by the Bogus Legislature. I thought White was going to burst a blood vessel there and then, but instead he just stomped away."

"I was merely stating my opinion," said Father Brown.

"So, after he left and a few followed him, we got down to business and repudiated the legislature's authority—though that's perhaps not the right word, since we never

147

acknowledged it to begin with—and pledged mutual assistance to each other in defying the laws. And if anyone appointed by that legislature tries to collect taxes, they shall do so at their peril."

"No taxation without representation," Wealthy agreed.

"An excellent point." Father Brown gave her one of his rare smiles.

"Do you think Judge Cato will actually enforce the laws, though?"

John glanced at his gun on the wall, well out of Johnny's reach. "Not if the Pottawatomie Rifles can help it."

~ ~ ~

"We had a fine turnout," John told Wealthy a few days later. "We stored our weapons in an old cabin near the tavern, and as many of us as could squeeze into Dutch Henry's fine establishment walked in while Cato was giving his jury charge. It took him a while with his Alabama drawl. We listened very politely, and then I submitted in writing the question of whether the court intended to enforce the so-called territorial laws. In due time, the judge finally looked over the writing, but did not bother to read it aloud or even give a reply. So, I walked outside, called the company together loudly enough so that the judge was bound to hear it, and read the resolution we passed at Osawatomie. It was approved through everyone shouldering arms, and then several of us marched in, unarmed, and presented the good judge with a copy of our resolution. Again, he said nothing, but I believe we made quite an impression on him and the jurors."

"Who were the jurors?"

"I didn't recognize some of them. But a couple of the Doyles were on the jury or serving in the court. Wilkinson was a district attorney. They gave us some hard stares."

Along with Dutch Henry Sherman and his brothers, the Doyles and the Wilkinsons were some of the more virulent pro-slavery settlers in the region. Wealthy was on nodding terms with Mrs. Doyle and Mrs. Wilkinson but nothing more. There were women on the Shermans' claims, but they were not the sort one nodded to. In any case, she had seen Wilkinson, the Doyles, and the Shermans only occasionally; the Free-State settlers, and even some of the other settlers, kept a distance from them. The men were a rude, crude bunch, given to vague muttering about what they would do to various Free-Staters, but so far their threats had been idle.

"Will you go back tomorrow?"

"No, I think we made our point. But we'll keep our ears out."

The court broke up a day and a half later, with no indictments for anything more serious than killing another man's hogs. "I think the men were almost disappointed that it didn't come to a fight," Wealthy told Ellen afterward. With the weather so fine, she and Johnny had walked to Jason's cabin to visit.

"I know, and it worries me," Ellen said. "They're courting trouble."

"They're passionate about the cause. Isn't that one reason we married them? For their convictions?"

"I married Jason because he was kind and gentle and liked to grow things."

"Well, he still is. And does."

"I know. It's your John and the rest who are so militant these days. If there was a Bastille, they'd storm it."

"They have to be. They can't simply stand back and let the Border Ruffians have their way."

"You're not much better than they are. Mind you, I want a free state as well. I'm just not sure if antagonizing these people is the right way to go about it."

"Our side hasn't used violence. Theirs has."

"True." Ellen gazed around her. Despite the couple's grief and Jason's inability to entirely shake off the ague, Jason and Ellen had managed to put in a flower garden and a vegetable garden, and the trees that had survived the trip from Ohio were growing nicely. Soon it would be time to plant corn. "We've made this a pretty place. I could learn to enjoy it, I suppose. But I can't help thinking that something is about to kick up."

Wealthy sighed. "Me too," she admitted.

Even as they spoke, things were indeed kicking up.

In Lawrence, the sheriff, a man named Samuel Jones, picked up a matter that had lay dormant over the winter and proceeded to arrest a number of Free-State men on dubious charges. For his pains, he was shot. Even while Free-State leaders denounced the violence, the pro-slavery papers were soon reporting his ghastly murder and demanding vengeance, undeterred by the fact that Sheriff Jones was neither dead nor even seriously wounded.

Frederick, who regularly went to Osawatomie to stop at the post office and call upon the Adairs, brought back more alarming news with each visit. A judge had issued warrants for the arrests of leading members of the Free-State party, including Governor Robinson. Risen from the dead, Sheriff Jones was threatening to lead an attack on Lawrence. An Alabamian named Jefferson Buford had gathered hundreds of men from Alabama and Georgia, ostensibly to settle the territory. By early May, they had arrived and fanned out around Lawrence and Osawatomie in large, unruly groups, one just two miles from Brown's Station. "Uncle Adair says that they're drunks who spew profanity," Frederick said. "Especially against Free-Staters. And they're armed to the teeth."

"Do they expect trouble there?" John asked.

"Every waking moment. But they are also trying to prepare for Lawrence being attacked. The men are running bullets, and Aunt Florella is busy baking provisions for the militia—as a matter of fact, she gave me a taste."

Frederick's guilty look made Wealthy smile in spite of herself, but Father Brown's lips tightened. "I have a mind to pay a visit to Buford's men," he said. "No, not a social visit. I think I shall go among them in the guise of making a survey and see what they say to me."

The next day, he did indeed take his surveyor's tools—with Owen, Frederick, Oliver, and Salmon as his assistants—to the Buford camp near Pottawatomie. "How did the spying go?" Wealthy asked when they returned that evening.

"Good," said Oliver. "I think we might have a vocation for this."

"Father said we were surveying for the government," Salmon said. "The Bogus government—not that we called it that. None of us could pass as Southerners, but we nattered on about how the abolitionists—"

"The *damned* abolitionists," Owen said.

"—were spoiling everything and that we just wanted a free white state."

"Emphasis on the 'white.'" Oliver smirked. "I thought one was going to offer his sister in marriage to me."

"Poor Father couldn't have stood much more of it," Frederick said. "Anyway, we got them talking quite freely."

"So, what did you hear?" John asked.

"Quite a bit," Owen said dryly. "The liquor was flowing there."

"During the day? Oh my."

Owen snapped his fingers. "Get the smelling salts! Wealthy is shocked!"

Father Brown coughed, and the merriment subsided. "We heard nothing but what we had suspected. Some are indeed here simply to stake claims. But most are spoiling for a fight. And even some of those who want to settle have notions of running us Free-Staters off our claims and taking over our houses and stock. The Doyles and their friends have been visiting Buford's men and have been so helpful as to pass on information about the settlers in the area and where everyone's sympathies lie."

"Including ours?" John asked.

"Yes. You might even say especially ours. Our abolitionist beliefs have been noted."

"Are we in danger?" Wealthy asked.

"Trouble is going to come somewhere anytime. It could be here. It could be everywhere." Father Brown trained his intense eyes upon them. "But we will put up a fight no matter where the trouble arises."

~ ~ ~

The next day, they had a visitor: Miss Mary Grant and some of her brothers. About twenty, Mary was a novelty in the area, being an unmarried woman of marriageable age, and a very pretty one at that. She and the rest of the family had recently come from New York to join their father. As Mary was a cultivated, artistic young woman, Wealthy had taken to her instantly. "So, who has asked you to marry him since I last saw you?" Wealthy asked after admiring Mary's latest sketches of Kansas's wildflowers.

"Now, I am the luckiest woman in the world. I have had a proposal from Dutch Bill Sherman."

"Oh, you poor thing."

"Well, needless to say, there are no approaching nuptials. Father lived with the Shermans when he first came to Kansas, you might remember, and they got on reasonably well, but the Shermans were always in their cups and quarreling. It was all Father could do to keep the peace and not bear the brunt of their anger himself. Somehow the Shermans came out liking him, despite Father being a Free-Stater, so of course when Father brought us to the territory and introduced us, we were pleasant to them. But evidently Dutch Bill took politeness on my part for something else and asked to marry me. The only thing I can say in favor of his proposal was that he delivered it sober."

"I daresay he wasn't pleased when you turned him down."

"No, indeed. I wasn't expecting it at all, so all I could do was stammer that I had no plans of marrying so young and that I was quite happy in my present state of life. He stomped off, but that wasn't the end of it. The next day, he came back in a drunken rage and threatened to drink my heart's blood—charming image, isn't it?—and my mother's too. I have no idea what made him drag her into it. Father was sick in bed, or it never would have progressed so far. Mother was on the verge of calling him in, but as it turned out, my brother Charley was at hand and managed to coax him out the door."

Frederick, who had been trying to teach Johnny's dog to sit, turned. "He threatened you, Mary? And your mother?"

"It was just the liquor talking, I'm sure, Fred. Even that Sherman lot wouldn't harm a woman."

"For his sake, I'd better not see any of them try. Or even speak of it."

He clenched his fist. Was this chivalry in general, Wealthy wondered, or had Frederick developed some interest in Mary? He still wrote to Lucy, but she had the disadvantage of being in Ohio.

Mary said, "Don't worry. He's all talk." But even Mary sounded a little uncertain.

Frederick said, "Well, I'll be stopping by with the lead, so let me know then if he's been bothering you."

The lead was for running bullets to aid Lawrence in its peril. Wealthy too would be running bullets in her cabin with Ellen's help. It was the Kansas equivalent of a sewing circle.

~ ~ ~

"I had a little run-in with the Doyles and Sherman today," Frederick said the next day just as Wealthy, John, and Father Brown had finished supper. "Your lead, madam."

Wealthy took the bar of lead Frederick held out to her. "About Mary? Heavens, surely they know she would never give any of them the scrapings off her shoes, much less her hand in marriage!"

"No, about us in general. I went to old Morse's store to buy the lead, and while I was going over to give the Grants their share, I had to pass by the Sherman place. Dutch Bill and the Doyles were all perched on the fence, drinking as ever."

"Don't they ever work?"

"I suppose they were taking a well-earned break from loafing in their cabins. They asked me what the lead was for, and I told them that we were running bullets for Lawrence.

That didn't sit too well with them. They told me that we damn Browns should mind our own business. I told them that we were doing just that—our business of making Kansas a free state. Then I walked away. They were cursing up a storm, threatening to murder all of us damn abolitionists—man, woman, and child."

"I am glad you did not let them provoke you, son," Father Brown said.

"How serious do you think they are?" Wealthy asked.

"I do not know." Her father-in-law stroked his chin. "For now, I think we must worry about Lawrence. If that town should come to harm, none of us will be safe."

~ ~ ~

The Browns had been expecting a call to arms for so long without receiving it that they began to think it would never come. Then early on May 21, a man galloped to the cabin where Wealthy, having produced a fine lot of bullets, set sewing on the front step. "The men must ride to Lawrence immediately," he called. "It's under attack."

In remarkable time, the Brown men were off, having first taken Wealthy, Ellen, and the boys to the home of Orson Day, Mother Brown's brother, who had arrived in Kansas from New York with his family in tow just weeks before. As he lived close to Brown's Station in a cabin the Browns had built for him, he had agreed to stay behind and make sure that no harm came to the women and children. "I certainly picked a fine time to settle here," he said as the men departed, John waving a farewell.

"An exciting time," Haskell Day, age twelve, said. "There was *never* anything like this in Whitehall."

"A bit too exciting," Wealthy said, ignoring Mrs. Day's protests that she did not need any help with breakfast. If she did not keep busy, she would go wild fretting over John and the other men.

~ ~ ~

For several days, Wealthy and Ellen heard nothing from their husbands or anyone else. Then, early in the morning of May 25, the women, sleeping with their sons and the Day children in the cabin's loft, heard a commotion outside. "Wealthy! Ellen!" someone called.

Clad only in nightshifts, the women clambered down the rough ladder and unbolted the cabin door to find Henry Thompson. "You and the boys need to leave here and go to Adairs'. There's no time to waste."

Wealthy caught him by the shoulder before he could remount his horse. "Why? What on earth happened? What about Lawrence?"

"Sacked. It was given up by the cowardly townspeople before we could even get there."

"Where are the others?" asked Ellen.

"They're safe, as far as I know. I need to go, and so do you."

"But why?"

"Five men were killed last night. Three of the Doyles, Bill Sherman, and Wilkinson."

"Really?" Wealthy tried to summon up some feelings of regret for the men but found it difficult. Who had they antagonized to get five of them killed? "Their poor wives," she said. "But why does that mean we must leave?"

Never would Wealthy forget the expression on Henry's face, blending shame and a certain pride as he said the next words. "Because we did it. We killed them."

11

May 1856 to June 1856

Word had gotten about, Wealthy saw as the oxcart—driven by Haskell Day, who was beaming with the exciting responsibility conferred upon him—approached Osawatomie. Men stood by the side of the road, staring hard at each passing conveyance, each horseman. When they looked at the Day cart, containing only a young boy, two little boys, two gray-faced women, and a couple of hastily packed trunks, they scowled and stepped back. In the back of her mind, Wealthy acknowledged the wisdom of sending Haskell instead of his father; they surely would have been challenged otherwise.

John could not have killed those men. He had never hurt a soul in his life. But Henry had said "we," and Wealthy would have thought him nearly as incapable of doing violence as John. This was the man who, last New Year's, had walked all the way from his lodgings to Brown's Station just to bring them a plum cake he had baked. How could such a man do murder?

Surely, they must have had some provocation or killed in self-defense. That had to be it. Oh, why had Henry not stayed around long enough to explain instead of bringing his horrible message and disappearing into nowhere?

"Madam!" She blinked to find a Border Ruffian questioning her, apparently not for the first time. "Do you know a man named John Brown? Stringy fellow in his fifties? Sharp-eyed? Dresses like an old-fashioned preacher?"

There could have been no better description of her father-in-law. Under her breath, Wealthy thanked the Lord that the children were dozing as only young children could doze, for both, who adored their grandfather, would have most certainly replied with a resounding yes. "I don't think I've seen him," she said coolly.

"Well, if you see him, you tell someone, you hear?"

Wealthy nodded. "Why?"

"Murder, that's all, madam. Cold-blooded murder. Last night a group of abolitionists went to three cabins, dragged out the men who lived there, and cut them to shreds."

Haskell, who had been diligently obeying his elders' orders that he not say anything that would identify the women as Browns, let a faint whistle escape his lips.

Without further interruption, they made their way to the Adair cabin. As the Adair boy, Charles, hurried out to help Haskell see to the oxen, Mr. and Mrs. Adair drew the women and their sons inside. "You're here because of the killings," Mr. Adair said bluntly.

"Yes, Henry Thompson said we should come."

"You can stay—you and the children—but I can't have the men here. Not if they did what they're accused of. This house would be burned down over our heads if we sheltered them."

"There has to be an explanation," said Ellen. "Jason doesn't even like to slaughter a pig. We'd probably eat only vegetables if he had his way."

"John couldn't have done it either." Wealthy felt her tears began to flow. "He couldn't—"

"Sit," Mrs. Adair said gently. "Both of you, rest. The Lord knows what happened and why. And soon, I trust, so shall we."

~ ~ ~

Throughout that miserable Sunday afternoon and the Monday following, visitors knocked at the door. Each time, Reverend Adair answered it, rifle in hand. With the exception of two or three people who were content to scream vitriol and then depart, however, the visitors were fellow Free-Staters come to deplore the terrible deed, to impart or ask for information, or in a few cases, simply to gawk at the murderers' relations.

Wealthy and Ellen sat silently during these visits, which at least allowed them to get a better idea of what had happened. Lawrence, as Henry Thompson had informed them, had been abandoned without a fight. That had not stopped the pro-slavery forces—Sheriff Jones and his men, Buford's men, and even a contingent of federal troops—from destroying the Free-State Hotel, Lawrence's largest building, tossing the printing presses of the two Free-State newspapers into the river, burning Governor Robinson's house to the ground, and plundering the other homes, some of them quite comfortable, that had begun to fill the city.

On the Saturday evening after the sack of Lawrence, as it was being called, a group of men roaming around the vicinity of the Pottawatomie River had knocked at the door of the Doyle cabin, identified themselves as being from the Northern Army—a vaguely Cromwellian touch, Wealthy would reflect in a calmer moment—and demanded that Doyle and his two oldest sons, both grown men, come with them as their prisoners. Mrs. Doyle had begged them to leave a third son, still a boy, with her, which they had done. Then the party had disappeared into the night, after which Mrs. Doyle had heard the sound of gunshots.

Sometime after midnight, Mr. and Mrs. Wilkinson had been awakened by the sound of a dog barking as if his life depended upon it. The men had ordered Mr. Wilkinson out, not even allowing him time to put on his boots, ignoring the pleas of the ailing Mrs. Wilkinson to allow him to stay with her. After that, Mrs. Wilkinson had heard nothing but the sound of her husband's querulous voice raised in protest.

Finally, at around two in the morning, the party had visited the house of a James Harris, where Dutch Henry Sherman and Dutch Bill Sherman were staying. Unable to find Dutch Henry, who happened to have been out searching for some cattle, they had questioned the other occupants of the house, leaving all but Dutch Bill undisturbed. He too had been led out into the night.

The next morning, the Sabbath sun had risen to reveal five dead bodies, all slashed with swords, and some shot as well. It was Mr. Harris who had identified Father Brown as the man in charge of the killing party, and the widows Doyle and Wilkinson had agreed that an older man had led the expedition.

Wealthy thought of all the fuss her father-in-law had made about keeping the Sabbath holy. Evidently, he had been willing to make an exception.

Sick to her stomach and disheartened, she had just climbed wearily to one of the spare beds in the loft on Monday evening and had tried to shut her eyes, only to see visions of the mutilated bodies dotting the banks of the Pottawatomie Creek, when she heard a knock. "Uncle Adair! It's Jason and John. Please let us in!"

"You can't stay here," Mr. Adair said. "Your families are here and safe. But none of us will be safe if you stay here."

"Please! We've eaten nothing since this morning, and John is . . . ill."

Wealthy all but fell down the ladder. "Please let them in!"

"Nephews, answer me truthfully," Mrs. Adair said. "Did you have anything to do with those murders."

"No. Neither of us did."

John was innocent!

Mr. Adair sighed and unbolted the door. "You can stay until morning."

The men tumbled in, and their wives ran to embrace them. Then Wealthy saw John's face and nearly dropped to her knees. It was utterly without expression.

She might as well have embraced a stranger. "John?" she asked timidly.

"We're back."

She stared at Jason, who hissed, "Wealthy, he's not himself."

Mrs. Adair rubbed her eyes wearily. "Let me cook something up for you two, and you can tell us about it."

As Wealthy, bewildered, held John's unresponsive hand, Jason said, "We set off in high spirits for Lawrence, John and his company, Father, Henry Thompson and the boys, all ready to fight. When we got about twenty miles outside the town, in

Prairie City, a messenger told us that it was all over with Lawrence. I suppose you've heard what happened there. Anyway, we decided to camp for the night and see what happened.

"By morning, a few men had joined us, some from here but some from Lawrence. One of them told us a telegram had arrived there telling of Senator Charles Sumner's caning in Washington. You've not heard of that?"

Wealthy shook her head. A senator from Massachusetts, Charles Sumner was the most fervent abolitionist in Congress.

"During a debate about Kansas, he made a great speech on the Senate floor, accusing Senator Butler from South Carolina of having a harlot—that harlot being slavery. The next day, Butler's nephew, who is in the House, walked into the Senate while Sumner was doing some work. He began slashing at him with his cane, almost killing him."

"It was a metaphor," John said as all eyes turned to him. "The fool couldn't understand a metaphor." He resumed staring at his shoes.

"Do eat something, John," Wealthy said.

John obediently nibbled at a corn cake.

"Father—the rest of us too—were already furious that the leaders of Lawrence had been so passive. When he heard the news from Washington, he was as angry as I've ever seen him—in that slow burning way of his. But that was just the beginning. He and his men started to talk about all the threats, all the mouthing off by the Shermans and their friends. Threatening the Grants—especially Mary Grant. Threatening Frederick about the lead he bought. Other things that you might not have heard about, like our friend Theodore Weiner. They've been harassing him and his friends since they got here, and just the other day they

162

threatened to run him off his claim. Morse, who sold that lead. They went to his house and threatened to string him up just for that. It terrified the poor man. It all came down to this: all of us felt that our lives were at risk, and that now that the Ruffians had had their way in Lawrence, that we would be next. Finally, Father said, 'This cannot go on. Something has to be done.' And after breakfast, he asked who wanted to go with him on a mission. Owen, Salmon, Oliver, Frederick, Henry Thompson, and Weiner volunteered. They spent the rest of the afternoon sharpening their swords."

"Did you know what they were for?" Mrs. Adair asked.

"No, but I suppose we should have guessed. Perhaps we didn't want to. Or perhaps Father wasn't even sure what he was going to do at that point. John did beg Father not to do anything rash. Anyway, Pa got a man named Townsley to drive them; he told him that he had heard there was going to be trouble by the creek and wanted to be prepared. They set off that afternoon. Afterward, we broke camp and moved to Palmyra.

"On Sunday, we were all restless and hadn't heard anything from Father and his party, so John decided to ride to Lawrence. Would you like to tell this, John?"

Wealthy's husband shook his head.

"John got to Lawrence and looked at the damage, talked to some people, and realizing how hopeless it was, headed back. He stopped to buy something to eat from a man when he heard the fellow's wife directing a torrent of abuse at someone. They were two slaves, a man and a woman. John and his companion drew their weapons and told the couple to give up their weapons and their slaves and to get out of town. They did, and John got back to the camp with the slaves that evening—"

"Wait," Wealthy said. "You actually freed two slaves?"

"Not for long," John said quietly.

"Half the camp were furious, and the rest were nervous. They hadn't come to free coloreds, they said, but to defend Lawrence. They took a vote, and all but a few voted to return the slaves to their master. So, someone loaded them into the cart and caught up with the master and his family, heading for Missouri, and handed the slaves back over to them. For his pains, he was given a saddle."

John stared bleakly into space.

"Soon after that, John got word from an army lieutenant that all gatherings of armed men in the area were to disband. We agreed and prepared to break camp. Then, three men came into camp in a perfect panic and yelled, 'Five men have been killed at Pottawatomie Creek, and old Brown did it!' I was never so shocked and horrified in my life. I wanted to believe that it could not be true, but then I could not but think it could be true. John was no better. He tried to put the best face on it, but he was shattered, and the men were furious. He finally felt that he had no choice but to resign his command.

"We went to our friend Ottawa Jones's house to camp overnight, and finally Father and the others returned with horses that had belonged to the murdered men. I found him alone and asked him point-blank whether he had had anything to do with the murders, and he said only that he had approved of them but not personally committed them. I told him that I thought it was a wicked act. He said that it was a necessary act for the defense of ourselves and others, and that God would be his judge. He seemed almost hurt that I did not understand. Soon afterward I asked Frederick about it, and he said that he had not been able to bring himself to do that manner of work but had stood guard.

"In the morning, we went our separate ways—John's old company their way, Father and the rest of the boys toward our homes, and John and I here. Henry told us we would find our families here. And that is all I know—except that we were lucky to get here without getting captured." Jason shook his head wearily. "I know we can't stay here, but I don't know what to do next."

"We will think of something in the morning," Mrs. Adair said. "In the meantime, the two of you must get some rest."

"Come along, Jason," Ellen said. "Thank God you didn't kill those men."

Jason obeyed, flopping down on the bed the Adairs had made for him.

"John, you need to rest too," Wealthy said. When he made no move to rise, she added, "Please, my love, isn't there anything you have to say to me?"

John looked up. "I believe I am going insane."

~ ~ ~

Jason did manage to sleep a bit, but John remained wide awake, staring into space and groaning once in a while. Wealthy considered putting Johnny in his arms in hopes that the sight of his son might draw him from the abyss into which he had fallen, but seeing his father in such a state might only terrify the lad.

She had known, of course, that there was insanity in John's family, but never in their courtship or marriage had he shown any signs of the malady. Oh, he had his moods at times, but didn't everyone? Certainly nothing like his present state. Was it the shock of the murders? Or had madness been creeping up on him for years? Would he ever be himself again? Or was *this* his true self?

Exhaustion sent her to sleep. When she woke, she was startled to find John smiling at her. Had this all been a dream, then? Quickly, she cast her mind back, trying to remember where the nightmare had started. The poor slave boy being strung up by the thumbs? Austin's death? The sickness? The murders? Leaving their little farm in Ohio in the first place?

"I have to be off, darling. Wake up."

"Off where?"

"To the ravine," John said a bit impatiently. "I am going to hide there until we can regroup and recapture Lawrence. We'll raise the flag of freedom there. It will be the Free-State capitol."

Wealthy looked at Jason, who shook his head. "We do have to go," he said. "Uncle's right. If the Ruffians find us here, we'll be strung up, and so will our uncle for harboring us. I'm going to give myself up to the army. I'll take John with me if he'll go."

"Never," John said firmly. "I have an excellent horse and a Sharps rifle. I can last for days."

"You don't have a horse, John."

"Actually, he does have a horse," Jason said. "Unless it's run off."

"Where did he get a horse?"

"Stolen, where else?" John said happily. "I've turned horse thief, and I'd say I'm quite an accomplished one."

Wealthy wondered if she might be going mad herself. It seemed almost a reasonable alternative to the reality that had fallen upon her.

~ ~ ~

The Adair cabin sat not far from the ravine, in which a man could indeed hide himself. Wealthy watched, her tears falling, as John set off on his horse, carrying his gun. No one had been able to talk him into leaving it behind. When he had gone, Mr. Adair said, "Wealthy, don't think we don't care what happens to him; we do. But in his state, it seems best to let him have his way. Jason said he hasn't slept for days. My hope is that he'll get worn out and sleep. Then perhaps he'll be rational."

"And then what?"

"I fear Jason's solution—giving himself up—may be the only one."

Following dinner, Wealthy took the extra provisions that the women had baked and walked to the ravine, deep in the back of the Adairs' property. To try to get down it would be nearly impossible in her skirts, so she had to settle for calling softly, "John!"

"Halt!" John's rifle was pointed straight at her.

"It's me, John."

Just a few hours in the ravine had given John a wild look, and nothing suggested that he had gotten any sleep as Mr. Adair had hoped. "What do you want?"

"I came to bring you some food. Please—come here and take it from me."

"Leave it there."

"Don't you know me, John?"

John appeared to be considering the matter. "I think I do," he said after thinking about it. "Toss it down, then."

She obeyed. After nibbling at the bread she had brought, John began to take more generous bites, having evidently decided it was not poisoned. "Thank you," he said. "I think you had best go now."

"Why, John? I can sit here and keep you company."

"No. It's no fit place for a princess here in the brush."

Her eyes filled with tears, but she managed to say, "Then come with me, please."

"No. I have to stay here. Up there—it's full of enemies. Enemies and treacherous men who smile at you one day and turn their back on you the next."

"All right, John," she said quietly. "I'll come again soon."

As she left, she could hear him scuttling deeper into the brush. She wiped at her eye but did so purely out of habit, as she seemed to have reached a point where no more tears would come.

~ ~ ~

A few hours later, having offered to watch Charlie while Ellen took a much-needed rest, she took him and Johnny out near the ravine, hoping that the voices of the children at play might tempt John out of hiding. But it was another man leading a lathered horse who stepped out of the shadows. "Owen!" She embraced him.

His voice trembled. "You don't shun me because of what we did? You know what we did?"

"Yes, and I understand. You felt it necessary to protect us all. Perhaps you saved some lives."

"I hope we did." He lowered his voice. "Father Brown sent me to find John. We have heard rumors that he is . . . not himself."

"No. He's . . . confused."

"Do you know where he is?"

"Somewhere in the ravine."

"I'll find him and see if I can bring him to Father's camp, then."

"He wouldn't come to me," Wealthy said. Painfully, it occurred to her that she was speaking of her husband as if he were a stray dog or cat. "Do you think he'll come to you?"

"I don't know, but I'll do my best. But I'd best be quick about it. I can't stay in the open long. I almost got caught by the Ruffians myself getting over here." He nodded at the horse. "He outran them."

"Just one thing—you're all safe?"

"Yes. And more have joined us."

With parting pats on the head for his nephews—who appeared to be getting used to the strange comings and goings of the adults around them—he led the horse toward the direction of the ravine.

For the rest of the afternoon and evening, there was no sign of Owen or John, only a thunderstorm of the fierce variety that Kansas seemed to nurture. As she and Ellen lay in the loft that night, their sons huddled next to them while the thunder clapped, Wealthy watched the lightning through the chinks of the cabin and fretted. Was John safe with Owen? Or was he huddled in the ravine, imagining horrors in every flash?

The night was well advanced when she heard a rap at the door, followed by Mr. Adair's calling upstairs. "Wealthy! It's John."

Wealthy scrambled downstairs to find John soaked to the skin. Beside him was not Owen but an entirely different Brown: Mr. Orville Brown, whose surname had occasionally caused confusion at the Osawatomie post office. He was the founder of Osawatomie and had attended the settlers' meeting that had outraged Martin White so much.

"I'm here to surrender." John looked around. "But it appears there's no one to take my surrender."

"All in due time," Mr. Brown said. "You can get dry, get something to eat and a change of clothing."

"I'll get you some fresh clothes," Wealthy said, removing John's sodden jacket. "Fortunately, I brought some of your things with me. Did you see Owen?"

"Yes."

"You wouldn't go with him?"

"No." He shrugged. "I'm tired of all this. I just want to sleep."

Wealthy nodded and proceeded to put him into dry clothes and make up a bed. He fell asleep nearly as soon as he lay down. "I don't think he's slept for days," Wealthy said.

"Probably not." Mr. Brown cleared his throat. "You mustn't suppose, madam, that your husband is without friends here. The Border Ruffians and the U.S. troops have been looking for him. We told them that the citizens of Osawatomie ran him off, and that Mr. Adair had barred his door to him. That threw them off his track for the time being—but only for the time being. Anyway, some of us have been keeping an eye on him as best we could. Tonight after the storm, I went down there and saw him wandering around like King Lear on the field, shaking and shivering. He was so wet and miserable that he consented to talk with me, and I broached the idea of surrendering. After all, he's innocent. It will give him some time for public sentiment to cool."

"But do you think he'll be safe in custody?"

"Safer than anywhere else in Kansas. If I thought we could get him safely to the States, I would do that. If there were an asylum he could be placed in until his head cleared, I would put him there. But I do not see those as possible with our present troubles."

"I think you have forgotten that I have some say in this, sir."

Mr. Brown was graceful enough to look abashed. "True, and I apologize. But we are concerned for his welfare. I think you will agree that he can't stay as he is, out of his head and hiding in the ravine. If the Border Ruffians don't grab him, some sickness will."

Wealthy looked at John sleeping peacefully, no signs of his recent troubles upon his face. Perhaps he would wake up with his sanity restored and could decide the matter entirely for himself.

When the sun broke, John stirred. He did seem more clear-minded as he yawned and said, "A bite to eat, and I'll be ready."

"You're sure of this, John?"

"I'm sure." He peered through the cabin's solitary window. "Besides, it seems I have no choice."

The little cabin was surrounded by mounted men, some in army uniforms, others in the motley attire of Buford's men. Somewhat incongruously, a closed carriage sat in their midst.

Calmly, John ate his breakfast, then walked outside with the rest. A man nodded at him. "U.S. Marshal Donelson. I believe I've seen you in Lawrence, sir."

"Yes, I was there after the destruction there. The needless destruction, I might add."

"I have a warrant for your arrest. For treason."

He read it sonorously. It appeared to relate to John's assembling with his men after the abortive attempt to defend Lawrence. That was treason? She expected John to protest, but his last effort seemed to have exhausted him. His eyes began to assume the distant, indifferent look she had seen in the ravine. Interrupting the reading of the warrant, she stepped in front of John and asked, "Please, can I accompany him?"

"No, madam. There's no place for a woman where we're going."

"Then he shouldn't go with you. He's ill." She grasped John's hand. "He's not going anywhere."

As if pulled by strings from above, every man present shook his head. Orville Brown said, "He must go, Mrs. Brown. I told you, there's no other way to guarantee his safety. You don't know what it's like out there since those killings."

"If he doesn't come with us, he'll be strung up on a tree and hanged. Not for this spot of treason, but for the murders of those men. He and every man who shelters him. Mark my words, madam."

John's mind took that inopportune time to right itself momentarily. "I'll be fine, sweetheart. Don't worry. Can I say goodbye to Johnny?"

With even John set against her, Wealthy nodded and went to fetch Johnny as the marshal made a great point of checking his watch. Upon her return, John kissed his son, then her, and climbed into the carriage. She supposed the closed carriage was a necessity to keep him hidden from those who might want to exact vigilante justice and perhaps a kindness to keep gawkers at bay, but she could not help but feel a sense of unease as John waved goodbye and a hand drew the curtain shut.

Mr. Adair put his arm around her. "It's for the best, Wealthy. Trust us—and trust in the Lord."

Watching the carriage disappear, Wealthy found it hard to trust in either.

~ ~ ~

Through the inquiries of Mr. Adair and Orville Brown, Wealthy learned that John had been taken to Baptiste Paola, where he would presumably await trial. Jason was said to be there as well. In recent weeks, there had been a flurry of arrests, so a number of other Free-Staters were being held captive at various locations, including the Free-State Governor, Charles Robinson, and George W. Brown, the editor of the *Herald of Freedom*, the printing press of which lay in the bottom of the river after the sack of Lawrence. It gave Wealthy some comfort to realize that John and Jason were in such illustrious company, especially since Governor Robinson's wife had some sort of family connection to President Pierce.

When she was not busy helping Mrs. Adair around the house, Wealthy got into the habit of sitting near the road, watching Johnny play, so that she might hear bits of conversation or ask for news. She was so engaged one hot afternoon at the end of May when she heard the sound of cavalry approaching. That was nothing unusual these days, with the authorities still searching for Father Brown and any other Free-Staters who might fall into their net, but this dragoon unit appeared to be coming at an especially smart pace. She pulled Johnny closer to ensure that he did not run out into their path. Then she clapped a hand to her mouth.

Amid the horses' flashing hooves scuttled a man on foot, his arms tied behind his back. A rope leashed him to a mounted soldier, riding like the rest at a trot. One misstep, one slowing of his pace, and he would surely be trampled to death. He was hatless, and he was sweating so profusely that Wealthy at first could hardly make out his features until he turned his head slightly. "John!" she screamed. "John!"

"Pa!" Johnny cried.

Breaking free of Wealthy's grasp, which she had loosened in the shock of recognition, Johnny ran toward the horses as one of the soldiers, cursing, fended him off. "Get back, you brat!"

"You sons of bitches!" Wealthy seized Johnny. "How dare you treat my husband so? Let him go! Let him go now, you whoremongers, or—or—"

Clutching Johnny, she collapsed to her knees as Ellen and the Adairs ran to her side and the soldiers moved on, the hooves of their horses kicking up a cloud of dust that obscured the obscenity she had just witnessed.

~ ~ ~

"From what I could find out, it appears that the army is convinced that your husband is feigning insanity," Orville Brown said a while later. "Hence its terrible treatment of him. No one would give me an outright answer, but I believe he is being held at the army camp near this place. I went there and asked if you would be allowed to see him wherever he was, but of course I was refused." He shook his head sadly. "I would have never encouraged him to surrender if I thought he would be treated so. You must believe me, Mrs. Brown."

"I do," Wealthy said hollowly. She had just soothed Johnny to sleep after an hour, during which he had sobbed and begged for John. "He didn't seem to recognize Johnny and me, or even realize where he was. I hope he was too far gone to realize it. That is my only comfort."

"There are two others I can give you."

"I am always ready to hear comforting news."

"First, while the Border Ruffians and the army—which has pretty much become the Border Ruffians too—have muzzled the Lawrence papers, they can't do the same to the Northern press. There are reporters wandering about, and I told one of them—from the *New York Tribune*, I believe—of the atrocity you witnessed. He was indignant. Such stories going about and getting to the halls of Congress can only help our cause."

"In the long run, yes. But for now—"

"The second you may find more cheering. The Border Ruffians and their ilk are absolutely terrified of old John Brown now. That might not keep them from mistreating your husband and Mr. Jason Brown, but that will keep them alive."

"Unless they capture him," Wealthy said gloomily.

Mrs. Adair looked from her knitting. "Don't underestimate my brother," she said. "He'll outrun those rascals."

~ ~ ~

He did better than that a few days later; he defeated them in battle. He and his small band, joined by another Free-State force, had heard that a Captain Henry Clay Pate was planning to capture the Browns. Instead, the combined Free-Staters had surprised Pate and his men at their camp at Black Jack and ended up taking their surrender. There was even a rumor that Father Brown had forced Pate to agree to a prisoner exchange, with John and Jason among those to be returned to the Free-Staters.

But just a day or so afterward, young Charles Adair hurried in, his face grim. "They're bringing prisoners by. Uncle John and Uncle Jason are among them."

Ordering Emma, the Adairs' daughter, to stay inside with the little boys, the women ran outside. Chained together at the ankle two by two, a group of men hobbled down the road, surrounded by dragoons. Jason, chained to a man who was a stranger to the women, gave the women a grim nod, but John, muttering something unintelligible, stared at the man in front of him. There was a bruise on his cheek, and he was still hatless.

As both Wealthy and Ellen ran toward their husbands, the soldiers pushed them back. "No interference!"

"We're their wives!" Wealthy waved to John. "Don't you know me, my love?"

"He's crazy," offered one soldier unsympathetically.

Mrs. Adair planted herself in front of the procession. All of a sudden, her family resemblance to Father Brown, her much older half-brother, became readily apparent to Wealthy. "What a sight this is in the land of the free, driving these men like cattle and slaves!"

"At least allow us to give them some food," Ellen pleaded.

The lieutenant in charge reluctantly consenting, Ellen and Wealthy rushed inside, leaving Mrs. Adair in her spot of obstruction, and returned with all of the bread and fruit they could grab from the kitchen. As the prisoners, some of whom seemed on the verge of fainting, eagerly grabbed at the provisions, Ellen asked, "Where are you heading?"

Jason said in a low voice, "Tecumseh, I think."

"But that is nearly seventy miles! In chains?"

"It's a ways off," snapped the lieutenant. "So, we need to get on with it."

"Please!" Wealthy thrust a hat at one soldier, who looked kinder than his lieutenant. "Please give this to my husband."

The soldier obliged, passing it along until it reached John's companion, who placed it on John's head. Startled, John looked toward the women, and a flicker of recognition crossed his face. "Thank you," he said.

"We've got the haberdashery taken care of. Now onward!"

The march of the prisoners, Wealthy and her companions soon learned, was the prelude to a general abandonment of the military camp at Osawatomie. What consequence this would have became apparent on June 6, when Spencer Kellogg Brown, Orville Brown's fourteen-year-old son, galloped up to the Adair cabin, which Mr. Adair had left not long before to go to the post office. "The Ruffians are looting Osawatomie! Grab what you can and hide yourselves!"

Obeying, the family snatched up the children and the little cash and jewelry they had on hand and rushed to conceal themselves in the ravine. When they had reached a place of safety, Spencer said, "They're a group of Missourians, mean and drunk. They're grabbing all the weapons and money they can, even forcing women to give up their earrings and wedding rings. Fortunately, they're not, er, doing more to them."

Somehow, the possibility of being raped was the least of Wealthy's worries. "Are the men resisting?"

"Some, but for the most part, everyone was caught by surprise."

"I wish my father-in-law was there," Wealthy said fiercely.

"So do I," Spencer said. "I'd fight with him if Father would let me."

Soon they heard the sound of horses, followed by a great deal of shouting and banging about. After another series of noises announced the Ruffians' departure, Spencer cautiously crawled out, then returned to help each lady and child scramble up the bank.

Wealthy looked around the cabin and felt an unfamiliar sensation—relief. Trunks had been broken open, and clothing was scattered everywhere, but aside from Mr. Adair's Sunday suit and his rifle, nothing appeared to have been taken. Evidently the wardrobes of the women and children had not been of interest. Spencer said, "They probably couldn't handle much more, as loaded down as they were from their thievery in town. At least everything is still standing." He nodded at Wealthy and Ellen. "Some feared that they were going to do to Osawatomie what they did to your cabins."

"Our cabins?" Wealthy asked. "What do you mean?"

Spencer blanched. "Oh, my Lord. You didn't hear?"

"No!"

The boy bowed his head. "I'm so sorry; I thought the news would have reached you. I suppose it reached the town first. Anyway, before Pate and his men reached Black Jack, they stopped by your cabins and grabbed everything they thought worth taking. Then—then they burned them to the ground."

~ ~ ~

Wealthy stared at the ruins of the cabin John had led her into just four months before. Everything—the quilts she had made, the linens she had brought from Ohio, John's library and phrenological aids, their framed marriage certificate that had hung on the wall—had been reduced to ash and cinders.

Beside her and Ellen, Mrs. Day said, "They would have burned ours too, but my husband and I were sick with the ague, so they settled for taking him and our son captive for a few days. They're home safe and sound now. Anyway, that's why we couldn't get word to you. They were cackling like demons as they watched it burn. They said that all of your husband's books were making a splendid blaze."

Ellen looked toward the field behind what had been the log cabin. "I suppose they drove away the cattle as well."

"Yes, yours and ours, but some have strayed back, and we've found others. In fact, Orson and Haskell are out looking for more cattle now."

Charles Adair said, "Do you want me to drive you to your claim now, Aunt Ellen?"

"I suppose." Ellen dabbed at her eye. "But I don't know if I can stand it. All Jason's fruit trees were looking so pretty . . ."

Mrs. Adair said, "I'll go with you, dear. Are you coming, Wealthy?"

"No. I'm going to see what I can dig."

"It's an exercise in futility, Wealthy," Ellen said, not unkindly.

"I'm going to try."

Donning a pair of heavy gloves lent to her by Mrs. Day, Wealthy began to sift through the cabin's remains, finding here and there a remnant of their lives—a saucer, a boot, a key covered with soot. She tossed aside the boot and the key but kept the saucer, part of the wedding china she had dragged to this godforsaken place.

Her fingers struck a rectangular shape—one of John's books, Elizabeth Barrett Browning's *Sonnets from the Portuguese.* She opened it carefully, expecting it to crumble to the touch, but other than its singed cover, it was intact down to its inscription: *To my dear husband on the fifth anniversary of our marriage, from your loving wife, Wealthy C. Brown.*

Another hour of work and she was exhausted, with only a few objects to show for her efforts. As she rose, she saw something shining in the ruins: John's watch, another gift from Wealthy. He must have forgotten to take it with him in the excitement of his departure. The crystal was shattered, but it could surely be fixed. Tenderly, she tucked it into the pocket of her dress.

Someday, surely, she would get to hand it and the book to John again as tokens of her love for him. She could only pray that John recognized the giver.

12

June 1856 to July 1856

"Now here's what I told you about," Rachel Garrison said, descending from her loft with a contraption made of buckram and steel. "A crinoline! David and his father said it was impractical, but I said that going to Kansas with all of the trouble here was impractical, so they gave in and let me buy one in St. Louis. I figure I can at least wear it to church once Sam gets his meeting house built."

"It actually looks quite practical," Wealthy said as Rachel, who—since there were only ladies and small children in the house, had stripped to corset, shift, and drawers—stepped into the crinoline and donned her petticoat. "You don't need to wear nearly as many petticoats now."

"Precisely!" Rachel twirled around in it. "I saw quite a few women in St. Louis wearing them. They're quite the thing back east now. I bet I could even milk a cow with it."

Rachel, whose husband, David, was a cousin of Mr. Adair, was a very recent arrival to Kansas, coming, as had the Day family, at precisely at the wrong time. She and her family had settled not far from the Adair cabin, and in the midst of all the troubles, had become friendly with Ellen and Wealthy, whom she had invited for a short visit.

Just as Rachel had taken off her hoop, as it was called, and resumed her usual rural attire, someone knocked. As was second nature now with everyone, male or female, Rachel reached for her husband's rifle as she called, "Who is it?"

"August Bondi to see Mrs. John Brown and Mrs. Jason Brown," a voice with a Viennese accent overlaid with a faint Missouri drawl called. "I am a stranger to you, but not to them."

"Mr. Bondi!" Wealthy rose. "He's a friend to us, Rachel."

Rachel set aside the rifle and opened the door, revealing a thin, dark young man in his early twenties, dressed in what appeared to be a fairly new linen coat, jean pants, and palm-leaf hat, but with his toes protruding from his shoes. He swept a courtly bow.

"Mr. Bondi! What are you doing back in the territory?" Wealthy asked.

"It was too dull in St. Louis," their visitor said. "And when I returned there, I found that my parents had found a perfect wife for me—a Jewish boy must have a wife, you know—but I did not wish to have a wife just yet."

"Well, you certainly picked a bad time to come back," Ellen said.

Mr. Bondi nodded. "Immediately upon my return, the Border Ruffians threatened me, and soon I happened across the encampment of the senior Mr. John Brown. What a wonderful man! I have been among his guerillas." Mr. Bondi pronounced the word with a flourish. "My purpose, though, is to tell you that I have seen your husbands."

"Are they well?"

"Is John sane?"

"After our encounter at Black Jack—oh, how splendid it was!—we heard that your husbands were being held in a camp not far from us, and Mr. Brown wanted me to see them and report on their condition. The captain allowed me to see them and two others under guard. They seemed healthy, but they were chained together, and they were not allowed to speak freely to me. John appeared in his right mind but somewhat dazed—if that is the right word. They did ask about their families, yet all I could tell them was that I had heard no bad news. I asked John how they were being treated, and Captain Wood said I was being impudent. I told him that we had treated our own prisoners well and had the right to ask the same, and he allowed John to answer. He said that the food was good, but that the chains hurt. He smiled when he said this."

"He knew who you were?"

"Oh yes."

"And he was lucid?"

"He made perfect sense in answering me. Considering that the soldiers had their rifles aimed at us the entire time, I thought he spoke very well." Mr. Bondi gave a grim chuckle. "In fact, I heard later that after I left, the captain ordered that if any rescue attempt was made, the prisoners would be shot."

"You have brought the first good news we've had in a long while," Wealthy said.

"There is bad news too. Poor Henry Thompson was shot at Black Jack, and Salmon accidentally shot himself afterward. They are recuperating nicely, though."

It was a sign of the times, Wealthy realized, that news of two of her family being shot hardly fazed her. "Thank goodness for that."

"How are the other boys?" Ellen asked.

"Oliver is well. Owen has spells of ague. Frederick was splendid at Black Jack. He had been left to guard the horses and supplies, but when it seemed that the tide was turning against us, he galloped onto the field and yelled, 'We have them surrounded and cut off their communications!' It confused the enemy terribly. I think he saved the day for us."

"What have you been doing since?"

"Well, Oliver and Frederick visited a store and impressed some clothing for us—as you can see from my own appearance—and a Colonel Sumner forced us to disperse and release our prisoners, including Pate, which meant of course we couldn't trade them for John and Jason. So, for now we are living rough, hiding until the boys can fight again."

"I think you could use a good meal," Rachel said. "Will you stay for supper?"

"Well, Captain Brown is adept at scrounging up food for us, but I wouldn't say no."

"Good," Rachel said. "I'll give you some to take back as well."

As the women prepared the meal, Mr. Bondi kept the children—including Rachel's little girl, Mary—well entertained, as evidenced from the gleeful shrieks that emanated from outside. "It's so good to see the boys enjoying themselves," Wealthy said after stepping into the doorway to observe. "They miss their fathers terribly, and while Mr. Adair has been very kind to us, he's not the sort to roughhouse with the boys. Their son has so many responsibilities, he seems practically an adult himself."

"And Charlie still misses Austin," Ellen said. "As do the rest of us, of course."

"Poor mites, this has been hard on them. Do they understand anything of what's going on?"

"We've only told them that their fathers have been called away, and that we don't know when they'll come back," Ellen said.

Wealthy nodded. "Of course, Johnny saw poor John being mistreated as he was, and that upset him dreadfully. He's stammered more since then, I've noticed, and he sometimes cries for him, especially when he's tired. But I don't think he understands the danger his father and Jason are in, and I suppose it's a good thing he doesn't."

After Mr. Bondi, trailed by three exhausted children, returned to the cabin and everyone sat down to supper, the conversation turned to more pleasant topics. Mr. Bondi regaled them with tales of his past adventures—as a mere boy, he had been involved in the student revolutions in Vienna in 1848, which had delighted John—and Wealthy told the group of some of the strange characters she and John had encountered when he was studying phrenology in New York.

"And Jason and I were running a nice little farm," Ellen said wistfully. "Nothing exciting, but we were quite content. Who would have dreamed then that we would all wind up here?"

"John says that all things work for the best," Wealthy said with a faint smile. It was something she had forgotten lately. "I do hope he's right."

~ ~ ~

Since arriving at the Adair farm, Wealthy had taken over the milking from Mrs. Adair. She found it a soothing task, and on the days when she despaired of the future, she could lean her head against the cow's warm flank and cry to her heart's content without making a scene. One day toward the end of June, after about two weeks with nothing heard of any of the Brown men whatsoever, she had a good stream of milk going into her pail and a modest stream of tears flowing down her face when she heard Ellen's joyous cry, "Jason!"

Muttering a quick apology to the cow, Wealthy jumped up and ran to find Ellen and Charlie clasped in Jason's arms. "No John?" she asked in a small voice.

Jason stepped back. "I'm sorry, Wealthy. There was a hearing at Tecumseh before Judge Hoogland. Most of us were set free for lack of evidence, but John and two others were held, mainly for being in the Free-State legislature. John hasn't been indicted, but apparently he is being accused of treason, slave-stealing, and horse-stealing. They will be sent to an army camp near Lecompton to be held with Governor Robinson and the other Free-State prisoners."

"I'm glad to see you back," Wealthy said quietly. "I truly am."

She embraced Jason but could not keep the tears from coming, especially when Johnny ran up and asked, "Uncle Jay! Where's Pa?"

"He's still away, Johnny, but he's well. He sends his love to you and your mother."

Wealthy wiped her eyes. "Come, Johnny. Help me finish milking."

Having given Jason a decent interval with his wife and son, Wealthy returned, and everyone sat down for breakfast. When Jason had finished, having first given Mrs. Adair many compliments about her cooking and coffee, he said, "Come take a walk with me, Wealthy."

She followed Jason out to the pasture, where a few of the Browns' cattle, retrieved by the Days, grazed, no worse for wear from the stay with the Border Ruffians. "I was telling Ellen before breakfast, I'm very pleased to see how well the two of you have taken care of the cattle."

"Never mind the cattle, what about John?"

Jason, unruffled, stroked his beard. "First, let me tell you that John's as well as I've seen him since this whole business began. Second, I think I should tell you that at one point, he was as bad as I've ever seen anyone."

"Before or after he was led by that rope?"

"You saw that?"

"Yes, and so did Johnny. It broke our hearts."

Jason put his arm around her. "After I gave myself up, I was held in camp for a few days—I thought they were going to hang me, but there were a few decent men there who prevented it. Then John was brought in. He was much as you saw him when we were both together here, with his mind prone to wandering and generally a little confused. The soldiers thought he was feigning madness, and since they were also convinced that he was one of those who killed those five men, they set out to teach him a lesson by binding his arms as tight as they would go and making him trot in front of the horses from Paola to Osawatomie. That's what you saw, the lesson. Seven miles."

Wealthy shuddered.

"Wealthy, I'm of two minds whether to tell you the rest, but I suppose you should know. Anyway, the lesson didn't work. I was brought to Osawatomie by wagon, and when I got there, poor John was a raving maniac. There's no other way to describe him. He was chained to a tent pole and was heaving himself around—I could only think of the bear baitings I've read about from olden times. He didn't recognize me or anyone else. Somehow he had gotten the idea that he was in charge of the camp, and he was screaming orders. They told me to make him be quiet. I tried my best, but I couldn't do anything with him. Finally, three men came in and kicked and beat him until he lost consciousness. I was in irons and there was nothing I could do."

Jason caught her as she staggered against him. As she leaned on his shoulder, he continued grimly, "He came to after a few hours, and they let me take care of him after that. I was able to at least keep him quiet, and gradually he came more and more to himself. He hasn't been mistreated since then, except that all of us were made to march for a long distance in chains, as you saw. But once we finally reached Tecumseh and appeared for that hearing, he was quite rational. He actually seemed interested in the proceedings and even snorted at some of the wilder testimony about us. Of course, under the law, none of us defendants could speak; we just had to listen. Anyway, the judge released me and most of the rest, and before we parted, John gave his love to the two of you. He said he would write as soon as he was allowed. It's going to be all right, Wealthy. I promise you."

He let her weep on his shoulder, patting her on the back gently as she cried herself out. Finally, she wiped her eyes and managed to ask, "What are you going to do now?"

"For the time being, Ellen and I will stay in Kansas. It's not safe to travel on the river these days if you have a Northern accent, I'm told, and the Ruffians are harassing people on the roads. Besides, I told John I'd look after you and Johnny. I'm sure you don't want to leave while he's still in prison."

"No. He needs me." Wealthy stared at the thin band of gold on her finger. "And I need him."

~ ~ ~

Although Wealthy had not seen an Eastern newspaper in some time—they seldom reached their destination in Kansas these days, and one Free-Stater had been beaten just for walking around with a *New York Tribune* protruding from his pocket—the letters that she began receiving from Ohio made it clear that the recent events in Kansas and John's part in them had become known far and wide, despite Wealthy's reluctance to alarm her family and friends with a complete account of the past few weeks. Hannah and Eunecia, her sisters, begged her to come back, while her uncle Riverius Bidwell, a man well in his sixties, offered to come well-armed and take her home personally. Wealthy had the distinct impression that he would not be averse to joining Father Brown's band of guerrillas.

Various former classmates of Wealthy wrote to her, all more or less promising to shoot any Border Ruffian they might encounter between the eyeballs, in the groin, and in various other picturesque spots. Wealthy would have encouraged them to come to Kansas had not all of the correspondents been from the female department of Grand River.

Ruth, having been given a complete account of events by Jason, wrote so tenderly to her that Wealthy could not forebear from crying, even though Ruth did not miss the opportunity to urge her, as she had been doing for years, to move to North Elba. It was indicative of the hardships of the past year, Wealthy thought, that for the first time she could consider the prospect of a nine-month winter with equanimity. Thirteen-year-old Annie contributed a short, bloodthirsty missive admixed with a certain longing to partake of the excitement herself. Even Mother Brown sent a letter, a typical Mother Brown composition which showed that she was taking the past year's events—her husband gone for months and now an outlaw, Salmon and Henry wounded, her stepson reduced to a raving maniac—very much in stride, it all being God's will. Wealthy would have preferred God to be somewhat less willful.

In their various ways, though, the correspondents each gave Wealthy cheer, and Eunecia and Hannah sent practical help as well in the form of dress patterns and materials for Wealthy to replenish her burned wardrobe. Even Mother Brown's stoicism had a bracing effect. But she heard nothing from the one person on earth she most wanted to hear from until one day in early July when she opened an envelope from a stranger, a Mr. Babcock, and saw John's familiar handwriting.

At first, she dared not believe it but scanned the letter over and over again. Indeed, the hand was a shaky one, and the signature lacked John's usual flourish. But she was not mistaken.

Better yet, the letter, though short, was rational. John was being held in Camp Sackett, named for its commanding officer, a humane man who allowed the prisoners to send and receive letters. He had granted John's request that Wealthy and Johnny be allowed to stay with him. Wealthy would not be the only woman in camp; Governor Robinson's wife, a formidable woman, was also there, as was another prisoner's wife, Mrs. Jenkins. The army would even give Wealthy a stipend for tending to John's meals and laundry. He desperately missed her and longed to clasp her in his arms again.

Wealthy sent a reply through Mr. Babcock, who turned out to be a lawyer in Lawrence who accepted correspondence for the prisoners. She would set off immediately.

Instead, she fell sick with the ague.

For days, Wealthy sat listlessly in a corner of the Adair cabin, shivering and shaking. As one who had seldom been sick, even as a child, her sympathy for her ailing companions the previous year had been tinged with the faintest contempt. Now, at last, she understood why no cabins had been built, no fences erected, and crops allowed to rot. She wanted only to coil up upon her pallet and sleep.

Soon, poor Johnny was ill as well. When he could stammer out coherent sentences, they concerned the same themes. He wanted Pa. He wanted home and the nice little bed that had been fixed up for him there. And finally, on his sickest day, he announced that he wanted Ohio.

So, by now, did Wealthy.

She was just beginning to feel herself again when another letter from John arrived, every sentence in it a stab to the heart. John had been ill with quinsy. He was so anxious to see her again, he could not sleep, and he feared he might lose his reason again. He begged her not to let Johnny forget him. But it was the shortest sentence that affected Wealthy the most: *Please come.*

Wealthy strode outside where Johnny sat listlessly stroking one of the Adair cats. "We're going to go to your father."

"When?"

Wealthy set her jaw and ignored the fresh shiver that ran through her. "Now."

~ ~ ~

Young Spencer Brown, always up for adventure, volunteered to take Wealthy to Lawrence, with a stop at the camp near Middle Creek where Father Brown and his sons were holed up. Once in Lawrence, Wealthy could get someone to take her to John's camp near Lecompton, which, as the capital of the Bogus Government, was only miles away but worlds apart from abolitionist Lawrence. Although Wealthy was reluctant to expose Spencer to danger, he told her that at the moment, boys were far safer traveling than men.

Everyone on the road looked askance at everyone else, Wealthy being no exception. Each time someone came into view, even an old lady on her mule cart, Wealthy, ready to defend herself, gripped the pistol on the seat beside her. This hadn't been the life she'd planned for herself when she was a schoolgirl at Grand River Institute just ten years before.

Neither Spencer nor Wealthy knew precisely where the Brown encampment was, a problem that resolved itself when Frederick Brown appeared carrying a rifle. He looked thin and worn but quite sane, and he smiled broadly when he recognized the travelers. "How's my nephew?" he asked, placing his rifle in the wagon and taking Johnny in his arms. He grinned at Wealthy. "Remember all the helpful advice I sent you and John when he was a baby?"

"It was well meant, at least. And some of it was even useful."

Frederick tapped Wealthy on the nose. "Just some of it?"

He led their wagon toward a cabin crammed with ailing Browns. Salmon and Henry Thompson, still recovering from their wounds, sat hunched over outside, looking wan and chilled even though it was a hot day. Inside, Wealthy found Father Brown sitting by a pallet on which a shockingly thin, almost skeletal Owen lay dozing. Father Brown himself looked nothing like the man she had first met as a schoolgirl. Then, he had been dressed immaculately in his dull, old-fashioned and drably colored clothes. Now his toes were protruding from his shoes, and his clothing was an odd mix of tattered pants, a brightly checked shirt that must have been picked up by Mr. Bondi on his raid, a colorless duster, and a rather jaunty straw hat that was presumably another one of Mr. Bondi's contributions. He nodded at her as if they had last seen each other just the day before. "You're going to stay with John?"

"Yes."

"Good. I will be taking my other boys to Nebraska to recuperate, and some of them will be heading back to the States afterward. I will be easier in my mind knowing that you are looking after John in my absence. I always did approve of his marriage to you, you know."

With this compliment burning in her ears, Wealthy set about making the men a bit more comfortable. They were not lacking for medical care—that being provided by Lucius Mills, a cousin who was also a physician—nor for provisions, but the cabin and the men's linen needed a good cleaning. Having done the best she could in that regard, Wealthy sat down to supper that evening with a good conscience.

No one seemed inclined to speak of the killings along the Pottawatomie River, and Wealthy forbore to raise the issue. Nor did anyone recount the party's valorous deeds at Black Jack, though Wealthy suspected that the younger men might have done so had their father's serious presence not discouraged such braggadocio. Instead, they talked of the plans of those intending to leave Kansas for Nebraska. Henry Thompson wanted to return to Ruth and their children, including a baby daughter, as soon as he was well enough to undertake the journey to North Elba, while Oliver and Salmon were contemplating working in Ohio for a time. All three seemed entirely weary of Kansas. Frederick, on the other hand, was uncertain, as was even frail Owen. Wealthy suspected they were reluctant to leave John and Jason behind. "Will you be coming back to Kansas, Father Brown?" Wealthy asked.

Father Brown fixed his eyes on her. "With John still here in prison and Jason destitute? Most certainly. And besides, my work is not done here."

~ ~ ~

Wealthy had just dressed the next morning when Frederick handed her a letter. "If you have a chance to mail something, I'd appreciate you sending this to Lucy."

"I'll do my best."

"She was thinking of coming here. I had to tell her that now's not a good time, that I might end up leaving here forever. I also had to tell her that if she hears any bad of us, to hear me out first."

"She'll understand, Fred. I do."

"Well, yes, but you're a rarefied creature." Frederick looked down at the letter in Wealthy's hand. "That was a horrible night's work. But what were we supposed to do? Wait to see if they would carry out their threats? Have them do unspeakable things to Mary Grant and Ellen and you?" Frederick clenched his fists. "No one has harmed any of you, have they?"

"Fred! Calm yourself. Nothing like that has happened, I assure you."

Her brother-in-law paced back and forth before he said in a milder tone, "I do hope I can stay here, though. It's been good not being known to one and all as Crazy Frederick. I haven't had a really bad spell since I came here, even after—" He lifted his eyes. "You're worried about seeing John, aren't you?"

"Yes. It was terrible seeing him in that condition. I'm afraid I'll say the wrong thing. I'm afraid he'll have a setback."

"Just be kind to him, as everyone in the family—you included—has been to me during my spells. He's still John. And I think seeing you is what he needs most of all."

194

~ ~ ~

About thirteen miles outside of Lawrence—the city's most prominent landmark now being the ruins of the Free-State Hotel—was the prison camp. Wealthy was surprised to see that it looked like a quite ordinary clump of tents, only with a United States flag flying amid the canvas houses and men with rifles on their shoulders marching about. The driver, a man from Lawrence who Wealthy had learned often carried messages between the prisoners and their lawyers there, said, "Looks like you're in luck, ma'am. Usually there's a crew standing out here, wanting to get in."

"Why?"

"Oh, some are friends of the prisoners. Some just want to get a glimpse of them. And some are Border Ruffians who just want to make trouble. Don't worry, though, ma'am. Captain Sackett keeps them in line."

Wealthy looked at the armed soldiers with a new sense of appreciation.

The sentinel at what passed for the camp's gate waved them through. After Wealthy had stated her business, Captain Sackett himself appeared. He was a large man—enough to be suitably intimidating to the Border Ruffians, Wealthy thought—and he spoke with an Eastern accent, which was reassuring. "I'm glad you're here, Mrs. Brown. Mr. Brown has been wor—"

A scarecrow of a man ran toward the tent. "Wealthy! Johnny!"

John helped Wealthy from the wagon and flung his arms around her. Any self-control the couple had been exercising vanished as they clung together, their tears melding. It was left to Johnny to bring them to themselves with a plaintive, "Can't I get out, Pa?"

In response, John lifted Johnny out of the wagon and kissed him while Wealthy wiped her cheeks. "I missed you, Pa."

"And I missed you." When Johnny at last squirmed away, John straightened, allowing Wealthy to take in his appearance. He'd always had to watch lest he become too fleshy, but now he was thin with gaunt cheeks, his haggard appearance matched by his ragged clothes and unkempt hair. At least he was wearing the hat she had found for him.

Johnny had been studying his father as well. "You don't look good, Pa."

"You're right, but I hope I'll be looking better soon."

"Let's get you settled in, Mrs. Brown," Captain Sackett said kindly. "Now, we do have to search your belongings, purely as a matter of course."

Wealthy glanced at the trunk on the wagon. "It won't take you long."

Captain Sackett nodded and briskly riffled through the contents of the trunk until he reached Wealthy's extra corset, at which point he drew his hand back as if encountering a snake and halted the search. Smiling at this, Wealthy looked to see John's reaction; he did not change expression.

"Now that your family's here, Mr. Brown, I've got a tent for you. It's an old one, I'm afraid, but it will have to do until I can find something better."

John thanked him somewhat absently.

Presently, Captain Sackett conducted them to a row of tents, in front of which a pavilion of sorts had been erected to afford shade to the group of civilians who sat outside them. Some were reading newspapers, some were playing cards, and some—for there were two women among them—were knitting. "Welcome to Traitors' Row," the younger of the women, Governor Robinson's wife, said after a flurry of introductions. "Sit here while the men pitch your tent."

Wealthy nodded and settled on a crate as Johnny followed his father. She was relieved to see that John was taking most of the work of pitching the tent upon himself and was doing it quite competently. "Has my husband been—himself—lately?"

"He's been rational, if that's what you mean, but his pacing around is about to drive us mad—if you'll pardon the phrase."

Mrs. Jenkins, the other woman, said more kindly, "He's been quite nervous and agitated, and he talks quite wildly at times, but he'll be much better now that you're here, I'm sure. He's been fretting about your safety a great deal and imagining all sorts of things in your absence." She patted Wealthy's arm. "I can assure you that my husband and Sara's did much better after we arrived. Married men generally do, although they'll never admit it."

"I certainly hope so," Mrs. Robinson said. "His walking back and forth is very distracting."

"Mrs. Robinson is writing a book about Kansas," Mrs. Jenkins explained.

"Yes, and I never realized that I would be supplied with so much material. We can thank your father-in-law in part for that, Mrs. Brown."

Despite his difficulties of the past month, John had not become less efficient at pitching a tent—although this one left much to be desired. It was smaller than the one they had brought to Kansas, and Wealthy had her doubts as to whether it would withstand a good rainstorm. But it was a haven of sorts, into which she and John stepped, leaving Johnny in the kindly care of Mrs. Jenkins, when the men's work was done and their meager belongings had been placed inside. Wordlessly, she sat on the trunk with John, leaning her head on his shoulder. She knew she didn't look all that much better than he did; the small mirror in the Adair cabin had shown a sad little woman, and she had even spotted a few gray hairs on her brush. *What a battered little family we are*, she thought as they sat in silence.

At last, John said, "I thought you'd never come."

"I would have come earlier, but I fell ill, and then Johnny fell ill, and—"

"No. I mean that I thought you'd never come, literally—that you'd take Johnny and go back to Ohio and your family and leave your crazy husband behind. I thought I'd never see you again, that if I got out of here, you'd try to have me put away."

How long had he been tormenting himself with these thoughts? "How can you think that, my love? I would have come so much sooner, sick or not, if I knew you were thinking these things. And now that I am here, I will never leave. I promise."

She took his hand to seal her pledge. Then she saw his wrist, encircled by an area that was red and raw, nearly worn to the bone. "That's where they bound you?"

John nodded. "The other looks the same."

"Those whoresons," she blurted out. How Kansas had expanded her vocabulary!

"I agree with that," John said with a slight smile. "But I was mad—raving mad—most of the time I had them on, if it's any comfort."

It was not. She steeled herself to examine his wound more closely. "Has no one given you anything for them?"

"The doctor gave me some salve when I was ill—I've had the dysentery, followed by quinsy— but I kept forgetting to put it on. Or I just didn't care."

"Have you been sleeping?"

"Not much. I just lie there at night and fret. George Brown will be glad to be rid of me. I think I keep him up too."

"Well, you're in my charge now, and we're going to fix you up. Starting with getting you healthy again. You're so thin. Don't they feed you here?"

"Quite well, actually, but I was ill, and some days I just don't bother." He stared at his hands. "Wealthy, I don't care to talk about—about the way I was when I was captured. Not yet. But I do have to warn you, it could happen again, my spell of madness. It did with my mother. It does with Fred. Do you understand that?"

"I do, and if it does, we will deal with it together. I will never desert you."

For the first time, John's lips twitched into a smile. "Well, thank you, Mrs. Micawber." The smile faded. "Even though I've got us back into a tent? Even though I don't know how long I'll be here or what will become of me? Even though we have almost nothing but the clothes on our backs?"

"Yes. Yes to all those things. Now let me show you what we do have left."

He nodded, and she delved into the trunk and pulled out its contents, most of which had fortuitously been among the belongings she had taken with her to the Adair cabin before the fire. Some letters from various friends and relatives. John's guide to legislative procedure. A textbook on phrenology. John's memorandum book and diary for 1856. Daguerreotypes of each of them, taken years before. "Here is what I found in the ruins. Look."

John wiped at his eye as she placed his watch in one hand and the book of poetry in the other. "Thank you. I'm glad to have them back. But it's you and Johnny I'm most glad to have back. And you don't want to leave?"

"No! Get that nonsense out of your head. I will follow you to the world's end in a white petticoat, or however that story went."

This time, John's smile was broad. "That didn't end so well for either party, sweetheart. But I appreciate the sentiment."

13

July 1856 to October 1856

There were worse places one could be in Kansas than in Camp Sackett, Wealthy had to admit. Captain Sackett was a kind man, and although there was an ongoing debate between various governmental officials as to which was obliged to pay for the prisoners' board, no one went hungry. Friends and sympathizers regularly sent in provisions, so the real danger was that the inmates, with very little to do in the way of physical exertion, might grow plump. Wealthy was spared only because she resumed her school habit of doing calisthenics, much to the amazement of those around her, and because, more conventionally, she suffered another attack of the ague. Each day the shivers came on like a bothersome visitor who hadn't figured out he was unwelcome.

The treason prisoners had real visitors as well. They fell into roughly three categories: friends and well-wishers, Border Ruffians, and gawkers. The first, naturally, were quite welcome, while the second seldom made it into the camp but were chased off by the captain and his men. The third group came merely to gaze at the traitors, especially the hard-shell abolitionist variety, who in their captive state could be observed with perfect safety to the beholder. John, who had actually stolen a man's slaves and was said to be crazy to boot, was a particular favorite. Captain Sackett apologized for letting in the gawkers but said that it was necessary in order to appease those who would have kept the prisoners' friends away as well.

Disagreeable and zoo-like as such visitors' presence could be, it did provide some diversion. Though the ladies, of course, were not prisoners, they could not escape being seen other than by retreating into their tents, which they scorned to do. Instead, they coolly went around their business. If Wealthy was cooking or working in the little garden she and Johnny had planted, she would don her bloomers, which added to the enjoyment of the guests. At least they weren't interested in the ladies' sanitary arrangements, which featured a series of sheets strung between some accommodating trees. Mrs. Robinson had made that her particular concern.

As for John, under Wealthy's care, he had rapidly regained his physical health, although Governor Robinson, who had been a physician, opined that the injury to his wrists would leave permanent scars. But he still had days when he was listless and despondent, and others on which he was anxious and overtalkative. Still, at other times, he was nearly his old self, and if he was particularly John-like, he would exert himself to argue with the gawkers about the institution of slavery. He even offered to read Mrs. Jenkins's head.

John and Wealthy fell into the habit of taking a walk to the creek each afternoon. Although it was an undertaking which required an armed sentry to trail along behind them,

Captain Sackett allowed them this daily excursion for the sake of Johnny, whom most of the soldiers were inclined to indulge. There, under the eye of their guard, John, whose interests had expanded over the years to include geology, would search for specimens—the only thing they could afford now, he joked when he had recovered a bit of his old sense of humor—while Johnny would launch boats of twigs and leaves and Wealthy would sit on a log and enjoy the shade afforded by the trees. A couple of weeks after Wealthy's arrival, however, John settled with Wealthy on the log instead of attending to his collection. "I wanted to talk to you about the killings."

"You don't have to, John. I know it's a subject that troubles you."

"I need to, though. I know that some here—George Brown, for one—condemn the killings and the men who did them. Do you?"

"Not the men, John. I love them as if they were my own father and brothers. As for the killings, I was horrified when I heard of them, and I was very glad when I learned that you did not participate in them. But as I told some of your brothers, I know that they had their reasons. They felt threatened."

"Yes. More than felt; we were threatened."

She had to ask the next question. "Did you know what they had planned?"

"I guessed. I made a very feeble protest, which Father of course disregarded."

"Do you think your father would have heeded even a vigorous protest?"

John smiled slightly. "No. And in truth, I didn't want to protest vigorously. I felt that he was in the right. But that was purely in the abstract. When I found the deed had been carried out, part of me recoiled nonetheless, and part of me was ashamed I hadn't helped Father and the rest. That, and everything else atop of it, was just too much for me. I thought I was stronger than that, that having gone all these years without any spells like my mother had, it would never happen to me."

Wealthy patted his shoulder and glanced back at the guard. He did not appear to be losing patience—indeed, there were far worse places, such as in the broiling sun, where he might be doing his duty.

John went on, "Assuming that we are not hanged for treason—and Governor Robinson is optimistic that Congress won't allow it—I have been thinking about where we can go after this. I just can't see going back to our claim. I need to get to someplace quiet if I am to recover."

"I certainly don't object to quiet." Wealthy looked at their son, who was skimming stones. With so many long hours to fill, John and Wealthy had had plenty of time to devote to teaching him, but despite their combined efforts, he had yet to learn to recite the alphabet. True, he was not yet four, but poor Austin at the same age had been able to recite his letters with gusto, as Ellen had pointed out on occasion. "I think it will be better for Johnny too. All this disruption has made him a little—well, slow, I think."

Johnny turned his head. "What, Mama?"

"Just that I love you, darling."

"I love you too, Mama." Johnny crawled into her lap, heedless of his muddy feet. "And Papa," he added as he leaned against his father's shoulder.

Strangely, Wealthy at that moment felt as safe as she ever had been since they crossed into Kansas. Almost, in a way, content.

~ ~ ~

Father Brown, having left the boys and Henry Thompson safe in Nebraska, was back in Kansas. He had met up with James Lane, a former congressman from Indiana whose sense of adventure had lured him to the territory the previous year. This John learned from Father Brown himself, who, in a letter passed to John through his lawyer, offered to help him escape. Lane had made a similar offer to Robinson and the rest of the prisoners. "I don't doubt Father's ability, nor Lane's," John said, tearing up the letter. "But Robinson thinks we'll be released soon, either through a writ of habeas corpus or on bail, or that we might be transferred for trial in the States. I'd prefer that to being a fugitive, assuming we survived an escape attempt."

"Especially if we had to part." Wealthy shivered, half from the thought, half from her daily attack of ague. "I couldn't bear that."

John wrapped his arm around her. "Then we stay."

~ ~ ~

Although the bugle call unfailingly summoned the camp awake, Wealthy did not need its prompting. Even if years of farming had not accustomed her to early rising, her lodgings were hardly conducive to lying in. She had made the best bed she could by raking some straw together, and John's knapsack served her as a pillow, but sleeping was still an uncomfortable proposition. As usual, she tried not to think of the four-poster of her girlhood, which also had happened to be her wedding bed.

She dressed and began making breakfast for the prisoners with Mrs. Jenkins. They at least had a stove, courtesy of Mr. Jenkins, who had sold them in Lawrence before his imprisonment. As they worked, she listened absently to Mrs.

Jenkins's complaints: although the government was supposed to be paying the women for boarding the prisoners, she hadn't received a payment since June. "And I imagine you haven't received a thing either, Wealthy."

"No." Wealthy frowned. "Why, what's that?"

"Gunfire," said John, who, along with the rest of the men and Mrs. Robinson, had straggled into the pavilion and settled down with the latest Missouri newspapers. "From the direction of Titus's camp." He hopped to his feet. "Could the scoundrel be under attack?"

Colonel Titus, as he was called, was a Border Ruffian from Florida who had been swaggering around Lecompton, prophesying that all Free-State men would be driven out of the territory within two weeks. Lately, however, although the Border Ruffians had caused their fair share of trouble, the Free-Staters had gone on the offensive as well, attacking Border Ruffians at Franklin and at Washington Creek. Rumors had reached the camp that Father Brown, who had returned from Nebraska after leading his sons to safety there, had been among the forces. "I certainly hope so," Wealthy said.

A clap of thunder followed by a general opening of the skies forced everyone to grab his or her plate and retreat into the tents, which, while not impervious to rain, were better than the leaking cover of their pavilion. As the Browns ate, John counted the gunshots. "At least two hun—"

"Good lord!" Mrs. Robinson shrieked.

A cannonball had sailed down the pavilion. Wealthy shuddered to think what would have happened if they had still been dining there. A few more scattered rounds of gunshot, and all was quiet. "Smoke!" John said, venturing out to look around him. "I think it's Titus's house." He hailed a passing soldier. "What's going on?"

"Supposedly about eighty Free-Staters pitched into the Titus camp. And now you know all I do."

"Splendid," John said. He headed back into the tent. "I'm going to write to Jason."

Mrs. Robinson called over. "If your father is among those men, Mr. Brown, I would request that he not send any more of his cannonballs flying toward us. I am trying to write, and it is not at all conducive to my concentration."

"I will," John said. He grinned at Wealthy.

Titus and a number of his men had indeed been taken prisoner, a messenger confirmed shortly, but this was the last favorable news they had. The current governor having fallen into disfavor with the Pierce administration, a new one, John Geary, had been appointed, but he had not yet assumed his duties. This left Kansas at the mercy of the lieutenant governor, Daniel Woodson, who was on the best of terms with the Border Ruffians. Rumors drifted about of yet another incursion from Missouri, with Osawatomie and Lawrence as the targets.

Peace-loving Jason, who had constructed a shed of rails near the Garrison cabin and was living there with his family, wrote grimly that he was preparing to fight with Father Brown. John began to pace again, tossing and turning so much at night that Wealthy thought he might bring their little tent down upon their heads. "I wish I'd accepted Father's offer to help me escape," he said during one sleepless night. "I'm useless here."

Wealthy could offer him little comfort. Thinking of their friends and relations in Osawatomie—including Mrs. Adair and Rachel Garrison, both of whom were with child—she felt useless herself.

Lieutenant Governor Woodson did nothing to protect Osawatomie and Lawrence, but Colonel Philip St. George Cooke, a Virginian, arrived at Camp Sackett with five hundred men, lest, John muttered, any Free-Staters get out of line. Meanwhile, Lieutenant Governor Woodson proclaimed the territory to be in rebellion and asked for assistance in suppressing it. "A blatant invitation for the Ruffians to do their worst," John said. He spoke in a low voice; although Colonel Cooke seemed a decent sort, he kept the prisoners under closer watch than had his subordinate Captain Sackett. "And I have no doubt whatsoever they'll do it."

They did not have to wait long. In the afternoon of August 30, a messenger rode into camp and headed straight for Colonel Cooke's tent. Despite their reservations about the new commander, the prisoners crowded around the tent and were waiting when the colonel emerged. "What happened?" Governor Robinson asked.

"My goodness, you look grim," Mrs. Robinson added.

Colonel Cooke nodded. "This morning, Osawatomie was attacked by a force led by John Reid." He glanced in John's direction. "A much smaller force led by John Brown opposed them—valiantly, it seems—but to no avail. They were routed, and the town was burned."

Wealthy clapped her hand to her mouth.

"What of my father?"

The colonel said, "He was last seen trying to cross a river. Whether he succeeded is unknown." He hesitated. "Do you have a brother named Frederick? I know there are other Browns in that area. Then I am sorry to tell you that before the battle, a preacher named Martin White was riding in advance of Reid's troops, apparently as a scout. He encountered Frederick Brown in the road and shot him. He seems to have died instantly."

As John staggered and Governor Robinson steadied him, Wealthy asked, "Why was he shot?"

"I don't know, madam."

"For no better reason than he was John Brown's son, no doubt. And nothing will be done to Martin White or those other scoundrels. Don't even try to tell me otherwise."

Colonel Cooke did not try.

As the other prisoners asked questions of their own, Governor Robinson gently led John back to his tent while Wealthy followed. "Let me be alone for a while," John said. He smiled faintly. "I'm not going to go mad again. I promise."

Reluctantly, Wealthy and Governor Robinson obeyed. Mrs. Jenkins having kindly offered to look after Johnny, Wealthy stole off to the creek where, for once unaccompanied by a soldier, she wept. Frederick! She had always been fond of him, but since John's troubles had begun, her affection for him had grown.

She had kept her promise to mail Frederick's letter to Lucy, enclosing it in a letter of her own in which she dwelt at length upon Frederick's superior qualities and—lest Lucy be tempted by someone closer to home—of the happiness they were bound to find together. And now, she supposed, she or John would have to write with their sad tidings.

About an hour later, Wealthy ventured into the tent to find a red-eyed but composed John reading a letter. "One of the ones Fred wrote when we were living in Ohio," he said. "The dear boy. How bravely he bore his affliction, and how cheerful he was in his good periods. *I want to know what you call the 'Bold Sonny.' He must be a fair horse by this time if W has fed him clear cream all the time.*"

Wealthy put her arm around John. "I shall miss him terribly. Shall I write to Lucy or should you?"

"I will, or perhaps both of us can; she will want all the comfort she can get. Poor girl. I know little of her, but

Frederick always described her as a lovely, sweet person, and I have no reason to think otherwise. For all of our flaws, we Brown men do attract most excellent women."

~ ~ ~

Amid their grieving for Frederick, John and Wealthy had to fret as well about the fates of Father Brown, Jason, and their other relations. This anxiety, at least, was relieved a little over a week later, when through Mr. Babcock they received a letter in Father Brown's distinctive handwriting. Father Brown declared himself entirely alive and in Lawrence, with Jason by his side.

From Father Brown and the Adairs, who had also managed to get a letter through, John and Wealthy learned that Frederick had returned to Osawatomie just a day before his death and had lodged with some friends. Having offered to convey some letters for the Adairs—no mean task in those days when carriers of mail to and from Free-State towns risked being captured or killed by the Border Ruffians—he had set out at sunrise to fulfill his promise and was not far from the Adair cabin when Mr. Adair, hearing a commotion, rushed out to investigate and found Frederick lying dead in the road, the weapons at his side still in their holsters. David Garrison, who had spent the night in the Adair shed, had hurried out as well. As the men examined the body, they found themselves the prey of Reid's men, coming down the road. Mr. Adair had escaped into the ravine, where he and young Charles hid all night before returning to a tearful Florella. Mr. Garrison, fleeing in a different direction, had been shot in the back and killed. Spencer Kellogg Brown, having joined Father Brown's tiny force, had been captured but was apparently not being treated badly. The only bright spot was that Reid's men had spared the Adair cabin—then crowded with women and children, some of them ill—from destruction.

"It appears that Frederick hadn't an inkling of what White and his men were up to," John said before handing over Mr. Adair's letter to Wealthy. "White later boasted about the killing, the scoundrel, and it seems that Frederick assumed that they were Free-Staters, or at least no one with any animosity toward him. He said something to the effect that he thought he knew White, and White said, 'I know you,' and shot him straight through the heart."

"And Reid's men shot poor Garrison while he was in flight," Wealthy said bitterly. "I'd like to shoot them myself." Guiltily, she looked over at Johnny, who fortunately had not overheard this homicidal declaration.

"Uncle Adair does have some comforting words. The night before he died, Frederick stopped by his house, and they talked about the state of things. Uncle Adair asked Frederick whether he feared falling into the hands of the Border Ruffians. He said no, that if it was God's will that he die in the cause of freedom, he was ready to die. Even if they got his body, he said, they would never get him. And they got neither."

~ ~ ~

Early on the morning of September 10, the prisoners crowded into a military ambulance, headed for their trial, or something, in Lecompton. No one from the government appeared to be prepared for a proceeding of any sort. John had yet to even be indicted. "There are plenty of things that could happen," John said. "We could be moved to Fort Leavenworth, as I think Colonel Cooke is rather tired of us. Or we could be bailed. Or we could be tried and released. Or we could be tried and committed to prison or hanged. But I do think the last is exceedingly unlikely, as we have some support in Congress, so I won't spend nearly as long embracing you and Johnny as I'd like to."

He took a long time about it anyway.

"You certainly are an affectionate couple," Mrs. Robinson said as the ambulance drove away.

Wealthy nodded. "You can include that in your book," she said sweetly.

After a few hours, the wagon returned, this time full of men waving their hats. "Are you free?" Wealthy called.

"Out on bail, actually," John said as he hopped down from the wagon. "After all the trouble of bringing us there, we found they weren't ready to go forward. After a great deal of back and forth, the judge decided to continue the case to a later date because he didn't think it would be possible to get a fair trial in the present state of unrest. Everyone certainly agreed with that. I wasn't included in the order as I've never been indicted, but Colonel Cooke is finding our presence burdensome."

"No disrespect to you, sir," the colonel said.

"So in the end, the judge treated me as if I had been indicted, and I was bailed with the rest. George Brown was kind enough to stand bail for me."

Wealthy blinked. "It hardly feels real." Somehow she had assumed that the government might keep John locked up just for spite.

Her relief at her husband's being free, even on bond, was tempered by the reality that they had no place to return except to their barren claim and the ashes of their little cabin, but as George Brown had offered to let them stay in his house in Lawrence for the time being, they quickly packed their meager belongings to be loaded in the military wagon. Johnny, who had assembled his own rock collection, carefully added it to the trunk. "Are we leaving for good, Mama?"

"Yes, dear."

"Papa too?"

John ruffled his hair. "Papa too. We're sticking together."

Colonel Cooke offered a military escort to Lawrence, which the men refused at first but finally accepted after a bit of dickering, rather to Wealthy's relief.

"Everything looks so desolate now," she said, gazing around at a landscape she had not seen in weeks. A cabin, which could not have been built but recently, stood lonely and forlorn.

A wagon heaped with goods came toward them. "Where are you headed?" one of their escort called.

The head of the family, a ragged, grim-looking man, answered, "Out of this damned place."

By arrangement, and to everyone's mutual relief, the soldiers left the prisoners about a mile and a half outside of Lawrence, where the town's militia, the Stubbs, soon turned out to escort them into the town, which had the look of a place expecting trouble. Some rude fortifications had been erected, and more militia men stood at the entrance to the town. But with the Stubbs as their escort, the prisoners needed no introduction. Instead, the men set up cheers, which the crowds lining the road took up as the wagon proceeded into the heart of the city. Although Wealthy knew that most of the huzzahs were for the more prominent men of their party such as Governor Robinson, she could not help but be touched. Even John, who had been lost in thought since leaving camp, broke out in a smile.

That evening, once all the former prisoners had settled into their various lodgings and, if John and Wealthy were indicative, had taken refreshing baths and put on fresh sets of garments, a meeting was held in the town. It doubled as a celebration. After Governor Robinson and a few others gave speeches, John, rather to his and Wealthy's surprise, was called upon to say a few words. He obliged graciously, paying a brief but heartfelt tribute to poor Frederick, predicting that Lawrence would heroically resist the threatened invasion, and winding up on a more cheerful note by hoping that he would soon be reading the next issue of the *Herald of Freedom*, suspended during George Brown's imprisonment.

"You did wonderfully," Wealthy said as they walked the short distance to George Brown's home, where the hired girl had been kind enough to keep an eye on Johnny.

"Thank you, my dear." John snorted. "Although I suspect some might have been disappointed to not see a raving maniac."

They found Johnny fast asleep in the trundle bed, a state of affairs that encouraged them to have their own private celebration in the handsome four-poster without the need for any speeches whatsoever—their first such encounter since May. They had barely disentangled themselves the next morning and gotten Johnny scrubbed for breakfast when the hired girl brought them a note. "Who is Isaac Smith?" Wealthy asked as she glanced at the signature.

"Father. He likes common names."

After a hasty breakfast with George Brown, who made no secret of his desire to get the meal over with so he could attend to the business of restarting his newspaper, Wealthy and John went to the place Father Brown had appointed, an office belonging to Mr. Edward Whitman. Evidently, Mr. Whitman had bestowed a change of clothing upon Father Brown, for the latter looked much more presentable, albeit weather-beaten and worn. "Son," he said simply when the trio was alone and father and son had embraced at length. "I am thankful that you have been preserved to us."

John wiped a tear from his eye. Wealthy thought Father Brown's eyes were moist as well.

"I am sorry not to have seen you yesterday, but I heard a rumor that Governor Geary might be here and seek to have me and others arrested. Until I know the measure of the man, it seemed best not to take the chance."

"I agree."

"I shall remain at my camp unless it appears that I can be of some good here at Lawrence. In the present unsettled state of things, I fear that every man will be needed. But what are your plans?"

John shook his head. "I don't know. I think it best after my—lapse—that I live a quiet life, and I doubt that will be possible here. I have thought of going to Minnesota or some other western place, or the Dakotas. Ruth, of course, would like to see me settle in North Elba. And Wealthy—"

"Ohio," Wealthy said.

Father Brown did not give the expected opinion. "I trust Providence will guide you."

"Are you planning to stay in Kansas, Father Brown?"

"Probably not for much longer. I have an idea, but it will take money, men, and planning, for which I will have to go east. I have long thought of such a plan, but it impressed itself again on me with overwhelming power as I watched Osawatomie go up in flames. Even if Geary can contain the troubles in Kansas and the Border Ruffians are driven out, there will be more Kansases and more savagery as long as slavery exists. I will give the South something else to do besides extend slave territory. I will carry the war into the South itself."

~ ~ ~

John soon made arrangements with Mr. Whitman to stay in his house a couple of miles outside of Lawrence in return for cutting hay. Jason, who was still with his father, planned to bring Ellen and Charlie to join them as soon as he could get them there safely.

Their future was still uncertain, but Mr. Whitman's place was pleasant enough, particularly now that the nights were turning crisp. But the unease over the fate of Lawrence remained. John, though quite sane, had been noticeably affected, sleeping little and eating almost nothing.

It was almost a relief, then, on the morning of September 14, when Wealthy and John, while at breakfast, heard the sound of a horseman who called, "The Ruffians are at Franklin! You can see them from Lawrence."

John threw down his napkin. "I'm leaving now."

"I'm coming with you."

"Dear, you'd be safest here."

"That may be, but I'm coming with you. So is Johnny. We—I, at least—can be of more use there than we can possibly be skulking around here." She did not add that the last time John had rushed off to defend Lawrence, he had returned a madman. "I can help with something, I'm sure."

"Very well, but you must clear out in case of danger."

Wealthy gave a slight incline of her head that could not really be taken as a promise.

With Johnny sometimes walking, sometimes squirming in John's arms, they made their way as quickly as possible to Lawrence, where they found Father Brown, who, like John, bore a rifle on his shoulder. "They say that there are twenty-five hundred or more Border Ruffians moving toward us, and several hundred already at Franklin," he said. "You don't need me to tell you what an unequal fight that will be, especially since so many of the militia here—and their Sharps rifles—are out with General Lane."

Wealthy nodded. At best, Lawrence could muster a few hundred men, and that was if the elderly and the invalid townspeople tottered up to join the fight.

"Robinson and the other leaders have sent a message to Geary. They seem hopeful that he will order the troops to help in our defense, but I have my doubts, given past experience. So, it appears, do the townspeople. They know they must prepare for battle. What's more, they are in fine spirits. A marked contrast to the last time the town was under attack."

"What can we do?" Wealthy asked.

"Well, you, my dear, can pack cartridges. I believe the ladies are busy with that over at George Brown's."

Wealthy dutifully hurried to that residence, where she found the editor's wife and a number of other ladies seated around a table, twisting paper into cylinders, stuffing the resulting package with powder and a bullet, and neatly tying up the combustible package with a bit of thread. With their bright dresses and neat hair, they might have been making a quilt. "Be careful," John warned her and the others. "A mistake, and you could all be blown to bits."

A few years later, when dozens of young girls and women, some toiling for the North, others for the South, suffered precisely that horrible fate at various times and places, Wealthy would realize just how true her husband's words had been, but with this knowledge far in her future, she simply nodded and attended diligently to her work. Meanwhile, smoke began to drift toward the city, causing all the women to cough. "The Ruffians are burning buildings in Franklin," John explained when he popped in the next time. "Some of our best young men have ridden out to meet the advance forces."

"No word from Governor Geary?"

217

"Not a murmur."

Wealthy sighed and returned to her work.

Around four, with her back aching and Johnny begging to go outside, she took a break from her duties and found Father Brown standing on a dry-goods box, addressing a rapt group of citizens, men and women alike, some bearing rifles or muskets, some holding pitchforks or even hoes. A young Englishman named Richard Hinton stood at his side, jotting in shorthand. He was a correspondent for one of the Eastern papers and, like most of the newspapermen in Kansas, also fought for his chosen side on occasion. "This is probably the last opportunity you will have of seeing a fight, so you had better do your best," Father Brown said. "Wait till they get within twenty-five yards of you, get a good object, be sure you see the hindsight of your gun, then fire. A great deal of powder and lead and very precious time is wasted by shooting too high. You had better aim at their legs rather than their heads."

Mr. Hinton scribbled intently as the crowd cheered. Wealthy longed to give the advice a try.

Throughout the afternoon, what remained of the militia made excursions into Franklin and appeared to be holding the invaders at bay. There was yet no word from the governor, nor from the army.

Even as darkness fell and the sound of firing died off, no adult dared to sleep, and even the youngest children found it hard enough. Wealthy at last succeeded in putting Johnny to bed at George Brown's —it took twice as many stories as usual—and then, after sitting in thought for a while, kissed him and left the house, which crowded full of women and children who had taken refuge from the fighting around Franklin. Pitchfork in hand, she made her way to the fort—

really only an earthwork that a man could crouch behind—and found John there, along with his father. "I've come to keep you company. And fight if I need to."

"The first I like. The second I hope won't be necessary. But with less than three hundred against twenty-five hundred, at least history will say we died fighting."

"I regret not having a rifle for you," Father Brown said. "Do you know how to manage one in case one of us falls and you pick his up?"

"Yes, I know how. I practiced at Mr. Whitman's."

"Good." In the light of a lantern, she saw him give one of his rare smiles. "I have been thinking a great deal of having a sort of weapon built to my specifications that a slave untrained in arms or a woman could easily manage if need be. A blade mounted on a sort of shaft, perhaps."

John said quietly. "I hope to God this won't become necessary. But if I do fall—or you fall—know that I love you dearly and have done so as long as I've known you. Nothing on earth is more precious to me than you and Johnny."

Wealthy could do nothing but cling to him.

But watching and waiting was a tedious business, and eventually she allowed John to coax her to rest her head in his lap and take a catnap, which turned into a deep sleep. When she woke, the dawn was breaking. "John? What has happened?"

He smiled down at her. "Quite a bit, my dear. Look up on Mount Oread."

She obeyed. Atop Mount Oread—the rather absurd name for the hill that overlooked Lawrence—flew a United States flag next to a good-sized cannon. Looking around, she saw troops encamped all about the town.

"They arrived past midnight. I'd have woken you, but when it became clear they were for our protection, I saw no need. I'd have roused you for a massacre, trust me."

"Where's Father Brown?"

"He thought it wise to lie low once it appeared that he could be of no further use. I hope, though, that the army and the governor have more pressing matters than arresting him and Lane." John helped her to her feet. "Go to Johnny, dearest. I'll find you later."

She obeyed but kept her pitchfork just in case.

~ ~ ~

Governor Geary arrived in town later that morning, accompanied by their last keeper, Colonel Cooke. After addressing the townspeople, the two men rode out to find the Missourians, who were every bit as numerous as had been reported. But Captain Cooke's courtly Virginia manners—and his pleasantly worded assurance that he would not hesitate to use the cannon to enforce the governor's will—succeeded in persuading the Missourians to return from whence they had come. "Do you think this means peace?" Wealthy asked John as they and Johnny trudged back to their lodgings at Mr. Whitman's.

"Perhaps. We shall see if Geary continues to hold the Border Ruffians to the laws—and if the President will let him." He set down a squirming Johnny. "You want to go to Ohio."

"Yes," she admitted. "I miss my sisters and my friends, and—well, everything. And I miss feeling safe. I miss *being* safe."

"Then we shall, as soon as it can be managed. I have said I need a peaceful life, but you and Johnny need one too. Even though I'm sure you could have wielded that pitchfork admirably."

"Or the rifle."

"True. Never underestimate a woman." His expression turned somber. "I must say, though, I feel somewhat of a failure leaving Kansas, especially with the Adairs and the Days staying, as far as I know. But I suppose it is for the best."

She took his scarred hand. "It is for the best. And it's not failure. It's home."

~ ~ ~

Mrs. Hotchkiss, Mrs. Sherbondy, and Mrs. Dehart, with their two small boys, one small girl, and one dog, did not stand out much from their fellow passengers on the steamer bound for St. Louis. They were dressed prettily, albeit sensibly, and their hoops swayed gently beneath their petticoats as they walked from the ladies' cabin to the deck from time to time to take the air and exercise the dog. They were friendly toward their fellow passengers, if somewhat reserved, and they were most polite to the servants. If there was anything unusual, it was only that they never got off the steamer, even when all of the other passengers took the welcome opportunity to stroll on dry land, except when the usual sandbars made it necessary for all to leave, and even then, they were the first to scramble back aboard. No one could have guessed that Mrs. Hotchkiss had seen her husband reduced to madness and her home reduced to embers, that Mrs. Sherbondy had buried her eldest child just a year and a half before and had spent the last few weeks in a shed made of rails, and that Mrs. Dehart's husband had been shot in the back as he ran for his life.

Although Wealthy, Ellen, and Rachel Garrison might have gotten along fine on the steamer without the ruse of traveling under their maiden names, the ladies had decided to take no chances. There were still occasional assaults of Northerners on the Missouri steamboats, and while it could be hoped that ladies would be unmolested, the Brown name was notorious enough in these parts to possibly warrant an exception. Sitting at table in the steamer's dining room, Wealthy and Ellen had heard Father Brown and his sons accused of everything from scalping old men to slaying newborns. It was because of such undying Missouri hatred that Father Brown, John, and Jason had concluded that while the ladies would be safe traveling through Missouri on the river, the men would have to make the journey out of Kansas across land and bypass its Southern neighbor altogether.

So, the ladies and the children had set off alone, trusting to Providence and the men's Sharps rifles that the Brown men would make it safely out of the territory. The women's first step had been to replenish their wardrobes in Lawrence with the help of funds from relatives from Ohio and the New England Emigrant Aid Society; their next, after they arrived in Kansas City by stage and found the streets full of women in hoop skirts, was to add this embellishment to their undergarments. Wealthy still had to remember to sit down just so in order to prevent the contraption from springing up with a life of its own. So attired, they looked to be who they said they were: married ladies from Ohio whose husbands, afflicted with wanderlust, had gone to Kansas and dragged them along. Having taken a look at the primitive conditions there, the trio had determined to return to their families and not set foot into the territory until a proper home could be provided for them. The ladies had no opinion on slavery; indeed, they seemed aghast that a lady should have an opinion on anything other than the necessity for a comfortable home.

Being a ninny was rather hard work, so the ladies spent most of their time in their family-sized cabin or on a secluded area on deck, watching their passage to Kansas in reverse. "Waverly," Wealthy said as they approached that fateful port. She put her arm around Ellen. "Look, there's the graveyard. And there's the house of the man who sent his servant to help us."

Ellen shook her head as she followed Wealthy's gaze. "I still wake sometimes in hopes that all this has been a terrible dream," Ellen said. "But at least we're going home."

Rachel, whose brightly colored dress belied her recent widowhood, nodded in agreement. "I'm glad to be going myself. And yet, much as Kansas broke my heart, there's something in me that would like to come back."

～ ～ ～

They did get to Ohio without incident and, after Wealthy and Ellen wished Rachel a safe delivery and Rachel wished for the safe return of the Brown husbands, went their separate ways—Rachel to her parents' farm in Greene County, Ellen to her family in Akron, and Wealthy to her sisters in Ashtabula County. She thought they would never stop hugging her and Johnny, or she them. "We'll never let you leave Ohio again," Eunecia said.

"Or maybe a trip to Chicago if you're good. But no farther!" Hannah said.

"My wanderlust—if I had that much to begin with—is sated," Wealthy said.

Both her sisters assured her that Wealthy and her family had a home with them as long as they needed it. Little Eunecia had married while Wealthy was in Kansas and was now

Mrs. Alex Fobes. Wealthy liked her new brother-in-law, a prosperous farmer who was a thorough-going abolitionist like many others in the county. All were eager to have Wealthy over to tea and hear about the indignities inflicted upon the Free-Staters, so while Wealthy fretted a great deal over the safety of John and the other men, at least her days passed quickly.

Then a letter arrived assuring her that the men had safely reached Iowa and were heading east, followed by an even more welcome letter announcing that John would be taking the train from Chicago to Ashtabula. Borrowing some cash from Eunecia, who was well set for pin money, Wealthy took the stage to Ashtabula and haunted the depot there for several days until, at last, she saw John step off the train. "Thank God you're safe," she said after he released her from his embrace. "I was so fearful I'd never see you again."

"We had some misadventures—Captain Cooke came within a few feet of capturing Father, for one—but we got through them fine. So did our secret cargo."

"Secret cargo?"

"A Missouri slave we ran into. Said that he had heard of Mister John Brown and that he would be mighty glad if we could carry him to Iowa. So, we did, under a heap of hay. He got a job in Tabor, Iowa right away."

"So, you did free a slave after all."

"We did. It's good to know that one man, at least, is better for our coming to Kansas." He looked around him. "Ohio again. I've mixed feelings, as you can guess, but in a way it's good to be back. Even though I've no idea what the future holds for us, other than some role in my father's rather mysterious plan."

"We'll find out together, won't we?"

"No doubt." He took her hand. "So, Mrs. Brown, are you ready to begin again?"

She kissed him. "I am, sir."

Part III

Annie

14

June 1856 to July 1859

Annie spent much of 1856 trying to figure out whether her father and brothers were murderers. In late June, her mother had been reading aloud a letter from her father in Kansas—a litany of disasters, including Brother John's madness, his and Jason's imprisonment, and the sacking of Lawrence—when she had read the words, *We were accused,* then stopped short.

Accused of what? What had Mother censored? Annie could not be at peace until she found out. Fortunately, her mother could never bring herself to destroy a letter from her father, and she had sorely underestimated Annie's curiosity, so Annie had only to procure the letter while her mother was cooking, then take it out with her to feed the chickens. While the chickens enjoyed a nice meal, Annie quickly scanned the letter to arrive at the words:

We were accused of murdering five men at Pottawatomie, and great efforts have since been made by the Missourians and their ruffian allies to capture us.

Murder? She read and re-read the letter, going through it more slowly each time, but at no point could she see a denial of the accusation.

Could it be true? Certainly, Kansas, judging from the family letters and the newspaper accounts, was a wild and lawless place where anything could happen and apparently did. But surely . . .

Diligently, Annie eavesdropped on Mother's conversations with Watson, but only learned a great deal about crops for her trouble. They probably knew no more than she did anyway. She scoured the newspapers but could find no more than the fact that Father had indeed been accused. How strange it had been the first time she picked up a newspaper and realized that the Browns mentioned in it were not just any Browns, but Father and the boys!

Then the boys and Henry Thompson straggled home from Kansas. All were in various states of disrepair, with Henry and Salmon still suffering from their gunshot wounds and Oliver skinny and shaking from ague. Either because Salmon and Oliver didn't want to alarm Mother with their stories, or perhaps just because Kansas had worn them out, they didn't have much to say for themselves but were content to appreciatively munch their food—plain enough, but far better than what they had had in Kansas—and enjoy the luxury of actual beds and a roaring fire that didn't smoke a bystander to death. Mostly, they teased Watson, who had been finding a lot of excuses to visit the Thompson farm in the past few months. His interest had coincided precisely with the arrival home of the Thompsons' only daughter, Bell, who had been teaching school but had come back to North Elba to help on her family's farm.

Annie bore this as long as she could. Finally, though, she cornered Oliver as he was chopping some wood. After he had completed a stroke, she said, "Oliver, Father said he and the rest of you were accused of murdering some men in Kansas."

"We were accused of lots of things in Kansas."

"But this was murder. And the newspaper mentioned it too. Something must have happened."

"Nothing that you need to worry about."

"So, something did happen."

"It was more in the way of self-defense. Now stop pestering me."

Annie stared at him. "You did actually kill someone?"

"I told you, stop pestering me. Go!"

"Let him be," Mother said. Annie hadn't even noticed her approach, although Mother, being tall and somewhat stout, was not exactly built for sneaking up on people. She took Annie's shoulder and firmly turned her in the direction of their house. "He doesn't like to talk about what happened there."

It was at least an acknowledgment on her mother's part that something had happened. "The murders?"

"Annie, you're too young to know about these things."

"But I do know," Annie pointed out. "I read the papers."

"Your father and the boys thought their lives were in danger. Theirs and everyone else's. That's all I know, and all I really care to know. We weren't there, and it isn't for us to judge."

Annie did not press further. There was a limit to what one could get out of Mother, and she had apparently reached it. But her mother added, quite gratuitously, "Don't press the boys too much. They went through a lot there. Sometimes I think Kansas broke their hearts."

~ ~ ~

It was not long after that when their hearts broke again. Frederick had been murdered.

Mother, who was not much for crying, stole off by herself and wept while Salmon vowed to go to Kansas to kill the Reverend White. Then Watson—gentle, easygoing Watson—announced his intent to accompany him. Mother barely tried to talk either out of it. She'd been more of a mother, less of a stepmother to Frederick than to any of Dianthe's other children.

But the boys met up with Father on their way to Kansas, and he sent them back, forbidding them to take vengeance against White, who, to the general disappointment of the other Browns, remained unmurdered. As if nothing at all unusual had gone on for the past few months, Watson turned his attention back to Bell Thompson, and Salmon soon took an interest in a girl of his own, Abbie Hinckley.

In early February, Father turned up along with Owen. They both looked rather gaunt and pale, although their clothing was in unexpectedly good shape—nothing like the tatters in which the boys and Henry Thompson had arrived home. He and Mother embraced in their usual unshowy style, but Mother brushed something off her face afterward, and Father was a little hoarse when he turned his attention to the children. One by one, he greeted them all, except for little Ellen, who fled behind Mother. Named for the sister who had died just before they moved to North Elba, Ellen, the baby of the family, had been only about a year old when Father had left for Kansas in 1855. "I'm afraid she doesn't remember you," Mother said.

"What if I sing you my favorite hymn before you go to sleep tonight?" Father asked Ellen. "Would you like that?"

While Ellen considered this from her place of safety, Annie asked boldly, "Are you staying put here, Father?"

The older Brown children had often told the younger ones that they could get away with things the children from their father's first marriage never could. Father did not scold Annie for her impertinence but said mildly, "We shall see."

"Ellen won't forget you again if you do stay."

"Very true." Father sighed.

Shortly after that, Father asked Mother to show him around the farm. Annie hoped he wouldn't be upset. Although he had regularly dispensed advice about its management, the mails from Kansas had been such that it often came too late. Oftentimes, Mother had already done something quite different, and even when the advice was timely, Mother was entirely capable of ignoring it. While eavesdropping, Annie had heard her tell Watson that she'd been farming on her own too long to not know what she was doing.

Finally, they reappeared, looking solemn and chilled. Neither said anything of consequence until the next afternoon, when everyone walked over to Henry and Ruth's house. Ruth had a baby girl—yet another Ellen—born while Henry was in Kansas and didn't want to take her out in the cold. Father wrapped up their own Ellen carefully and carried her himself. She seemed to be warming a bit toward him.

Ruth, knowing Watson's proclivities, had invited Bell Thompson to spend the evening, and her brother Dauphin, the youngest member of the large Thompson clan, was there as well. He was a handsome lad with a cloud of curly blond hair. Babies loved him, and Ruth's was no exception. He was one of the few people who could soothe that very fussy infant, and so it was he who was holding her when the Browns entered the house. Annie suspected that Ruth and Mother regarded him as a future husband for her—once she reached the proper age, of course—so she greeted him rather coolly. She had every intention of deciding this matter for herself and was in no hurry to do so.

With tears, Ruth greeted her father, then with the other women's help turned to the practical business of getting dinner ready. Father led them in prayer, which his sons endured politely. None of them shared their father's faith anymore. Annie herself had her doubts, although she had not yet acquainted anyone with that besides her friend Martha Brewster.

With the prayers and the meal over, Father said, "I regret to say that my stay at North Elba will be a short one, much as I would wish it longer.

"When I watched Osawatomie burn, stood over the grave of our poor Frederick, and saw the scars on John's wrists, I realized that there was never going to be a peaceful solution to the scourge of slavery. And these are just the sufferings of white men. My health has not been good lately, and although the Lord may grant me more years, I have decided to devote what remains of my life to eradicating slavery from this land by whatever means necessary. I do not flatter myself that I alone can accomplish this, but I mean to do my part, in Kansas or elsewhere. But to do it right, I need funds, and it is seeking those funds that has kept me away from you and will draw me back again."

"Mr. Gerrit Smith?" Ruth asked.

"Him and others. There are several men around Boston who have shown an interest in my work and who have the means to support it. One has introduced me to another, and that one to another, and so on."

"And bought you clothes," Annie said.

"You miss nothing, child." Father looked around him. "I hope that some of you, if not all of you, will join me in my endeavor when the time is right. I know that for some, what happened in Kansas is a raw wound. I will not press anyone as yet, but Owen for one has made his choice already and will be in for any fight."

Owen nodded modestly.

"I know this calls for a sacrifice on your mother's part. I have spoken to her, and although I must admit that I would probably follow my own course regardless, I have gained her consent to what I must do. I do not forget how much she has put up with in the past, and what she will in the future."

"I'd like to help," Dauphin said, jiggling the baby. "Can I, sir?

"Certainly, if your father consents."

Bell, who had taken advantage of the attention being riveted on Father to slip her hand into Watson's, sighed very faintly.

~ ~ ~

Having announced his plans, Father did not linger. The very next day, after breakfast, he bade them a tender farewell and set off with Owen, promising to write to them regularly.

"You're not sad that Father spent so little time with us?" Annie asked as she helped with the dishes that evening. "He was gone for so long."

"Of course, I'm sad, but he is doing noble work, and as he said, he needs me here minding the farm so he can do it." Mother handed her a sopping dish, which Annie dried somewhat haphazardly. "Besides, I took a vow with your father and the older boys. Ruth was too young, and so was poor Frederick."

"When, Ma?"

"Oh, it must have been twenty years ago, well before we moved to Akron, back when—back before those deaths in Richfield. It wasn't so long after the murder of that poor man Elijah Lovejoy in Illinois. I'm sure you've heard your father speak of him."

Annie nodded; it was a tale she knew better than anything from a storybook. "Yes, he was killed protecting his printing press from a mob. A pro-slavery mob."

"It upset your father dreadfully. He was visiting his father in Hudson at the time, and there was a meeting at the church there to honor Mr. Lovejoy's memory. Your father stood up after the sermon and swore that he would devote the rest of his life to ending slavery. It was probably not long after this that he asked us to do the same. Of course, we all agreed."

"Because he asked you to?"

Her mother wrung out the dishcloth. "No. Because it was for the right."

~ ~ ~

For the time being, though, no one else at North Elba showed much inclination for Father's plan. Oliver went to Connecticut to work for a man there—a venture supported by both his parents, who thought that the guerilla life in Kansas had made him a bit wild. Watson and Salmon were busy with their farm duties and with their girls, not necessarily in that order. Brother John and Jason, back in Ohio, were farming. Henry Thompson, still feeling some effects from his wound, did what he could on his farm and enjoyed his new daughter.

The boys are resolved to learn and practice war no more, Mother wrote to Father. His return letter, which Mother of course read to the family, was philosophical enough, but still Annie brooded over the matter. Was he disappointed in the boys? It was a pity she couldn't make it up to him by going herself. Even Wealthy had wielded a weapon in Kansas, albeit without having to use it. Annie knew, though, that Father wouldn't approve of her going at her age—just over thirteen—even if she wasn't laboring under the disability of being a girl. He had been reluctant to let young Oliver go to Kansas, although in the end, Oliver had just up and went anyway.

Annie felt even worse when Father, who had fallen ill with the ague that still plagued him from time to time, came home in early April to recuperate. But he said little about his plans and allowed Mother to nurse him, much to her gratification. With her ministrations, he was soon well enough to stand in the Thompson parlor and watch Watson marry Bell. "It's good to have another Thompson in the family," he said, surprising Bell by kissing her on the cheek.

Annie studiously ignored Dauphin's glance in her direction. She was way too young to worry herself with that sort of thing.

The wedding was barely over when Father announced his intention to set off; he planned to do a little more fundraising before finally heading to Kansas. When he might return to North Elba, no one knew, so this time, Annie watched for her chance to catch him alone. "Father," she asked coaxingly, "what happened with those men in Kansas? Doyle and the rest?"

To her father's credit, he didn't tell her that it was nothing for her to trouble her silly girlish head about. "It is something about which I care not to speak."

237

"But can you tell me if you and the boys killed them, yes or no? I won't blame you if you say yes."

Her father gave a glimmer of a smile. "That is very rational and thoughtful of you. Still, it is a question I prefer not to answer."

"But—"

"You're a clever girl. I think you know the answer to that question already."

She did, in fact. It was written on the faces of all the boys, and it explained their war-weariness now. With her father all but confirming her belief, she found that her love for all of them had not lowered a whit. "I wish I could help in Kansas."

"You're better off staying here and going to school. This country needs more sensible women. And the conditions there were very, very hard. The ague is as vicious as the Border Ruffians."

"Wealthy and Ellen went."

"They were grown women. I had no say over their choices. I'm not sure their husbands did either; they can be rather forceful ladies when they care to be. You are too young and, to be quite frank, you would be a drag upon the rest because our first concern would have to be your safety. I cannot let you go to Kansas." Seeing her scowl, he added, "But that does not mean I may not need your help in other ways, or that you cannot be of use when you are older. In the meantime, you can be most helpful by assisting your mother with the farm. I think I have made it quite clear that her service is valuable."

"Yes, but—"

"No buts."

It was clear that they had reached an impasse. Annie nodded, but as she began to retreat, her father said, "We never know what we may be called upon to do or when. Remember that, Annie."

~ ~ ~

A group of the younger people in North Elba decided to celebrate the Fourth of July with an excursion to Whiteface, the mountain that towered over North Elba. It seemed like a somewhat frivolous activity to Annie when so many were suffering, but after she was invited to go along, her pleasure in being included outweighed her misgivings. The last such outing, she had been left behind as too young.

The newlyweds, Watson and Bell, were going, and Salmon decided to go too when he learned that Abbie Hinckley would be one of the group. To allow Annie to traverse the mountain paths more easily, Mother made her a pair of bloomers, which made Annie feel both quite comfortable and quite daring, although that feeling was diminished slightly when Bell and Abbie, who were old friends, turned up in their own bloomers, which matched.

Mother herself had never been up on Whiteface. She said that she was quite content to look at it.

At dawn on the third of July, the party of twelve, mainly consisting of Browns, Hinckleys, and Thompsons, set off on their journey. From Paradox Lake, they sailed up Lake Placid, where they docked and walked to the foot of the mountain. There, Annie studied the expanse of white stone created by a landslide years before that gave Whiteface its name. Brother John, who was reported to be quite sane now but still prone to fits of melancholy, would appreciate a detailed description of it. With that in mind, she collected a few stones to add to his collection of specimens.

"Better not weigh your pockets down too much before we climb," Simeon Hasbrook warned her. A few years older than Annie, he was the eldest son of one of the black families who had settled in the area. Annie supposed it was a sign of progress that he felt as free to tell her her business as the white members of the party. Still, it wasn't bad advice, so she carefully placed her stones in a pile to retrieve later.

After a rest, they began their ascent. Over the years, the mountain had attracted its fair share of climbers, like the Mr. Dana who had stopped by their cabin years before. There was a sufficiently worn path for them to tread without too much difficulty, although Abbie proved to be rather slower than the rest. Fortunately, Salmon was there to help her along.

Watson devoted his attention to Bell, leaving the rest of the men and boys to assist Annie when needed—not that it was often necessary, as Annie was as good a walker as any of them. Holding the stick that Watson had provided her, she made her way carefully along the trail, inhaling the delightful scent of the trees that lined the path. It was her favorite thing about the summer in these parts, aside from the respite of its being summer.

By early afternoon, they had reached the summit of the mountain. As the men planted a flag on top to mark their success, Annie found an accommodating rock on which to sit and stared around her. What a heavenly view! She could see the Green Mountains of Vermont, the St. Lawrence River, and Lake Champlain—even the boats skittering upon it. She felt simultaneously very tall and very small.

As she gazed around her, she felt an intense ache of loneliness, a strange thing to feel surrounded by so many people, but felt nonetheless. Was it Father's absence, so prolonged before, and now indefinite? Poor Frederick's death? Watson's marriage? Or was it something to do with the monthly bleeds that had begun troubling her a while back, much to her disgust? Thanks to Ruth, as well as to Annie's general ability to pick up on things, Annie hadn't really needed the talk Mother had given her the first time she had one, but no one had told her that she would have the blues for two or three straight days prior to a bleed. Perhaps it was different for other girls. Annie had been told by various people that she tended to take things harder than other people. There was a theory that this was because her mother had undergone so much sorrow with those four children dying while Annie was in the womb. Annie sometimes wondered if she'd been a poor substitute.

A tear coursed down her face just as Watson's hand, firm but gentle, rested on her shoulder. It sent another tear splashing down. Watson had hardly spoken a private word to her since his marriage. In her head, Annie knew that this was perfectly reasonable, but in her heart, she missed him dreadfully.

"Are you all right, Annie? You've been quiet today."

"I've been concentrating on the trail." But she knew Watson knew better, so she said, "I'm just out of sorts, that's all. I don't know why. It's so pretty up here."

"When the girls are gabbing together tonight—if Salmon lets Abbie, that is—we'll look at the stars together. How's that?"

She brushed a tear away irritably. "I'd like that."

They camped a little ways down the mountain, on the Wilmington side. The fire smoked terribly—Salmon said that it reminded him of Kansas—and they could hardly sleep, so they passed the time telling stories and singing. Bell had a nice, clear voice, not as good as Wealthy's but still quite serviceable. Annie had to give her credit for that. And although Watson's plans for looking at the stars did not quite go as planned—Salmon and Abbie proved to be inseparable and given to lurking at the outer perimeter of the fire to spare Abbie from the smoke—Bell obligingly talked with her brother William while Watson and Annie admired the stars. It was a splendid night for stargazing, with both Dippers present.

"I've been thinking about going to California," Watson said.

She turned to him in horror. "California! Why, that's so much farther than Kansas!"

"Yes, but I keep thinking I should be a bit more adventurous."

"You should have thought of that before you got married."

"Funny, that's what Bell said. Of course, we'd go together, or I'd send for her once I got safely settled."

"I just wish people would stay put for a bit."

"Well, it's not a certainty yet. And who knows? You might get a hankering for the west yourself."

"Maybe," Annie said dubiously. "You don't want to go to Kansas?"

"No, not after all that happened there." He studied the stars. "I feel guilty for saying that with Father and Owen headed out there, but that's the truth of it."

"Do you wish you'd killed that man Martin White?"

"Sometimes. But then I wouldn't want it on my conscience. Not I think that Frederick's death troubles his." He glanced up at the sky again. "I'm not a spiritualist, but I do like to think that Frederick's presence is with us. I feel it in nature. He was a good brother to us boys. He got us out of fixes with Father plenty of times by covering up for us. It does bother me that he sacrificed his life for the cause while I've done so little."

"You've done more than I have. I even offered to go to Kansas with Father. He wouldn't let me."

Watson kindly did not reiterate the annoying facts that she was a girl and but thirteen. Instead, he said, "You never know what might happen. Now shall we attend to the stars again?"

She assented happily. When everyone at last made a feint at sleeping, she was one of the few who actually managed it.

~ ~ ~

A few weeks after this, a stranger turned up at the Brown house. This wasn't so unusual these days; in the years since the Browns had settled in North Elba, more people had come to explore the beauties of the area, and Henry Thompson and others had even started earning money guiding them around. He was driving a buckram wagon of the sort that the Browns and most of their neighbors had, but he did not seem particularly adept at it. Amused, Annie watched his progress from the doorway, which was open to let the breeze in. Fortunately, Salmon and Watson (who, to everyone's relief, seemed disinclined for California for now) were working nearby and stopped to talk to the stranger. Presently, Salmon took charge of the horse and wagon, and Watson led his visitor to the house. He was a dark, rather good-looking young man, no more than thirty, but he was not dressed for hiking, camping, or fishing; he wore the type of clothing that Annie associated with Boston, although she had never been there. "Ma," Watson said, "we have a visitor. Mr. Frank Sanborn of Concord, Massachusetts."

As Annie congratulated herself on getting at least the state right, the man took off his citified hat. "Mrs. Brown, I am honored to meet you. Perhaps your husband has mentioned me to you?"

To Annie's surprise, Mother nodded. "Many times."

"Your husband is engaged in a noble cause, Mrs. Brown, and he has told us of the support and loyalty you have offered to him. It has been a concern of his that should something befall him, you and your daughters would be left dest—"

Mother drew herself up. "I have told him often that we would manage, and that he need not distress himself."

"Precisely what he said," Mr. Sanborn said. "He told me that you had gone so far as to take in washing while the men were in Kansas."

"I did."

"I helped," Annie said.

Mr. Sanborn included her in his approving glance. "Still, your husband's friends have determined to relieve his anxiety because his concern is our concern. We have taken a collection to purchase one hundred sixty acres of land contracted for by Mr. Brown, which I understand to be owned by Mr. Henry Thompson's brothers, and to place it in the names of you and Mrs. Ruth Thompson. It will provide some security for you. And I expect that when all is paid for, there will be twenty dollars or so to spare, which shall be turned over to you."

"Contracted for by my husband? I knew nothing of such a plan." Mother frowned, then added hastily, "Of course, I am grateful for the kindness of his friends. Do come in and have something to eat."

Mr. Sanborn agreed and was soon seated in what Annie thought of as Father's chair, although Mother used it more than anyone else. To his credit, he didn't turn his nose up at the little sitting area, although Annie knew as well as anyone else that it wasn't much of one, which wasn't to say that Henry Thompson hadn't done a fine job of building their house. It just was very simple, especially when she remembered Mr. and Mrs. Perkins's grand house in Akron. Even their plain frame house in Springfield compared favorably to this place. Still, Mr. Sanborn looked around him as closely as was polite, as if he were impressing the scene on his memory.

Mother had nothing fancier to serve than tea and toast, but Mr. Sanborn seemed to enjoy it. Soon it emerged that he had grown up on a farm but had ended up at Harvard, which had pretty much wiped out all traces of the farm. A man named Ralph Waldo Emerson, whose name was vaguely familiar to Annie, had helped him set up a school in Concord. Annie gathered it was somewhat of a more rarefied affair than the little red schoolhouse which she still attended, somewhat reluctantly, in North Elba. Their teacher had to do several jobs to get by, which probably wasn't the case with Mr. Sanborn.

"Are you married, Mr. Sanborn?" Mother asked.

"I am a widower." Before Mother could respond with the expected condolences, Mr. Sanborn added, "It's an odd story; my wife was a few years older than I was and encouraged me to improve myself before I married her. It was much because of her influence that I went to Harvard. She was always delicate, but I learned while I was at school that she was fading quickly and did not have long to live. I hurried home and married her, and eight days later, she was dead."

Annie had never heard anything so romantic in her life.

Later, though, she wondered if she should have heeded the warning and realized that Mr. Sanborn had somewhat of a passion for hopeless causes.

~ ~ ~

In just a couple of days, Mr. Sanborn had completed his business and handed the deeds to the land to Mother and Ruth, along with twenty-five dollars. "I hope I don't seem ungrateful," Mother said as he prepared to leave. "I certainly do thank you and the others for doing this. It's just strange to have him planning all of this as if he doesn't expect to return."

"It's no different from his insuring his life, Mrs. Brown. Simply a precaution."

"That's a good way to look at it," Mother conceded. But she was quieter than usual for the next few days, even as she took out her pen and paper and figured out to the penny how the windfall could best be spent.

~ ~ ~

In October, Salmon finally married Abbie in her family's parlor. Given Abbie's personality, which was a forceful one, Annie was surprised the wedding hadn't happened sooner. Mother, who had been pleased enough about Watson's wedding, seemed even more pleased about this one. She made Annie and her sisters new dresses for the occasion, and even refurbished her own best dress. Not since she had taken the notion to have a daguerreotype made of herself, Annie, and Sarah a few years back had she made so much fuss over clothing. "I think this will be good for Salmon," Mother said as Watson drove them home. "Abbie will settle him."

"That's putting it mildly," Watson said dryly.

Mother ignored this rare bit of snideness from Watson. "Now there's just Oliver to go. And, of course, Owen."

"Oh, Owen is a hopeless bachelor," Watson said.

"And busy in Father's service," Annie said wistfully.

They were quiet, thinking of Father. What were he and Owen up to? From what they could tell from the newspapers, Kansas was rather peaceful at the moment. The last they had heard, Father himself was at Tabor, Iowa, putting his small band of men on a more warlike footing. His future movements were uncertain. Not even the newspapers, which had been full of his exploits in 1856, had had anything to say about him recently. It was almost as if he didn't exist.

~ ~ ~

By early 1858, Oliver was back in North Elba. After persuading the one tavern in the area to stop selling whiskey, he began to devote himself to a new cause: Martha Brewster, Annie's good friend. Martha was pretty and blond, noted in North Elba for her refined manners and for being the best turned-out girl at Sunday meeting. Annie would have thought that to be frippery had she not known how hard Martha worked for her finery—she hired herself out to all of the housewives in the area to do chores and fine sewing, all because her father, who was not well regarded, could not be bothered to outfit her and her sisters properly. Oliver could harp for hours about the indignities heaped upon her.

After yet another sermon from Oliver about Martha's plight, Mother said quietly, "Oliver, are you in love with the girl?"

"In love?"

"I mean, son, you certainly seem to have her on your mind a great deal. She's pretty and quite sweet."

"I'm just interested in her well-being," Oliver said. "And in justice."

But the next Sunday, he turned up at meeting—hardly his natural habitat—looking uncommonly well turned-out himself, and he offered to walk Martha to the house where she was working. Soon he was finding more excuses to walk with her, each more ridiculous and hopelessly transparent than the last.

"People always did think your brother was slow in some ways," Mother said. "But once he gets hold of an idea, he grasps it quickly."

Annie looked out the window and spotted Oliver and Martha by a tree. If they stood closer together, they would need a marriage license. "He certainly does."

While Oliver and Martha's relationship was progressing, just as the spring of 1858 arrived—on the calendar in chilly North Elba, at least—Father came home. Ellen, who had become tolerably used to him at his last visit, took one look at him and scurried behind Mother, for Father had a noticeable beard. "It is a disguise in part, but it is also easier than operating clean-shaven in the field," he explained in response to their chorus of comments.

Father had left Owen in Iowa but had Brother John with him. Annie watched John carefully, but he showed no signs of insanity, although he was not as talkative as he had been in days past. After she had observed him for some time at supper at Henry and Ruth's house, he turned to her and smiled. "I hope you're not expecting some ranting or raving out of me."

Annie blushed. "I'm sorry."

"No matter. People can't help but wonder after what happened. Do you want to see the scars?"

She nodded with some trepidation, and John slid back his sleeves, cut longer than was normal, to reveal a distinct ringed scar on each wrist. Annie shuddered. "I can't imagine how much that hurt."

"That time still affects my spirits now and then. Fortunately, I have a most excellent wife who puts up with my gloomy spells."

It was flattering, but also somewhat awkward, to have her oldest brother confiding in her thus. "How is Wealthy?" Annie asked after a too-long pause.

"Good. She's happy to be back near her sisters and family."

"And Johnny?" She wondered if he was still slow for his age, but that would be an even more awkward conversation.

"Doing well. He has collected a whole menagerie around him. When I left, his cat was ready to have kittens." His smile, which had been somewhat forced before, turned genuine. "I enjoyed the letter you sent about the camping trip, in case I did not tell you adequately in my return letter. If it was summer, I would climb it myself."

Father, having led everyone in less than enthusiastic prayers (at least Mother and Ruth did their part), had been somewhat quiet during the meal, devoting his attention to little Ellen, who had sufficiently overcome her fear of her father's beard to sit beside him. When the table was cleared and the dishes washed, and the younger children had been sent to the next room to play, he said, "There is something I wish to say to all of you who are old enough to be trusted to hear it. I have included you, Annie, because I know you can keep a secret. Can you?"

Annie nodded, then realized a nod was not good enough. "Yes, sir."

"Good. Do not make me regret taking you into my confidence. I will not be returning to Kansas. I have determined to go to the mountains of Virginia—with a body of men, of course—and free what slaves we can—"

Mother gasped. "Like you told Mr. Douglass so long ago."

"Why, yes, how did you know?"

"I overheard."

Unperturbed, Father went on. "I have indeed been turning this idea over for many years, waiting for the right time, and perhaps thinking that it might be attempted—more effectively attempted—by others. But the thought has occurred to me that the Lord has ordained that I am the one to undertake it. I do not say that boastfully, merely as a matter of fact. At the same time, I have come to believe that there is nothing to be gained by waiting any longer. Every day of delay, more are born into bondage, and more die in it. So, with a group of well-trained men, black and white, who are avid for the cause, I shall first go to Canada, and from then, onto the South."

John, whose expression showed that none of this was news to him, said, "You may wonder about Canada. The hills of Virginia will not only be a base for our operations; it will be a refuge for those slaves who escape from their masters. So naturally, it will require a government. Father has drafted a preliminary constitution for it. That and the details of his plan will be discussed in Canada at a town called Chatham, which is home to many fugitive slaves."

"Do you have weapons?" Mother asked.

"A very practical question," Father said approvingly. "We do, my dear. John has been storing them for us in Ashtabula County. I should add that for now, John will not be joining us in the South, but has been and will be assisting in a myriad of other ways. Wealthy knows of the plan too and approves of it. And this brings me to my next point. I know my dear wife wrote that those of you who had been in Kansas wished to make war no more. I understand, and yet I hope at least some of you will change your minds. I will not press you today; I know all of you wish to think upon the matter, and some of you must consult with your wives."

Mother did not point out that Father had not consulted with her.

As the boys began to pepper Father with questions, Annie listened. Leading slaves into the hills? Setting up one's own government? It would have all seemed a bit mad if poor John had proposed it. No one seemed shocked, though, but sat calmly discussing the various aspects of Father's plan as if every father in America had contemplated freeing the slaves and drawing up his own constitution at some point in his life.

"Father? Do Mr. Sanborn and the rest know about your idea?"

"Of course, Annie, at least the vital parts of it. And they approve of it."

This seemed somehow reassuring.

~ ~ ~

Salmon refused to take part in the plan. He thought it ill-advised, although Annie suspected that Abbie had had a say in the matter. Certainly, Ruth had a role in Henry Thompson's decision to stay aloof; he still suffered from the effect of the bullet he had taken in Kansas, she told Father, and she simply could not bear to put him at risk again, especially now that he was a father three times over, Ruth having borne another daughter just weeks before. Watson, however, agreed to join in if he could be spared from the farm. And Oliver agreed as well, although he said that he first had some business to take care of.

The nature of the business became clear in mid-April, not long after Father had started on his way to Canada, when Oliver came in to breakfast, clearly with something on his mind. "Ma," he said finally. "Do you think you might have time to make a cake?"

"What kind of cake?"

"Well, a wedding cake, actually."

"For you and Martha?"

Oliver nodded. "That's the size of it. I was going to wait until she got a little older"—Martha was fifteen, a year older than Annie—"but with father's plan, I wanted her to have a claim upon the family in case anything happened to me."

"Of course, she will have a claim upon us. When were you planning to marry?"

"I thought this evening would be good. The justice of the peace is free."

"What do her people say about this?"

"They say we're half crazy, or maybe not half, and that Martha is a fool for marrying me. Otherwise, they're not opposed."

Mother's jaw set. "Annie, go over to Salmon's and see if Abbie can do some cooking. I'll get started on the cake. Sarah, fix up the parlor. We're going to have a beautiful wedding."

And so they did. Sarah, who had an artistic bent, decorated the parlor with ribbons and a few of the flowers that had ventured out of hiding, and Abbie and Salmon rode over with a freshly baked ham. Annie, who was a decent enough seamstress when she cared to be, mended Oliver's best coat, then gave it a good brushing. Even Ruth, busy with her little baby, found the time to fashion a wedding veil. When Martha arrived with Oliver and her younger brother Byron, the latter bearing Martha's worldly goods in a small trunk, the scent of freshly baked cake filled the house. "It's the wedding day I always dreamed of," Martha said as Annie and Mother helped put on her veil.

Mother patted Martha on her shoulder. "I don't think Oliver could have possibly chosen better."

Although Byron, who had worked for the Browns from time to time, was the only member of Martha's family at the wedding, some of the blacks who still lived in North Elba attended, as did a few of the Thompsons and the Hinckleys, so the parlor turned out to be quite full. When the justice of the peace, whom everyone knew, began to ask Martha if she would love, honor, and obey Oliver, the groom said, "Not obey. That's tyranny," and the officiant nodded resignedly and went on with the ceremony. When everyone had pronounced the refreshments delicious and congratulated the couple, they all cleared out of the house, including Mother and the girls, who had arranged to spend the night at Henry and Ruth's so the newlyweds could enjoy an evening of privacy.

"Now you're next," Sarah said to Annie as the wagon jounced its way to the Thompsons'.

"Not anytime soon."

"Dauphin Thompson might want to change that."

"How would you know?" It was true that Dauphin had attended the wedding and had stood next to Annie, but they had been so tightly packed in the parlor that he had been standing close to three other people as well.

"Girls!"

Sarah crossed her arms. "I have eyes and ears," she hissed.

~ ~ ~

But Oliver's hasty wedding was for naught, because in June, a disappointed-looking Father returned to North Elba. The convention in Chatham had been a success, with a good turnout of local supporters. But disruption had come in the form

253

of a man named Hugh Forbes, an Englishman with a revolutionary background whom Father had engaged to drill his men back in Iowa. When the two fell out over tactics and money, Mr. Forbes had attempted to blackmail Father and his supporters and had then gone to Washington, D.C. to tell his tale. Although he had found few listeners in the Capitol, one had taken him seriously enough to give the alarm to Father's supporters in Massachusetts—by now, they had a name for themselves: the Secret Committee of Six—who had conferred and insisted that Father confound the tattling Mr. Forbes by postponing his Southern plan and returning to Kansas.

"Perhaps it's for the best," Mother said. "You'll have more time to plan and recruit."

Father agreed, albeit without a great deal of enthusiasm, but did indeed go to Kansas. For months, they heard little of him other than periodic assurances that he had not succumbed to the ague, so the North Elba contingent of conspirators began to lose heart. Oliver began to talk about moving to Ashtabula County, Ohio, the abolitionist nest where Brother John lived. Watson sold what livestock and household goods he had and set off for California, intending to send for Bell once he got established. In the end he got no farther than New York City, where he was cheated out of his passage money, and he returned to Bell and North Elba in a sheepish, penniless condition.

Then, just after 1859 rolled around, the Browns opened the newspaper to find that around Christmas, Father had made a run into Missouri and liberated eleven slaves from their masters. That was an accomplishment in itself, but evading the law and the professional slave-catchers was another thing; for weeks, the Browns hurried to the post office to get the once-a-week delivery of newspapers so they could follow

Father's perilous passage north. Soon they learned that the number of people in their father's charge had increased to twelve; one woman had given birth while in hiding.

At last, in March, the newspaper informed them that the escapees had safely reached Detroit and boarded the ferry to Windsor, Canada. "That will please his friends," Mother said as the family's cheers died down, and so it did. Soon, Father was back in North Elba with an announcement: the Southern plan was back on.

For weeks, Father made his rounds, gathering funds and meeting with his supporters, while in North Elba, Mother, with the girls' help, made bandages, assembled medicines, and put the men's summer clothes in order. She directed these proceedings calmly and was as intolerant of slacking off as a factory forewoman might have been—indeed, Annie was inclined to think that her mother might have had some aptitude in that direction—but Annie caught her from time to time looking pensive, and on more than one occasion, on her knees praying. "Are you frightened?" Annie asked in her straightforward way.

It was flattering to Annie that Mother did not brush her off with some soothing reply. "Of course, I am. It has always been my greatest fear that your father would fall into the hands of his enemies, and he is walking into the midst of them there. But it is in God's hands." She gave a very faint smile. "At least, as far as your father will allow it."

In June, Father and Jeremiah Anderson, a young man Father had met in Kansas, stopped by North Elba and then left with Owen and Oliver for the South, promising to send for Watson and anyone else in due time. "Remember, I shall be known as Isaac Smith," Father told them as he embraced them all in turn. "And therefore you will be Smiths as well when you write to me."

Annie wished he had come up with something more interesting.

But just a few weeks later, Oliver appeared back in North Elba. "Why, what are you doing here?" Mother asked.

Oliver spoke the next words casually, as if they were of no consequence whatsoever. As if Annie would not spend the rest of her life remembering them.

"To fetch you and Annie. You're needed down South."

15

July 1859

"Father's rented a farm in Maryland, not far from Harper's Ferry, Virginia," Oliver said to the assembled family, his arm firmly ensconced around Martha's waist. "It's set back quite a bit from the road, with neighbors on either side, though they're a ways off. Southerners are friendly, though. They'll talk your head off, as a matter of fact. They're also on the nosy side. Father's worried that people are going to come around, then get suspicious when they see a household full of men and no women. So, Father wants Mother and Annie, or maybe Annie and Martha, to come down and stay for a few weeks. Chat with the neighbors, invite them in if necessary, but keep them in the dark. The more men arrive, the more secrecy will be required, and the more we'll need their help."

Father had written in the letter Oliver carried, *I want you to come right off. It will be likely to prove the most valuable service you can ever render to the world.* Annie needed no further persuading.

But Mother read the letter again and frowned. "He says it would be fine to leave Ellen here, and I'm sure that she and Sarah would be well taken care of, but she's never been away from me. What if we had to stay there longer than your father thinks? And the weather? Is it as bad as Kansas?"

"It can be miserable," Oliver said. "Hot and humid. Like walking around in a wet wool blanket."

"If I took her, she might fall ill like poor Austin. And I know Bell has her own mother to help her, but she's so far gone with child, I hate to leave her. But I don't want to disappoint your father."

Martha said, "He did say that Annie and I could come instead. I would like to go and be with Oliver."

Oliver squeezed Martha's hand. "I'm sure the two of them will please Father."

"Yes, I suppose so." Mother sighed. "Still, I feel that I'm letting him and his cause down. But I just don't feel right about leaving Ellen or taking her. And—"

"And what, Ma?" Oliver asked.

"I just don't know if I can lie to all those people."

"I can," Annie said.

"I'll do my best," Martha put in.

But Annie doubted that Martha had much of a talent for this either. Annie would have to supply the deficiency.

~ ~ ~

"I heard you're going down South," Dauphin Thompson said. He had somehow materialized in the Browns' yard. Since it was laundry day and a second pair of hands was always useful for hanging clothes, Annie couldn't really complain.

Somewhat to the annoyance of the rest of the family, Annie had not fallen in love with Dauphin, who at twenty-one was the youngest of the Thompson clan. There was nothing at all objectionable about him; indeed, in a larger place than North Elba, he probably would have had quite a following. He was tall and well-built, with light blue eyes and a head of curly blond hair, and he worked hard on his father's farm. He didn't smoke or drink, and the only time Annie had ever seen him lose his temper was when someone around him had been mistreating a horse. He hadn't been a star of North Elba's red schoolhouse, but he hadn't been a dunce either, and he did like to read. If he had a flaw, it was perhaps that he had hardly ever been out of North Elba and didn't seem to mind.

But he did support Father's cause, so Annie bestowed a smile upon him. "Yes, we're going as soon as everything is ready."

"I'll be going when Watson goes. I'm eager to do my part." Dauphin blushed, which he often did. "I never really thought about slavery much until I heard your father speak over at the schoolhouse. He really opened my eyes." Dauphin picked up a shirt and pinned it neatly to the line.

"Father can be very persuasive."

"He did warn us that it could be dangerous. He didn't really need to, of course; I knew that from Henry. If he'd caught the bullet just another way—well, I don't even like to think about it, and I'm sure you don't." Dauphin stared hard at a pillowcase. "Anyway, there's something I would like to ask you. You know I like you."

"You haven't done a great deal about it," Annie observed.

"I thought perhaps I should wait until you were a bit older. But we've always been friends. Haven't we?"

Annie had to concede this. She liked Dauphin, as did everyone in North Elba, and they had had some pleasant times hiking together. Although Annie preferred to walk alone, Dauphin was quiet, so he made for a reasonably good companion on these excursions. It was only now that he had developed this irksome tendency to talk. "Where are you going with this, Dauphin?"

"I'm asking if you would think about marrying me. Not if you will marry me. Just if you'll think about it."

Mother had told all the girls about her unusual proposal from Father: in writing. Brother John had declared his love for Wealthy in the freezing cold. Did strange proposals run in the family, then?

The strangest part, perhaps, was that she really couldn't say no. She liked Dauphin, and there was something pleasing about having someone devoted to her, even on this oddly informal level. Maybe watching Oliver and Martha mooning around was making her just a bit jealous. "I suppose."

"Thank you."

There was an awkward silence that even Annie thought could probably be remedied only one way. Fortunately, Dauphin had the same thought. He stooped—there was quite a difference in their height, which Annie had never had occasion to consider before—and after some deliberation, gently kissed her.

It wasn't bad at all, Annie had to admit. Still, the things that she'd read about in the novels and ladies' magazines that Wealthy or Ruth occasionally sent to her hadn't happened— no fluttering of her heart, no dizziness. Were the writers making all this up?

~ ~ ~

If their semi-engagement had been a secret—Annie wasn't sure whether it was supposed to be one—Dauphin soon let it slip, which wasn't disagreeable, as it gave Annie a dignity which she hitherto had lacked. Mother praised her good sense in accepting Dauphin, who, although he was the youngest of the Thompson sons, could expect a little land from his father, and also her good sense in not rushing to marry, as she would not be sixteen until December. There was plenty of time to know her own mind better.

In the meantime, however, there was the other family matter to see to.

With everyone's help, they were ready to set off for the South in mid-July. Even so, it had taken them longer than expected; Mother, usually so efficient, had dawdled more than usual and almost always found something else to command her time. "You must tell your father to send you girls back as soon as possible," she said for about the fifth time the morning of their departure as Annie packed some wash towels into their trunk and Martha checked the loft to make certain nothing had been left behind.

"Don't worry, Ma. He will," Oliver said. He had a tendency to be brusque, even with Mother, but marriage had softened him quite a bit. "They'll be just— Martha!"

Martha lay in a heap at the bottom of the stairs leading to the loft. "It's all right," she gasped. "I was hurrying and missed the bottom stair. Ouch!"

Oliver picked up Martha deftly and sat her on the bed. "Your ankle?"

Martha nodded as everyone gathered to stare at her ankle, which was scraped and beginning to swell. Mother took it into her hands and prodded it deftly, shaking her head whenever Martha let out a squeal of pain. "It's only a sprain,

I think, but a bad one. You can't set out for Virginia like this. You must wait until it's better."

"No." Martha drew her ankle back. "I'm going with Oliver and Annie now."

"Then maybe Oliver can wait."

Oliver shook his head. "I can't, Ma. I've kept Father waiting long enough."

Mother sighed and put a hand out to stop Martha, who was trying to wriggle off the bed. "At least let me bandage it up for you. There's a walking stick you can use too."

Martha consented, and Mother carefully bandaged it, showing Annie how to do it in her absence. "We could have used you in Kansas, Mother," Oliver said, admiring her handiwork.

"I almost wish I could go with you now. I just have a feeling."

"It's a good cause, Ma."

"I know." She sighed and embraced them one by one, holding Oliver the longest. "Godspeed you all."

~ ~ ~

It wasn't at all like Mother to just have feelings or to be teary-eyed, and that along with Martha's painful ankle put a damper on their departure. But the interest of their journey soon supplanted the gloomy atmosphere, especially for the girls, who had not been out of their near neighborhood for some time.

When they reached Troy, from which they were to travel to New York City by steamboat the next morning, Oliver consulted his watch and nodded in satisfaction. "There's something I would dearly love, Martha. Your photograph. Would you oblige?"

"Can we afford it?"

"We'll manage. When I left for the South before, all I had was that lock of your hair you gave me. I wanted so badly to look at your face."

Beside them, Annie rolled her eyes. But still, she was glad when Martha said, "All right. But I have to freshen up first at our hotel."

Oliver grinned. "Of course."

They were stopping at Father's favorite hotel, the American House, a temperance hotel. He was a frequent guest there, and a popular one, for all they had to do was mention his name to get a considerably discounted room. After they had stowed their luggage and Martha had arrayed herself in her best dress, they walked over to the daguerreotypist's, taking their time to accommodate Martha's ankle. "We can get your likeness taken too, Annie," Oliver said. "Thanks to Father's influence here, we've a little more to spare than I thought."

Annie shook her head. She disliked the only photograph of herself, taken when she was quite young, and wasn't sure that time had improved her.

"Come," Martha said, "I've never had one done, and you must keep me company. As your elder, I command you."

"Oh, if you insist."

The deed having been done, they rested and admired their photographs at the hotel after eating a good supper. Oliver and Martha had decided upon a daguerreotype of themselves, somewhat old-fashioned by then but producing an excellent likeness, as well as a tintype of Martha. Annie had also elected a tintype, which was so cheap that she'd had a couple made. Dauphin might like one, although it was hard to imagine him staring at it the same way that Oliver was gazing at Martha's likeness. One would think they were still courting.

Early the next morning, they boarded a steamer and began sailing down the Hudson River to New York. With John
and Wealthy's travails on her mind, Annie had been reluctant to travel by water, but the vessel glided silkily down the
river without incident, and the only annoyance was having
more food pressed upon them at meals than they could possibly eat. In between repasts, Oliver settled Martha into a
deck chair and propped up her ankle like a vassal serving his
queen. "This is heavenly," Martha said as they passed
through a particularly scenic bend of the river. She squeezed
Oliver's hand. "I would have never seen this in all my life if
you hadn't married me."

Oliver blushed in a way that would have made Dauphin
proud.

"It is very pretty landscape," Annie said.

"Harper's Ferry is arguably prettier, but you and Martha
can soon be the judge of that."

They passed West Point, then Sing Sing—such different
institutions!—and presently it became time to look out for New
York. Martha, who had begun to doze in her chair, had strictly
charged Oliver not to let her miss the approach to the city, but
her worrying proved to have been for naught. As a jumble of
buildings began to appear on the horizon, mothers began to
shout for their children, the men who had been enjoying the
steamer's saloon ambled out to the deck, and the crew commenced a general yelling. To spare Martha's ankle, the Browns
did not join the general stampede to dry land but waited until
the steamer had nearly emptied itself of humanity.

Annie had thought that she would be equal to New
York—after all, she had lived in Akron and Springfield—but
as they waited for the horse-drawn streetcar that would take
them to the depot, she found herself gaping around her in

the most hopelessly rustic manner she could have mustered. Women in silk bobbed in and out of carriages, careful not to catch their hoops—they all wore hoops here—on the steps. Their male companions were hardly less well dressed, wearing top hats that surely would not withstand a gust of wind and carrying walking sticks that did not seem at all required to help them walk. Those traveling by foot were for the most part attired more humbly, but the boldness with which they shoved their way along made up for any deficiencies. Annie was pleased to see a good admixture of black faces in the crowd, pushing their way along as briskly as the rest.

Oliver, who fortunately had some experience with New York, paid their fare. As the horses tugged their streetcar along its tracks, Annie continued to stare about her. Never had she seen so many edifices huddled so close together, never so many signs advertising so many different things for sale. No wonder poor Watson had been cheated when he came here; his senses had probably been completely bedazzled.

She had little enough time to gawk, though, because they were soon at the depot where they were to take the cars for Harrisburg, Pennsylvania. Martha, it turned out, had never been on a train, and to the delight of the other passengers and the conductor, Oliver sought to educate her from the workings of the engine to the intricacies of the various lines and their interconnections. "Don't worry when we tilt a little when coming to a curve," he said near the end of the disquisition. "It's quite normal."

"Don't worry, Martha," a passenger called as they approached the next curve.

Martha blushed and giggled.

Late at night, they disembarked at Harrisburg, then stumbled onto the train that would take them to Harper's

Ferry. Annie and Martha, who now considered herself an old hand at riding the rails, promptly dozed off until Oliver nudged them. "We'll be at the Ferry soon."

And soon, after their train passed through Sandy Hook, Maryland and crossed a bridge, they were.

Oliver had not exaggerated the beauty of the area. Surrounded by blue-tinted mountains, the Potomac and Shenandoah Rivers conjoined, tumbling over rocks that peeked through the water. Yet at the same time, machinery clanged around them and smoke filled the sky, for like Springfield, this was the site of a thriving federal armory.

"I'll show you a prettier view after we eat," Oliver said. "We've some time before I need to find Father."

Next to the railroad platform stood the Wager House Hotel. "Is this a temperance hotel?" Martha asked primly.

Oliver could not restrain a snort of laughter. "Lord, no. They'd abolish slavery before they'd abolish their liquor here. Come to think of it, maybe that would be the way to go about it—telling them that if they had one, they couldn't have the other. Why, look at that man; he's started early."

Martha looked disapprovingly at a man half-sauntering, half-stumbling by and clutched Oliver's arm tighter.

"Are there many slaves here?" Annie asked in a low voice.

"Some, and quite a few free blacks here as well. But there aren't that many big plantations in these parts. There's plenty of misery here, just not on a large scale."

He led the way into a hotel, where the man standing behind the counter nodded at Oliver. "Good morning, Mr. Smith."

Annie looked around in confusion before she remembered that they were all traveling under aliases. Up until now, they'd never had the occasion to state their names.

Mr. Oliver Smith nodded suavely back.

"Are you settled at the Kennedy Farm yet?"

"Not quite," said Oliver. He indicated the girls. "My wife and my sister are here to help us along."

Mr. Fouke, as Annie soon learned he was, inclined his head. "Welcome to Virginia, ladies."

Mrs. Smith and Miss Smith smiled graciously.

"Have you seen my father in town?" Oliver asked.

"Not since yesterday. I guess he's busy at the farm. Hurry, boy, the gentleman and ladies are waiting for you."

A porter bustled over and relieved them of their luggage, earning a curt nod from Oliver. When they reached their room, Oliver said, "Thank you, sir," and handed him a coin.

"Does everyone here know you, then?" Annie asked when the porter had left them.

"Pretty much. Even with all the people the armory employs, it's a small enough place for everyone to notice a stranger passing through and to inquire about his plans. So, don't forget, Father is interested in buying cattle and driving them up north."

"Not sheep?" From her years in Akron with the Perkins-Brown flock, Annie could talk sheep nearly as well as Father and the boys.

"Cattle," Oliver said firmly.

In the dining room, two gentlemen greeted Oliver, as did the waiter. Surrounded by all these Virginians, all of whom knew the Browns' business, or at least thought they did, Annie had never felt more Northern in her life.

Their breakfast over—Martha had barely touched hers—Oliver turned to the girls. "Are you up for a little climbing? It's worth it, I promise."

"I'm going to have to rest," Martha said apologetically. "Besides my ankle, I'm still tired. I don't know why; I slept beautifully last night."

"Probably the travel," Oliver said.

Annie had her own thoughts on the matter, but she kept them to herself.

Leaving Martha to her slumber, Annie and Oliver began their ascent from Harper's Ferry's Lower Town, where the armory and a few factories held sway, to the Upper Town, where the town's leading citizens dwelled. They passed the town's Catholic church, which earned a glare from Oliver (it was the Puritan in him), and then an Episcopal church, which merited only an "Almost there." Turning onto a heavily trodden path, they zigged and zagged along until they reached a clearing. There stood a large rock—or, Brother John could have told them, masses of shale piled upon each other—surmounted by a shale platform resting upon stone pillars. Beyond it lay a perfect vista of river, mountain, and sky.

"Jefferson Rock," Oliver said. "Thomas Jefferson himself stood here in 1783. He said that this was a view worth crossing the Atlantic for."

"He was right," said Annie. Not bothering with Oliver's help, she hitched up her skirts and clambered upon the platform, erected by someone in the Ferry to give some protection to the layers of shale on which Mr. Jefferson had stood. "It's splendid!"

"John Cook got married here," Oliver said. "I forgot, you don't know him, but you will soon or later. I met him in Kansas. He's quite the charmer. His sister is married to the Governor of Indiana, if that gives you an indication of the people he comes from. He's been staying here in town, picking up information for Father."

"Spying?" Annie asked.

"Well, if you put it like that, yes. Anyway, he married his landlady's daughter back in April. She's not exactly his kind, I've heard, but it was a matter of some urgency. Their baby was born in June."

"Was Father distressed?"

"Well, Cook did do his duty by her, and he's been all in for Father's plan. And he's an excellent shot. He brought down quite a few birds for us in Kansas."

After they had enjoyed the view a little longer and Oliver had added his lover's initials to the rock, as had hundreds before him, they strolled back down to the Lower Town, where the armory was humming at full speed. It was gated off from the public, of course, but from the street, Annie admired its neatly placed buildings and the fire engine house that appeared to double as the armory's guard house. Something about the latter building kept her eyes turning back to look at it.

What it was, she could not say. But still she looked and looked again.

16

July 1859

The Kennedy Farm, as the locals called it after its late owner, was ideally placed for secrecy. A modest farmhouse, it was set well back from the road, as Oliver had said, and was shielded by shrubbery. Six hundred feet behind the main house stood a small outer building nearly obscured by the growth around it. Neglected since the death of Mr. Kennedy had left his estate in litigation, both structures were home to a thriving colony of fleas, as Annie discovered her first night at the farm. They penetrated everywhere, even to the tender skin beneath her corset and chemise, and it was all she could do to stop from scratching herself as she sat on the porch with Jeremiah Anderson, Father's comrade from Kansas.

Annie hadn't paid much attention to Jerry, as he had instructed everyone to call him, when he turned up with Father in North Elba. There had simply been too much going on. Still, she had observed that he was a dark, good-looking young man in his mid-twenties, compact and of the medium height. When he had been in North Elba, he had been growing a beard, which had since come out in its full glory. It suited him.

The porch, running off the house's main living area, which sat above a floor used chiefly for storage, commanded a fine view of the blue-tinted mountains. From the porch, it was also possible to see anyone passing on the road, including a face that had become very familiar in the short time Annie had been a resident of the farm. "There's Mrs. Hoffmaster," Annie called to Martha.

"How many chicks with the hen?"

"All four of them."

A small, barefoot woman of about thirty or so with a faded sunbonnet, Mrs. Hoffmaster had rented a patch of land on the farm to grow vegetables; why she did not grow them on her own land was never clear to Annie. At least since the "Smiths" had moved in, she found it necessary to tend it at least once a day, and usually two or even three times.

Nearly always, Mrs. Hoffmaster was accompanied by some combination of her four small children, three girls and a boy. Annie, of course, had to invite the lot of them to sit on the porch and rest after they had finished their business in the garden. "It's important that we be good neighbors," Father had said when they first moved in. "Of course, that is what we are commanded to do anyway. But prudence obliges us to be especially good neighbors."

"But if we are too obliging, wouldn't that be suspicious?"

"I hadn't realized until we came here what a talent for dispute you have," Father said. He sighed. "Just use your good judgment, Annie."

Though more men were expected to come to the Kennedy Farm, for the time being there were only Father, Oliver, and Owen, along with Jerry, who had not acquired any notoriety while in Kansas and thus had no reason to assume a false name. Sometimes the men worked around the farm, improving the stabling for their horse, mule, cow, and pigs; other times, they went on scouting expeditions around the area disguised as hunting trips. Usually one man stayed on the premises just in case there was trouble, and today that man was Jerry, reading the *Baltimore Sun* on the porch. Or rather, he *had* been holding the newspaper in his hand and talking to Annie, whose spirits had rather sunk upon sighting the familiar sunbonnet.

She managed a smile, however, as Mrs. Hoffmaster waved. Jerry, whose grandparents hailed from Virginia, rose and handed Mrs. Hoffmaster and the children up the stairs one by one. "Now, Mrs. Smith is busy cleaning," he warned the children, who were edging toward the open door to the kitchen. "She gets to be a regular bear when she's cleaning, so I wouldn't go in there if I were you. It's nicer out here anyway."

Defeated, the children ranged themselves around the porch as Mrs. Hoffmaster settled onto a bench and took the water that Annie handed to her. "You were right, Mr. Anderson. It's so nice up here, I hate to leave and work in that hot garden."

"Stay as long as you like," Annie said, attacking the shirt she was mending with some ferocity.

"Now, refresh me, sir. You are kin to Mr. Smith?"

"No, ma'am. No relation. Just an old friend of the family. I thought coming down South might do my health good." This, Annie knew, had a kernel of truth; Jerry, like everyone else, had suffered from ague after Kansas.

"I don't know why, but I thought you might be fixing to marry Miss Smith."

"Well, no," Jerry said. "I have been batching it for some years and have no plans to change my status at the moment."

Mrs. Hoffmaster looked a bit disappointed. After some chatter about the Kennedy family's affairs, she took her leave, having forgotten about the garden entirely.

"Thank goodness they didn't come in," Martha said, poking her head out. "Father Brown has all these maps spread out on the kitchen table, and I was afraid I'd have to move them or find some explanation."

"Oh, Annie could explain them away," Jerry said. "She has a knack for this."

Annie glowed with pride. It was a relief that Mrs. Hoffmaster's odd supposition hadn't created any awkwardness between her and Jerry.

Martha came out on the porch. "Time to take a break," she said. "Go on with what you were saying before the hen and her chicks showed up."

"I was just telling Annie about my time in Kansas, but I don't want to bore you."

"Oh, please," Annie said. "Tell."

She might have sounded more insistent than she realized, for Martha said, "Actually, I think I'll go out back and read a little. Oliver bought a couple of books at the Ferry for me, and I fear he's going to quiz me on them."

Martha waved a cheery goodbye, leaving Jerry and Annie in possession of the porch. Jerry wasn't so reluctant to talk about Kansas as her brothers were, and soon Annie had learned quite a lot about Jerry's time there and about Jerry himself. He had studied for the Presbyterian ministry but had decided that he was a Universalist instead. After running a sawmill for a time, he had sold his interest and moved to Kansas, half for the adventure and half to aid the Free-State cause. His father, despite being born to a slave-owning family, was an abolitionist who had raised his children to hold similar beliefs. In Kansas, as a member of James Montgomery's militia, Jerry had fought against the Border Ruffians, earning himself a couple of stays in prison at Fort Scott. Finally, after his path had intersected with Father's in 1858, he had joined his raid into Missouri and, learning that Father had plans for the South, had decided to leave Kansas for good. Since then, he had stuck close to Father. "I remember in North Elba, someone asked if you were Father's bodyguard," Annie said.

"And he said, *Try him, and you'll see.* And I certainly would defend him to the death. I've never met a man so firm in his convictions—good convictions, anyway. In fact, your entire family impressed me deeply in that regard. Including you and Martha. Your father's told me more than once what confidence he has in the two of you. It must have been hard coming here, so far from your home and your mother."

"I did get terribly homesick the first night I was here," Annie admitted. "But mostly it was the fleas biting me half to death. Martha and I killed at least seventy apiece yesterday, but they keep coming."

"I will try to slay my share too, then. Chivalry demands it. Now, tell me something of yourself. Do you like North Elba?"

She nodded. "Mother doesn't care much for it. I think she liked being in town better. But I like the mountains and being able to go off by myself and look at all the beauty around me. Of course, our winters are long and hard, so I must get my fill during the summer."

"And you will be missing it this summer. But the country around here is beautiful as well. While it's quiet, would you like to go pick some berries with me? Tomorrow, perhaps? If, of course, your father agrees and it won't trouble Martha."

Annie readily agreed, as did Father, because in this lull before more men arrived, it was sensible to be seen about doing ordinary country things. Oliver agreed to help Martha guard against any incursions by Mrs. Hoffmaster. Only Martha raised an objection of an entirely specious sort. "You don't think Dauphin would mind?"

"That I am berrying with Mr. Anderson?"

"He is rather good-looking."

"Well, he can't help it."

That being irrefutable, Martha made no further protests.

Supplied with a basket apiece, the two of them set off early the next morning, heading in the direction of the Potomac River. By mid-morning, they had filled their baskets with an assortment of wild berries. "Should we head back?" Jerry asked. "Are you tired?"

"No. Besides, we're almost at the river. We can rest there."

"And eat our spoils."

Finding a hospitable stone, they settled on it and enjoyed the view of Harper's Ferry across the river. "Have you had the chance to see Jefferson Rock? Oliver showed it to me when we first came here."

"I haven't been on it."

"Would you like to?"

"It would give me great pleasure. Especially if you were to show it to me."

"Then let's go."

"Aren't you going to let me eat a few berries first?"

"Well, I suppose. Don't take all day."

He grinned at her. "You're quite the taskmaster. I must say, though, I've known country girls all my life, and you still have more energy than most of them. Or, I should say, more energy than most of them pretend to have."

"You certainly are free with the compliments."

"I can give more. Just say the word."

Annie snorted, but when Jerry helped her up, she found herself not caring that he might have retained her hand a little longer than necessary.

After admiring the Potomac River skipping over the rocks, they crossed the bridge, where the Baltimore and Ohio railroad ran on one side and a road for wagons and pedestrians on the other. In Harper's Ferry, Jerry bought them some lemonade, then they began the ascent to Jefferson Rock, Annie pointing out the way rather proprietarily. When they had reached their destination, Jerry stared about him. "This is sublime, Annie."

"I thought you would like it."

Jerry helped Annie mount the rock's platform, then stepped up beside her and knotted his hand in hers. Somehow, Annie had been expecting—and in fact, wanting—him to do just that. Her heart was beating in a way it hadn't before. It was most peculiar.

"Do you read poetry?" Jerry asked after they had gazed in silence at the converging rivers for a while.

"No."

"I didn't think so; you take after your father in many ways, and he's not a poetical man. But he does feel the beauty of things around him, as I learned when we traveled together. And I know that you do too. May I read something to you?"

She nodded, and Jerry withdrew a little, well-worn book from his pocket. "I do read poetry, and write it, although I

won't inflict my own doggerel upon you. Let me read this to
you instead.

> For thou art with me here upon the banks
> Of this fair river; thou my dearest Friend,
> My dear, dear Friend; and in thy voice I catch
> The language of my former heart, and read
> My former pleasures in the shooting lights
> Of thy wild eyes. Oh! yet a little while
> May I behold in thee what I was once,
> My dear, dear Sister! and this prayer I make,
> Knowing that Nature never did betray
> The heart that loved her; 'tis her privilege,
> Through all the years of this our life, to lead
> From joy to joy: for she can so inform
> The mind that is within us, so impress
> With quietness and beauty, and so feed
> With lofty thoughts, that neither evil tongues,
> Rash judgments, nor the sneers of selfish men,
> Nor greetings where no kindness is, nor all
> The dreary intercourse of daily life,
> Shall e'er prevail against us, or disturb
> Our cheerful faith, that all which we behold
> Is full of blessings."

"That's lovely. Who wrote it?"

"A man named William Wordsworth. It reminds me of
you, Annie, except in one respect."

"What is that?"

"I don't think of you as a sister."

She hardly recognized her own voice. "I don't want you
to."

He took her hands and placed them on his chest, which was beating in the same odd way as hers. As she looked up at him, he reached for her bonnet strings. "This is a bit in the way. May I?"

Somehow, she had lost the power of speech. She nodded.

Carefully, Jerry pushed back her bonnet—Annie would have just thrown the stupid thing aside—and kissed her, gently at first and then with a growing intensity that Annie herself matched. She felt weightless, at the same time conscious of her body in a way that she'd never been before.

A report sounded in the distance, startling them apart—a snapping twig. "Another pair of lovers," Jerry said. "We had better leave them to it, darling."

Annie shook her head. "We have a moment," she whispered and presented herself for another kiss.

Most willingly, Jerry obliged.

17

August 1859

"I have written to North Elba asking Watson and Dauphin to come on," Father said after leading his usual morning prayer. "And I have heard that we should be getting some guns soon as well. Sharps rifles, the best."

Annie gulped. Somehow she had neglected to inform Jerry of her semi-engagement to Dauphin, and needless to say, she had not informed Dauphin of her kissing Jerry, both on Jefferson Rock and on numerous occasions afterward.

Nor had she been entirely honest with Jerry about another matter. When they had first come to the farm, she had informed Mrs. Hoffmaster, with Jerry overhearing, that she was seventeen, soon to be eighteen, and had given her to understand that Martha was about the same age. It was a perfectly sensible lie, one which made Mother's absence all the more plausible. She'd never got around to mentioning the deception to Jerry, though. At the time, it had hardly mattered.

"It'll be good to have some more hands," Owen said. "Are they just going to come on, or do we need to pick them up?"

"They can just come on. I have told them to identify themselves as precisely what they are, a married son of mine and his brother-in-law, but the next arrivals will have to be sec—"

"Someone's here," Annie said. She had been sitting closest to the door, all the better to survey the approach to the house.

"Annie never misses a thing," Jerry said rather proudly. "But wait! It's only Cook."

"In broad daylight." Father shook his head. "When will he learn discretion?"

A man of around thirty was making his way toward the house on foot. As he drew closer, Annie saw that he was blond, though not as splendidly blond as Dauphin, and rather slight. He was dressed more snappily than the Brown men and Jerry, wearing a brightly checked vest. Under his arm he carried a couple of books. "Good morning," he called brightly. "Might I interest you in some most excellent books? Eminently suitable for family reading."

"Show us them," Jerry called.

Mr. Cook bounded up the stairs to the porch and inside the room that served as a parlor. Father said, "Cook, I am always glad to see you, but do you think it wise to come this time of the day, in full sight of the neighbors?"

"That's why I brought the books," Mr. Cook said sunnily. "I actually do earn some money as a book agent, you know. Teaching a little, lecturing a little—mind you, not on any topic that would upset the populace—that's all part of my work here. Now, you must be Mrs. Brown and Miss Brown—or should I call you Mrs. Smith and Miss Smith? I do hope you will allow me to call you Martha and Annie; we are all essentially brothers and sisters here in the cause of righteousness. And it's easier as well."

"Certainly," Martha said, and Annie nodded assent.

"Excellent!"

"What type of books do you sell, Cook?" asked Jerry.

"Dull ones, I'm afraid. The publisher does offer some poetry and even some novels for the ladies, but most of what they have is rather plodding and practical. Books of conduct. Books on agriculture. Bibles, of course. I do my best sales with Bibles. Poetry sells the worst. The people here are quite religious and not at all poetical in nature, except for the gentry, of course. There's a Mr. Lewis Washington I plan to visit one of these days; he has a nice library. He is a great-grand-nephew of George Washington and is said to have some delightful mementoes. But no one has asked me about my son yet."

"I was meaning to," said Father.

"He is thriving. Very forward for his age, I think. I could swear that he tried to say 'Papa' the other day."

"I do think that is a little young," Father said.

"Well, I bow to your experience as a father. I was the youngest of seven—and a quite pampered youngest, I might add—so I have little experience of babies. But mine is charming." Cook turned to the young ladies. "But I have been terribly rude. I trust you had a pleasant journey here?"

"Yes, it was very interesting," Martha said. She blushed. "I've never left Essex County before, so it was all quite new to me."

"I enjoyed going down the Hudson," Annie said. "I wish I could have seen a little more of New York City."

"Mr. Brown and I were there for a little while," Jerry said. "I felt and looked like quite the rustic, but I did enjoy myself."

"We both looked the rustic," Father said. He smiled at Jerry. Annie couldn't help but notice that Father had taken quite a liking to him, which boded well for her future.

Oliver snorted. "Well, I hope poor Watson makes it through New York without getting fleeced this time."

"Now, son," Father said, "don't be hard on your brother. I know he regrets being taken in."

"Oh, I know," Oliver said. "He won't get fooled again. Besides"—his grin widened—"he has Dauphin to look after him."

Even Father smiled, but he added, "He's a good young man. He will be an asset to us."

"I got taken in by the sharpers more than I care to admit," Mr. Cook said. He downed the cup of milk Martha had given him and rose. "Well, I just wanted to pay a call more than anything, and to say that everything still looks promising for our enterprise. Do you think your near neighbors would care to buy some books?"

"I don't think the Hoffmasters are bookish people," Annie said.

"No matter. I shall call on them anyway and see what they have to say about their neighbors the Smiths. Then I can assure them that you seemed like most excellent people, interested in mining and cattle and absolutely nothing else. By the way, ladies, did you get a look at the Ferry?"

"We did," Martha said. "It was lovely."

"I particularly enjoyed seeing Jefferson Rock," Annie added.

Somehow, Jerry's hand found hers without Father noticing.

~ ~ ~

A few days later, just after a visit from Mrs. Hoffmaster (who had been talked into buying a family Bible by Mr. Cook), Watson and Dauphin arrived. With them was a third man, Dauphin's older brother, William. Father beamed at the sight of another Thompson in their midst. "We hadn't expected you."

William shrugged. "Well, I didn't want to miss the fun."

"He said it wasn't right to stay when Watson was leaving Bell and his new son," Dauphin said.

"So, she had a boy? Is she well?" Annie asked.

"She did, and both are fine," Watson said. "We named him after Frederick."

"I thank you for that," Father said. He batted what could have been a gnat or a tear from his eye.

~ ~ ~

William Thompson's arrival was not only good for the cause, but a relief to Annie. Dauphin was close to William, as he was to all of his large family, and he would not be left without someone to console him when Annie broke the news.

It took Annie a bit of time to catch Dauphin alone, which strengthened her resolution. Wouldn't a more ardent lover be seeking out such opportunities himself? Jerry certainly was. She'd allowed him a little more liberty the last time he had caught her alone, which made it all the more important that she have the conversation she now initiated. "There's something I must tell you," she said as they walked to draw some water.

"I'm sorry I didn't write."

Even though Jerry was in the same house with her, he had found the opportunity to write a verse or two and leave them in the book she was reading. Really, Dauphin was making this almost too easy. "Dauphin, I'm sorry to say this, but I can't marry you."

"Why? Have I said something wrong?"

"No, not at all." She forestalled another question. "I'm very fond of you, but all my feelings are those of a sister. And I am your sister, for all practical purposes, through Ruth and Watson. I've missed you since I came here, but not in the way a future wife should."

"I missed you very much." Hurt filled his blue eyes. "I knew I should have written, but there were the crops—"

"It's not that, Dauphin. Truly. It's that you're more family to me than anything. And I'm still very young."

Saying that was ill-advised, she realized immediately; she'd given him a kernel of hope. "But really, Dauphin, it's mainly that my feelings are just sisterly."

If she had to say "sister" or a variation one more time, she would scream. But Dauphin said, "Well, if that's how it is, it's over. I won't bring it up again."

"We're still friends. Aren't we?"

"Yes. And relatives, as you keep pointing out."

She hadn't expected that last flash from mild-mannered Dauphin. Almost regretfully, she watched him as he grabbed the pail of water and strode to the house. Annie assumed that he would go to William, who was rumored to have had a flirtation or two before his marriage. She could almost hear his sensible advice to Dauphin. "Women. They're fickle. You're better off discovering it now than later."

She could hear it so vividly, in fact, that she almost ran after him to defend herself. But what defense was there? Nothing, except that she hadn't had the faintest inkling of what love was until Jerry had kissed her on Jefferson Rock.

~ ~ ~

A few days later, the first and largest shipment of guns arrived, having made the journey from their hiding place near Brother John's house in Ohio to Chambersburg. There were far too many for Father's little mule wagon to handle, so Owen had engaged a Pennsylvania Dutchman to haul them while Owen rode alongside them. "Admire his team while we unload," he hissed to Annie after the Pennsylvanian and his freight had arrived at the farm. "Ask him questions so he doesn't realize how heavy these boxes are."

It was indeed a fine team of five massive horses, strapped to a single harness. Annie's equine conversation was limited, but she did her best as the men went about their work. William Thompson recounted her efforts that evening while Father, who had gotten into the habit of leaving the young people to themselves in the parlor, sat in the kitchen with his newspaper. "'What splendid horses!'" he said in a high voice.

"Surely I don't sound like that," Annie protested.

"You do, a bit," Dauphin said to the delight of Oliver and even Watson.

"'How do you keep them from running into each other? What if they all take a notion to run away? Can I pet one? How big and strong you must be to manage them!'"

"I did not say that last."

"Well, no, but he was a rather strapping fellow."

Annie scowled.

Martha said, "Now, boys, Annie did an excellent job of distracting him. Give her credit for that."

"He did mention to me that it was uncommon to find a young lady so interested in wagon driving," Jerry said.

"Maybe Annie learned enough that she can spell one of us on our way to Chambersburg."

"No," said Father, passing through. "Annie's presence is absolutely necessary here."

Jerry smiled at her. "Well, I tried," he said softly.

~ ~ ~

Not to anyone's surprise, Mrs. Hoffmaster turned up the next day, chicks in tow. "I saw that man driving here the other day," she informed Annie.

Annie forbore from pointing out that the man had in fact made his delivery only the day before. She brought out the lie which she had spent some time crafting. "Our furniture arrived."

"Oh, let me see!"

Before Annie could remonstrate, Mrs. Hoffmaster, swift in her bare feet, had scurried into the parlor, followed by the four children. The Hoffmasters stared around them in puzzlement. "Oh, you haven't unpacked yet."

Annie nodded. "It's our new parlor set," she said, indicating the largest of the crates, which could have held a small sofa but in fact was bristling with Sharps rifles.

"Oh, it must be lovely." Mrs. Hoffmaster looked at the box longingly. "I reckon you'll be opening it later today."

If there had been a crowbar within reach, Annie thought, her neighbor might have forced open the crate herself. "No. My mother is very particular. We are not sure how long we will be staying here, and she does not want us to put everything out until we are permanently settled and she is here to supervise."

"Oh," said Mrs. Hoffmaster. "She sounds right strict."

"She is," Annie said. "But she's always been that way."

Poor Mother could never come to Maryland now, Annie realized. No one would recognize Mother, who'd never owned a parlor set in her life, in this high-nosed creature she'd summoned up.

~ ~ ~

Several days after Father and Owen took the wagon to Chambersburg, something awoke Annie in the middle of the night. That wasn't unusual; she shared a room with Oliver and Martha, only a calico curtain furnishing her (and them) some privacy, and more than once she'd come out of a sound sleep to hear furtive rustlings from the other side of the room. Once, awakened from a particularly pleasant dream, she had asked what they were up to, and Martha had replied that they were stirring some softness into their mattress.

So that was what they called it. Just thinking of it now made Annie snort again.

But it soon became apparent that Martha and Oliver were not the culprits, for Father's voice called softly. "I'm back. With some friends."

Oliver, awakened by the commotion, arose to unbolt the front door as Annie peered out of the open window. Father stood alone on the porch. "Do you need me?" she hissed.

"No, child. The fewer people up and about, the better. You and Martha stay where you are. Go back to sleep. You too, Oliver."

As Oliver trudged back into the room, Annie obeyed the first command but not the second. Soon she heard a series of footsteps passing into the house and up to the loft, followed by nothing but the usual country sounds of frogs peeping and crickets chirping rather crossly, as if knowing they had been interrupted.

When she and Martha awoke the next morning, Owen, who was a rather good cook, had already started breakfast. With the rest of the men were two strangers who promptly rose at this feminine entrance. The first had the look of a good-natured pirate, and as for the second, Annie could not but observe that his physique, even in his shabby clothes, could only be called magnificent.

"Morning, ladies," Owen said. "Meet our new arrivals. These two gentlemen are Charles Tidd and Aaron Stevens, two of the bravest men I've ever met. They also happen to have beautiful singing voices, as I'm sure you'll find out soon. Men, these are Oliver's wife, Martha, and my sister Annie. As I told you on the way down here, you can trust them with anything."

Annie liked the looks of them immediately. "Welcome."

"With Mr. Tidd and Mr. Stevens joining our numbers, we have reached the point where we cannot pretend we are simply a family and a friend or two," said Father. "These men and the ones who will come after them must be kept out of sight of the neighbors. Their presence would awaken too much suspicion, which is why I brought them in darkness. As Martha prefers to do the housework, Annie, your main duty will be to watch. To keep them invisible from the outside world."

"My invisibles," Annie said solemnly.

~ ~ ~

Over the next couple of weeks, more invisibles arrived. The Coppock brothers, Edwin and Barclay, who had met Father in Springdale, Iowa. William Leeman and Albert Hazlett, Kansas veterans. A young Canadian, Stewart Taylor, a spiritualist who seemed to be in the spirit world half the time.

Annie liked them all, but her special fondness—aside from Jerry, of course—was for the first of the arrivals, Stevens and Tidd. Each night, the last thing Annie heard before she fell asleep was the sweet sound of their duets coming from the attic where they slept.

Martha had not been feeling so well lately, so Father had instructed Annie to do the laundry herself, with the help of one of the un-invisibles Father assigned in rotation. Last week, it had been Dauphin, which had been awkward, but they had gotten through it cordially enough by discussing whether Father's Constitution could be construed to give women the right to hold office. She had pretty much succeeded in persuading Dauphin that it did.

Today, her washing companion was Jerry, Father and Owen having gone to Chambersburg. "This is one way to spend some time with you," he said as he lugged the washboard, laundry club, and washtub down to the creek. "Though it's not what I would like to be doing."

"What is that?"

"Oh, I don't know. Traveling with you, maybe. Seeing Niagara Falls with you. Or just kissing you."

He set down the tub and took Annie in his arms. "The laundry won't do itself," she said sadly after they had kissed for a while. "We need to get back to work."

"Yes, ma'am. Give me the worst of the shirts, and I'll leave you to the rest. I promise not to look at your unmentionables."

Jerry had been "batching" it long enough to become quite adept at laundry, and together they made good progress and developed a friendly competition over who could produce the whitest shirts. "And here's Mrs. Hoffmaster, come just in time to judge," said Annie as their intrepid neighbor walked toward them and the array of clothing just hung out to dry. "Which shirt is cleaner, Mrs. Hoffmaster, that one or that one?"

Mrs. Hoffmaster studied them for some time, then pointed to the one on the right.

"Drat," said Annie.

"I just finished doing my own laundry," Mrs. Hoffmaster said. "I sat a spell with your sister-in-law and thought I shouldn't leave without saying a word to you." She looked again at the clothing as a soft breeze rustled it. "Your menfolk sure do have a lot of shirts."

"They're not used to this heat yet," Annie said. "They have to change them twice a day sometimes. Quite a nuisance, really." She glared at Jerry.

"Guilty as charged."

"Well, I'd better get back," Mrs. Hoffmaster said. "Mrs. Smith is keeping an eye on the children. They'll be overstaying their welcome before long, I reckon."

It took another five minutes' worth of pleasantries—Mrs. Hoffmaster was the sort who always thought of one more thing to say—before Annie and Jerry were alone again. "I guess we had better go back ourselves," Annie said regretfully.

"Stay awhile. We've earned the right to a little time together, I think."

She nodded, and he started to draw her to him again. "No! I look a fright after all that work."

"You look beautiful. Your hair's coming out of that tight knot, and your cheeks are glowing."

"Really?"

He kissed her. "Really."

Annie let him draw her into a more secluded spot and onto his lap. His kisses were more intense than they had ever been, and his hands were wandering quite a bit. As her corset was presenting an obstacle to him, she unhooked the front clasps herself and was rewarded most pleasantly for her initiative.

"Jerry? *Annie?*"

They sprang apart, Annie sprawling backward onto the grass as Dauphin stood over them. Jerry recovered his dignity first. "What the devil are you doing here?"

"Martha sent me to look for you. Mrs. Hoffmaster told her that you were finished with the washing and she's tired of watching. And it certainly looks like you were finished with the washing." Dauphin's blue eyes blazed. "Did you know that she was engaged to me, Anderson?"

"Semi-engaged," Annie whispered as she pulled the bodice of her gown together. The corset would have to wait.

"She told me that she thought of me more as a brother and friend than as a lover," Dauphin said in a high voice. He was nearly as good a mimic as his brother, something Annie had never known up until now. "So what could I do? I took it as truth. I didn't know she'd been playing me for a fool all along, that she was rutting around with you."

Jerry stood and stepped close to Dauphin. "Don't speak of her like that."

"She also said that she thought she was too young. If she's too young for me, she's way too young for you, Anderson."

"She's seventeen."

"Seventeen? Try fifteen."

Jerry stared at her. "Is that true?"

Never had Annie felt so absolutely fifteen. She hung her head. "Yes."

Annie had read about people "blanching," but she had never seen anyone do it until Jerry did then. Jerry bent and reached for his jacket. "I'm sorry, Dolph. I didn't know any of this. I'm going for a walk."

"Jerry—"

"I don't like lies, Annie."

"All we're doing here is lying!"

"For liberty. Not for our own convenience." He turned and strode away.

Annie turned to Dauphin. "Please let me explain. I didn't mean to hurt you."

He studied Annie, her hair falling around her shoulders and her dress askew. "I'm not in the mood for explanations," he said curtly. "I'm going to Cook's." He stomped off, taking a different path than Jerry had.

Neither man had bothered to help Annie up from the grass. She rose, fastened her clothing, arranged her hair as best she could in its usual tight knot, and trudged toward the house, choking back tears.

Martha was at the head of a delegation gathered to meet her. Even the invisibles had come from the attic. "What on earth has happened? Jerry stormed in here and said he was going to Cook's to spend the night, and we just saw Dauphin stomping down the road. He didn't even bother to come in."

"But Dauphin is going to Cook's!"

Watson grimaced. "Then it looks as if poor Cook is going to have his hands full."

In her lovely, relentless way, Martha continued, "But what on earth could have made them angry? Dauphin never gets angry."

"Me," Annie said.

William frowned. "About you breaking your engagement? But that was weeks ago."

"Wait," Martha said. "You broke your engagement? And never told me?"

"Semi-engagement! No."

"Why?"

Annie shrugged.

"That's terribly hurtful," Martha said.

"Well, you never told me you were expecting. So there."

Oliver dropped the *Baltimore Sun* he had been holding. "You're *expecting?*"

Martha blushed beautifully. "Yes. I hadn't envisioned telling you like this."

Oliver clasped her in his arms. "My love. I'm so very happy."

Tidd and Stevens looked at each other. Tidd began, "Mother, dear mother, 'tis sweet to know, in stemming the current through life's ebb and flow—"

"Though heartless and fickle all else may be," Stevens chimed in, "thou'rt ever, ever faithful to me."

They were still singing when Annie quietly slipped away.

~ ~ ~

Walking through the woods with no direction in mind, she came to a creek and considered, quite seriously, the possibility of drowning herself in it. It looked deep enough, if she weighed herself down with stones or whatever people did. Yet what would that accomplish, except to upend their whole point in being here? She could picture poor Father explaining to his friends in Boston that he would have to give up his plan, for the time being at least, because his fool daughter had had a spat with her lover and ended it all.

Maybe it just made more sense not to bother with men at all. Or people, for that matter.

She sighed and walked on, trying to find some comfort in the beauty around her, which was abundant, and in the August day, warm but not oppressive as it could be in Maryland.

She munched on some wild berries she found and picked a few wildflowers. They would look pretty set on top of the crate of rubber blankets that served her as a dressing table.

When the sun began to set, she turned back. All the men were gathered in the parlor, and she tried to enter as nonchalantly as possible. "Where were you?" asked Tidd. "You shouldn't wander off like that without telling anyone."

"Walking," Annie said. "A human being has a right to walk."

"A horde of Hoffmasters could have invaded while you were gone," Oliver said.

"We'll have to court-martial you," Stevens said. He smiled at her. "Dereliction of duty."

Watson put his arm around her. "Don't tease her, boys."

They obeyed. In a few minutes, they were back to their original conversation, which turned out to be naming Oliver and Martha's baby. Already Tidd had started calling them "Mother" and "Father."

~ ~ ~

Dauphin and Jerry turned up together the next morning, looking sheepish but apparently in harmony with each other. They had brought doughnuts from the Ferry to the especial delight of Stevens and Tidd, both of whom were strapping men. "And we brought a little present for each of you girls," Dauphin said bashfully.

"Mrs. Cook picked them from her garden," Jerry said.

They were two matching nosegays. "That's so sweet of you," Martha said, and Annie echoed her thanks. Jerry being the one who pressed hers into her hand comforted her a little.

By and by, Annie went out to the porch to do some mending and watching. A little while later, Jerry appeared.

"Walk a little with me, Annie. Just to the road. You can keep an eye on the place from there."

She obeyed. When they had traveled out of earshot from the house, Jerry said, "First, I apologize for the liberty I took yesterday. It was inexcusable."

"I enjoyed it."

He smiled faintly. "I know you did. I don't like to think of what might have happened if we hadn't been interrupted. After all the trust your father has placed in me . . . Which brings me to my next point. Why didn't you tell me that you were promised to Dauphin? Or that you were barely out of short skirts? You must have known that these things would matter to me. I'm not a knave or a cradle-robber."

"Everything happened so quickly, and I fell in love with you so hard and so fast, I suppose I didn't want to spoil things."

"Then Cook was right."

"You told Cook about this?"

"To some degree. You see, when Dolph and I turned up at Cook's within a few minutes of each other, he knew something was up, so he held a hearing of sorts. Cook's more a man of the world than either of us, so it was helpful to hear his opinion."

"About me?"

"More about our own follies. Cook was hard on both of us. Dolph admitted that he knew you weren't in love with him, but he had been hoping you'd come round eventually. Cook told him that it wasn't 1830 anymore, and it wasn't right to expect you to marry where your heart wasn't. Dolph agreed that he might want to see a bit more of the country himself before he marries. He has been thinking of getting a job on the railway when our work here is done. For me, Cook said I shouldn't have moved things along so quickly. He said I should have gotten to know you a bit more before overwhelming you with poetry and kisses. He thinks it's the frontier life I've been leading and our peculiar situation here that made me act so rashly. I didn't mention the liberties."

"Well, that's something."

"He actually had a sensible idea, which I'll put before you. That I speak to your father about my intentions—which I assure you are entirely honorable—and abide by what he says."

"You mean you don't want to end things now that you know the truth?"

"It's the last thing I want to do, Annie. But no sneaking around as we have been."

Jerry—and Cook—made sense, Annie had to admit. She wasn't even sure why they had been sneaking around. Dauphin's feelings had some part to do with it, at least as far as she had been concerned, but perhaps it was more that a secret romance fit in well with the rest of their outlaw activities that summer. "But what if he doesn't approve? What if he sends me back to North Elba? What if he sends you away?"

"He loves you, Annie, and he likes me. I think at worst, we'll have to wait until you're older. Whatever he says, we'll have to abide by it, at least until you're of age. But I'll try to catch him in a receptive mood."

Father was in gloomy spirits, however, when he returned from Chambersburg. He had tried and failed to recruit his old friend Frederick Douglass into their scheme; although Mr. Douglass had traveled from his home in Rochester, New York to hear him out, that was all he had done. "Mr. Douglass would have brought so many more of his race in,"

Father said. "But there is still time to change his mind. I hope he does."

"Why didn't he agree?" Annie asked.

"He is a cautious man. I suppose I cannot entirely blame him, having built a successful life for himself in the North after spending so many years in bondage in the South. But I did, in fact, gain one more adherent—a black man who operates a clothes cleaning establishment in Rochester. His name is Shields Green. Owen is escorting him. He felt it unwise to take him in our wagon as we would have to stay overnight in Hagerstown, and Mr. Green could not join us inside our hotel."

Annie frowned. She had expected better of Mr. Douglass. Still, she was pleased to hear the news of Mr. Green, their first black recruit. He would require especial vigilance as his presence at the house would be simply too hard to explain, even with Annie's growing adeptness at telling tales.

But when the time Owen and Mr. Green should have arrived at the farm came and went, they all grew alarmed. Had they been captured? Would poor Mr. Green—a city dweller—be sold into slavery to one of the enormous plantations in the Deep South, a fate arguably worse than death? Would Owen be clapped into jail?

Father began to pace about as the hours dragged on. In his turns around the room he was followed by the Kennedy Farm's latest arrival, Cuffee, a yellow dog that a poor family had bestowed upon Father for his services in cutting a carbuncle from the wife's neck. He had taken a shine to Father, as most animals did. "If they are not here by tomorrow morning, we must go make inquiries at Hagerstown," he said, which somehow caused Cuffee to wag his tail. "And if they are in jail there, we must break them out somehow. What that will do to our plan, I do not know."

"Those of us who are known already can break them out," Jerry suggested. "The rest—and you—can still carry out your plan. We can all join together eventually."

"It may have to come to that," Father said sadly.

Everyone had straggled off to bed in a state of deepest dejection when Cuffee began barking with a vigor none of them had heard before. (He knew Mrs. Hoffmaster from the neighborhood and never so much as whimpered when she made her daily incursions.) William Thompson, who had guard duty that night, called, "Who is it?"

"Me!" Owen sang out.

They all rushed into the parlor to see Owen leading in a worn-out looking black man. Father beamed at him. "Mr. Green, I am glad you made it safely."

"Well, sir, I had my doubts."

"Did he ever!" Owen said. "We were half a mile away when he told me that we were forty miles away from the place, that I would never see any of you again, and that he wished he had never left Rochester. Mind you, though, we had our fair share of danger getting here."

He and Mr. Green began to tell a tale full of narrow escapes, but Annie only half listened. She was looking at Father's smiling face and hearing what Jerry whispered in her ear. "I'll talk to him tomorrow."

~ ~ ~

Late the next afternoon, while the men were engaged in a game of cards, Father nodded to Annie. "Come out to the lawn with me, Annie."

Annie could not tell from her father's impassive face whether to expect good news or bad. Her heart pounding, she obeyed as Cuffee tagged along.

"As you might guess, I have had a conversation with Jerry. I must say this is business I did not expect to be conducting here, given that I have other preoccupations." He stroked his beard. "If your mother had come down as I had asked, this would not have occurred, I'm sure."

"I'm sorry, Father."

"In any case, Jerry spoke to me this morning. He was very straightforward, which I appreciated. He said that he had fallen in love with you, thinking that you were somewhat older, and that when the truth was revealed to him, he found himself unable to change his feelings. He asked my permission to marry you."

"Father—"

"I told him he must wait. I told him that while I did not object in principle to girls of your age marrying, and that while I had offered marriage to your mother when she was but sixteen, the times were different then, and she was mature beyond her years in many ways. Even then, I waited until she was seventeen for the wedding, and she still had certain difficulties, mainly managing Dianthe's children, that an older wife might not have had. I told him that while you had a good head on your shoulders, you needed to develop better business habits. And finally, I told him, because you are precious to me and it is not in my nature to mince words about an entirely natural aspect of existence, that I feared the consequences of your getting with child at such a young age. It is something that has concerned me with Martha, although I have hopes that she will do well. Jerry is a sensible man. He agreed with me on all points, except that he gave you credit for more business sense than I. And there is the matter of Dauphin Thompson. Jerry told me that you had had an understanding with him, evidently of a somewhat uncertain nature."

She nodded miserably. "Yes."

"Don't toy with a good man's heart ever again, Annie. I am also disappointed that you did not choose to mention that to me yourself. That is all I have to say on that painful subject. Now, don't look so unhappy, child. I told Jerry that when you are seventeen, the two of you can marry. I also told him that I had never known you to let go of a notion in my life. He assured me that his feelings would not change either, and that he had never felt so strongly about a woman before. You may keep company with each other and, once you leave here, write to each other as far as our circumstances will allow it." He grimaced. "Although I commend Jerry for asking my permission to do these things, I am worldly enough to know that you would likely do so anyway."

"Thank you, Father." Though neither she nor her father were usually demonstrative, she could not forebear from embracing him.

"Well, well," Father said. "I suppose you'll want to be finding him now."

18

September 1859 to October 1859

"Upstairs!" Annie called into the kitchen.

By now, the men needed no further instructions. Each grabbed his plate and hurried up to the attic. Hazlett, the last to go, snatched up the tablecloth. The invisibles safely out of sight, Martha sat at the table and calmly picked up a newspaper as Mrs. Hoffmaster approached the house.

This time, however, she was accompanied not only by the chicks, but by Mr. Hoffmaster, who up until now had never come to the house except when Father, having slaughtered a pig, had invited his near neighbors to take a portion home with them. It was the custom of the neighborhood, and Father's adherence to it and his regular attendance at the local church had won him much approbation in the area.

Would they have to be on guard now for both Hoffmasters? Annie frowned, then put on her usual welcoming face as Mrs. Hoffmaster came up the porch stairs. "I have a bit of a favor to ask, Annie. George here has been working so hard lately—well, to make short work of it, last night he was sitting at home when he heard the sweetest singing coming from your house. It just relaxed and eased him so to sit back and listen. I wonder if your menfolk might favor him with a little tune."

"Well—"

"I know it's a bit much to ask, but it did his head wonders last night. Didn't it, George?"

Mr. Hoffmaster looked at his feet. "Yes," he said bashfully.

There was no help for it; they would have to oblige. Unfortunately, the beautiful singers were Tidd and Stevens, stowed in the attic. The visible ones—the Browns, the Thompsons, and Jerry—were passable at best. She turned and walked into the kitchen. "Mrs. Hoffmaster wants the men to sing."

It took a lot to ruffle Martha, fortunately. "I'll get them."

Father and Owen were away, but in due time Oliver, Watson, the Thompsons, and Jerry ambled in. After a few pleasantries, Watson said, "What you would like to hear?"

Annie forestalled the Hoffmasters from answering. "Perhaps something they haven't heard before. Wouldn't that be nice?"

"Try 'Old Memories,'" Jerry suggested before the Hoffmasters could reply.

One could never go wrong with Stephen Foster. Annie gave Jerry an appreciative look.

With the girls chiming in occasionally, they sang, "Old Memories," "Jeanie with the Light Brown Hair," and after a couple of more selections, finished up triumphantly with Father's favorite, "Blow, Ye Trumpet Blow," which everyone from North Elba could sing in his or her sleep. Mr. Hoffmaster, however, did not look exactly transported, although he did jiggle his foot when the Thompsons sang "Camptown Races."

"Much obliged," Mrs. Hoffmaster said as they departed.

Mr. Hoffmaster, a man of few words, nodded. "I must say, though, it sounds a little sweeter from afar."

"Probably something to do with the way the summer breeze travels," Oliver said.

~ ~ ~

A few days later, Father took Annie to a camp meeting of a sect known as the Winebrennerians. He had heard that they were strongly opposed to slavery and was curious to hear what they had to say. Annie, eager for a break from her watching, accepted his invitation to come along to hear the preaching. "The sentiments were fine," he said as they walked home a couple of hours later.

"I thought the execution was lacking."

"Now, child, don't be so harsh. Why, what is Jerry doing here?"

Jerry was hurrying down the road. "I wanted to meet you," he said in a low voice. "There's a problem at the house. Mrs. Hoffmaster saw Shields Green."

"Oh dear," Father said.

"How? Wasn't anyone watching properly?"

"Martha was busy ironing, and Green came down to offer to do the ironing himself if she would mend his coat for him. Leeman was already sitting there, wearing that black oilcloth cap he's so fond off, and Barclay Coppock was there too. Anyway, while this little convention was going on, our man standing guard on the porch left his post and wandered into the kitchen."

"Who?"

"I won't say," Jerry said. "He's very ashamed of himself. Anyway, while Martha was looking at Green's coat and

Green was smoking his pipe, Mrs. Hoffmaster walks to the open door and sees all three of the men. Poor Martha could hardly think what to do, so she just gave her the flour she came to borrow and didn't even try to explain why a black man was sitting in our parlor, puffing away like the lord of the manor."

Father sighed. "I must think what to do. In the meantime, I will walk to the house by myself. You two linger a bit—I presume that won't be entirely unpleasant—and follow in due time. By then I will have a plan."

He hurried away. Normally, being left with Jerry with express permission not to hurry along would have been the height of bliss, but she was too worried to enjoy the arm that Jerry put around her. "It'll be fine," he said. "He'll think of something. Or you will."

When they reached the farm, the invisibles were stowed away and silent, although Annie could feel a sense of penitence flowing from the attic. Father said, "The best thing, I think, is for you to go over and visit Mrs. Hoffmaster. Going over myself, or having one of the boys go, would make matters worse. You are quite capable of dealing with the situation, I know. Find out what she saw, and if it looks bad for us, then you may have to bribe her to stay silent. I would prefer you bribe her with goods instead of money, as we have very little to spare, and I think that since she is poor, she will settle for that, but if it must be money, then the Lord will provide."

So now she would have to add bribery to her skills. It was proving to be an educational year.

Fortunately, she had visited Mrs. Hoffmaster from time to time, so just walking over there wasn't unusual. She could only hope the place wasn't aswarm with other visitors. Mrs. Hoffmaster was from Pennsylvania with but a few relations in

Maryland, but her husband's family sprawled all over Washington and Frederick counties in Maryland and into Virginia. Any gossip about the Hoffmasters' odd neighbors and their black houseguest would have the legs of a centipede.

For once, though, Mrs. Hoffmaster was alone, save for the four chicks. "I'm sorry we missed you this afternoon. We were at the meeting."

"So Martha told me."

"She is going tomorrow with Oliver. The preaching was very vigorous."

"I saw a colored fellow over at your house today. Him and a white fellow in a fancy cap, who looked rather sharp at me, I thought. I'd know him again."

"They were friends passing through. Father knows them from Chambersburg. They were thinking about coming out here."

That was a reasonable enough lie. Chambersburg did have a large black community, and probably more than a few white men with fancy caps as well.

"Some might wonder if you folks are running off slaves, you know."

"Oh, we don't do anything like that." Did her voice sound a little hollow? "They're interested in mining here, that's all. I don't know if they'll decide to take it up or not. They're also thinking of going west. So are we, actually, though we're not really sure yet. Time will tell."

Mrs. Hoffmaster nodded deeply. Annie sensed skepticism. It was time to move to step two: bribery. "Anyway, I thought you might like a little milk. Our cow's like a geyser these days."

"I sure could use some."

"Well, good." The rest was going to be awkward, so Annie plunged right in. "Maybe it might be best to not say anything about the colored man. Some might take him for a slave just because he is colored. He's been questioned a time or two, traveling about."

"I won't say a thing."

"Well, then. I guess I'll probably be seeing you soon. Just stop by if you need anything."

"I will."

And she did. Father and the men, who were in the habit of buying provisions from different places so as not to raise suspicions, soon got into the habit of buying a little more just to meet Mrs. Hoffmaster's needs. But she appeared to have kept silent, which became all the more important when Watson came from Chambersburg with a new addition to the household: Dangerfield Newby, a freedman of mixed race. He had made the journey covered over with blankets in the back of the wagon.

In his late thirties, Mr. Newby was much older than most in the house, save for Owen and Father. He had been freed in Ohio and had met Brother John there. "My wife and seven children are in Virginia," he said. "Shenandoah County. Every time I get near raising enough to buy them, their price goes up. Up and up."

"That's so sad," Martha said, her eyes welling with tears.

"I sure hope we can get our business started soon, because her master is having hard times. Ain't got much to sell, except for them."

Annie shuddered. What did having to keep Mrs. Hoffmaster in flour and milk matter when they had a chance to save the Newby family from the auction block?

~ ~ ~

In mid-September, Father and Owen returned from one of their journeys just before dinner with their man in Chambersburg, John Kagi, whom Annie now saw for the first time. He was a trim young man with lovely green eyes, but one pant leg had been stuffed into his boot, while the other rode outside of it. Annie supposed that it must have been dark when he dressed himself.

But what was he doing here? A couple of days before, Cook had visited, and since then, there had been some earnest discussions in the attic, which Annie hadn't been able to make out. Clearly something was up. She had asked Jerry, but he had been unusually close-mouthed, saying only that there were some matters to be resolved which needed all hands at the farm.

Since the table wasn't large enough to hold everyone, Annie and Martha usually fed the men first, then had their own meal and did the washing up with one or more of the men drying. Today, however, the men started doing the washing up even as the girls sat down to eat, and it was clear that they were not to linger at their meal. When Annie set her fork down—not having dared to do it before for fear that her plate would be snatched away prematurely—Father said, "You must watch now, and do so very carefully. By no means let Mrs. Hoffmaster or anyone else near the house. Not even on the porch."

Annie nodded. She grabbed everything she could possibly want—a book, a newspaper, and some sewing—and took her place, accompanied by Cuffee, who alternated between lounging on the porch and gamboling on the lawn. It occurred to her that she could attend to her duties and still throw sticks for him, which they both enjoyed, but that would prevent her from hearing what was going on inside.

It wasn't, of course, hard to hear; the walls of the farm-house weren't that thick, and an early September day in Maryland did not allow for the house to be shut up. Father's voice, soft but firm, easily trailed out to the porch. "I have heard that there is some objection to our plan."

"Yes," Tidd said. "For one thing, not everyone knows exactly what your plan is. Is it the Kansas raid but on a larger scale, as I was led to believe? Or is it a plan to seize the arsenal at Harper's Ferry, as Cook tells us?"

"It is both," Father said calmly. "We seize the arsenal, take what weapons we need, and move out to the mountains."

Seize the arsenal? Annie dropped her sewing.

The arguments and counterarguments volleyed off the walls of the little house. The arsenal was too well guarded. It was not that well guarded at all. With the telegraph lines and the railroad, it would be too easy to summon assistance. The element of shock would prevent anyone from sending for as-sistance quickly enough. The slaves in the town were too settled to join in the raid. The slaves outside the town would gladly join in.

"That town is a death trap," Oliver said. "Hemmed in by the mountains and the rivers. If we go in, we need to go out quickly."

On and on they went as Annie gave up any pretense of sewing or reading and Cuffee of being played with. He gloomily flopped beside her. When the door finally opened, it was only Martha. "It's so contentious in there, I can't stand it anymore. Do you want me to watch for a while?"

"No. Father said I must stay here."

So, the two of them watched, but not a visitor came into sight. Inside, the voices grew less distinct until the door banged open, revealing Tidd. "I'm going to Cook's."

"Why?"

"Because this is madness, that's why. I should never have left Kansas for this."

He stomped off down the road as Father emerged. He didn't call Tidd, who was already on his way. "Come in, girls."

They obeyed to find the discussion breaking up. Some men were stretching while others were already heading upstairs to their lair. "Are you really going to take the Ferry?"

Father nodded. "It has been settled. Yes, we are."

It was plain from the faces around her that not all were reconciled to the decision, but Annie wisely did not continue the discussion. Instead, she tugged Jerry aside at the first opportunity. "What happened?"

"Your father said that if all were opposed to the plan—and many were and are—he would resign as our captain, and in fact, he did resign. And then, after five minutes, we chose him as our leader again."

"Harper's Ferry and all?"

"Harper's Ferry and all. Kagi's all for the plan. So is Owen. So is Shields Green. So am I. Your other brothers have their doubts. But there are those who told your father that the Kansas raid would fail too, and instead, a dozen people are free. So, we will abide by his decisions."

"And Tidd?"

"He'll be back. He just needs to cool off."

But she could not forget Oliver's words. *A death trap.* That night, when they had all retired to their room, she called softly behind her calico curtain, "Oliver? Do you really oppose taking the Ferry?"

"Yes. But it makes no difference now. We're going through with it."

"But why, if you feel so strongly against it?"

"Because he's our father. He's not going to change his mind. We can't let him go into this venture alone. And he's going to go in one way or another."

~ ~ ~

The next morning, Kagi had both pant legs arranged properly, but his necktie was untied, which was terribly bothersome. She pointed to it as he stepped onto the porch. "May I?"

"Certainly."

Annie made a neat bow. "Better," she pronounced.

"Thank you," Kagi said. "In Chambersburg, Mrs. Ritner is usually kind enough to check if I'm presentable before I leave the house. I see you're on duty again."

"Father wanted me to watch until you're safely off. By the way, you shouldn't be standing out here, in case the neighbor lady comes."

Obediently, Kagi stepped just inside. "Your father places a lot of trust in you."

"He always has, in all of us."

"Yes, he's often talked to me about you and the rest of the family. He's very proud of you all."

"Yes, I am," Father said, making them jump. He stroked his beard. "One thing I regret is being so harsh on my children, especially the older ones. I have learned something from my travels in New England, where I have stayed with many upstanding families, which is that it is better to bind a child by love than by fear."

Stevens, who along with the other invisibles had ventured downstairs, said, "I think you have no reason to feel guilty if the four children you have here are representative of the whole."

"Well, that is kind of you, Stevens. But it is one thing I wish I could do over."

He sighed, and Annie squeezed his hand. Was he forgetting the little presents he'd always brought home from his travels, the loving care he had given them and Mother when they were sick, the songs he would sing them to sleep with?

There was no way the boys—or any of them—could leave him to carry out his plan alone.

~ ~ ~

A few days later, just after nightfall, Tidd appeared at the farm. "I'm back," he said gruffly as Annie blocked the door with her figure.

"I see. Why'd you come back?"

"None of your business."

She crossed her arms and leaned against the door. In a softer tone, Tidd said, "Because, while I still have my doubts, we all need to stand together, whatever differences we have. Because it's a noble cause."

"You could have just told me that straightaway," Annie snapped.

"True. I'm sorry. You think the old man will see me?"

"Yes, but you don't deserve it."

"True again." He chucked her on the chin. "Now will you let me in?"

"I suppose." She stepped aside.

That night, she lay on her mattress, waiting for Tidd and Stevens' duet. Sure enough, their voices soon filled the air—joined presently by the rest of the men. A good omen, she thought. Smiling, she rolled over and drifted off to sleep.

~ ~ ~

On September 24, their third black recruit arrived: Osborne Anderson, another mixed-race man, who had gone to Oberlin College in Ohio and set up shop as a printer in Chatham, Canada, where he had met Father during his convention there. He was the one man who didn't fuss about being cooped up. "The print shop's far worse," he told Annie.

But she hardly got a chance to know him, because the very next day, Father said, "I am going to Philadelphia in hopes of raising some more money—and some more men. Kagi will accompany me. After that, we will be commencing operations soon. That means I must send you girls back to North Elba."

"Can't we stay?"

"No. I promised your mother that you would not be exposed to any danger. And there is the matter of Martha's child as well. It is best that she be sent to bear it among friends, instead of remaining here in uncertain circumstances. But I will be sorry to see you go; you have done good service."

"But who will watch? And what about Mrs. Hoffmaster and the other neighbors?"

"We will manage. As for Mrs. Hoffmaster, you had best explain that you are leaving. I doubt she will come by when there are nothing but men here."

Annie was not so certain, but the day before their departure, she and Martha, bearing an impressive array of foodstuffs, paid a call on Mrs. Hoffmaster. "We are going to visit some relations in Pennsylvania," Annie said. "We may be gone for a month or so. The men will be keeping bachelors' hall while we are gone, so I'm sure you won't want to see them in their uncivilized state. They'll probably be smoking."

"Spitting tobacco everywhere," Martha added. She wrinkled her nose prettily.

"I never seen them do any of that," Mrs. Hoffmaster said.

"Only because we made it clear we wouldn't put up with it," Annie said. This was actually true; she'd given the men a fine lecture when she had found tobacco juice on the floor—Hazlett had turned out to be the culprit—and she had gotten so sick of filling Shields Green's pipe, she'd put pepper in it one day. There was no telling what depravity they and the other smokers might revert to in the women's absence. "But when the cat's away, the mice will play."

Having warned Mrs. Hoffmaster off this lair of men the best they could, they returned to discover that the men had put together a farewell program of sorts for them. Shields Green, the pipe incident evidently forgiven, made a speech. Osborne Anderson presented the girls with a nosegay apiece. Dauphin Thompson imitated Martha, while William mimicked Annie. Stewart Taylor read a spiritualist poem. Hazlett promised that he would abstain from tobacco when their mission was complete. Dangerfield Newby read from the Book of Exodus. Owen and the Coppock brothers had baked some bread for them to take back home. Cook had sent some preserves, put up by his wife, from the Ferry via Leeman, who was fond of sneaking over there. Jerry had compiled a list of each item Mrs. Hoffmaster had ever borrowed, which he read aloud with a great deal of flair.

Oliver, who would be escorting Annie and Martha as far as Troy, and Watson, who would be driving the three to Chambersburg, said that they would be seeing more than enough of the girls on the way north, so they hadn't prepared anything. "But I love them," Watson said.

"Me too," Oliver said.

"You know what we have," Stevens said, and he and Tidd began to sing, "Home Again."

At last, everyone went to bed. Annie went to her room like the rest but only to get her shawl, which she wrapped around her as she stepped out onto the porch. Sure enough, in a few minutes, Jerry emerged from the shadows and glided up the stairs. "I knew you'd be waiting."

"I knew you'd come," she said as he took her into his arms.

"I'll going to miss you so much."

"I wish we could be alone together before I left. Really alone." Since news of their attachment had become known at the farm, it was as if they had a dozen chaperones.

Jerry stroked her cheek. "Since you mentioned that, I must confess I thought the same. I have a proposition for you. I'm not going to do anything that would violate the trust your father has put in me—in us, actually. I respect him too much, and I love you too much. But I would like to simply lie close to you and hold you before we part. I think you'll like it too."

"It would be heavenly."

"Then follow me to our fairy bower."

He guided her down the stairs and pushed open the door to the lower floor, used only for storage, mainly of the pikes—shafts with blades upon them—that Father had had specially made in Connecticut for use by slaves who hadn't been trained in the use of arms. The room was lit by a single lantern. In a corner, Jerry had placed a few blankets, and he appeared to have taken a broom to the premises.

She settled herself down in their nest, and Jerry held her fast against him. Inevitably, their closeness led to caresses and more. Annie, who had never dreamed such passion lay within her, would have given herself up to him entirely, but Jerry shook his head. "I'll not risk leaving you pregnant and alone, should the worst happen."

That brought her down to earth. "Jerry, what if the plan fails?"

"We'll be regarded either as traitors or fools. Or more likely, both. But I prefer to think that we'll succeed, that many will be free through our efforts, and that I'll come back and marry you." He traced the finger where she would have worn a wedding ring. "My brother has been advising me—since I am the youngest, my brothers regularly give me advice—to settle down and read the law. I generally make a point of not following their advice, but I admit it makes sense for a man who wants to marry. Would you like me to do that, when I feel that I have done my part here?"

"I would like that."

"I'll take you to see my folks in Iowa. Then we'll settle in a place where a man can make a steady living but where we're surrounded by beauty."

She leaned on his chest, which she had lovingly laid bare. "I love you so much, it's frightening. I can't bear to think of the worst happening."

"But you're not asking me to back out of the plan."

"No, of course not."

"I knew you wouldn't. None of you Brown women would; you've too much pluck." He set a kiss on her lips. "I do know the dangers of this, for all that I am an optimist. We all do; we've had some grim talks upstairs. Stevens asked Watson the other day why he had come here with a son just born to him, and he said that he couldn't justify living only for his own happiness and contentment with so many suffering. I think that's how we all feel, although he put it more eloquently." He stroked her unbound hair. "If I don't come out of it, I will have two things to console myself with: I have done my part to liberate people from bondage, and I have had the love of a good woman. Some poor souls can't say yes to either of these, and most can't say yes to both. I am lucky."

Annie supposed that she could console herself similarly, but the thought was too gloomy to pursue. Instead, she nestled against him and fell into a sweet sleep.

~ ~ ~

When the sun's rays began to penetrate into the basement, they arose and made themselves seemly. Jerry handed her a book. "I read from this the day I kissed you at the Ferry. I want you to keep it safe for me."

"Always."

After a parting kiss—if they extended it for much longer, they'd been on the blanket again—Annie slipped back to her room, where Martha was already primping at her gun box/dressing table. "Annie, I hope you didn't do anything foolish."

"No." She hugged Martha. "It was the most beautiful night of my life."

Martha sighed, then nodded in understanding "I know."

Breakfast, then another round of goodbyes. Annie took Dauphin's extended hand. "Friends?" she said softly.

"Friends. Give my love to my folks. Especially Bell and little Freddy."

"I will."

Jerry took her hand.

"Kiss her," Dauphin said resignedly. "You know you want to."

Jerry obeyed. "I'll write when I can."

"Tell us when the baby's born, Martha," Tidd said.

Martha blushed.

"Name it after me if it's a boy," Dangerfield Newby said.

"Well . . ."

"A joke, ma'am."

Martha grinned in relief.

Outside, Owen was loading their trunks onto the wagon. As Annie brought the last of her things outside, she turned to look at the worn old house. "I'll never forget this place," she said softly.

Owen followed her gaze. "I was thinking the other day, if our plan succeeds, one day this place will have a United States flag flying over it. If not, it'll be known as a den of traitors and thieves."

~ ~ ~

It was the practice of the men to take a horse and a mule to Chambersburg, with one beast pulling the wagon and another going along beside it. As the Browns traveled on the National Turnpike that led to Hagerstown, Oliver driving the wagon and Watson riding aside, a man turned his horse off a side road and veered in his direction. "I've seen him before," Oliver said.

"Who is he?" Martha asked.

"I don't know if he's a patrol of some sort or just a local busybody. Our wagon is getting a bit too familiar. One reason Father's starting operations soon."

As they watched, the man caught up with Watson, who had slowed to ride behind them. "Morning," they heard him say.

"Morning," Watson said politely.

"What are you hauling today, if you don't mind me asking?"

"Girls," Watson said. "We're hauling girls."

Annie and Martha poked their heads out of the back of the wagon and waved at him.

"Begging pardon, ladies," the man said. He studied the interior of the wagon, which held nothing but the girls' two small trunks and four carpetbags. "But what are you usually hauling?"

"Whatever needs to be hauled for whoever wants me to haul it."

"Wool?"

"Sometimes."

"Well," said their inquisitor. "I guess I'll be seeing you again."

"Most likely."

The man galloped off in the direction from which he had come.

"He's going to send someone to arrest us," Annie said.

"For traveling with two girls? No. But it's something to be concerned with." He snorted. "I wasn't lying entirely. Newby has a fine woolly mass of hair."

Although Annie continued to worry, they made it to Hagerstown without incident, and from there, to Chambersburg, where they were to spend the night at Mrs. Ritner's before Oliver and the girls boarded their train. "How much does she know about us?" Annie asked Watson, who had taken over the wagon at Hagerstown.

"More than she lets on, I suspect. She's an abolitionist who's hidden escaped slaves from time to time, and so were her late husband and her father-in-law—he was the Governor of Pennsylvania. We've never made a secret of our views with her. But we've always told her that we're in the mining business, and we've never given our true names, and neither has Kagi. He's her pet, you'll find. I think if he was older, she'd find a way to marry him."

Mrs. Ritner's house was trim and tidy, as was its land-lady, a refined-looking woman in her thirties who beamed at them when she opened the door. "Mr. Smith and his sons are the best lodgers I've ever had," she informed Annie and Martha as she led them inside. "Them and Mr. Henri." That was the name that Kagi, who had relations in Virginia, went by. "No tobacco, no liquor, and what perfect gentlemen! And Mr. Henri makes charming conversation."

"Don't we?" asked Oliver.

"Well, of course you do! But Mr. Henri truly excels at it."

Watson nudged Annie.

A little girl scurried up and hugged Watson. "Mr. Smith, will you give me a ride tomorrow?"

"Of course."

"They always let me ride on their wagon for about a mile," the girl explained.

Mrs. Ritner served them a delicious supper, and they conversed with a couple of her other boarders, who seemed nearly as fond of Father and the rest as their landlady. As Mrs. Ritner questioned them about the slaves living near the Kennedy Farm and the four of them answered, Annie reflected that it was pleasant to be in a place where they did not have to conceal their opinions, even if they were still traveling under assumed names. When Mrs. Ritner rather wistfully mentioned that Mr. Henri was in the habit of reading the evening newspaper to her, Watson obliged, although Annie suspected his efforts were not as well received as Kagi's.

After a good night's sleep—Annie had nearly forgotten what it felt like to lie in a real bed with no marauding fleas—they bid farewell to Mrs. Ritner, who was delighted by the news that Father and Kagi were expected in Chambersburg that day, and would in fact be meeting the girls and Oliver as they changed trains at Harrisburg. At the station, just around the block from Mrs. Ritner's, Watson handed Annie two letters, one for Bell, and the other for Mother and everyone else. "I told Bell this in my letter, but tell her I would like to have a proper love letter from her. The last one was too businesslike. Kiss Freddy for me."

"I will," Annie promised.

"Both of us will," Martha said. "We'll treat him like a little king."

Annie handed her brother a thick envelope. "I have a letter for Jerry if you'll give it to him."

"That's quite a missive," Oliver said.

"I wrote it last night." It was the first love letter she'd written. Seated at the writing desk in Mrs. Ritner's parlor, she'd thought she had made a fairly good job of it. At least Jerry would have no cause to complain that she was too businesslike.

"I'll deliver it safe and sound," Watson said. He patted Annie on the shoulder. "He's a good man and a good choice for you. If everything goes well, I'll be proud to have him as a brother."

"*If*," Annie said. "I don't like that word."

"When," Watson said cheerfully. "Better?" When Annie nodded, he hugged them all goodbye before they boarded the train, then stood waving his hat at them as their train chugged away.

~ ~ ~

As promised, when they got off the train at Harrisburg, they found Father and Kagi waiting for them. Kagi's tie was undone, a situation soon remedied by Martha. "I have very little money to send home," Father said, handing Annie some gold coins. "I know, however, that your mother will spend it wisely, and I trust that John will send some once business operations commence."

"Was your business in Philadelphia successful?" Annie asked.

"Sadly, not entirely. But it will not prevent us from commencing business operations."

"Do you need this?" Annie held out the money she had just been given.

"No, child. The Lord has provided before, and he will provide again." Father turned to Martha. "My prayers will be with you for a safe confinement, my dear. I know that between my wife and Ruth, you will have the best attendants."

"Thank you, Father Brown."

Kagi took Martha's hand, then Annie's. "I am pleased to have met both of you. I hope that someday all of us will be reunited."

"Will you be leaving Chambersburg?" Annie asked in a low voice.

"Yes, when operations commence. I'll miss it there."

Annie could not help but feel sorry for Mrs. Ritner. She hoped that the time would come when she and her model lodger would be reunited as well.

Father said, "Now, Annie, let me speak to you in private, and quickly. Your train will soon be here; it is always quite punctual." Expecting a lecture on the duty she owed her mother in his absence, Annie followed Father a ways. Instead, he indicated his battered coat. "Check inside this pocket, as you did when you were little."

Annie obeyed, and pulled out a dainty linen handker-chief. "Father!"

"It's very little, child, but I bought your sister Ruth a gift when she turned sixteen, and there is little or no likelihood I will be present when you turn that age. So, I wanted to give you something pretty and practical. And I will also give you a promise: when we see each other again, we will talk more about your marriage to Jerry."

Annie flung herself into her father's arms as a whistle blasted in the distance.

"There, there," Father said, gently putting her aside. "You must get ready to board. God bless you, Annie."

~ ~ ~

Although Father had impressed upon them the need to exer-cise the strictest economy, when they reached the hotel in Troy, Oliver told the clerk, "Two rooms." He would be set-ting off for the trip back to Maryland the next morning, leaving Martha and Annie to take the train to Whitehall by themselves. Annie took advantage of her solitary room to compose yet another love letter to Jerry, this time with the pleasant addition of Father's good news. This being accom-plished, she settled into her maiden's bed and thumbed through the book Jerry had given her until she reached a wildflower pressed into the page reading "Tintern Abbey." Jerry had marked a passage:

If solitude, or fear, or pain, or grief,
Should be thy portion, with what healing thoughts
Of tender joy wilt thou remember me,
And these my exhortations! Nor, perchance—
If I should be where I no more can hear

Thy voice, nor catch from thy wild eyes these gleams
Of past existence—wilt thou then forget
That on the banks of this delightful stream
We stood together; and that I, so long
A worshipper of Nature, hither came
Unwearied in that service: rather say
With warmer love—oh! with far deeper zeal
Of holier love.

Her eyes filled with tears, and she dropped the book. "Come back," she whispered. "Oh, please, my love. Come back."

~ ~ ~

Although Oliver and Martha had had ample opportunity to say anything they wanted to say to each other the night before, they didn't see it that way, and they huddled together in the railway station before the platform started to tremble with the approach of the train to Whitehall. Then Oliver turned to Annie. "I want to apologize if I've ever hurt your feelings, Annie. I know I can be brusque."

"Not lately."

"Well, that's good. Take care of yourself." In a lower tone, he added, "Please take good care of Martha. See that she exercises. See that she eats well."

"I will. I promise."

"Thank you." Oliver kissed Martha, then helped her onto the train and settled her into her seat by the window. "Comfortable?" he asked.

"Oliver, you'll be in Whitehall too if you don't get off this train."

"True." He sighed and gave Martha one last kiss.

~ ~ ~

The goodbyes were over now. Henceforth, there would be nothing but greetings: Thomas Jefferson, the man who had first guided them to North Elba, waiting with his wagon at Whitehall to take them home. Then Mother, Sarah, Ellen, Salmon, and Abbie. Then Henry and Ruth. Annie hadn't realized how much she had missed them all.

The Thompsons stopped by as well, but the meeting was just a trifle chilly. Dauphin had informed them of the broken engagement, it turned out, and while this relieved Annie from having to give awkward explanations, she knew they must think of her as fickle and even cruel. Even Bell was a little remote. But in time, she hoped, Dauphin would bring someone home who was far better for him than Annie would have been with her moods and general orneriness, and Annie herself would be living in Iowa or wherever Jerry and she decided to settle, far away from reproach.

She found it hard, though, to adjust back to her old routine. No watching, only farm chores. She wondered whether Mrs. Hoffmaster had found some way to plague the men, whether any new ones had arrived. Had the wagon been stopped again? Were the invisibles sticking to their attic lair? And—most important—had the plan been carried into effect?

Father sent a letter dated October 8, telling them of Oliver's safe arrival and little else. Since then, there had been silence, although Mother said this wasn't unusual, given that Father was in the habit of sending and receiving all of his mail at Chambersburg.

Following Oliver's advice to exercise, Martha had taken it upon herself to go to the post office for the weekly mail. She returned home one day in the latter half of October frowning. "There's a rumor that Father Brown has been captured. I don't think it true, though."

"Father has been reported captured ever since he went to Kansas," said Annie. "Even dead."

"And the marshal's caught him how many times?" Salmon asked.

"Who told you the rumor, Martha?" Abbie asked.

"The postmaster. He heard it from someone passing through, but he hasn't got a paper to confirm it yet." She held up the mail, which included several issues of the *New York Tribune*, as well as the usual anti-slavery papers. "None of these mention it that I can see."

"What do you think, Mother?" Annie asked.

"I don't know what to think. Each time I hear such news, I fear it may be true." She looked at the mantelpiece, where Father's daguerreotype held pride of place. "Where is he supposed to have been captured?"

"They didn't say."

Annie brightened. "Surely if it was true, they'd have said Virginia. Right?"

"Or Maryland, or Pennsylvania even." Martha's cheeks began to bloom again. "It's clear now. It's just a rumor. For all those people know, he might as well be in Kansas."

~ ~ ~

The next day, Martha's young brother Byron appeared at the door—hardly an event in itself, as he often came over to help Salmon with the heavy chores. But he was as white as Martha had been the day before, and he carried a newspaper under his arm. "Mrs. Brown, one of the neighbors was at Vergennes yesterday. He brought me a *New York Times.*"

He faltered. They all stared at the newspaper as if expecting it to unfold and speak for itself. Finally, Byron removed it from his arm. "You'd best read it, Mrs. Brown."

The headline on the paper, dated October 20, read: THE HARPER'S FERRY REBELLION. REVELATIONS OF CAPTAIN BROWN.

Mother closed her eyes. "Please read it aloud for us, Annie. You read better than I do."

Annie read. She read slowly, carefully as the rest listened in complete silence.

The raid, in Father's mind for ever so many years, had utterly failed.

Father was a prisoner.

Stevens was a prisoner.

Edwin Coppock was a prisoner.

Cook was a fugitive.

Oliver was dead.

Watson was dead.

Dauphin Thompson was dead.

William Thompson was dead.

John Kagi was dead.

Dangerfield Newby was dead.

Stewart Taylor was dead.

William Leeman was dead.

Jeremiah Anderson was dead.

Two things had been taken from Jerry after death, the reporter noted: his commission as a captain in Father's army and a memorandum book containing a poem:

> I look upon her as she stands
> Free from all woman's tricks of art,
> And in my own I clasp her hands
> And lay them on my beating heart.

"*But that heart is now still in death, and his body lies upon the grass surrounded by those of his deluded and miserable companions,*" Annie read in a flat voice. "*And no more cared for than the carcasses of so many dead swine.*"

She must have stopped reading for a moment, she supposed, for someone said quietly, "Go on, Annie. Can you go on?"

She nodded, commanded her voice, and resumed reading.

That was what you did—what a Brown woman did, anyway—when everything fell apart. You went on.

Part IV

Mary

19

October 1859 to November 1859

Watson and Oliver had taken most of their wearing apparel to Maryland, having anticipated being there for all seasons. But they had left their oldest hats at North Elba, hanging on pegs by the door. Until the news had come, people—even Mary and the girls—had often plucked them off the pegs when going outside for chores. They were easier to work in than bonnets, and what did the livestock care? The younger girls and their cousins liked them as well when they played dress-up games.

But now the hats remained undisturbed on their pegs. One day, Mary supposed, she would have to take them down. But she hadn't had the heart. None of the Browns or the Thompsons had much of a heart for anything.

Some of the details as to what had happened were still unclear in their minds, and it was painful to dwell on the ones they had gleaned from the newspapers, which were already stale by the time they had arrived in North Elba. One thing was clear: John, having taken Harper's Ferry with his men on the rainy evening of October 16, had lingered there too long, so that he was trapped. "Why did he stay so long?" Martha asked over and over again. "Why?"

No one had an answer.

One by one, his men had met their fates. Annie, wandering about the house at all hours, sleepless and pale as a wraith, had known nearly all of the fallen and the imprisoned. Most of the dead had perished in exchanges of fire between John's men and the motley group of locals who had turned out to defend the town. Dangerfield Newby, the first of the men to be slain, carrying a letter from his enslaved wife in his pocket. John Kagi, taking a bullet to the head as he tried to escape across the Shenandoah River. William Leeman, shot in the face as he tried to surrender. Stewart Taylor, whom Annie claimed had predicted his own death, gunned down. Lewis Leary, the last of John's black recruits, his throat slashed by a passerby as he lay captive. Aaron Stevens, wounded while carrying a flag of truce, was one of the few who had survived the fighting.

And then there was Oliver, shot at John's side in the arsenal's engine house, to which John's men had retreated on October 17. Watson, also wounded while carrying the white flag, lingered in agony for two days. William Thompson, North Elba's favorite young man, had been captured. But after the town's mayor was killed in the fighting, a group of drunken, vengeful citizens had dragged the bound William from the Wager House hotel, shot him, thrown him off the bridge into the Potomac River, and then, finding him still alive, finished him off with a fusillade of bullets.

By the morning of Tuesday, October 18, John's force had dwindled to five men: John himself, Jeremiah Anderson, Shields Green, Edwin Coppock, and Dauphin Thompson, holed up in the engine house while Oliver lay dead in one corner and Watson lay dying in another. There, as the local slave owners they had taken hostage and a few of their slaves huddled against a wall, John and his men had faced an assaulting force of United States Marines commanded by Colonel Robert E. Lee. Their glittering bayonets had slammed Jeremiah Anderson against a wall and pierced Dauphin Thompson as he took cover under the engine. Lieutenant Israel Green had concentrated on John. Having failed to bayonet him, he'd beaten him into unconsciousness with the hilt of his sword instead. But John had confounded the lieutenant by surviving. He, along with Stevens, the unharmed Shields Green and Edwin Coppock, and John Copeland, a black latecomer to John's ranks who had had the good fortune to escape the ire of the crowd after being captured, had been taken the next day to Charlestown, Virginia, the county seat, to await trial.

And that was all anyone in North Elba knew.

"I knew Father would get himself trapped," Salmon said on a day when Martha and Bell happened to be out visiting North Elba's third widow, Mary Thompson. "That's why I didn't go with the other boys."

"The other day you said that you didn't go because Abbie was expecting," Annie said. "And then the day before that, you said that you were needed on the farm. And the day before that, you said you would have gone later, when you were called for. And the day—"

"Maybe they were all true," Salmon snapped. "Anyway, aren't you glad I'm still here?"

"Of course I am! But if you knew what was going to happen, why didn't you say so?"

"Who would have listened? Anyway, Watson wanted to go after missing his chance in Kansas; you know that. And Oliver did too."

"Please," Mary said. "I am grateful that the Lord has spared one son to me."

"I'm sorry, Ma." Salmon's shoulders slumped. "I wish I had gone too. Maybe I could have helped them."

"Maybe you would have gotten killed too."

"Just stop it," Mary said. This time, she succeeded.

It was some relief, though, to see Annie finally showing a glimmer of life. Even before the girls' return from Maryland, Mary had heard from Henry and Ruth that she had thrown off poor Dauphin, although Mary had privately hoped that the girl just needed some time and maturity. But she hadn't realized until Ruth wormed the truth out of Annie that there was another man at the root of it all, the Anderson fellow who had accompanied John on his visit to North Elba in May. (Mary couldn't bear to think of it as John's *last* visit to North Elba.) He had been friendly and obliging, and John appeared to think a great deal of him, but Mary didn't like the idea of him starting a romance with her daughter right under Dauphin's nose. Worse, Mary couldn't shake the idea that there might be something else amiss. Even under the weight of the sorrow she was carrying, Annie seemed more knowing.

Later that afternoon, when Annie grabbed her old cloak from its peg—it pained Mary to realize just how old a cloak it was, a cast-off from Ruth—Mary followed her outside. "Where are you going?"

"For a walk."

Annie went on these walks daily, disappearing for hours at a time. Ruth had said that she reminded her of someone out of *Wuthering Heights*. Mary had no idea what this meant but was fairly sure it wasn't anything good. "Let me walk with you a little ways."

Her daughter grumbled a consent.

"Annie, how well did you know Mr. Anderson?"

"I told you, we were to be married."

"Should you have been married?"

"Of course we should have. We loved each other." Annie's voice cracked.

"I know." But how well could someone love someone she'd known for only a matter of weeks? "But I mean—could you be with child?"

"No."

"Are you sure?"

Annie regarded her with eyes of steel. "Yes. I started bleeding today."

Mary drew a breath of relief, even as she reflected that Annie hadn't protested the impossibility of her getting with child. She would take this one ray of comfort.

"I wish I was, though. I would have carried it proudly. It would have been my one consolation. Now will you let me walk by myself?"

She stomped off before Mary could even answer.

~ ~ ~

Not a man to leave things to chance, John had always included minute instructions in his letters, quite often about things that Mary knew perfectly well how to do. Sometimes the advice had amused her, sometimes, especially in the last few years when John was so seldom around, it had irritated her. Did he think that she just sat around helplessly, letting things go to rot while she waited for his advice?

But he had left absolutely none in this instance: what to do if his plan failed and he was a prisoner of the State of Virginia.

Their first thought had been for Salmon or Henry Thompson to travel down to Charlestown. But any man named Brown or Thompson was at risk of being imprisoned. No one except for little Ellen could plead ignorance of John's plan. Everyone had known at least some of its contours. Annie had offered to go, but Mary would not permit it. No telling what she would do if she was allowed to go to Virginia.

There was Mr. Sanborn, the man who had come to pay off their land a while back. Mary knew he lived in Concord, and she also knew the names and locales of some of John's other benefactors. But to write to them would to be incriminate them, if they hadn't been so already, although John seemed to have been scrupulous in mentioning no names to his interrogators. John Jr. was equally at risk. Jason, though absent from the plan, would likely be deemed guilty just by being a Brown.

And there was the matter of Owen. He hadn't been mentioned among the dead or the captured, so there was hope that he was a fugitive, as John Cook was known to be. No one wanted to do anything that might put his life in jeopardy. And if he or others happened to arrive in North Elba in need of shelter and perhaps wounded, someone would have to tend to them.

So, the Browns remained where they were, not having heard from any soul outside of North Elba since their last letter from John—unless one counted the letters that arrived from Watson, Oliver, and Jeremiah Anderson, mailed before the raid and received after they had gone to their deaths. It still hurt to recall the wild hope that rose in all of them when they opened the letters, only to see the dates.

There seemed nothing to do but wait for the next mail and pick at their wounds.

Then Mr. Thomas Wentworth Higginson, one of John's New England supporters, turned up.

He arrived in a horse and buggy, both the worse for wear—later, he confessed to Mary that they had gotten away from him on the snow-covered, twisty roads leading to North Elba—but to the Browns, he might have descended from heaven, lapsed minister though he was. He brought the assurances that although some of John's friends had fled for cover, fearful of arrest, others were standing by him.

"I feared my husband's friends might be disappointed in him after the failure of his plan," Mary said.

"Disappointed? You can have no idea, Mrs. Brown, in your seclusion here, what a sensation your husband has wrought. His courage and manly speeches have won the respect even of his captors. And he was not the only hero there. Stevens, wounded and thought to be dying, staring down a mob that came to kill him, to the effect that the citizens backed out of the room, ashamed of themselves. Your noble son Watson, lying at the point of death, telling a Baltimore reporter that he had come to Virginia to do his duty. William Thompson shouting before his death that tens of thousands would rise to avenge him. The black men, fighting side by side with the whites. The sheer audacity of a small band of men stealing into Harper's Ferry and taking it."

"There were no more gallant men than those," Annie said fiercely.

"The raid may have been a failure, technically speaking, but it was a noble one, and mark my words, the slaveholders of the South will never have a good night's sleep again."

Mary asked, "Do you have any other news for us, sir? We are desperate for it."

"Better than that." Mr. Higginson indicated his carpet-bag. "I have newspapers—a day old, to be sure, but full of fresh tidings for you. I will read from them to you anon. But let me start by saying, in case you did not know, that Mr. Brown's trial—if you can call it that—began a few days ago. The result was a foregone conclusion. He was found guilty of treason and of murder—for the deaths of various towns-people who engaged with his men, and for one of the marines who stormed the engine house. He has not yet been sentenced, but I think we know what his sentence will be."

Mary sighed. "Yes."

Mr. Higginson brought out his precious newspapers, and the widows of North Elba, who had staked out a corner of the parlor for themselves, excluding even Annie from their sisterhood of sorrow, joined the rest around the table. Rapt, they listened as their visitor read to them John's answers to his interrogators just hours after his capture.

Had John gone to Kansas under the auspices of the Emigrant Aid Society?

No, sir, I went under the auspices of John Brown.

"So much like Father," Ruth said affectionately, brushing a tear from her eye.

You may dispose of me very easily. I am nearly disposed of now, but this question is still to be settled—the Negro question, I mean. The end of that is not yet.

"Very true," Salmon said grimly.

When Mr. Higginson had ceased reading, Ellen brought out the Bible that John had given her, and for good measure, her rag doll, which had nothing to do with John but which Mr. Higginson duly admired. Salmon and Henry talked of

John's days in Kansas. Sarah scurried about, collecting the family daguerreotypes to show to their visitor. Martha quietly produced her own photograph of Oliver. Annie told Mr. Higginson about each and every one of the young men she had known in Maryland. Ruth sang John's favorite hymn. Even Mary found herself talking much more than usual— about John's favorite Bible verses and Oliver's favorite books and all the improvements Watson had made to the farm. "I hope I'm not boring you, sir."

"No. Go on."

But Mr. Higginson had a purpose for his visit, which he unfolded soon enough.

"I told you, madam, that I expect the harshest sentence for your husband. And that, Mrs. Brown, is where you come in. There are plans to try to free him from his prison, which we think could succeed. It is our understanding from his lawyer Mr. Hoyt—a young man we sent to him both to aid in his defense and to keep in communication with us—that he does not wish to escape, that he believes that he can do our cause far more good by dying for it. We will do nothing against his wishes. Still, we do not wish him to forfeit his life. It is our hope that you would be willing to go to Charlestown and persuade him to let us carry out our plan."

Mary almost smiled. "If my husband has made up his mind, it won't be changed by me. Or anyone."

Mr. Higginson nodded in understanding. "I have sufficient acquaintance with your husband so as not to doubt what you say. But if anyone can change his mind, it might be you. You can plead that he escape for the love of you and his family. No one else has that hold on him."

"If there is one person who could have done that, it was my husband's father. John revered him. But he has been dead over three years, and John didn't always take his advice either."

Mary looked at the earnest young man. "Still, I want to save him too, and at the very least, I want to see him. I will go."

~ ~ ~

"Was all of this a surprise to you, Mrs. Brown?"

Mary was ensconced on a train headed toward Boston, where Mr. Higginson wanted her to meet some of John's supporters before heading south. She shook her head. "Only as to some of the details. I always knew my husband wished to strike a blow against slavery."

"And you never complained about his absences? Some women—I think most women—would."

"No. Why would I? He was doing the Lord's work. I would not have complained if he were preaching or in the missionary field. This was no different."

"Extraordinary." Their train was approaching a station. "I believe today's papers will be out by now. I'll hop out and get some for us."

It was a longer hop than Mary would have expected, but Mr. Higginson returned presently, laden with freshly printed newspapers. "I am sorry, Mrs. Brown," he said as he handed her one.

John had been condemned to death, his hanging scheduled for December 2. Her eyes filming, Mary read the speech he had made before his sentence was pronounced.

Now, if it is deemed necessary that I should forfeit my life for the furtherance of the ends of justice and mingle my blood further with the blood of my children and with the blood of millions in this slave country whose rights are disregarded by wicked, cruel, and unjust enactments—I submit, so let it be done!

Mary bent her head against the seat in front of her. "Amen," she whispered.

~ ~ ~

At the American House, John's favorite hotel in Boston, Mary prepared for what she thought might be half a dozen visitors— the Secret Six, give or take a few. Instead, her suite was soon awash with men and women. Mr. Sanborn was there, as was his maiden sister, Miss Sarah Sanborn, who taught at her brother's school. "You will want to put your daughters in the way of making a living for themselves, as I do," she informed Mary. "I suggest my brother's establishment. No doubt some will urge other schools upon you," she added darkly, "but Mr. Sanborn is a far better teacher."

Mary's head whirled.

Dr. Samuel Gridley Howe, another member of the Secret Six, swept into the room, followed by his wife, Julia Ward Howe, a striking redhead considerably his junior, who appeared very far gone with child. Dr. Howe was about John's age but looked younger and far more dashing, and Mary could not help but think he was a bit of a peacock. She was reproaching herself for this uncharitable opinion when a tearful Mrs. Howe flung her arms around her in parting and Dr. Howe said, "Now, Julia!" as if scolding a child. "You mustn't upset yourself in your condition."

Mary wished Mrs. Howe a safe delivery and gave her a parting embrace nearly as extravagant as had been bestowed upon her. John had never fussed over her in such a silly manner when she was pregnant; more often than not, she'd been busy with her chores when she had felt her labor pains come on.

All who came pressed various items upon her. Money, plenty of it, for her journey south. Gloves—mostly too small for her, but roomy enough to accommodate her daughters and daughters-in-law. Handkerchiefs, enough for two weeks. Someone even brought a pair of shoes, which surprisingly fit her. Had Mr. Higginson surreptitiously measured her feet?

Everyone had his or her favorite quotation from John's interrogation and trial to recite to Mary. Everyone had a kind word for her to pass on to John and to his fellow captives. Everyone was worried about Owen and the other fugitives.

Mr. Amos Lawrence, who had done much to fund the Free-State settlement of Kansas—Mary knew that the city of Lawrence was named after him—turned up with money and a very specific request. "Mrs. Brown, you must have a photograph made of yourself."

"Whatever for?"

"His supporters wish to have one of Mr. Brown's noble wife to place alongside their photograph of her brave husband."

It would have been churlish to argue further, so Mary agreed and presently found herself at a Mr. Heywood's studio—the first time she had had her photograph taken since the time she had sat in Springfield with a sulky Annie and a game Sarah. For some reason, she'd never gotten around to having herself taken with any of the boys, including Watson and Oliver. But they had had the foresight to sit for their photographs as grown men before it was too late, and now she at least had the comfort of having their faces before her on the mantelpiece. "Photography is a wonderful thing," she told Mr. Heywood as he adjusted the neck brace on his posing stand.

"I agree, madam."

Well, he would, wouldn't he? Her half-smile softened her face as she gazed at the camera.

~ ~ ~

With more baggage than she'd arrived with in Boston, Mary boarded the train that would take her to Worcester, where she and Mr. Higginson would part, as he lived in that town and it would be unwise, given his connection with John's plan, for him to accompany her south. She would continue to Connecticut, where she would board a steamer that would put her in New York City by dawn. There she would travel by rail to Philadelphia, and from there, to Baltimore, and ultimately to Virginia and John.

"I want to tell you before we part, Mrs. Brown, what a privilege it has been to meet you and your family," Mr. Higginson said, gathering up his things. "Your husband has always spoken of you and his children with the greatest respect, but still, I did not know what to expect when I came to your door at North Elba. I feared that you might be bitter and despairing, but instead I found you heroically resigned to your circumstances."

Mary shook her head. "We're not the perfect people you think we are. We've been lost these last few days, not knowing what to do. Lost and squabbling among ourselves. Salmon is glad about being alive and guilty over not going to Virginia with his brothers. Annie is wearing herself to rags over a young man she knew for only weeks. And I—I love my husband dearly, but sometimes I think I could strangle him before the State of Virginia does when I think of my poor boys dying as they did. It's hard when they die as children, but it's hard too when they die as adults. Why didn't he just leave that terrible place when he could?"

"Oh, Mrs. Brown."

Mary could not help but think that a minister, even a lapsed one, should have been able to come up with something more. "I do comfort myself that my sons died for a noble cause. If the Lord had to take them, I am glad it was for that. But I would rather that their lives had been spared. I miss them so very, very much."

"I understand, Mrs. Brown. Still, I must admire you for your fortitude. You and your children are worthy of your husband."

If Mr. Higginson was determined to think the best of them, she really couldn't argue with him.

~ ~ ~

On Monday, November 7, Mary reached Baltimore and nearly the end of her journey. From there, she would travel to Harper's Ferry, and then, assuming that the authorities allowed it, to Charlestown. Mr. James McKim, an abolitionist from Philadelphia, had accompanied her to Baltimore.

Jiggling her foot and repeatedly glancing at the station clock, Mary was sitting in the depot at Baltimore when a man entered and began to look around him. In no time at all, his eye fell upon Mr. McKim and Mary, who knew she was conspicuous with her country attire and the newspapers protruding from her carpetbag. She gathered as many as she could at every opportunity and read them from front to back, looking for any mention of John and his men. "Mr. McKim?" the man said in a low voice. "I believe I met you some months ago. Is this Mrs. John Brown?"

"Yes, sir."

"My name is Charles Fulton, an editor here." He nodded at the *Baltimore American* in Mary's hand. "You are reading my newspaper, as a matter of fact. Thank you." He cleared his throat. "Mr. McKim, I have received this telegram from one who heard that Mrs. Brown might be here."

Mary's companion frowned as he scanned it. "It appears, Mrs. Brown, that for some reason your husband does not want you to proceed to Charlestown. He has sent word through his lawyer to that effect."

"Why?"

"He gives no reason. I am sure he has a good one that cannot be conveyed in a telegram, though." Mr. McKim drew his arm through Mary's. "Come, Mrs. Brown, let me escort you back to Philadelphia. You can stay with us until this is cleared up."

Mary acquiesced numbly. Barely thanking Mr. Fulton, she let Mr. McKim retrieve her baggage and hail a carriage to take her to the depot that served Philadelphia-bound trains. Why did John not want her by his side?

One lady, the very pretty and very young Mrs. Nellie Russell, had already been admitted to John's cell. Her husband, Judge Thomas Russell, who had known John in Kansas and sheltered him in Boston when he was in some danger of being arrested, had hurried to Virginia to see his old friend after receiving a letter from John asking him to procure counsel for him and the other prisoners. Mrs. Russell had become fond of John during the week he had hidden at her house, and she had insisted on accompanying the judge to Charlestown, where the couple had been allowed by John's jailor to visit with him for a short time. By chance, Mary had met the Russells at the depot in Boston when they returned from their journey south. "I cried when I parted from that brave old man," Mrs. Russell had told Mary, and her lovely eyes had glistened again at the memory of it.

It was pure foolishness, Mary knew, to feel a stab of jealousy. Mrs. Russell hadn't seen John alone, and John hadn't even known she and her husband were coming. But she couldn't suppress it.

At the depot, Mr. McKim went to the newsstand and returned with the *New York Tribune*, the most sympathetic to John of all the New York papers. Eager for a distraction from her unworthy thoughts, Mary opened it to page six, where news from Harper's Ferry usually appeared, and read slowly on to page seven, where she learned that her husband's friends had sought and received permission from the authorities for her to visit. "*But when the matter was mentioned to Brown, he directed that this message should immediately be sent: Do not, for God's sake, come here now. John Brown.*"

Mary snapped the newspaper shut. Her eyes stung with tears, necessitating that she reach for one of the fine handkerchiefs she had been given in Boston.

~ ~ ~

"*I long to nurse you, to speak to you sisterly words of sympathy and consolation,*" Mary read to Mr. William Still, her host.

"*Sisterly* words," Mr. Still reminded her gently.

The newspapers were full of a Mrs. Lydia Child, an authoress and abolitionist, who had gotten it into her head that she should proceed to Charlestown and nurse John as if he didn't have a perfectly good wife waiting in Philadelphia to do just that. The intrepid Mrs. Child had written to both Governor Wise of Virginia and to John himself, whose reply, if he had given one, had not yet been made public. "She could have written to me."

"She probably had no idea of where to reach you," Mr. Still said reasonably.

Mary scowled.

A black conductor on the Underground Railroad, Mr. Still, who was also a friend of Mr. McKim, had invited Mary to stay at his house on Locust Street while she awaited further word from John or from the newspapers, whichever came first. Mr. Still had helped dozens of people to freedom over the years and had also assisted two of John's men to safety. These were Osborne Anderson, whose name Mary recognized from Annie, and a Francis Meriam, whose name Annie had not mentioned. From what Mr. Still had gathered, the latter, who came from a wealthy Boston family, had joined John and his men just before the raid, bearing hundreds of dollars in gold, and when all hope was lost had escaped with Owen, John Cook, Barclay Coppock, and Charles Tidd. The five, freezing and short of food, had spent days secreted in the mountains until Owen, finding Meriam to be unfit for the life of a fugitive, had escorted him to Chambersburg and directed him to walk in a blizzard to the next railway station, from which he had boarded a train to Philadelphia and sent a message to Mr. Still. Mr. Cook, Mary knew from the papers, had left the group later in search of food and been caught. Another fugitive, Albert Hazlett, had also fallen into Virginia hands, but Owen, Mr. Coppock, and Mr. Tidd were still at large. "I hope they can find their way to you as well," Mary had said.

"If they do, Mrs. Brown, never fear, we'll get them to safety. But I think they've probably already reached it. Our men have been looking for them too, and I must say they're good at it."

But while Mr. Still was undoubtedly adept at shepherding wandering men, his attempts at reassuring Mary about John's refusal to see her fell as flat as Mr. McKim's, especially when Mrs. Child's letters entered the picture. "I am sorry if I seem ungracious, sir. I just can't believe he won't see me. I really don't mean to be so much trouble."

"No trouble at all, Mrs. Brown." He chuckled. "Now Meriam was trouble. Strange little duck. Blind in one eye, and in dreadful shape physically. Very well brought up, very bright. But touched in the head a bit. He had the idea he should go back and rescue your husband single-handedly, when, by his own admission, it took your stepson Owen to get him to Pennsylvania alive. It took a great deal of persuasion to get him packed off safely to his people in Boston."

A one-eyed boy from Boston, an authoress, Mary herself—all wanting to go see John. Mary wondered if any of them would manage it.

~ ~ ~

That afternoon, George Hoyt turned up at Mr. Still's house. He was a young man, only in his early twenties, and he looked like a mere stripling. Sent down to Virginia by John's Boston friends after news of the disaster at Harper's Ferry, Mr. Hoyt had rendered John some legal services but had mostly gone as a spy. It was he who had advised Mr. Higginson that John did not wish to escape. The Virginia authorities had been suspicious of him from the start. After John's trial had concluded, he had found it expedient to return to Boston, where he and the Russells had met Mary at the railway station as she was heading South. "But now I am coming back to continue to keep his friends informed," he told Mary, who wondered if a beard might help the youth, assuming he could grow one. "And Mr. Higginson has given me this to bring to you. It is a letter Mr. Brown wrote to him when he learned that you were coming. He wanted you to be acquainted with its contents."

Mary's heart leapt at the familiar handwriting.

If my wife were to come here just now it would only tend to distract her mind, ten fold; *and would only add to my affliction; and cannot possibly do me any good. It will also use up the scanty means she has to supply Bread & cheap but comfortable clothing, fuel, &c for herself & children through the winter. DO PERSUADE her to remain at home for a time (at least) till she can learn further from me. She will receive a thousand times the consolation AT HOME that she can possibly find elsewhere. I have just written her there & will write her CONSTANTLY. Her presence here would deepen my affliction a thousand fold. I beg of her to be calm and submissive; & not to go* wild *on my account.*

Go wild? When on earth in their twenty-six years of marriage had Mary ever gone wild? Not in the early days, when she had been a seventeen-year-old bride faced with five scowling stepchildren. Not on the day she watched the government's man haul their goods away. Not on the days the fever took her four children in Richfield. Not on the day poor Kitty had gasped her last. Not on the day when she had heard that Watson and Oliver had been killed. And not just a few days ago, when Mr. Higginson had handed her the newspaper that told her that John had been condemned to die.

After all those years, couldn't he give her more credit?

Still, her worst fear—that she had somehow displeased him—seemed unfounded. When Mr. Hoyt had taken his tea and was preparing to leave to meet his train, she said, "I do hope I shall be able to see my husband again in this life. But tell him that I can spare him for the sake of his—our—great cause."

Surely John would not consider this *going wild.*

~ ~ ~

While Mary was at a standstill in Philadelphia, yet another a lady had arrived in Charlestown—not Mrs. Child, as the press thought at first, but Mrs. Rebecca Spring, the wife of a wealthy merchant from Perth Amboy, New Jersey. Thinking to meet Mrs. Child at Charlestown, Mrs. Spring had not bothered with writing to the governor or anyone else but had simply conscripted her son as an escort and headed down South, where she had found herself less than welcome but had finally managed to gain admission to John's cell.

Mary knew all this not only from the newspapers, but from Mrs. Spring, who had stopped in Philadelphia after leaving Virginia with a letter from John, a tale to tell, and an invitation for Mary to stay at her home in New Jersey. Mary had accepted, despite being quite at home at Mr. Still's. She did not want to drain his limited resources, and in any case, Mrs. Spring was not a lady who took no for an answer, as evidenced by her experience in Charlestown. "They treated me like a regular shuttlecock, sending me from person to person," she informed Mary. "Finally, I met one of Mr. Brown's lawyers, and he got me permission, even though Mr. Brown hadn't wanted to see me at first. But when he realized that I only wished to bring some comfort to him, he agreed. Your husband is a perfect gentleman, which is more than I can say for most of the men down there. What an uncouth lot! They stared at me in a most disagreeable way, spit their awful tobacco near me, crowded as close as they could, and said the most hateful things to each other with the intent that I should overhear them. Mr. Brown is quite wise not to let you come, trust me."

"Yes, I'm sure he is," Mary said, fingering John's letter in her pocket. "But I wish more than anything to see him."

Intended for the entire family to read, the letter from John Mrs. Spring had carried to her had been more palatable than the one John had written to Mr. Higginson.

I wrote most earnestly to my dear & afflicted wife not to come on for the present at any rate... The little comfort it might afford us to meet again would be dearly bought by the pains of final separation . . . If she comes on here, she must be only a gazing stock throughout the whole journey . . . it is my most decided judgment that in quietly and submissively staying at home, vastly more of generous sympathy will reach her without such dreadful sacrifice of feeling as she must put up with if she comes on.

It was full of solicitation for her, as was the next letter, forwarded to her by Mr. Hoyt, safely arrived back in Charlestown.

I need not tell you that I have a great desire to see you again, but that many strong objections exist in my mind against it . . . I am under renewed obligation to you, my ever faithful & beloved wife, for heeding what may be my last but earnest request.

With those words ringing in her ears, she could hardly defy John and travel to Charlestown, especially since it turned out that Mrs. Child had heeded John's polite request not to come. But the letters, which she pulled from her pocket and re-read whenever she found herself alone, had not quenched her desire to do so, especially since John was still recovering from the wounds he had received at the hands of the assaulting marines. Young Mrs. Russell had mended John's coat, and Mrs. Spring had brought him autumn leaves to decorate his cell and, more practically, arnica, bandages, and toiletries. But what had Mary done?

Seated at the handsome rosewood writing desk in Mrs. Spring's sitting room with a stack of thick, ivory-colored writing paper at her command, Mary fiddled with her pen as she tried to summon up words that would get John to relent.

I am here with Mrs. Spring, the kind lady who came to see you and minister to your wants, which I am deprived of doing. You have nursed and taken care of me a great deal, but I cannot even come and look at you. O, it is hard! But I am perfectly satisfied with it, believing it best . . . When you were at home last June, I did not think that I took your hand for the last time. But may Thy will, O Lord, be done. I do not want to do or say anything to disturb your peace of mind; but O, I would serve you gladly if I could.

Surely staying away was not the best service Mary could render John.

In the meantime, she did at least have the satisfaction of making some shirts and drawers for John, most of whose clothing had vanished from the Kennedy Farm. This was accomplished in the sewing room, for Mrs. Spring's house was of such an immensity that there was a special room for doing almost anything, including bathing.

Mrs. Spring owned a sewing machine, which was mainly operated by a servant, but Mary eyed it for so long and so closely that Mrs. Spring asked if she wanted to try it. Despite her embarrassment at being caught out, Mary didn't demur but stepped right to the machine and took her place. She listened politely while the girl explained the workings, but all she really needed was to try the thing herself. In what seemed no time at all, she had produced a machine-sewn shirt for John.

"You catch on very fast," Mrs. Spring said.

"I've been spinning all my life," Mary said. "This is much easier."

She was pleased enough with her new accomplishment to sew another shirt, this one made of such fine linen that it could likely last John a couple of years before being relegated to the ragbag. Then she remembered that it had to last him only for about three weeks.

~ ~ ~

As Mary's time with Mrs. Spring drew to an end, her hostess ushered a young man into the sitting room. "This is Mr. Theodore Tilton. He writes for the *New York Independent*."

The *Independent*, the *Tribune*, the *Herald*, the *Times*, the *Observer*—Mary had at first had difficulty keeping all these New York papers straight. The *Tribune* was sympathetic to John; indeed, Mr. Hoyt and the Russells had told her that it was banned from Charlestown, although its correspondent was there, his identity a secret. The *Times* and the *Herald* were far less supportive, but Mary found their coverage bearable. The *Observer* was so rabidly anti-John that Mary refused to read it. The single time she had, it was all she could do not to tear the hateful rag in half. The *Independent*, a weekly, was firmly abolitionist, but as John in recent years had been constrained by his finances to limit the papers he took , Mary had only seen it once or twice.

Mr. Tilton took her hand. "Mrs. Brown, I hope you might grant me a favor. An interview, to be precise."

"About my husband?"

"Well, yes, but about you as well." Seeing Mary's look of doubt, Mr. Tilton added, "I have heard nothing but laudatory things about you and your support for your husband's cause. It can only help the cause for the public to know what a small circle of people already have learned in these past few days."

Mary had to concede that Mr. Tilton had a point.

Gently, he drew out answer upon answer from her, all the while scribbling in a little notebook. It was unnerving at first to see it. Who had thought in 1832, when Mary arrived at Mr. Brown's house as hired help, that anyone would possibly be interested in hearing what she had to say, much less take notes about it? But gradually, Mary's eyes stopped wandering to the moving pen, and Mary even grew quite warm in her remarks, especially when given the opportunity to correct some misconception about John. He did not go about brandishing weapons; only since his Kansas days, when he and the boys were constantly under threat, had he been in the habit of carrying arms, and even then, no more than strictly necessary. A cruel man? Far from it. He was only too generous, too kind-hearted. No one had tended her and the children more tenderly in sickness than John.

Mr. Tilton had a delicate question which he hoped would not offend her. Did she believe Mr. Brown to be insane, as so many people were saying?

"Nonsense. His head is as clear as yours, mine, or anyone's." She smiled grimly. "I never knew of his insanity until I read it in the newspapers."

"I believe you, Mrs. Brown. His plan was a daring one, an audacious one, but not a mad one."

"My husband would not have asked my boys to go into a scheme for which he had no hope simply to make a point. He loved them." She could not suppress a tear.

"I know." Mr. Tilton rose to leave. "It has been an honor, Mrs. Brown. And I do not say that as a mere politeness."

~ ~ ~

354

Only ten minutes' acquaintance is enough to show that she is a woman worthy to be the wife of such a man . . . Her manner is singularly quiet and retiring, although her natural simplicity and modesty cannot hide the evident force of her character and strength of will and judgment which have fitted her so long to be a counselor to her husband's enterprises and a supporter in his trials.

Mary blushed and put the *Independent* aside.

~ ~ ~

John was keeping his promise, writing regularly. He had little to say about her staying away, but even less to say about her coming. But Mary had not given up. She had let him know that she wanted to come, and now there was nothing to do but wait and hope that he talked himself around to it. There was not much time; the day of execution was fast approaching, and he had made it clear to everyone that he had no intent of cheating the hangman by escaping. Mary's original purpose in leaving North Elba had long since become moot.

In the meantime, having been staying with Mr. McKim and his wife, Mary accepted an invitation to visit Mrs. Lucretia Mott. Mary knew that Mrs. Mott was in the habit of speaking in public, advocating not only against slavery but for the rights of women. She had not heard a woman lecture since her time in Northampton, when a party from the water cure went to hear Miss Lucy Stone speak about abolition, so despite the cloud gathering over her of John's impending execution, she went to hear Mrs. Mott with a certain eagerness and was not disappointed when the prim-looking Quaker lady spoke with passion about John. "Your sermon did me good," Mary said as they drove home.

"I meant what I said, Mrs. Brown. I do not condone violence, but your husband is a moral hero. There will be a meeting in Philadelphia on the day of his death. If you are not in Virginia, I hope you will come."

"I will if I am still here. But I hope my husband changes his mind."

"The Lord will steer him in the right direction," Mrs. Mott said.

There was a letter from John the next morning—perhaps, Mary realized, the last she would ever receive while John was alive. She read through it hastily. Some kind words about Mrs. Mott. Some money John had been given for his family's benefit. John's health. His time passing quite pleasantly. The difficulty she might have in getting the bodies of John and the boys. (Mary winced.) Some sensible advice about carrying home the money she had been given in gold. And:

I will close this by saying that if you now feel that you are equal to the undertaking, do exactly as you feel disposed to do about coming to see me before I suffer. I am entirely willing.

Mrs. Mott smiled at Mary as she looked up. "I think you received the answer that you wanted, Mrs. Brown, didn't you? God is good."

20

November 30, 1859, to December 8, 1859

"You think old Brown's wife will go see him hang?" the man sitting across the aisle from Mary asked his companion.

"It'd take a peculiar sort of woman to do that," the second man said. "But then look who we're dealing with."

Mary stared out the window while Mr. McKim's wife patted her hand.

Since Mary, the McKims, and Mr. Hector Tyndale—a china merchant from Philadelphia whose militia experience and soldierly bearing had recommended him as a suitable escort for Mary into hostile territory—had boarded the Harper's Ferry train at Baltimore, her fellow passengers' talk about John's execution, which was to take place in two days, had not ceased. Only Mary's quartet had been silent on the matter, a fact that Mary suspected was making them somewhat conspicuous. Mrs. McKim had suggested that she and Mary retire to the ladies' compartment, where they might escape the cruder comments about Old Brown, but Mary had suspected that she might be even more conspicuous there in her simple black gown and heavy face veil; uncovered, her face plainly showed her heavy grief. Besides, having heard some ladies in the waiting room at Baltimore holding forth about how Old Brown hadn't cared a fig about sending his sons to their deaths, she doubted that a change of car would be much of an improvement.

"How long do you think it will take him to die?" the first man asked. "I mean, he's a tough old buzzard from what the newspapers say."

"Sir!" Mr. Tyndale stood up. "Please, I beg you. There are *ladies* present. This is not a topic for their delicate ears." He looked at Mrs. McKim, who did look somewhat delicate.

"Well, apologies," the man mumbled. He resumed his conversation in a much lower voice, although Mary doubted it was any more pleasant.

Chivalry having triumphed, Mary fingered her carpetbag. It bristled with letters smoothing her way, including the most important one: a letter from Governor Wise of Virginia giving her permission to retrieve John's body when the time came. Gentlemanly and proper, it had shattered Mary's last hope, which up until then she had not realized she cherished—that John would be spared the gallows. She had been unable to restrain a flood of tears.

It was so strange, having John's death scheduled for a specific day and place. Had they set a time too? Mary wondered if it would have been easier to bear if he had died of his wounds, as had her sons. But at least she would have the chance to tell him goodbye, to give him a final embrace.

The men, meanwhile, had moved to a new topic. "Fellow in line ahead of me at Baltimore wanted a ticket to the Ferry. Almost got laughed out of the station. Virginia's not letting anyone ride to the Ferry or to Charlestown unless they have a damn—a very good reason. Fellow said he was an editor for a Northern rag."

"They'd skin him alive if he went down there."

"And it would be well deserved. Last thing we need is more Northern meddlers." The man's eyes fell again on Mr. Tyndale. "Where are you headed, sir, with your ladies?"

Before Mr. Tyndale could reply, a third man rose—a hulking man with two sidearms. Mary had no idea why she hadn't noticed him before. "Say another word, sir, and I will toss you off this train. Without the necessity of stopping at a station."

Sulkily, the men subsided as Mary remembered what the station manager at Baltimore had told her when she had shown her paper from Governor Wise and he'd authorized her ticket. "Don't worry, madam, the train will be full of our men. You might not know it, but they'll be there."

By the time the train reached Sandy Hook, the last stop in Maryland—had not John and the boys stayed there for a time?—the train was almost empty. When the last of the passengers had disembarked at Sandy Hook—had been shooed off more accurately described it—the burly man said, "Well, Mrs. Brown and party, we got you through safe, didn't we?"

"I thank you."

A man in a military uniform entered the car. "Mrs. John Brown, I presume?" He had a slight Irish lilt to his voice.

"Yes."

"I am Captain Patrick Moore of the Montgomery Guard—part of the Virginia militia. Please allow me to escort you and your company to your hotel. It is a but a short distance from the depot, but as you might have gathered, feeling against Northerners is high in these parts."

Not knowing whether she could refuse even had she been inclined to, Mary thanked him.

Soon they pulled into Harper's Ferry. Night had already fallen, so Mary could make out little of her surroundings except for the rivers gleaming in the lamplight and the darkness of the mountains surrounding them. Still, she could not help but feel the presence of her sons and the rest who had lost their lives in this place.

As a few people who had been idling near the station fixed their eyes upon Mary and her companions, Captain Moore led the travelers into the Wager House and to the desk, where a lady of about Mary's own age stood. "This is the party you were telegraphed about, Mrs. Fouke."

"So I guessed." She shook her head. "Your husband and sons often came around this hotel, madam. Your daughter and daughter-in-law were here too, I believe. It was rather a poor return for our hospitality."

Mary could think of no good reply.

"That business in October prostrated me for a week," Mrs. Fouke continued. "Just ask anyone here. But at least we found out that our colored people were loyal to us; they stayed put through all of it. I suppose you'll be preferring to take your meals in your room."

"If it's not too much trouble," Mary said. The tipplers at the hotel bar, she had noticed, had ceased their conversations and were not even pretending not to stare.

"It is, but it will better keep the peace."

She handed them their keys as a porter gathered their luggage and led them to their rooms, which probably had excellent views during the day. As the porter set down Mary's bags, heavy with gifts from Philadelphia for John's fellow prisoners, he said, just above a whisper, "Don't believe what some white folks here will tell you, ma'am. Some of us did join your husband and his men. Some were killed in the fighting. Some have disappeared—maybe escaped. Others slipped back to their masters only when all was lost. More would have joined Captain Brown if he'd made it to the mountains."

"Thank you." She batted back the tears that always seemed to lurk. "People have called his plan insane—it was no such thing. My husband is as level-headed as anyone I've known. And so many don't understand him or even try to. They think he was trying to murder all the slave owners. He didn't want to do that at all. He just wanted to set people free. Every innocent life lost grieved him."

"I know. But I'd better get moving. They're watching us mighty closely nowadays. We'll be praying for him on the day he dies—and for you."

~ ~ ~

Although Mary had risen early on December 1 in hopes of starting off to Charlestown as soon as possible, a dejected Captain Moore informed her that she could not leave the Ferry until orders were received from the militia commander at Charlestown, Major General Taliaferro, who Mary had learned pronounced his name as "Tolliver." No one in Virginia found this at all peculiar.

"But the governor gave me permission to come here," Mary protested.

"Well, he gave you permission to take your husband's body," Captain Moore said. "That could be construed as being allowed to see him only after he was, er—"

"Dead."

"Well, yes. I agree, though it does seem harsh." He brightened. "Colonel Lee is here. Perhaps he can help."

361

Colonel Lee, the man who had directed the final charge which had killed Dauphin Thompson and Jeremiah Anderson and had almost killed John. Mary could not think of a person she wanted to see less, but she said, "Please take me to him, then."

"I'd best bring him here, madam. You see, there are orders to watch the four of you, so you might find venturing outside unpleasant."

"Watch us?" Mr. Tyndale said. "Watch us?"

"That seems excessive," Mrs. McKim said.

"I'm sure they're for your own protection," Captain Moore said suavely. "Now I will go find the colonel."

"These orders must come from General Taliaferro," Mr. McKim said. "Watch us!"

"As if the entire populace wasn't doing that anyway," Mrs. McKim said.

"Fine talk from a man who can't pronounce his own name correctly." Mr. Tyndale scowled.

Sooner than Mary had expected, Captain Moore returned with Colonel Lee. He was a darkly handsome man, beginning to gray, and he seemed to want to see Mary as little as she wanted to see him. "I am sorry, Mrs. Brown, that your husband's folly has brought you to this pass. That being said, I see no reason that you should not be allowed to visit him, but it is a matter for the Virginia authorities in which I cannot interfere. I am here solely to protect the arsenal against any disturbances which might occur. You must apply to General Taliaferro."

"We have, and have heard nothing yet," Mary said.

"No doubt he has applied to Governor Wise for orders. The wheels of state take time to turn, Mrs. Brown. I am sure you will hear something presently. I cannot imagine why anyone would keep you away." He bowed. "Good luck on your quest, madam."

He hurried from Mary's hotel room. Mary was almost relieved that he had done nothing for her. It would be hard indeed to be obliged to the man who had given that order to storm the engine house, the order that had left John a captive, not to mention poor Dauphin and that Jeremiah Anderson wallowing in their own blood and her Annie a heartbroken waif. She was glad to see the last of him.

But for all practical purposes, she hadn't. In just a year and a half, she would see his name in the paper, and would see it again and again until he surrendered to General Grant at Appomattox. Most people, even in the Union, would feel a certain sympathy for the man at that time.

Not Mary. She would growl, "At least no one ran a bayonet through him," and toss the paper aside. A woman had her limits.

~ ~ ~

By early afternoon, word at last arrived from Charlestown. She could visit John, but her companions could not ride with her there—not even Mrs. McKim. She could not visit any of the other prisoners. She could stay only a couple of hours. Oh, and she could not see him alone.

"Surely under the circumstances, Mrs. Brown could be allowed a lady companion," said Mr. McKim. "My wife is hardly a threat to Virginia."

"I'm sorry, sir. The orders come directly from the governor."

"The misnamed Wise," Mr. Tyndale grumbled.

But as Mary could see that arguing would be futile, she said, "How will I go there? By rail?"

"Oh no," Captain Moore said. "By carriage, and with a military escort. The carriage is on its way here now."

In due course, a closed carriage appeared, surrounded by mounted men. After Mary bade goodbye to her companions, Captain Moore handed Mary in, and she settled into her corner. She hoped that she might be left to her thoughts.

The captain, however, was a man who believed that silences needed to be filled. As they wound through the Ferry to catch the road to Charlestown, he said, "I am sorry, Mrs. Brown, that you must endure this because of your husband's actions. It is a pity when the innocent suffer."

"It is a pity that my husband is suffering. He does not deserve death for his actions, even though he has most willingly submitted to his fate."

"Still, it must have come as a shock to you to find him acting as he did."

"It did not. I have known of his plans for some twenty years. Not in this exact form, of course—even he did not know exactly what he would do—but I knew about them in general."

"And you never begged him not to go through with them?"

"No. Why would I? I knew what my husband thought of slavery when I married him. It would have grieved him terribly to think that I did not support him."

"Still, he should have thought of the effect on his family. On their prospects, not to mention the loss of support."

"Our farm is owned free and clear. We get what we need off it, and if it proves not enough, we will have to decide what to do. But my husband's friends have been generous, and my son Salmon—the only son of my body left to me—is a hardworking man. We will survive."

"But what of your daughters? Did your husband ever think of their marriages? What will happen?"

"My husband's friends have offered to educate the older girls so they can become teachers. But we are not society people, so I do not think they will be harmed much." Mary sighed. "Of course, there are not many girls who have been in their position, I grant you that."

Captain Moore seemed to take this as an admission of defeat. Then Mary added, "They are proud of their father and always have been. And I am proud to be the wife of such a man. He is dying as a martyr, not a common criminal."

The day was a mild one, more like early May than December, and they passed a group of black children playing near the road. "Look at them, Mrs. Brown. Do they look ill-treated to you? Do they look unhappy?"

"No."

"Because they aren't. They are as well taken care of as any white children in Virginia."

"Are they enslaved or free?"

"Well, I don't know about these particular children."

"I think it makes a difference, sir."

"What your husband does not understand, Mrs. Brown, is that it is in the best interests of a slave owner to treat his people well. I certainly do mine, as I think they would tell you if they were asked. Most of us do."

"I am glad to hear that."

"They'll even get presents this Christmas. Did you know we do that, Mrs. Brown?"

"I did not."

"Well, then!"

Mary glanced back at the children. "John told me that New Year's Day is when many slaves get sold or rented. Is that true?"

"Well, yes. But I haven't sold any of mine. Not even Minnie, and she's so old, she can hardly knit a sock."

"But what would you do if you needed money? Mortgage your land? Sell some livestock? Or sell a human being?"

Captain Moore scowled. "I understand what you're getting at, Mrs. Brown. Believe it or not, I would not be sad if slavery died out. But it must be a natural death, or there will be chaos."

"It cannot die out too quickly for me—or for the slaves, sir."

They were coming into a place that Mary supposed must be Charlestown. She had never seen so many men in uniform in her life. "Is this all because of John?"

"It is, Mrs. Brown." He pulled down the curtain of the carriage.

"The sun is not bothering me."

"I thought the people looking at you might."

Indeed, everyone who was not in uniform had his or her eyes riveted on their carriage. "Then I thank you." She peeked out from behind the curtain. How terrified these people must be, to put up such an array!

But it did have its uses, as she discovered when the carriage came to a dead halt outside of the Carter House, the hotel where Captain Taliaferro had his headquarters and where most of the press was staying. Evidently, most of the town's citizens had gathered there with the express purpose of looking at Mary. "Clear off!" one of the cavalrymen shouted.

Mary let down her veil. It had been given to her in Boston and had proven most useful.

After a few minutes, the carriage jolted forward, advancing a couple of blocks before reaching a building ringed by men with bayonets. "Here we are," Captain Moore said as more shouting commenced.

"This is the jail?" It hardly looked like the fortress Mary had expected.

"Captain Avis has his residence in one wing. The prisoners are held in another." Captain Moore stepped out and offered Mary his hand. Objectionable as she found the captain's views on slavery, she was grateful to have him guiding her up the stairs through the throngs of armed men, pressed closer to her by the crowd trying to observe her. She felt considerable relief when the door closed behind her.

As Captain Moore walked away, obeying an order that Mary did not hear, three men stepped before her—General Taliaferro, Sheriff Campbell, and Captain Avis. After greeting Mary courteously, the first two men spent considerable time informing her that it was regrettable that Mr. Brown had to die but that the law had to be upheld. "I hope, Mrs. Brown," the general concluded, "that you will not feel unwelcome in the future in Virginia. Should you return under different circumstances, Virginia stands ready to give you the best of Southern hospitality."

"Well, thank you," Mary said. "Everyone has been very kind." She nodded at Captain Moore, who had returned. "Especially you, sir."

"Thank you, madam. I have informed your husband that you are here."

Captain Avis took Mary's arm and led her into a parlor where a pretty young woman some years his junior awaited him. "This is my wife, Mrs. Brown. You and she are both Marys. I will tell you at the outset that she has an unpleasant task to perform. She must search you."

"Search me? For what?"

"Contraband," Mrs. Avis said apologetically. "It is by orders of the general, Mrs. Brown. Please come into this room, and we will get it over with."

Grimly, Mary followed Mrs. Avis into a bedroom. "Now, please empty your pockets and take off your clothing."

"Why is this necessary? Do they think that I have smuggled in a weapon?"

"More like poison for Mr. Brown to take," Mrs. Avis said pleasantly. She shook out Mary's bonnet briskly, then set it tidily upon a dressing table as Mary began to unfasten her dress. "No one here believes that he or you have any such intentions, but it has been deemed necessary. I am sorry." She sighed. "This may sound presumptuous, Mrs. Brown, but we have grown very fond of your husband. We shall miss him."

"My husband has always spoken well of Captain Avis in his letters." Mary handed over her dress, then her outer petticoat. She hoped that the smartly dressed, hoop-skirted Mrs. Avis would say nothing to the press about her inner petticoat, which was not a true petticoat at all but simply the skirt of a dress that still had enough life in it to escape the ragbag.

Mrs. Avis riffled through Mary's gown. Her searching was not interfering with her ability to converse. "My children—I have two little ones, plus the ones from my husband's first marriage—love to come to Mr. Brown's room, with his permission, of course. Sometimes they will just sit there and play while he writes his letters."

"Children have always loved John." Mary stepped out of her inner petticoat and removed her corset, then her shoes and stockings. She now stood in her shift, just as she had stood before John on her wedding night, except that now she also wore drawers, which hadn't been common among country people when she married. "Surely this is enough," she said as Mrs. Avis delved into one stocking, then another, and turned her corset every which way. Mary supposed it would have made a good place to store a little vial of poison.

Mrs. Avis pursed her lips. "Just give your chemise and drawers a good shake, ma'am." As Mary complied with no contraband flying out, Mrs. Avis said, "He speaks a great deal about your daughters."

"Our sons?"

"The ones who died? No. He finds that a very painful subject. We don't raise it. A pat here and there, Mrs. Brown, and we'll be done."

The search completed, Mrs. Avis adjusted Mary's skirt after she had redressed, then firmly pinched each cheek before Mary could react. "A little color, Mrs. Brown. Your husband will want to see you looking as well as possible."

She led Mary down a little corridor and into a room that had a barred door and windows but was otherwise indistinguishable from an ordinary, though sparsely furnished, bedroom. And there, for the first time in six long months, Mary saw John.

Without a word, he pulled her to him, and they stood clinging to each other for a good five minutes until finally John drew back and cleared his throat. "I am glad to see you, Mary."

"And I you." She wiped her eyes. "It would have broken my heart not to see you again."

She took a closer look at John. From weeks of confinement, he was much paler than usual, but his hair and beard were neatly trimmed, and he showed little signs of the wounds he had received at the Ferry. He was wearing a suit and slippers bought for him by Mr. Spring.

John led her to a chair and sat down on a bed while Captain Avis, whom Mary knew had to be in attendance, sat on a stool and studied a newspaper. "I have one thing that I must say, my dear. You know that I made some blunders at the Ferry. I do not care to dwell upon them, which I admit is due to vanity as much as anything, but I know that they cost dearly—cost us the lives of our own noble boys, and others as well. Can you forgive me for that?"

"I do, John. But it is hard—very hard—to have them gone." She could not suppress a sob.

"They are angels in heaven. You most certainly will meet them again. Tell me about the ones who are living."

"Salmon is—"

"Speak up, dear. My hearing is not all it could be after that blow to my head, and Captain Avis is a man of discretion."

"I last received a letter from home a week Tuesday. Salmon is well; he is grieved, of course, but he and Abbie are looking forward to their baby, and Abbie's health is good. Ruth is bearing up well, though of course she is very saddened. Sarah is interested in going to school, especially if she can study drawing. Ellen is being very good. She helps Bell mind little Freddy. Martha is doing the best she can to hold up for the sake of her coming child. Annie is still grieving for Mr. Anderson. I wish she had been true to Dauphin, although it would have ended the same."

"Don't be hard on the child, my dear. They did love each other, and I know neither meant to cause Dauphin pain. Both young men stood by me to the very end, and both were loyal to each other and their comrades. Some tell me that Jerry was run through when he tried to shoot my assailant."

"I will try to understand her better, then. I hope going to school, as our kind friends have offered, will help to take her mind off her troubles."

"I hope so too. Tell her I advised it."

"I am to see Captain Barbour at Harper's Ferry about getting the bodies of our boys."

John nodded. "As I wrote to you earlier, I am not certain that you will be able to get them—they may not be in a good state of preservation, and I see no reason why you should give yourself the pain of trying to identify them. But should you succeed, perhaps you could take my body and theirs and burn them before taking them north. It would be much more conven—"

"I cannot bear such a thought. Besides, I am sure the state of Virginia would not allow it."

"It would not," Captain Avis put in.

"Well, it was only a thought, my dear. Think no more of it." He patted her hand. "It really matters very little where their bodies lie, so do not grieve if you cannot get them."

Mary knew she would break down if they pursued this topic further. "Have you had many visitors?"

"Oh yes. Some want to argue, some want to gawk, and some are genuinely interested in hearing what I think. Captain Avis keeps the worst sort from pestering me. All sorts of people have come through. We had a young man in this morning—an actor, he said. He came here with a militia, the Richmond Grays, said that duty called him from the stage to accompany them here. A handsome fellow, I must say, and I don't usually notice things like that. What was his name, Captain Avis?"

"Booth. John Wilkes Booth. I saw him act once in Richmond."

"Ah, yes. He seemed to think I should have heard of him. I told him I wasn't much for the theater, which amused him."

"Did he come to argue with you?" Mary asked.

"No, he just asked me what I thought of Virginia. I told him that Virginians were some of the most excellent people I had ever met, but that they were burdened by this slave system of theirs. And since he was here and I was rather tired of talking, I asked him to recite some Shakespeare. The opening lines of *Richard III*. He was quite good, as far as I can judge such things."

Mrs. Avis, looking woebegone, brought in supper. There was a knife and fork for Mary but not for John, whose food had been prepared so he could eat it neatly with his hands. Mary wondered what tumult would result if she offered him her knife.

John picked up a biscuit and dipped it in some gravy. "Excellent," he pronounced as Mary nibbled at a chop before putting down her fork. "Now, this won't do, my dear. You must keep up your strength."

But after a few bites, he too gave up the effort. He must have realized, as did she, that every morsel brought them nearer to their final parting.

For a while, they spoke of practical matters—the girls' schooling, the state of the farm, the best route for Mary to take home, John's will, and the inscription he wanted on the tombstone that he had acquired some time before. It had been his grandfather's but had been discarded after a finer one had been purchased. Already, Frederick's name had been carved upon it. "I want to add my name to it, as well as Watson's and Oliver's. I shall write out the inscriptions for you."

For a man who didn't care what happened to his body, he was certainly particular about his tombstone. Mary smiled very faintly, then started to cry, and John took her hand. "Be of good cheer, Mary. I am. We shall all meet again in heaven,

I trust. In the meantime, I know that I have left everything in good hands—our children, the farm, everything."

"I know that you die in a noble cause, and I must trust that everything is for the best. But I shall miss you more than my words can say."

He pressed her hand gently. Mary wiped her eyes. "*Keep up courage, there is a better day a coming*,'" she said after a while.

"Who said that, my dear?"

"Watson. It was in the last letter he wrote to Bell."

"He was a wise man, our Watson. When you grieve for him and Oliver, and our Frederick, remember that you helped make them what they were. It is something to be proud of."

"Time," called a voice, and General Taliaferro appeared in front of the door. "I am sorry, Mrs. Brown. You must return to the Ferry."

John indicated a trunk—the same trunk that Mary had packed for him at the Spring house in Philadelphia. "This is ready for you to take tonight. These are a few items I had here, clothing and such, and the letters I have received since I was brought here. I think you will want to keep the letters, but do what you want with the rest." He glanced at Captain Avis. "Captain, have they set a time for my hanging?"

"Eleven o'clock." Captain Avis sighed.

"Well, then," John said. He took Mary's hands and kissed her cheek. "God bless you and the children."

He was gazing at her just as intently as he had when Mary came to his house as his hired girl, but now there was nothing but love and compassion in those gray-blue eyes. Mary returned his look for the last time. "God have mercy on you." Her voice cracked.

It was up to Captain Avis to separate them forever. He gently took her by the arm. "Come, Mrs. Brown."

The tears did not come until she reached the Avis parlor. "Do take good care of him tomorrow," she sobbed as Mrs. Avis helped her with her bonnet and shawl. "Do your best to make it quick."

"We will, madam." Captain Avis led Mary to the waiting Captain Moore and loaded John's little trunk into the carriage. "Goodbye, Mrs. Brown. We will be thinking of you tomorrow."

"Thank you for your kindness to my husband."

She settled into the carriage. With the soldiers surrounding the carriage and the jail, there wasn't a chance of catching a glimpse of John at his window, so she put down her veil. It was an excellent screen for the tears that rolled silently down her face all the way to Harper's Ferry. Even the chatterbox Captain Moore understood the barrier.

~ ~ ~

Early the next morning, Mrs. Fouke brought Mary and Mrs. McKim breakfast and a card from Colonel Barbour, the commander of the arsenal. Having given vent to her feelings upon their first meeting, Mrs. Fouke had warmed considerably toward Mary. "Good strong coffee for you this morning, Mrs. Brown," she said. "You're going to need it, poor thing."

Mary obediently took a sip. The coffee would have made her hair stand on end had it been any more potent. "Thank you, Mrs. Fouke. Please tell the colonel he may come up whenever he pleases."

"And I know you don't feel like it, but eat. You have to keep up your strength."

Colonel Barbour arrived shortly afterward, accompanied by Mr. McKim and Mr. Tyndale. He gave a neat bow. "My sympathies, Mrs. Brown. I have come here for several reasons. First, to apologize for the incident yesterday."

"Incident?"

"We were shot at," Mr. Tyndale said.

Mrs. McKim nodded. "While you were at Charlestown, we ventured out, and a bullet whizzed past us. We had to hasten back here. We didn't mention it to you, as we felt it would only cause you needless upset after your trip, but it was quite alarming."

"We don't know who did it, but such behavior won't be tolerated," Colonel Barbour said. "He—or she, as there are some ladies with strong feelings here—will be dealt with severely if we can find the miscreant. The next is a rather delicate matter. I would prefer that Mr. McKim talk of it."

Mr. McKim cleared his throat. "The body is but a mere vessel that holds the soul, Mrs. Brown. When the soul has fled, it is as mere dust."

"The governor will not let me have John's body?"

"That order has not been changed at all, Mrs. Brown. Do not fear. This concerns your sons. You know, I think that when the engine house was stormed on Tuesday morning, your son Watson was dying from the wound he received on Monday."

"While carrying a flag of truce," Mr. Tyndale said. "Disgraceful."

"He died on Wednesday. Jeremiah Anderson was mortally wounded on Tuesday morning and lingered until that evening. By the time they died, the bodies of their comrades, including that of your son Oliver, had already been collected. Some students from the medical college at Winchester happened to be in the area. They took the bodies of your son Watson and Mr. Anderson with them."

Colonel Barbour nodded gloomily. "I would not have allowed it if I had been here, ma'am. I was at our sister armory in Springfield. But it happened."

"So, my boy and Mr. Anderson are at the medical college?"

"Yes, Mrs. Brown. I am sorry. You will read it in the papers, so I shall tell you the rest now to spare you the shock. I know nothing about Mr. Anderson's body—I suppose he was dissected—but they say your son is being used as an anatomical display."

Mary had thought that what had happened to William Thompson would have inured her to the stupid, pointless cruelty of men. It had not. Her kind Watson to be poked and prodded by joshing medical students until he could finally be of no use and would be tossed aside like offal. Oh, she knew that his soul was in heaven. It didn't comfort her, not while his battered body was being treated so.

They could have hardly found a better way to hurt her, except for killing him and the rest all over again. "My son was a good man. He only wanted to make this a free land for all. He didn't deserve this. Neither did Mr. Anderson."

"You have my sympathies, madam." The colonel allowed a decent interval to pass. "As for your other son, we found the site where he and the others are buried and unearthed them. It's about a half mile up the Shenandoah River on the east bank. They were buried in two graves with no ceremony, and are in an advanced state of decay. You could perhaps distinguish the white men from the black ones, but I have my doubts that you could do more than that. I would not recommend trying, madam. I think you have suffered enough."

"They were all buried together, black and white?"

"Yes."

"Then let them stay that way. They would be honored."

"I will see to it that they are reinterred, then." Captain Barbour's relief to be done with this topic shone in his face. "I didn't come here simply to cause you pain, Mrs. Brown. I thought you and your companions might like to see some places of interest with the safety of an escort. I don't mean to be presumptuous, but there is some time before the—event."

"Thank you, Colonel. I would like to see those places."

"And with the press down at the—event—there will be more privacy for you. I heard they were bothersome last night."

Mary nodded. Mr. Tyndale and Mr. McKim had had to shoo off some of them from the very door of her room when she returned from Charlestown, and although she had agreed to speak with the more gentlemanly specimens, she had only been able to answer their questions for a few minutes before breaking down.

With a few other official gentlemen and a military escort to suitably intimidate anyone who might try to approach them, Colonel Barbour led the way out of the hotel and into the armory. He gestured toward a battered little building, its windows shattered and its doors—what was left of them after being battered through by Colonel Lee's men—pockmarked with bullet holes. "This is the engine house where your husband made his last stand, and where your son Oliver was shot and killed on Monday afternoon. Your son Watson died in the guard house side."

"They were a brave lot of men," one of the soldiers said. "I don't agree with your husband on much of anything, ma'am, but they were a plucky lot, facing down Colonel Lee's men."

"Thank you, sir. That means a lot to me." She turned to Colonel Barbour. "May I go in?"

"I would not, madam. It's still in much the state it was after the men were captured. Rather unpleasant for a lady."

"But I would like to see it anyway."

"As you wish, madam."

With Mr. McKim holding onto her arm, Mary entered the engine room, where, true to its name, sat a fire engine dented here and there with bullet marks, and stared around her. It was indeed a grim sight. Blood stained parts of the walls which had once shone bright with whitewash and had congealed on the floor. There was a particularly nasty stain on the rear wall. Dauphin's? Mr. Anderson's? Mary shuddered.

She turned so she was facing the entrance. So this was how John and his brave little band had stood, awaiting their fates. Never had she been prouder of them.

The men around Mary seemed rather surprised that she had not fainted. Colonel Barbour led her out and into the guard room, separated by a wall from the engine house. A guard, warming himself by the stove, startled to attention and yanked off his hat upon the sight of a woman. "Mrs. Brown just wants to peek in," the colonel said.

"Mrs. John Brown?"

"Yes."

"Your husband sure did shake things up, ma'am. I'll give him that."

Unlike the engine house, the guard room bore little signs of the strife it had witnessed. The guard indicated a bench. "Your son Watson died over there, ma'am. He suffered a great deal, but his comrade Coppock did much to ease him while they were being held together here."

Mary gazed at the bench, a narrow, short affair that could have hardly fit her tall Watson. She fought back a sob.

"I can wrench off a little of it if you like, ma'am."

"That's very kind of you."

Putting the precious bit of wood in her pocket along with a fragment of brick Colonel Barbour found for her, she followed the colonel for a few minutes around the armory, of which he was quite proud, then back into the town, the shop windows of which were bright with Christmas displays. As the colonel pointed out various spots where John and his men had taken their stands and where some had perished, the Ferry's conjoining rivers tumbled merrily over the rocks as if they had never been disturbed.

The colonel led Mary to the bridge that spanned the Shenandoah River. Pointing to a riverbank some distance off, he said, "If you look over there, madam, that's where the dead were buried. I wouldn't recommend going there, game as you seem to be. As you can see, the townspeople picked a place that was out of the way. And the hour is approaching."

"I will stay here, then." Perhaps, after all, it was best to picture the burial place from this pleasant vantage.

"I did get the men to gather up a few stones for you."

Mary looked at the stones he placed in her hand as she thanked him. They were still slightly damp from the riverbank.

A bit of brick, a piece of bench, and some stones. All she had to take with her of the boys and their companions in arms.

Still, it was more than she'd had when she had come to this place.

~ ~ ~

At the Wager House, everyone in the lobby fell silent when Colonel Barbour led Mary and the others in. Mrs. Fouke, handing over the room key, gave a sympathetic cluck. The porter, standing grimly at his post, hissed, "God be with you, ma'am."

The appointed hour was fast approaching. Tears running down their faces, the McKims and Mary joined hands and prayed in Mary's room while Mr. Tyndale sat outside, ready to face down anyone who might attempt to disturb their vigil.

A church bell, then another, struck eleven. But Mary somehow knew that John had not yet departed from the earth, and it was not simply because her recent experiences had made her realize that Virginians did not necessarily proceed on schedule. She prayed on with the rest a quarter hour more. "He is gone," she said in the middle of a prayer. "I feel it."

Mr. McKim said, "Then he is beyond all earthly care or pain, Mrs. Brown."

Mrs. McKim put her arm around Mary. "If anyone would know that he has left us, it is you. Would you like us to continue here? Or would you prefer to be alone?"

"I thank both of you very much for your kindness," Mary said. "But I would prefer to be alone for now."

The McKims each gave her a kiss and an embrace, then left her.

Alone, Mary did not resume her prayer, as had been her first instinct. Instead, she opened the trunk and looked at the belongings John had sent back to her. Letters—some of them from herself and the rest of the family, some from friends, some from people who identified themselves as utter strangers to John. Mary would read them later. A few shirts, the same ones that Mary had made at Mrs. Spring's. Some books. A double spyglass.

Carefully, since John had willed the spyglass to Owen, Mary picked it up and determined how to adjust it. She stood at the window, training it upon the distant hills.

The hills that John should have reached, had the Lord not willed it otherwise. With a sigh, Mary gently returned the spyglass to its case and placed it back into the trunk.

~ ~ ~

Late that afternoon, Congressman James Ashley of Ohio arrived at Mary's room, along with the McKims. A tall, well-built man who, through some recent mishap, was obliged to walk with a crutch, he was not an inconspicuous figure, which made the fact that he was there all the more surprising, as he was known for his abolitionist views. Mary had met him the day before while waiting to be conveyed to Charlestown. He bowed as he approached her. "Mrs. Brown, I promised you yesterday that I would attend your husband's hanging, if I was allowed, and would report to you what I saw. I am honored yet sorry to keep my promise. You perhaps have heard of the noblemen in days of yore who, after having displeased the crown for some trivial cause, went bravely to their executions. Your husband surpassed them."

Mary's eyes filled with tears. "Sit down, sir. Please tell us all about it."

"Through an acquaintance I have, I was tolerably close to the prison when he was brought out to the waiting wagon, which held the coffin intended for him. Mr. Brown took his assigned seat—on the coffin—and as he did so, a slave woman standing near me said, 'God bless you, old man; if I could help you, I would, but I can't.' I was somewhat infamous in Charlestown by that point, being known as a Northerner and an abolitionist, so I must assume she meant that I should hear her words, which I am happy to convey.

"He proceeded by wagon to the site, which is some distance from the main part of the town. I am told that on the way over, he admired the countryside but otherwise said very little, although he appeared thoughtful rather than despondent. The area around the gallows was ringed by soldiers; the only civilians present were those like me who had somehow obtained permission to be there. Mr. Brown got out of the wagon without a trace of reluctance. He did not even seem to be daunted by the sight of the gallows."

"I can believe it," Mary said. "When I saw him yesterday, he was the only cheerful person in the room."

"He walked up to the platform with the same sure stride. There was a slight breeze, and when it came time to place his hood on, the wind kept blowing it upward, so Mr. Brown indicated his coat collar, where he had some pins that the sheriff put to use."

Mary could not help but smile. "My husband always kept some there just in case. So do his sons."

"The only time he moved with less than a sure step was toward the trap door, and that was because with the hood on, he could not see where he was going and had to get the sheriff to guide him there. When the sheriff asked if he wanted a handkerchief to signal when it was time, he said he did not but asked that he not be kept waiting unnecessarily. After that, because there was a delay in getting the troops in place, he did have to wait, but he stood there calmly, never trembling. Finally, the order came, and he fell. I will not say that the death was as swift as I would have wished, Mrs. Brown, but after about five minutes, all was over."

"What time, sir?"

"About quarter past the hour."

"I knew it."

"I hope my telling you of these things has not added to your grief, Mrs. Brown. I thought you would want to hear the details from someone who had been there and who deeply admires your husband's bravery, which he showed from the first to the very last."

"I thank you for them. And I am glad to know that my husband remained strong to the very end. But I am not surprised. I would not have expected anything less."

With the congressman taking his leave, there was nothing to do but wait for the arrival of John's body. And early in the evening, the arrival of a one-car train at the station informed Mary that it had come.

It was time for both of them to go home.

~ ~ ~

In the dark and rain, Mary hardly recognized the familiar ground of Essex County and could only hope that the carriage driver knew where he was going. Certainly, her companions, Mr. McKim and Mr. Wendell Phillips, a prominent abolitionist who had joined them in New York City, could be of no help.

Behind them, a wagon held the precious cargo of John's body, resting in a walnut coffin supplied by a New York undertaker, who had also prepared John for burial. Mary had fretted that some mishap might befall the wagon on the slippery, twisting roads—wet for once instead of snowy—but all seemed well. In any case, no accident would have escaped the notice of the occupants of the carriage behind the wagon, which bore several men from the press. Each time the cortege stopped and the men alighted, a cloud of smoke would emanate from their equipage. They were well behaved, though, and Mary had almost gotten used to their presence.

At least she would be expected in North Elba; a young man in Elizabethtown, the son of the sheriff there, had volunteered to mount a fast horse and tell the family to prepare for John's funeral the next day. He was only one of the many people—innkeepers, railway attendants, the inhabitants of the towns they had passed through—who had shown kindness to Mary on this wearisome journey.

Taking care not to disturb Mr. McKim, who was dozing, Mary shifted her position and peered out into the fog. Then she saw them—men with lanterns heading toward the carriage, the driver of which understood the unspoken message. Led by the lights, the bearers of which maintained a reverent silence, the procession made its way to the house.

One by one, the girls ran into Mary's arms: Annie, Sarah, Ellen, Ruth, and Martha as well. Mary could feel Martha's burgeoning pregnancy as she embraced her. "My Oliver and Watson are not here?" Martha asked as the men, putting down their lanterns, began to bear the coffin inside the house.

"No, child. Mr. McKim has promised to tell you and the rest all that happened once everyone is settled. Oliver is with his comrades."

Martha nodded. Mary wished she had taken the news less placidly.

Neighbors, some of whom Mary had seen only a few times, fluttered about, serving a light meal, offering accommodations for the night to the newspapermen, and bearing John's coffin to the loft. When at last everyone gathered to hear Mr. McKim, who had most kindly agreed to acquaint those present with the details of their stay in Virginia, the men of the press scribbled and drank tea, except for a short, somewhat plump young man whom Mary doubted was even old enough to vote. He was drawing in a sketchbook, which quickly commanded Sarah's attention. "Don't disturb Mr. Nast at his work," Mary said gently as Sarah peeped over his shoulder.

"No, Mrs. Brown, it is all good. And I like Sarahs. There is a Sarah very dear to me in the city whom I hope to marry. One day!"

He smiled at Sarah, who watched his pencil strokes raptly until Mr. McKim began to speak. Mary sat in her familiar chair, cuddling Ellen and stroking the hair of Annie, who sat on a cushion, listening intently. Annie hadn't pulled away when Mary touched her, which was an encouraging sign. She had also declared her intention to go to school as her father wished but not to enjoy it, which was encouraging as well. Mary smiled undetectably, then turned her attention back to Mr. McKim.

It was slightly unreal, sitting here and hearing this account of her last few days told by another. Mary wondered what John might make of it all.

~ ~ ~

Just after daybreak, a group of neighbors carrying pickaxes and shovels arrived to dig John's grave at the site he had specified next to a huge rock. Approaching them with a pot of coffee and some hot rolls, Mary heard one say, "Mark my words, all of this is going to end in war. I don't know when, but sooner or later, it's going to happen."

"Sooner," Mr. Nast said. He was alternately sketching and blowing on his fingers. "I vote for sooner. You remember what Mr. Brown said to his captors—that the people of the South had better prepare for a settlement of the slavery issue sooner than they were expecting it. The man spoke the truth."

They all fell silent upon seeing Mary's approach. Perhaps they wanted to spare her feelings, or perhaps they assumed that as a woman, she would shy away from this talk of war. But if there was no alternative way to end slavery, if all other means had failed . . .

"Then let it be done," she said, half to herself. She served the coffee and returned to the house.

~ ~ ~

Soon the house was crammed full of people—Bell, little Freddy, William Thompson's young widow, and the rest of the Thompsons; neighbors, black and white; some friends from farther off; a few complete strangers come to pay their respects. One of these, the Reverend Joshua Young of Brattleboro, Vermont, kindly agreed to officiate. It had saddened Mary to think that John would have no clergyman at his grave, especially since he had refused a minister before his hanging on the grounds that he did not wish to be attended by any man of the cloth who supported slavery.

It was sad too that John's oldest sons could not be there. But at least they were well: Owen, along with Barclay Coppock and Charles Tidd, had made it to safety and was working for Mary's Delamater relations in the oilfields of Crawford County. John Jr. was quite sane, and although there were rumors that he might be arrested, all of Ashtabula County—and especially Wealthy—was determined that he would not fall into unfriendly hands. Jason was living quietly among his fruit trees near Akron. Ruth, who like all of John and Dianthe's children could spin out a letter for pages, had promised to give them all the details of the funeral.

Led by Lyman Epps and his family, who had been some of the first black settlers in North Elba and who possessed one of the best farms and the best voices in Essex County, the mourners sang John's favorite hymn, "Blow, Ye Trumpet Blow." Black and white voices joining—it would have pleased John. So would the rest of the service, held inside in deference to the North Elba weather: the prayer by Reverend Young, the tributes by Mr. McKim and Mr. Phillips honoring not only John but the others who had lost their lives and the ones in prison—John Cook, Edwin Coppock, Shields Green, John Copeland, Albert Hazlett, and Aaron Stevens, Annie's favorite—who would soon follow John to the gallows. Perhaps he would have even liked the moment, unrecorded by the newspapermen, when little Freddy, entranced by Mr. McKim's watch, snatched it with a contented gurgle.

While another hymn was sung, a group of young men mounted the stairs to the loft and carefully brought down John's coffin. Phineas Watson, a well-to-do farmer in the area, stepped into the room. "You may see him now."

Leaving the family to take the last view, the guests thronged forward and outside, where the coffin rested on a large table. "I can't bear to look at him so," Annie said in a trembling voice. "I want to remember him as I saw him at the railway station."

"You don't have to," Mary said. "He will understand."

At last, Mr. Watson made a signal, and the Browns and Thompsons went forward. The New York undertaker had done his work well; only someone familiar with John's history could have known that he had been hanged. His face had a slight flush to it, replacing the prison pallor that Mary had observed, and he looked, as was usually said of the dead, as if he were merely sleeping, except that in this case, it wasn't a mere platitude; one was tempted to try to shake him awake. Even Annie, lingering behind the rest of the family, could have probably borne the sight, but Mary didn't force her. Instead, she gazed at John's still face, then gave him a farewell pat on the cheek. "Let us lay him to rest now," she said.

Mr. Watson carefully shut the coffin lid, and the pall-bearers stepped forward.

In a line, they processed toward the great rock, Mary on the arm of Mr. Phillips, Martha and little Ellen on either side of Mr. McKim, the Reverend Young leading Bell, and Mr. Young's friend, Mr. Bigelow, escorting Mary Thompson. Behind the four widows walked Ruth and Henry, Salmon with Annie and Sarah, and the elder Thompsons. No one stumbled on the slippery ground, no one set a foot wrong, and no one lost his or her composure. It was as if they'd been born and reared to do exactly this.

Then, using straps, the men lowered the coffin into the grave. It was suddenly too much for Mary and the rest of the family, all of whom, men and women, gave way to sobs. But the Reverend Young stepped up and said in a fine voice, "I have fought a good fight, I have finished my course, I have kept the faith. Henceforth, there is laid up for me a crown of righteousness, which the Lord, the righteous judge, shall give me at that day: and not to me only, but unto all them also that love his appearing."

It was what they needed to hear. As the minister proceeded to the benediction, the Browns stood erect and brushed away their freezing tears.

Now there was nothing but a grave waiting to be filled in. Mary and the rest accepted their escorts' arms and slowly made their way back into the house.

~ ~ ~

It was three o'clock, and all the out-of-town guests were anxious to be on their way back home: to Vermont, to Massachusetts, to Pennsylvania, to New York City. The reporters from the *Herald* and the *Tribune* thanked Mary for her hospitality and wished her well. Mr. Nash presented Sarah with a little sketch of herself. To Mr. Phillips, Mr. McKim, and Mr. Young, Mary gave little mementoes of John. There were final embraces and promises to write.

And then there was no one in the house but Mary, the four children left to her of the thirteen she had borne, Martha, and Salmon's wife Abbie. No reporters, no well-wishers, no neighbors. Just the Browns and the memories of the brave men who had left this place forever.

Ellen broke the silence. "What do we do now, Mama, with Father gone?"

"We do as we always have. We keep the faith. We carry on. And there's a lot to be done."

A lot to be done, indeed. Choosing a school for Annie and Sarah. Bringing Martha's fatherless baby safely into the world. Guarding precious Freddy. Sorting through John's letters, which a Mr. Redpath was anxious to use in a biography. Placating the indefatigable Mrs. Child, who had also wanted to write a biography. Answering the mail, much of it from total strangers, heaped on John's writing desk. Providing for whatever waifs and strays might turn up at the Browns' door.

And there was the matter of deciding whether this was where Mary wanted to spend the rest of her life. As her carriage had navigated one hairline twist of road after another, the thought had occurred to her that that while she was bereft, she was also her own woman. She had a paid-up farm, she had her health, and she was only in her forties. There were possibilities.

But for now, all that would have to wait. The sky hinted at snow to come, and there were chores to do.

Mary drew on her cloak. Then she grabbed Watson's hat from its peg and walked outside.

AUTHOR'S NOTE

Some time after John Brown's death, an in-law of Salmon Brown visited North Elba, extolling the advantages of his new home, California. It made an impression. In 1864, Mary, her daughters, and Salmon and his family traveled by wagon train to that state, where Mary, Annie, Sarah, and Ellen spent the rest of their lives. Indeed, all of John Brown's surviving children, except for John Jr., ended up migrating to California, although Salmon and his family later moved to Portland, Oregon, and Jason in his old age ultimately returned to Ohio.

After moving west, Mary worked as sort of a practical nurse, tending her neighbors and occasionally delivering babies. In 1882, she traveled back east and was honored as John Brown's widow in Kansas, Chicago, and Boston. (Although John Brown remained a deeply controversial figure in Kansas, he had acquired his fair share of admirers there, and the Browns were generous over the years in donating family artifacts to the Kansas Historical Society, including a medal presented to Mary by a French group that included Victor Hugo.) While Mary was in Chicago, an Indiana surgeon came forward with the startling news that he had taken Watson Brown's preserved body from the Winchester Medical College during the

Civil War and still had it in his possession. The surgeon turned the body over to John Jr., and Watson at last was buried properly in North Elba alongside his father. Mary attended the funeral, as did Watson's widow, Bell, who had remarried, her second husband being a cousin of her late husband's. (Bell's son by Watson, Freddy, died of diphtheria in 1863.) Soon after Mary returned to California, her health began to decline, and she died in San Francisco, at her daughter Sarah's home, in 1884. She is buried at Madronia Cemetery in Saratoga, California. The funeral of this quiet, unobtrusive woman was heavily attended.

In the summer of 1860, an armed group of men appeared at John Jr. and Wealthy's rented house in Dorset, Ohio, and talked their way inside, where it proved that they were intent on kidnapping John, presumably to deliver him to Virginia authorities. Because no one wanted to shoot Wealthy or the other ladies who happened to be at the house, John and his friends, along with the would-be kidnappers, took their fight outside, where everyone seems to have rather farcically shot at each other in the dark until Wealthy devised some stratagem to divert the attackers. Annoyingly, the *Cincinnati Daily Press*, which recorded this, gave no further details of Wealthy's heroics.

Following the outbreak of the Civil War, John Jr. helped recruit troops for a Kansas unit and served as a company captain. Rheumatism put an end to his military service, which is perhaps most notable for the rather erotic letters, written in code, that he sent to Wealthy from camp. (Wealthy's side of the coded correspondence, sadly, does not appear to have survived.) After his return home, he, Wealthy, and Johnny (who had an intellectual disability) moved to the island of Put-in-Bay, Ohio, where they ran a vineyard. In 1866, Wealthy gave birth to a daughter, Edith, a talented pianist who married a stock company actor, Thomas Alexander, in 1893. Shortly after their daughter's wedding, Wealthy and John Jr. attended the Chicago World's Fair as guests of the state of Kansas, from which they had fled that turbulent year of 1856. After John Jr.'s death of heart failure in 1895, Wealthy remained in Put-in-Bay, where she died in 1911. Researcher Katherine Mayo, who interviewed Wealthy in 1908, noted the presence of no fewer than five fat gray cats at the house Wealthy shared with her daughter, her son-in-law, and Johnny.

Annie and Sarah went to Franklin Sanborn's school in Concord, Massachusetts in early 1860. Although Annie, deeply affected by the Harper's Ferry tragedy and the impending execution of her dear friend Aaron Stevens, found it impossible to remain at school for more than a few weeks, she returned with Sarah the following year. In Concord, the girls boarded for a time with the Alcott family, prompting a grumbling entry in Louisa May Alcott's diary that preparing for the newcomers was disturbing her writing routine. Later, the girls attended Fort Edward Institute in New York State. After finishing school, Annie briefly taught freed slaves in Union-occupied Norfolk and Portsmouth, Virginia before joining her family on its trek west. Having worked as a teacher for a while in California, Annie married Samuel Adams, a blacksmith, in 1871, and bore nine children, seven of whom lived to adulthood. Unfortunately, Annie's marriage was unhappy, due in large part to her husband's alcoholism. After he died in 1914, Annie lived for a time by herself, then near a daughter. The last surviving child of John Brown, Annie died in

Shively, California, in 1926 at age 82 and was buried in Rohnerville Pioneer Cemetery. Throughout her long life, she paid tribute to the young men she had known at the Kennedy Farm and cherished her own role in her father's raid. Although Annie never published an account of her adventures, the numerous written reminiscences she offered to John Brown's biographers and admirers remain a valuable source for historians.

Owen Brown never married. For a while, he lived in Put-in-Bay, spending his winters as caretaker at the Gibraltar Island estate of financier Jay Cooke. He spent his last years living with his brother Jason on a mountaintop near Pasadena, California. After attending a temperance meeting, he fell ill with pneumonia and died at Ruth's house in 1889. He was buried atop his beloved mountain with a temperance ribbon fastened to his breast. In 1874, Owen published a memoir, "Escape from Harper's Ferry," in the *Atlantic Monthly*.

For years, Jason worked on developing a flying machine but was never able to perfect it. After spending time in California, he returned to Ohio to be with his wife, who died in 1895. Jason then returned to California but spent his declining years in Ohio, where despite his years, he made a point of entering one of the "walking contests" that were popular at the time. He died at his son's home in Akron in 1912.

Ruth Brown Thompson and her husband spent their last years in Pasadena, where Ruth died in 1904 and Henry in 1911. A lover of flowers, Ruth enjoyed her surroundings and in 1899 wrote Wealthy a detailed description of the Tournament of Roses parade.

Salmon Brown volunteered for the Union army as a lieutenant but never made it out of New York, as the other officers in the regiment, objecting to his notoriety as a son of John Brown, successfully petitioned for his removal. After his emigration to California, Salmon prospered there for a number of years but sustained a blow to his finances during an economic downturn. While living in Oregon, he suffered a debilitating accident that left him increasingly dependent on others for his care. Frustrated and depressed about his deteriorating health and regarding himself as a burden, he killed himself with a shotgun in 1919. His widow, Abbie, died ten years later.

Like Annie, Sarah worked as a teacher but eventually found employment at the United States Mint in San Francisco, which she held until a change of presidential administration led to the loss of her position. Later, she taught English to Japanese immigrants—then a despised group—and became an accomplished painter. Sarah never married. Her younger sister, Ellen, married James Fablinger, a schoolteacher, with whom she had several children. The two sisters each died of cancer in 1916 and are buried near Mary in Saratoga.

In January 1860, Martha, Oliver's widow, bore a daughter, Olivia, who lived only two days. With little will to live, Martha succumbed to childbed fever in March.

Three of John Brown's surviving raiders, Barclay Coppock, Charles Tidd, and Francis J. Meriam (who did not arrive at the Kennedy Farm until the day before the raid), served in the Civil War. Coppock, who was commissioned a first lieutenant in the 10th Kansas Infantry, was fatally injured in September 1861, when Confederate "bushwackers" sabotaged a railroad bridge passing over Missouri's Platte River, causing his train to derail and flip into the river. Tidd, a first sergeant with the 21st Massachusetts Volunteers who enlisted under the name of Charles Plummer, died of enteritis on a troop transport ship in February 1862 as the battle of Roanoke Island (North Carolina) raged nearby. In 1863, Meriam was in South Carolina with the 21st U.S. Colored Infantry, for which he served as acting captain. The following year, he enlisted as a private with the 59th Massachusetts Infantry and was wounded in the right leg at Spotsylvania in May 1864. He died in a New York City boardinghouse in November 1865.

Osborne Anderson, the only black survivor of the raid, published a memoir, *A Voice From Harper's Ferry*, in 1861, though it has only recently received the attention as a source that it deserves. He died in Washington, D.C., of tuberculosis in 1871.

In 1899, Thomas Featherstonehaugh, an admirer of John Brown who had long been distressed at his followers' ignoble burial at Harper's Ferry, went to that town (much battered by the Civil War and flooding) and unearthed the remains. Packing them in ordinary luggage, he arranged for their reburial with due ceremony at North Elba. The Reverend Joshua Young, who had presided at John Brown's funeral, was again on hand to lay his men at rest.

A number of places associated with John Brown still stand, including the farmhouse at North Elba, the Kennedy Farm (in private hands and available for tours only sporadically), the Perkins mansion in Akron and the heavily remodeled Brown residence across the street, Mrs. Ritner's boardinghouse in Chambersburg, the engine house at Harper's Ferry (moved several times and reconstructed before ending up a short distance from its original location), and the Adair cabin in Osawatomie (also moved from its original location). Save for the Adair cabin and the interior of the Kennedy Farm, I was able to visit all of them over the course of writing this novel.

~ ~ ~

In the early 1900s, Katherine Mayo, a researcher for biographer Oswald Garrison Villard, interviewed hundreds of people who had known John Brown, as well as many of his surviving relatives, including Annie, Sarah, Jason, Salmon, Wealthy, and Henry Thompson; her notes and the rest of the Villard papers, housed at Columbia University, are invaluable for researchers. (And they make for fun reading: "I could have Potawatomie-d her on the spot," Mayo grumbled to Villard when Ellen Brown Fablinger proved unwilling to be interviewed.) It was Sarah who told Mayo the family stories of Annie jilting Dauphin Thompson in favor of Jeremiah Anderson (a tale which is supported by circumstantial evidence) and of Mary Day coming to help an unnamed sister keep house for the widowed John Brown and receiving a written proposal sometime later. In addition to the Villard papers, I read hundreds of letters from Brown family members, deposited in archives in New York, California, and everywhere in between. I also consulted, of course, a number of biographies, including those by Louis DeCaro, Jr., David Reynolds, Robert McGlone, and Stephen Oates, along with the older, but still quite useful, books by Franklin Sanborn, Oswald Garrison Villard, Richard Hinton, and James Redpath. Certainly one of the most valuable books I read was Bonnie Laughlin-Schultz's *The Tie That Bound Us*, a study of the Brown women, along with her underlying dissertation.

I have also been greatly aided by the research of Jean Libby. Any mistakes, of course, are my own.

As in all my novels, I have tried to stay true to history while sifting through contradictory accounts and filling in gaps. Almost all of the named characters actually lived, with one notable exception: Josie is a fictitious character, as is the episode in which she figures, but John Brown, Jr., remembered his father helping fugitive slaves as far back as 1825.

Although there is no record of a meeting between Sojourner Truth and Mary Brown, the former's biographer, Margaret Washington, places her at the water cure at the time Mary was there, and Sojourner's daughter was employed there. The other famous figures portrayed here as interacting with the Browns—Lucretia Mott, Frederick Douglass, Robert E. Lee, and John Wilkes Booth, to name just a few—did indeed do so.

Any direct quotations from letters and newspapers in my novel are from actual documents, although in some cases spelling and the like have been corrected or modernized.

Like many people, I grew up with the notion of John Brown as a crazed fanatic, a notion that was at its zenith in the mid-twentieth century and that has slowly been losing ground thanks in part to the historians I mentioned above. He will always be a controversial figure, but reading his own words and seeing him through the eyes of his family changed my view of him. I hope this novel has inspired you to read more about him—and about the strong women who made their own contributions to the cause of human freedom.

Acknowledgments

In researching *John Brown's Women*, I received assistance from the staff of a number of research institutions, including, in no order whatsoever, the Chicago History Museum, the Kansas Historical Society, the Columbia University Rare Book and Manuscript Library, the Rutherford B. Hayes Presidential Library, the Hudson Library in Hudson, Ohio, the Ohio History Center, Harvard University's Houghton Library, the Huntington Library, the Crawford County (Pennsylvania) Historical Society, the Feinberg Library at the State University of New York at Plattsburgh, the Humboldt County (California) Historical Society, the Chester Fritz Library at the University of North Dakota, the Gilder Lehrman Institute of American History, the Concord (Massachusetts) Free Public Library, the New York Public Library, the Library of Congress, the National Archives, the Washington County (Maryland) Free Library, the American Antiquarian Society, the Western Reserve Historical Society, the Ashtabula County (Ohio) District Library, the Historical Society of Pennsylvania, the Frederick County (Maryland) Library, the Harpers Ferry National Historical Park, and Smith College's Young Library. I have purposely avoided naming individual staff members, as I would most certainly leave out someone inadvertently. All of these institutions and their staff deserve our gratitude for keeping history alive and accessible.

I found two websites particularly valuable: Kansas Memory, maintained by the Kansas Historical Society, and West Virginia Memory Project, maintained by the West Virginia Department of Arts, Culture and History. These sites contain a wealth of material on John Brown and his associates, all of it free for public viewing.

Historians Louis DeCaro, Jr., and Jean Libby were kind enough to offer assistance to me on a number of occasions. Any historical errors I have fallen into are mine, not theirs. Alice Keesey Mecoy, a descendant of Annie Brown, offers a wealth of information about John Brown's descendants on her John Brown Kin blog. Another Brown descendant, Lucille Crisp Clement, has posted a number of seldom-seen photos of Brown family members on her Ancestry pages. Marty Brown kindly shared some photos of sites in Put-in-Bay, Ohio, connected to John Brown, Jr. I have also profited from conversations with Richard Smyth, Grady Atwater, Greg Artzner, and Mick Konowal.

Jenny Quinlan and Jessica Cale at Historical Editorial helped me bring this project to completion with their cover design and editorial services, and John Low at Ebook Launch saved me the headache of formatting. Working with them was a pleasure.

I have no doubt I have left out someone deserving of thanks. My apologies and appreciation.

Finally, I would like to thank my husband, Don Coomes, and my children, Thad and Bethany Coomes, for indulging my interest in all things John Brown, and Dudley, Emmy, and (occasionally) Harrison for helping me hone my powers of concentration through their melodious barking or meowing.

ABOUT THE AUTHOR

Susan Higginbotham is the author of a number of historical novels set in medieval and Tudor England and, more recently, nineteenth-century America, including *The Traitor's Wife*, *The Stolen Crown*, *Hanging Mary*, and *The First Lady and the Rebel*. She and her family, human and four-footed, live in Maryland, just a short drive from where John Brown made his last stand. When not writing or procrastinating, Susan enjoys traveling and collecting old photographs. Visit her website, *History Refreshed*, at www.susanhigginbotham.com, and look for her on Facebook as "Susan Higginbotham, Author."